PRAISE FOR THE SHADOW ARTIST

"THE SHADOW ARTIST is a classic spy story wrapped in a contemporary thriller and driven by a modern-day female protagonist. An artist by nature and a skilled operative by training, Alex Winter could step into the ring with Reacher, Rapp, or even Rambo, and I give even odds as to who would come out alive. Winter is exactly the sort of female hero I love to read, and I can't wait to see what Grayson tests her with next."

— VICKI PETTERSSON, New York Times Bestselling author of SWERVE

"A plot that Nelson DeMille would kill for, complete with propulsive action and twisted by secrets—both private and all-pervading—as heroine Alex Winter walks a high tightrope over order and obligation. Winter is an eidetic artist, but it is James Grayson who draws a memorable picture of greed and treachery. I couldn't put it down. Twice."

— THERESA SCHWEGEL, Edgar Award winning author of OFFICER DOWN

THE SHADOW ARTIST

JAMES GRAYSON

Alistern Press, LLC

Library of Congress Cataloging-in-Publication Data has been applied for.

ISBN: 978-1-940221-02-1

For my wife, V.
You believed from the start.

One

THERE YOU ARE, BEING CHASED BY SOMEONE, and along comes a river or canal or something—so you keep going, you dive right in.

Your pursuer, though, likely slows down as he approaches the water, maybe even stops. It's human nature. He thinks: Is it cold? Will the current wash me away? Or, this goddamned suit cost me a thousand dollars. Who knows what he's thinking, but he's standing there. Perhaps he's pulled his gun. He's aiming it, drawing a bead on you and thinking of shooting you in the back.

Meanwhile, you've already started swimming. If you've timed it right, you've taken a breath and gone under, making it harder for him to get that bead. He used to be mere yards from you, but now he's back there. Sure, he can jump in, start the chase again, but unless he's a better swimmer than you, you've created distance, gotten the edge.

Chances are, you've gotten away.

In forty minutes and for the first time in her career, Alex Winter will be the one all dressed up and left standing at the edge of an icy river. She'll be cursing herself for stopping.

She'll be wishing like hell that he hadn't gotten away.

The river was the Thames, and Alex had chosen the perfect view through the floor to ceiling windows of the chic Café Martin, the location of tonight's event. She tricked her subjects into sitting long enough to be sketched by having them stare outside where, with London anticipating its first white Christmas in over a century, the river's surface had congealed into an icy slush. The city'd had a handful of technical white Christmases before—the definition being a single snowflake falling on the roof of the queen's palace—but the last Christmas that snow actually blanketed London was in 1895. The mere chance of witnessing history had mesmerized most of her models all evening.

It also kept their gaze off of Alex in the little black dress.

Her employer, a master at exploiting the particular skills of each agent, had booked Alex for the black-tie event as a Royal College of Art graduate student working on her PHD. As one of the *entertainers* celebrating the homecoming of a Royal Air Force pilot, she was to make simple sketches of the patrons, focusing on the exaggerated features of each person and re-creating a likeness that would be suitable for amusement, elicit a few laughs.

Everyone loved a caricature. Even when it was of them.

Who knew how the operators managed to gain these entries or validated the credentials of the aliases, but The Company was able to put someone just about anywhere these days. The CIA had installed chief level executives inside foreign companies, servers within hostile government cabinets, and even a chef inside a certain Saudi royal family member's home. Gaining attendance to an event, even as posh as this one, was run of the mill.

As for this evening, outside of drawing, Alex's instructions were straightforward: Enter the UK as herself, Alex Winter, a US citizen from DC spending Christmas in London. Stay in a regular hotel, play tourist. On the second night, assume the identity of the budding artist until the right moment presented itself. Then slip away and intercept an attaché from slot number forty-four of the coat-check closet. Leave through the front entrance and deliver the attaché to a predetermined dead-drop. Do not contact anyone from the CIA, the US consulate, or any other bureau or agency until the drop is made.

No exceptions.

Simple enough, though those instructions included a few details she wouldn't think significant until later.

With party chatter and soft jazz echoing throughout the contemporary steel and glass restaurant, Alex motioned for her next victim to take a seat. Then, amidst a good deal of laughter from those crowded behind her, she elongated the poor chap's nostril holes to the shape of canoes and tightened the sprout of hair at his forehead to rise into a tall horn. Alex added the remaining features, a little texture to his pressed tuxedo shirt and shiny silk bow tie, and signed it. Then she nodded him over to have a look.

"Well," he said, "You've made me into something of an inquisitive unicorn."

More laughter behind Alex, and she said, "All in good fun." She winked, tore the sheet from the pad, and held out the souvenir to him.

He eyed her for a moment, long enough for it to be uncomfortable. Then he nodded, took the sketch, and folded it into his tuxedo pocket. As he strode off, Alex seized the opportunity to case the now-full room, allowing the images to etch into her memory like still lifes.

Two dozen guests gathered in several spots beside the main entry, straight across the floor, while another group had gathered behind a shiny black grand piano adjacent to the bar, though the pianist was still nowhere to be seen. A tall woman in gold sequins moved from group to group with the ease of a politician—the hostess of the event and mother of the soldier. The room was balanced in both groupings and gender, with half women and half men, almost to the number. Average age in low fifties. Considering the number of tailored tuxes, designer dresses, and gemstone necklaces in the room, most were in possession of the kind of wealth that gave way to the softness of affluent excess.

Good, she thought, no real opposition to her objective.

Assuring herself that she wasn't disappointed with the lack of challenge, Alex turned back around as a man wearing an RAF black tie and tailored coat approached the easel. "Time for one more?"

Angus, the returning pilot and guest of honor.

"Of course." Alex sat back down and reached up to begin, but then held her hand steady for a moment as she studied Angus's face. The first stroke was the most important as it became the foundation of the study, initiating a conversation for the artist. Not unlike first impressions, the opening line was also the most difficult to correct.

Angus had no extraordinary features, no wild hair or imperfect teeth. And though she could create a comical likeness of him, and as the gathering crowd behind her waited for just that, Alex changed her mind at the last second. She would let the veracity of Angus's face take over instead.

She opened her satchel, drew out the leather fold of pencils, and chose three, placing them aside. She would use the pencil with hardest lead to form outlines, edges, and then later, the tiniest of details. She would use the softest lead for the heaviest blacks and the need for dark expression in a single stroke. The semi-soft lead would act as something of a connector, blending the stark differences in each of the other pencils' depths. She closed her eyes for a moment, seeing the finished product before she had even begun, and then she went to work.

As Alex stroked the page, she blocked out the praise and the exclamations behind her and dove into the work until she found that place. There, she could not be disturbed. The safety and sanctity of creation, where the only voice she could hear was that of the self-critic. She knew she'd captured Angus's handsome likeness when she reaffixed her attention and realized the gathering behind her had fallen silent.

"For you," Alex said. Then she slipped a small knife from her pocket and slit the page from the pad.

"Truly amazing," Angus said. "Almost a photograph."

"Better than that," another said.

"Thank you," Alex said, even as she admonished herself for eliciting the extra attention.

Taking her satchel, Alex begged away from the circle of people inspecting the work. She swiped a flute of champagne from a passing server's tray and slipped across the room, changing her view. As she leaned against the enormous piano, Alex sensed a presence approaching from seven o'clock.

"The name's Patrick Donning."

Alex glanced back at the man she'd made into a unicorn and gave a flat smile. "Nice to meet you."

"A black-haired beauty with all that talent." He leaned close, sliding his hand across her bare shoulder so that the tips of his fingers were under the lip of her dress. His mouth touched her ear as he said, "I find you exquisite. And I wouldn't mind seeing what other talents you may have."

Alex pulled away, allowing the urge to reach for her knife fade as she searched her memory for Mr. Donning's details included in her pre-op packet.

Recalling the juicy snippet, Alex turned, leaned to his cheek, and whispered, "From what I hear, I'm almost ten years older than you like them. Schoolgirl anime, isn't it?" She lifted her glass, tilted it toward his precious bow-tie, then back to her mouth.

Mr. Donning's face flushed to the color of a deep bruise and he mumbled something unintelligible, then walked off. In his wake was the sudden and almost cloying scent of almonds. At first Alex thought it was his cologne, but the scent remained as he disappeared into the bathroom hall. She swirled her champagne, but the drink was crisp, stars on the tongue and all that—no almonds—and she didn't see a bowl anywhere nearby.

Strange.

Pushing from the piano, Alex decided to edge all the way around the back of the crowd until the entry popped into view again, then nearly dropped her glass when it did.

A man stood centered in the doorway, holding a metal attaché. He made no attempt to hide, and even gave her a slight nod. She almost shook her head, but afraid to ruin the illusion—because that's what it had to be—Alex stayed as stoic as she could, her next breath lodged in her throat like a swollen balloon.

He couldn't be here, not now. Not ever.

This man had died decades ago.

He tilted his head in a *follow me* motion, pivoted, and nearly knocked into the incoming piano player as he strode back down the narrow hallway.

Alex dropped her glass to the floor, evoking gasps, then kicked off her heels and avoided the piano player as she hurtled the corner of an empty table. By the time she reached the hallway, the man with the attaché was already down the stairs and heading out the front. Alex slowed long enough to peer into the coat-check closet—sure enough, slot forty-four sat empty—then raced down the marble steps.

She punched the doors open, and caught sight of the man directly ahead, running now and a good half block away. The large metal attaché thumped his leg between strides.

Alex darted forward just as a piano key chimed faintly behind her. Later she'd realize how dull and out of tune it'd sounded, but the thought was lost in the deafening boom that instantly followed tossing it from her mind and hurtling her forward. A searing blast bellowed above her as she tumbled across the cobblestones, one arm twisting below her. Her head cracked against the stones with an unheard grunt.

From a half-curl, Alex squinted back at the broiling flames now swallowing the restaurant behind her.

Whirling around, she saw that the fleeing man had also been thrown forward, but farther away, and already rising. Without a hitch, he picked up the metal case, lumbered a few steps, and began running again.

Ears buzzing from the explosion, Alex crept to her feet, holding her wrenched shoulder as scream-filled smoke and crackling flames billowed behind her. The fire roared and emergency sirens wailed, but the man never turned. She paused only to seize her satchel before racing after him.

He veered right, disappearing onto the next block just as she hit her stride. Gambling, Alex cut down an alley, thinking to head him off at the street parallel to the river. Twenty yards on, just as her thighs began to burn, she bolted from the street's end, and barreled into him full force, almost sending them both into the water. The attaché skittered and struck the railing with a clank, then popped open as it fell.

Laid out on her stomach and gasping for air, she found herself squinting at a translucent pouch encased in foam. A dark red passport that read British Isle of Man was cradled inside ... next to a man's severed hand.

A clack sounded behind her, and cold steel stung the soft skin behind Alex's ear.

Gun pressed tightly to her head, the man leaned to one side and gathered the case with his free hand. His movements were fluid but tense, professional but deadly, and she followed his progress with her eyes alone. When he knelt in front of her, eyes darting back and forth as he worked, he didn't look at Alex once. She saw him, though, and other than the lightest toll of years, he hadn't changed a bit.

"They will have questions for you. Answer them all honestly, except for one." He snapped the case closed and moved behind her again. "You never saw me."

His words clouded in the cold air above her shoulder, his warm breath—and that voice, his voice—sent chills up Alex's spine. It was really him.

"Where have—?"

But he just strode past and climbed over the railing, attaché in hand.

Alex scrambled. "Wait. What—"

He leaped into the river with the case and quick-stroked to an idling jet boat lurking in the darkness. He never glanced back.

Alex gripped the railing, chest heaving as a cacophony of sirens and flashing red lights swarmed the roads behind her.

And she watched her father disappear.

Two

Tuzla, Bosnia and Herzegovina
Ninety-three kilometers north of Sarajevo

Standing between the rented jeep and the door of a plaster-walled hillside mosque, Evan Lockard tucked the Ukrainian passport back into a fold in the suitcase and removed the last of his clothing. Bosnia was much colder than London, but Lockard was relishing the moment. It reminded him of the dark mornings in Coronado, when the crash of the frigid waves sounded like Mother Nature's laugh, an invitation to an evil dare. Those were the moments when his fellow classmates had dropped out. They just couldn't bear another frigid four-a.m., five-mile swim, a main component of BUD/S—Basic Underwater Demolition/SEALS training. In reality, it wasn't Mother Nature that beat them. It was their own minds.

Knowing this, Lockard stood there for an extra few moments, staring up at the mosque's wooden minaret, and concentrated on controlling *his* mind. Not that he was a masochist or anything. Quite the opposite. He liked pleasure as much as the next guy, and standing naked in the dark recess of a worn country, sucking on a fistful of snow, Lockard felt *alive*.

Twenty minutes later, geared in cold-weather-white, Lockard blended in better than a wolf against the shoulder-high snow drifts. He checked his watch. Josef Faris would retreat to his home office in twenty-six minutes and make the appointed phone call to his new Swiss banker. It would take Lockard sixteen of those minutes to navigate the hill and a small patch of woods before reaching the house. Three minutes or less to enter. A single minute to settle into Josef's office. At worst case, that gave Lockard six full minutes to spare.

Plenty of time.

He inhaled deeply, drawing in the scent of cheap burning firewood. He wondered if he should feel bad for what he was about to do. After all, Josef had been a critical piece to the success of the take. A Customs officer in charge of private plane arrivals at Tuzla International Airport, Josef had provided them simple and seamless entry to Bosnia and Herzegovina. Lockard could not have succeeded without Josef.

But then Josef made a major mistake and threatened to expose them all. The likelihood of fallout was not enormous, but the degree of violation did not matter in this instance.

Lockard remembered finding Josef injured and trapped on the Sarajevo street nicknamed Sniper Alley over a decade ago. He'd bought the man's loyalty with a pocketknife and four strips of black duct tape. Funny how money could make any man betray his loyalties.

Now, though, Josef was no different than a racehorse with a limp.

Lockard exhaled, watching the vapors of his breath disappear. Then he set off.

It turned out he was wrong, which pissed him off, but it took only fifteen minutes to reach the house, and he negotiated the garage's side door in less than three seconds.

It was unlocked.

Mistake number two, Mr. Faris.

He placed his hand on the hood of the car in the garage. Cold. Josef had been home for a while. Lockard couldn't make out the model of the car, but it looked to be some sort of Fiat or maybe Opel. Garbage, either way, and useless in the mountains, especially in this weather. Still, Josef hadn't been extravagant.

Yet.

Lockard took a knee to untie and slip off his boots. Holding them in one hand, he stepped to the interior door, placed them aside, and waited.

Faint sounds of an active household echoed from inside. Josef's two children were both home, and so was his wife. No sound from Josef, but Lockard was not concerned by that. The man was there, no question. He would honor the banker's requested time for this call.

Lockard reached up, swiveled the knob a hair, and then a bit more, feeling the latch yawn before pushing it open an inch. He paused again and listened. Same sounds, about twelve to fourteen feet away, and with no rugs in the hallway, they created a small echo. It sounded as if the whole family was in the living area at the other end of the house.

Lockard pushed the door fully open, swept inside, and eased it closed again, careful not to let the latch click. Taking in the smell of roasted pork—probably *odojak*, traditional whole piglet—he moved sideways down the hall and slipped into Josef's home office.

The lights were off, but that was fine. He had studied the layout on his last visit.

Lockard strode over to the desk and tested the chair. Well oiled, so he took a seat. Then, regulating his breathing to temper any excess adrenaline, he waited.

Eleven minutes later, Josef called to his wife as he walked down the hallway toward the office. He spoke in the South Slavic dialect used these days by most Bosniaks, the traditional Muslims who'd survived the ethnic cleansing war of the nineties to remain in Bosnia. Lockard did not speak the language fluently, but he understood enough from other Slavic training to know Josef had told his wife he needed some privacy and to keep the children from disturbing him.

By the time Josef closed the door and turned around, Lockard had his HK45 Tactical pistol trained on Josef's head. Though long retired from the SEALs, Lockard still favored the Heckler & Koch for its reliability, accuracy, and the extended threaded barrel, on which he'd fastened an Osprey sound suppressor for the occasion. Wearing the snow-whites, he must have looked like an apparition to the poor man.

Josef opened his mouth to yell.

Lockard shook his head an inch, side to side.

Josef closed his mouth, glanced at the door, then back at Lockard. "How did you—"

"Josef. We have been friends for many years, haven't we?"

"Yes."

"And how is your leg today, in this cold?" Lockard glanced down at his own winter gear.

Josef took a step toward the door. "It aches."

"Yes, old wounds do that," Lockard said. "Come closer please, Josef."

Josef eased forward, eyes wide.

"Where is the rest of it?" Lockard placed the HK on the desk.

"I don't—"

Before Josef could finish the sentence, Lockard had sprung from the chair, secured him in a headlock—not easy, as Josef was much taller than he—and stuffed one of his thick, synthetic-down gloves in the man's mouth. Josef grunted and Lockard pulled him to the chair. He drew four thick plastic zip ties from his pocket and secured each of Josef's limbs to the seat. He was careful to keep the straps over clothing, to avoid evidential rubs or bruises.

Immobilized and muted, Josef struggled for a moment, and then his eyes filled with tears.

"Josef?" His wife called from behind the door. "Are you all right?"

Lockard bent down and whispered close to Josef's ear. "Don't make me kill the children. Tell her you will be out in five minutes." He waved the HK and Josef nodded.

Lockard pulled the glove from Josef's mouth. He coughed, and said, "A few more minutes, then I'll be out."

She walked away without answering.

Lockard said, "Where is it?"

Josef glanced at the closet.

Lockard walked across the office and opened the double doors. A tall metal file cabinet sat flush against the wall. "Here?"

Josef looked away. "Behind the files. There is a loose board."

Lockard tugged back the cabinet—good thing it was empty—and peered behind it. He thumbed a long board, causing it to swivel open.

Well hidden, Josef. You should have kept it that way.

He reached in, found the handle, and pulled it out from the wall space. Josef had kept it in the same aluminum Zero Halliburton case Lockard had given him over a week ago. Placing the case on the desk before Josef, Lockard said, "I assume you changed it. Let me guess, your birth date, or maybe your wife's?"

"My son's," Josef said. "July, the fifth."

Typical. Lockard reversed the numbers – almost all Europeans, Eastern and Western, listed the day first and then month – and pressed the two latches open to find ninety-nine thick stacks of US dollar bills. Just under a million dollars.

Key word—*under.*

"You took a trip to London." He tilted his head at Josef. "And Monte Carlo."

"It was for my brother. He is sick." Josef paused, and looked down as he said, "And he likes the casinos."

"Where is the rest?"

Josef nodded to the desk.

Lockard pulled open the drawer and searched, careful not to thump Josef's fingers. The near-empty stack of hundreds sat under a sleeve of papers. He dropped the anemic pile into the briefcase, snapped it closed, then pulled out a small, clear vial of resin and held it up. "This will make you sleep. So I can leave without problems."

"I won't say anything, I promise it. Please."

Lockard uncapped the vial.

"You needed me," Josef pleaded.

"You were a great help. I appreciate that." Lockard grabbed Josef's hair and pulled his head back. Stuffing the vial between the man's lips, he shook the milky liquid into his mouth.

Lockard held Josef's mouth and nose shut as he waited for the swallow, and kept them covered until the convulsions began. Josef spasmed against the restraints, eyes bulging wide as the chemicals reached his bloodstream and his breathing became labored. Thirty seconds later, his bowels released and his body slumped in the chair.

The massively condensed dose of Gonyaulax tamarensis, a neurotoxin derived from mollusks, caused almost instant paralysis and lung failure. Any autopsy performed would show a simple shellfish poisoning. Josef hadn't suffered.

Lockard cut off the zip ties and arranged the body into a more natural position, leaving the eyes open. Lifting the case, he then walked to the door, turned, looked around the room, and listened. The three remaining people in the house were farther down the hall, one playing a mistuned piano as the other two laughed.

Satisfied, Lockard slipped outside and back into the white night.

Three

Evading the police was easy. Focused on the destruction of the restaurant, not one officer glanced at Alex as she'd snuck past, slipped a set of keys from the valet stand, and relieved the restaurant lot of a black Mercedes. Sadly, the owner wasn't going to need it anymore.

Alex steadied her arms on the steering wheel as she sat parked across the river from the restaurant, shielded by two large stone buildings adjacent to Victoria Embankment. Smoke twisted skyward in a giant black funnel, scarring London's picturesque skyline.

Did my father do that?

He was dead this morning. He was dead this afternoon. This evening, up until ten o'clock, Edgar Winter was still dead. Now he was alive, and dozens of innocent people were not. Alex gripped the wheel so hard her hands began to shake.

Eighteen fucking years.

Taking deep breaths, she loosened her grip long enough to pull the mobile from her satchel and switch it on. After waiting a full minute to sync to the data network and update, she checked for text messages, e-mails, phone calls. Nothing. As far as Operations was concerned, Alex was in a blackout. Deputy Director Moss would know she hadn't completed the assignment when she didn't report in from the airport later today.

Exhaling hard, Alex dug back into the satchel, trading the phone for her sketchbook, and clicked on the overhead light. She flipped the pages until she found the scene she'd drawn no fewer than a hundred times. From all different aspects, the illustrations ranged from simple line sketches to full-fledged, detailed drawings.

Alex chose a sketch that was midrange in perspective. It undulated with the snaking bend of a shallow chalk stream, its smooth white sides and bottom in milky pastels as it meandered through the countryside somewhere in the western UK. The summer sky glowed upon grass that was overgrown at the banks. The houses seemed smaller than they would in the stark graying months of winter and the large red brick mill lay unseen behind her vantage point, but the full meadow stretched all the way to the horizon. They'd fished the stream together that day. She could still smell the scent of ferns and the faint odor of live trout.

It was the last time she'd ever seen her father.

Alex did not have *daddy issues*. Of course, it'd been hell when her parents died. Terrible that it'd happened in an embassy bombing, but tragedy was an undeniable part of this world. Innocent people were hit by cars, paralyzed skiing. They crashed motorcycles or were victims of natural disasters. One did not forget the unexpected and sudden, but one could overcome any emotional trauma in time. Wounds closed up, scarred over, left a thickened patch of skin to protect any nerves that survived below that surface.

For Alex, her parents were there one day, and gone the next. A solid and full home-life erased and then replaced. Sure, she'd been pissed off at the world for a few years, cursed The Universe and all that. What pre-teen wouldn't? But she'd been well cared for, well loved, and eventually she came to the conclusion that though a person might yearn for order, she operated ever in chaos. Predict the next year? The next day? Most times you couldn't even predict the next minute.

And Alex was fine with that. This early understanding had made life easier on her in ways, and it'd certainly contributed to her success on the job. Yet tonight was different. No way in hell would she have ever predicted her father re-appearing from the grave…so much for deadened nerves. Suddenly, Alex was no longer an orphan, she was just left behind. Abandoned.

Alex realized, with a building hollowness in her stomach, that she had been discarded.

She flipped the pages forward to see if she'd drawn any other scenes of the chalk stream in this book, but the rest were places she'd traveled to on nonofficial business. Geneva, Sao Paolo, Costa Rica. She paused on a page that showed the Place du Bourg-de-Four in Geneva's Old Town, where Jack Pope— the self-described nomadic salesman—sat at the edge of the Mont Blanc Bridge. Also a last meeting.

Wearing dark wash jeans and a charcoal Harrington jacket, he held a baguette in one hand and an espresso in the other, as the alternating Swiss and Geneva flags flapped in the background. She could almost smell the melting snow mixed with the annual tulip festival, and remembered how he'd laughed while telling her—with the betrayal of an English accent—that he wasn't the sort of man who drank tea.

Jack's dark blond hair was short in the drawing, making him look younger than his mid-thirties. Alex used to run her hands through that hair as they made love. She swallowed hard and shook the thought away. It was her own doing. She'd kept Jack at arm's length, refused to let him get too close to her, after all.

Alex turned to a blank page, untied her leather fold of pencils, and closed her eyes for a moment.

Drawing to Alex was much like writing in a journal or deep meditative yoga was for others. They called it eidetic, but all Alex knew was it helped her process information, occupying her conscious mind while releasing the subconscious. Drawing was the primary tool she used to analyze complex situations.

This time she drew to remember.

Alex thought of her father standing in the restaurant entry, unmoving as the light cut across his face and he stared straight at her. She let her hand glide across the page, her pencil creating the long, oval contours of a face, eyes high-set, jaw strong. She outlined the hair and ears next, and finally the nose and lips. First the lines *of* the face, then the lines *on* the face. Each of them darkened as the image became more grounded, more certain. The person before her came to life.

Edgar Winter.

Breathing in easy cadence, Alex added line-by-line, long strokes and shorter ones, detail-by-detail, with fluid movements and a soft touch to the page. This was what she needed to calm herself, and she fell into the work, deeper and deeper, until she could finally hear words rising from the man taking shape before her.

"See?" her father asks, and she gazes to where he points, while standing up to her waist in the cool meadow stream.

"No. Where?" Alex bends low, careful to keep her rod's tip from disturbing the surface.

"Watch for the movement first." Her father puts a strong arm around her shoulder and bends with her, pointing to the same spot. "There."

A strip of dark silver flashes below the ripples.

"I see it!" Alex says, and moves to cast.

"Good," he says, but holds her arm down, preventing her from raising the rod. "Now watch the movement. Follow him with your eyes only. Stay still."

"He's right there, though. I see him. I can—"

"No," he says, without ever taking his eyes off the water. "You need to time it. Find the right moment. Then make your play."

"When he surfaces again?"

Her father nods. "This is why trout get caught, Alex. They have patterns. Remember that." And he peers at her for a long second.

Alex looks up and searches her father's face. It's an opening, an intentional one, and she knows it. How does she take it? How does she ask?

"You like fishing, Daddy?"

"Fishing is not something I do. It's something I am."

Alex smiles at him, but doesn't have the guts to ask him what she really wants to know.

Her father knows it. He says, "That's not the question you were thinking of, is it, Alex?" He glances up at Alex's mom sitting under a tree, reading, then adds in a low voice, "Your mother told me your concerns, so go ahead and ask. You're old enough to know... and you should, so you can understand why I'm not always here."

Holding her breath, she waits, unsure she wants to even hear the full truth, but certain she's tired of the half lies. So she asks, as bravely and brazenly as she can, "Where do you really go?"

She searches his eyes after he tells her. "Does Mom know?"

"Of course. Only in fantasy do the spouses remain ignorant. And how could that really work, me leaving for weeks or even months at a time?"

Alex stands silent, nothing to say to that.

"But she doesn't know details. No one does. The movies get that part right."

They stand there for what seems like a good while, the water lapping the rocks at the edge of the stream. Suddenly, without ceremony, her father squeezes Alex's shoulder and points to the water.

"Now."

Four

Alex startled awake to the sound of someone rapping the butt of a black pistol on the car window. With no gun of her own, she whirled away and shielded the back of her head with the hard bone of an elbow. Best she could do in the tight space.

"Easy now." The man's muffled voice sounded distant in the solid Mercedes chamber. "Just need to move your car, is all."

Squinting, Alex turned and peered through the glass.

The man wore a puffy down jacket and light brown gloves with black marks on them. He was holding up a black cell phone, not a pistol, and pointing to a truck in front of them, then the large wooden double doors behind. Alex was blocking his entrance.

"Right," she said, holding up a hand and wincing at the soreness of her shoulder.

Alex set aside the sketchbook and started the car, revving the engine to get the heat going. According to the digital read on the dash, the temperature had dropped to nine degrees Celsius outside, and felt like twelve or so in the car, which translated to the low fifties in Fahrenheit. She checked her watch as she pulled around the tall truck. Just after five a.m., no wonder it was still dark.

Alex drove alongside the river, cutting through Piccadilly before hitting Buckingham Palace. With white lights strung over the street in the shape of presents, bows, and huge umbrellas, as well as a row of twenty-foot-high blue Christmas trees, Oxford Street rivaled the winter displays of Saks and Rockefeller Plaza in New York City. At this hour, though, the roads were empty of people scurrying from store to store and lugging oversized sacks of purchases. She switched the phone on again, but there was still nothing from Langley so she kept her objective simple. Get back to the hotel and change out of the dress.

She was staying at the Marriott in Grosvenor Square, partly because it was the same hotel where she and Jack had stayed during their first trip to London last year.

Call her romantic.

Truth was, Alex liked the contemporary Maze bar there, and the Gordon Ramsey menu rarely disappoints. That, and she liked being able to look across the green at the US Embassy.

Call her practical.

As she drove, Alex couldn't help wondering what other cities Jack had been to these last months, after he'd disappeared. The thought still stung, but was no longer acute, and she was pretty sure it would disappear entirely in another couple of months. Pretend to feel nothing for long enough, and eventually it became true. For example, she'd already stopped wishing to see his face long enough to punch it. That was progress.

Of course, she'd done a background check on Pope after he stopped returning her calls. Actually, she'd also ordered one as soon as they'd met; spies did things like that. The Company almost required it. In any case, both checks were identical: empty files, criminal or otherwise. Only a birth certificate, the UK passport she'd already seen, and verification that he had, in fact, grown up New Cross, south London. Unlike Alex, he was who he said he was: a high-level microchip salesman assigned to territories in Europe.

With most of her assignments also in Europe, they could meet at a moment's notice and had even found themselves in the same city twice last year. Then he declined to meet up in Prague three months ago. When Alex asked him to the Cayman Islands a few weeks after that, he declined again, and that was it.

Two yellow cards and you're ejected.

Anyway, who was Alex to judge duplicitous behavior? She'd told him she was a private security consultant and that her job was confidential and sometimes dangerous. Even if she'd been allowed to tell him she was CIA, she wouldn't have.

Do you think you have trust issues, Alex?

No, doctor.

Then why won't you let anyone get close to you.

Because it's worked out so well for me before?

She didn't even want to know what the CIA psychoanalyst would say about the impact of learning about her father.

I fear you are currently experiencing the initial phases of the feminine Oedipus attitude. We call it the Electra complex.

You fear I'm becoming a superhero?

I fear you're blaming your mother for your father's death … and for the fact that neither of you have a penis.

But doctor, I can have a penis anytime I want.

Alex pulled into the lot at the Ukrainian Catholic cathedral and silenced the car before navigating to the phone's browser to check the news at The Times and The Guardian. Both papers were running an identical, single-paragraph article that described the explosion at the restaurant as a result of faulty natural-gas pipe fittings.

Damage Control 101. She just wondered which agency had gotten to the media first.

Beyond that, still no messages or voicemails for her. No revised assignment or new directives. That meant one thing and one thing only: Finish the original assignment. She thought of her father leaping over that river railing, never looking back, not once meeting her eye, and she pointed the car in the direction of the hotel.

Finishing this was exactly what she intended to do.

After wiping down the car and locking it, Alex placed the keys above the rear tire, leaving it in the Cathedral's parking lot. Investigators would notice it missing from the restaurant sooner or later, and she didn't want it to be too easy to trace back to her, but she still wanted to keep it near for emergency use.

Alex hurried down Duke Street, shivering but thankful for the short days of winter. The sun didn't rise until after eight and it disappeared again by four. It would make it easier for her to move around unnoticed.

When she entered the empty hotel lobby, the sleepy, mid-twenties front desk clerk raised her head, but gave Alex only a single raised brow. Alex countered her insouciant British reserve with a wave as she disappeared into the lift, as if it were perfectly normal to wander in after five a.m., shoeless and wearing a tattered black dress.

Arriving at the fifth floor, Alex slipped the key card from her satchel and stood before the door to the room for a moment and listened. She stared at the card insert, frozen by an image of her inserting the key, turning the knob, and being blown backward. Clearly still shaken from the evening, Alex brushed the image aside, and slipped the card into and out of the lock. The green light blinked, the door clicked, and she entered.

And stopped a single step into the room.

None of Alex's belongings remained. No suitcase, no clothes, not even her toothbrush. Whoever had taken it all had even swiped the novel from the nightstand. The Charm School by Nelson DeMille. The helicopter had just landed and they were about to escape Cold War Russia.

"Bastards," Alex muttered as she shut the door.

The only items left in the room were in the closet: a dry-cleaning bag holding a single dark pantsuit she'd have never chosen for herself, a pair of heels unsuited for running, and hose that lay atop a folded scarf. No coat.

Whoever left this didn't want Alex very mobile.

She tossed the dry-cleaning bag onto the bed, checked the tag—Palace Gates Dry Cleaning—and unsheathed the suit. In the jacket's pocket, she discovered a leather fold. Tucked inside, a dark blue passport with gold lettering and a crown with two flags on the front. Opening it, Alex saw her current passport photo staring back at her. Apparently she was now Canadian.

The name was Amanda Carr, not a legend she'd ever used, or any of those that the CIA had given her upon entering the National Clandestine Service. According to the stamps, she, Amanda, had traveled to the south of France, Australia, and Hawaii this last year.

"A recreational surfer, Amanda enjoys a good Bordeaux while drawing ocean sunsets," Alex murmured, closing the passport.

Behind it, she found a commercial plane ticket, complete with the thin perforated edge on one side. Heathrow to Dulles. Someone was trying to send her back home to DC, and fast. The flight was set to leave in four hours.

Alex shuffled through a few receipts from local shops and restaurants, all folded behind the ticket, along with a nominal amount of cash, both in euros and pound sterling. *Pocket litter.*

But was it from Langley? The Company had never delivered her a legend on a job before; it would be too risky. Plus, Moss had made it ultra clear that Alex was to see this assignment through without any contact until finished. This didn't mesh with that instruction or the complete blackout in communication thus far.

No, there was only one explanation, and it was as clear as the chalk-stream water of that long ago day. Her father had cleared out this room. He sent all this, set it up.

He wanted Alex gone again.

"Damn." Alex threw the passport and ticket fluttering across the room. "Damn you." She yanked the fabric of her dress, causing the side seam to tear wide open and expose the black tattoo on her ribs. The two eagles, talons outstretched, tumbling over each other in a circle of infinity, were the mark of a self-inflicted honor.

Talonstrike.

The sight of it in the dresser mirror stilled her, calmed her. Only two candidates from the CIA's Farm—one male, one female—along with the top team of Navy SEALs each year, were selected for a chance to earn it.

"I earned it," she said aloud, like *he* was still there to hear.

She'd driven vehicles at speeds of over a hundred miles per hour, *in reverse*. She'd learned to overtake and pilot commercial and military helicopters, mid-fucking-flight. She could pilot US, British, and Israeli fighter jets, both Soviet and North Korean MIGs. Alex could land any of them, wheels up on grass strips, gravel runs, desert soil, beach sand. And yes, even water.

"Sui cadere dulcis," Alex said loudly, defiantly. That was what the instructors had called piloting along white-capped waves in the middle of a thunderstorm, three-hundred miles offshore…in the middle of an engine stall. Roughly translated, it meant *sweet suicide*—as more than one candidate had signed their life away attempting it.

Well, she'd passed all their tests, beat almost every single Navy SEAL in scoring, too.

Pulling the dress over her head and off, Alex balled it up and threw it into the trashcan. "Patterns, Daddy. Everyone has patterns."

Five

Jackson Hole, Wyoming

CIA Deputy Director of Operations, William Moss—Bill to his handful of family and friends—eased toward the edge of a sage thicket and stopped four feet behind Georgia, his favorite German shorthaired pointer. Stiff as a morning pecker, her lean muscles were strung taut beneath the long brown spots and dirty white coat. She must have come up on a whole covey of birds. Maybe even a couple of pheasants, if she was lucky.

Moss ticked off the safety and nestled the stock of the side-by-side shotgun into his shoulder. A bit lighter than the Beretta he was used to, the Holland & Holland twenty-gauge felt balanced and would swing easy with the target. He contemplated doing the old shoot-from-the-hip move, but thought better of it. Georgia was new at the game and he couldn't be sure she'd find many more. And having bagged only one lousy grouse thus far, he wasn't about to risk his best opportunity of the day.

Besides, Moss was ready to roast his feet and have a lunchtime sip of the old tonic.

He glanced down at Georgia—poor thing was beginning to quiver—and whispered, "Get it."

Georgia pounced into the thicket and the bush exploded, four birds rocketing into the sky.

Moss took a single beat to make his decision, then swung right. The trajectory was a better line, and the grouse moving in that direction looked fatter. Two sharp pops later, he'd struck both birds, sending them tumbling to the frozen ground.

Georgia, having sat up straight from the flush to watch for prizes, bounded into the field to fetch them, her head down and tail swinging in violent spasms.

Moss cracked the smoking gun open and laid it across his forearm, savoring the smell of gun smoke as he waited for Georgia to complete her task.

Prancing back, she smiled as she approached.

That's when Moss realized why she was so smug.

The damn bitch had picked up both birds in one fetch.

"Out."

She dropped the birds, then panted, still smiling.

"Idiot," he said, leaning over and inspecting the take. The two blue grouse were now mangled from the grip. After slipping them into his vest, he poked Georgia's head with the butt of his gun and said, "Find 'em."

He'd have to go back to the training grounds with this one. Georgia seemed to have a stubborn streak in her, and Moss would have to break it.

As she began to circle the field in a wide arc again, nose to the ground and tail back up in the air, Moss's cell phone chirped twice.

He dug it out of his chest pocket and checked the message. The texted code, *Tempest 033*, meant it was a secure packet sent from a European CIA-controlled satellite dubbed *Oslo*. It could have come from only one person, a man who, for all purposes, didn't even exist.

As Moss braced for the report, he couldn't help but chuckle to himself. "Tempest" was a throwback to the mysterious NSA telephonic security acronym from the late sixties. It meant nothing in reality, just a middle finger to the competing intelligence group. Even more tickling to Moss, the satellite orbiting the Earth at seven thousand miles per hour had been designed and launched by the Central Intelligence Agency. In an internal test for "security robustness," the CIA had challenged the NSA to hack in and listen. The NSA failed, of course, seven times. A fact that the president himself both admired and disliked.

Too fucking bad. When the CIA needed privacy, it got it. Period.

Moss entered his own corresponding code and waited. Two minutes on the dot, and the phone chirped again.

He said, "Should I be worried?"

"You've seen the news, I assume." Edgar sounded weary for once.

"This isn't North Korea. Of course I have."

Edgar didn't answer.

Moss pinched his nose. "I wish you had neutralized the blast first."

"How long has it been since you were in the field?"

Moss looked at the long stretch of icy brush before him, Georgia still working her concentric circles, and contemplated a sly response, but instead said, "What's your point?"

"Things happen."

"Define things."

A long pause, then Edgar said, "I was made."

Moss sputtered, "By whom?"

"I think you damned well know, Bill."

Moss didn't have to answer to Edgar. Hell, he didn't have to answer to anyone short of the president himself. Edgar had been in the cold for the better part of the last two decades, and he would stay there for the next two, as far as Moss was concerned.

"Never mind that. Did you get it?"

"Of course."

Moss dug a toe of his boot into the frozen turf. "And?"

"It's not what you think."

Moss stopped. "Tell me."

"Not on these damn megaphones."

A drop of sweat trickled down his forehead. Moss calmed himself. He knew all along it'd be like this with Edgar Winter. Moss had been a fool to accept carrying the torch of this fantasy operation. He should have cut Edgar loose the moment he'd gotten him. He said, "Then dead drop it."

"Not acceptable," Edgar said. "And I'll need to go black for a bit."

"I'll cut you off!"

"One more thing," Edgar said, unfazed by the threat. "The Brits know about the account."

Moss closed his eyes as the words sank in. He had the sense he would remember this moment for the entirety of his life. The day his world had begun to unravel. Playing dumb, he said, "What account?"

A chuckle from the other end. The bastard was taunting him. "Zoran Draganic's. My intelligence says he's known in the money-laundering world as the Serbian Whale."

The back of his throat beginning to burn, Moss was unable to respond before Edgar said, "I'll be in touch," then hung up.

Dammit.

Moss squeezed the phone until he heard a crack. He'd put Alex Winter there for one damned reason and one only. Hell, he'd had her trained for this mission from her first goddamned day at The Farm. With Talonstrike, she should have been prepped for anything that went wrong. And as for Edgar, well, he had less of a conscience than Moss had even figured. The man should have locked up with a coronary when his own daughter appeared in the middle of a mission. As his opposition.

Instead, it sounded like the bastard was enjoying himself.

If you want something done…

Staring far into the horizon, where the sun played with the clouds, he saw Georgia's silhouette. She had stiffened again.

Fuck it, Moss said to himself, fetching two more shells and jamming them into the chambers.

Looks like I'll have to dig out my old legends one last time.

Chester, UK
Four hours west of London

Zoran Draganic dug the heel of a boot into the horse and swatted him across the nape again. The creature named Alabaster snorted and turned hard on the near-frozen turf. So hard that Draganic was taken off the line and he missed the ball with his mallet.

Again.

Draganic turned back around the goal and entered the play in full view of the stadium. Chester Racecourse was about four hours west of London, and Draganic understood why the English trekked all the way to it, even for a private polo match. Rich green grass stretched to the white grandstands and red stone walls. A placard stated it was established in 1539 making it older than most countries.

He kicked Alabaster and crossed back over the line of the ball, a clear violation of gentlemen's rules, but Draganic was no gentleman. Without an umpire present, it was a self-policing match, and since there was no real harm, there was no real foul, in Draganic's mind.

He raced back up to the ball, bumping the youngest of his opponents' thighs with one of his own. Being larger than the boy, Draganic almost knocked over him *and* his horse.

But the aspiring duke showed some spine and elbowed Draganic, causing him to lean too far and lose control. Alabaster pulled up and turned on him.

Then the boy gained the line alone and smacked the ball right into the goal.

Just as Alabaster dumped a pile of shit on the field.

The three opponents' wives—the lone attendees—cheered with loud claps and calls of the soon-to-be-duke's name.

Draganic was tempted to pull out his Katran knife and slit the animal's neck right there, let him bleed out on the pitch. Designed for Russian Navy combat divers and therefore nicknamed the *Black Sea Shark*, the Katran was long, thick, and constructed of carbon steel. The blade could slice right through the animal's spine.

Lucky for Alabaster, Dragonic was too determined to score by the end of this chukker, the last period of the match.

Draganic figured the Brits had fed the horse double to spite him, the lone Eastern European of the group. Financial envy ran deep in England, and it wouldn't surprise him in the least. Though his teammates weren't envious, they were just interested. Former bankers for Draganic, they had gotten word that he'd come into another sum of cash.

Of course they'd see none of it this time.

In his own little *fuck you* to the shameless trolls, Draganic showed up in a bright orange checkered shirt and lime green helmet; it must have embarrassed them to the limit. As usual, the lot of them looked like they'd been painted with the British boring brush—all khaki and brown.

As Draganic made his way back to his teammates, his cell phone rang.

All three of the men stopped their horses as Draganic fished the phone from his jacket and checked the caller. It was Pachai Randeep. A call he would take.

Draganic could hear the groans and whispers that included "uncivilized" and "Croat," as he turned the horse and trotted off to talk with some privacy.

Annoyed, Draganic used Pachai's despised nickname as he answered. "Poshdeep," he said, "you make me wait for your call."

After a pause, Randeep said, "I am sorry, Zoran. I was working on the model."

Draganic kept trotting away until he was near the edge of the racetrack. Then he unstrapped his helmet and flipped it off to hear better. The wives must have caught sight of his scarred neck because one of them gasped, and he could hear her even at this distance. His beard did little to hide the roped skin. Ignoring the reaction, Draganic said, "Always you are with these computers. This is why you never married."

"This is not why," Randeep said, sounding hurt.

"Never mind that. We have good news."

"How good?"

"We are ready to invest again."

"It is done, then?" Randeep sounded excited. "I can start?"

"Not yet. Soon. I have to make another call."

"What amount is it that we are talking about?"

Draganic turned back to see one of his teammates approaching. He held up a hand, stopping the man a good thirty yards away. Draganic smiled as he said, "More than before. And this time, it is protected."

"This is quite fortuitous, as I have just finished the model."

Draganic tapped the horse with a heel. "Of course, the model. Is it finally working?"

"Zoran, it is not only working,"—Randeep almost sang the last words of the sentence—"it is alive."

Six

One thing that Alex's father had taken the precious time to teach her: much like trout finning the deep shadows of a grassy riverbank, spies were most difficult to find when they were hunkered down—hidden in a safe house, unplugged from the world. Rather than trying to stir them up, it was better to wait them out. Watch for when they disturb the surface, because sooner or later, they always did.

And that's when they got caught.

After taking a scalding, if quick, shower, Alex changed into the suit that'd been left for her—a tailored fit, of course—pinned up her hair, and headed back downstairs. As she re-entered the black-and-white-checkered marble lobby, Alex was even more aware of the clerk's considering eye than before. Hotels like this one were found next to embassies and consulates because dignitaries and diplomats liked to stay near their respective home-bases, same as agents. The employees at these hotels were often used by the host government to monitor guests' comings and goings. Even allies like the UK and US play this little game with each other. As this clerk had allowed someone carrying a dry cleaning bag access to the upper floors, Alex figured she was on Scotland Yard's dime.

Which she immediately disproved by brightening as Alex approached. "Excellent. You've received it."

"Excuse me?"

"The suit. And he was quite right ... you needed it." She gave Alex a playful wink.

Alex crossed to the desk, eyeing her carefully. "The deliveryman."

"You mean your brother?" she said, then leaned forward and whispered, "Truth be told, he was a bit cross with you. Out so late on your own and all. But I assured him that's it right safe around here."

"My brother…" Alex nodded as she eyed her. "The short, dark-haired one?

Rough looking?"

She gave a look of confusion. "No. He was tall, though I couldn't see his hair. He was wearing one of those ball caps."

"My *step*brother, I have five of those. Same height as me?"

"Taller by a few inches, I'd say over six feet. And, if I might say so…he was a bit of alright. Though a spot old for my liking."

Maybe Edgar. "How old?"

She twisted her mouth. "Thirty-five, I'd say."

Scratch that. Alex leaned forward. "Did he have an accent? Or maybe a tattoo?"

"English accent, but not the Queen's. And no, not a single tattoo on his neck or face." She raised her brow and gave Alex the eye. "I fancy that these days."

Alex refrained from pointing out the row of stars tucked behind the lobe of the clerk's right ear, or the ankh tagged at her wrist. They'd become snapshots of memory as soon as she'd approached the desk. Alex would be able to return to this moment in her sketchbook without even concentrating.

"Tell you what, ring me if he shows again and I'll be sure to get him your number." Alex nodded.

"Count on it!" She beamed like they were bosom friends.

The cold, damp air rushed her as Alex exited the lobby, but she kept her hands free, both at ease and at the ready as she scanned the early morning faces around her. With temperatures dropping and the threat of snow later today, most people were bundled under dark trench coats and hats.

Edgar could be anywhere among them.

Having made a quick check on her phone's browser, Alex knew Palace Gates Dry Cleaners opened at seven a.m. With almost an hour to kill, she decided to take the Tube, then double and triple back to be sure she wasn't tailed. The habit had saved her hide more than once—most notably last year in Tangier when an over-zealous and under-savvy military type shadowed her following a small altercation in a local bar.

Another warm professional memory.

Alex headed north from Grosvenor Square toward the Bond Street station, but noted a couple reversing direction to pass her again. She canvassed their features with a quick gaze, locking in the shape of the man's bulbous bottom lip and the long curves of the woman's neck. Alex had not seen them before this day. Their body language was relaxed, and when they passed the second time, the man nodded at Alex and made solid eye contact. Alex was just about to nod back when a car screeched behind them. Alex leapt aside, grabbing the wrought iron park gate, ready to hurdle the fence and run.

A tall black carriage taxi sat ten feet away, wedged between two cars, with only inches separating all four bumpers. The couple who'd just passed Alex looked bemused by her reaction, but made no move toward her. She gave a flat smile and continued on, picking up the pace.

She reached the Bond Street Tube station three blocks later, and made her way underground. Though not yet mobbed with the bustle of rush hour, the station was already hot and smelled like animal sweat. Lots of damp wool around. She located the right tunnel and platform, and stepped onto the Tube without incident.

A dozen seats remained open, but Alex stood at the front of the train where she could survey the entire car behind her. The majority of passengers were barely present at all, either reading eBooks or texting or social networking on phones. The rest stared into space, maybe dreading the long day of ahead or still trying to wake to face it. The real activity came from a group of punks a few feet away, voices escalating as they spoke in Serbian, feeding off the other commuters' silence. They moved up the car and toward a young Indian couple seated across from Alex who had been whispering about student loan payments, as well as the man's final interview for a potential accounting job. The only interview he'd found in months. The woman wore a silk head scarf above the red bindi on her forehead, and man wore a semi-expensive looking suit. He had extended himself for a good impression at the interview.

The Serbs glanced around and spoke loudly as they edged closer to the couple, all but blocking their exit.

With a working knowledge of five of the major European languages, and having studied a few Eastern European ones as well, Alex understood exactly what they'd planned to do to them.

The woman gripped her purse tight to her stomach, and her companion put his arm around her. One of the Serbs sat on the other side of the woman and peered close to her face. She shrunk into her companion, turning away as he held her tighter. The Serb smiled at the back of her head and whispered something.

The next stop was announced over the loudspeaker, and the couple abruptly stood. Then, in a scurry of movement and body bumping, the largest of the men blocked the woman's exit, cutting her off from the Indian man who spun back to grab her hand.

The Serbs circled, confusing them.

It ended as quickly as it had begun, but Alex saw exactly what had happened.

The Serbs scattered, allowing the couple walk through them and off the train.

They laughed, watching the woman grip her purse like it was her last possession as the couple hurried away.

Alex carefully stood and kept her eyes on the two Serbs at her side as she made her way toward the doors. The one she needed to track was leaned against the steel pole closest to the doors, watching the departing couple with a shit-stained grin on his face.

The operator warned to clear the doors, the bell dinged, and Alex made her move.

Darting forward, she slipped her arm beneath the Serb's, took hold of his wrist, and twisted, pulling him off the pole.

He popped forward and stumbled through the closing doors with her.

"What are you—?"

They landed on the platform outside, the doors closed, and he was left alone with Alex—his punk buddies rolling away in the train.

Jumping to his feet, he yelled, "Fuck you are doing?"

Alex put out a hand. "Give it to me."

He brushed himself off and ignored her as the last of the departed passengers disappeared into the stairwell, leaving the two of them alone on the platform.

Perfect.

She spoke in Serbian, "Don't make me take it from you."

He gave her a long look up and down, smiled with sharp canine teeth that protruded forward from the others. "You should mind your business, yes?"

Alex kept her hand out, hoping he would try to take it, but he didn't.

Instead, he half-turned, as if walking away, then darted back, hand angled to strike her face. Alex sidestepped as she twisted the scarf from her neck and snared his arm. Pivoting behind him, she kicked straight up into his groin. Then she stepped back and let that sink in.

Talk about a great caricature. The man stood there, half bent, thick eyebrows in a tight V and his mouth in a distorted O. Then he stumbled forward, arms extended, and fell to the ground in a heap.

Alex dug a heel into his calf, and leaned over his writhing body to rifle through his pockets. Drooling on the pavement now, he attempted to speak, but it didn't come out in any of the five languages she understood, so she didn't answer back.

Giving him a toe-tap to his forehead, she eased her scarf free. Then she hurried toward the stairs and almost bumped right into the Indian couple who were scrambling back up to the platform. They stopped, stared at the Serbian flopping around behind her.

"He fell," Alex said.

They glanced at each other and then back at her.

"This is yours, I believe." Alex handed the man his wallet and watched as he opened it, flipped through the fifteen pound sterling inside, and gave a sigh of relief.

"Oh, and this." She dug into her pocket, retrieved an amulet on a gold chain, and handed it to the woman.

With a look of surprise, the woman felt her neck. Her eyes then filled with tears, and she hugged Alex. They thanked her profusely, began to walk away, and the woman ran back and hugged Alex one more time.

Keeping a low profile was overrated anyway.

Alex moved fast the rest of the way, the winter air a brisk relief after the heated altercation off the train. The Palace Gates Dry Cleaners was five blocks southeast of Buckingham Palace, and she walked past it twice, checking for any interested parties—those who would be much more circumspect than punk pickpockets—before striding once more all the way around the block. When Alex reached the shop again, she entered.

With a tall white storefront, neon lights in the windows, and two long counters inside, it was much larger than she'd expected. Alex had figured it for some dusty old shop with no customers, likely a front for deliveries within the intelligence community, be it CIA, MI6, or other. But from the half dozen customers queued up before her, and the strong scent of perchloroethylene in the air, the place was no operational beard.

Edgar was good.

Standing aside for an exiting man, garment bags flapping with a gust from the open door, Alex scanned the store for any tall, blue-eyed men, but the only two visible employees were compact, female, and Asian—one at the register, the other behind the long counter.

"May I help you?" the cashier asked, the strength of her British accent marking her as a native Londoner.

Alex held up the receipt she'd taken from the suit bag. "Can you give me the details on this?"

"What of it?"

"I'd like to know when the order was initiated and who delivered it."

She glanced at the other customers and then back at Alex. "Was there a mishap?"

"No, nothing like that."

The woman frowned, but held out her hand and Alex gave her the ticket. Keying the numbers into her computer, she peered at the screen. "According to this, the suit came in the night drop and was requested for this morning. Rush order, it was. See?" She spun the screen and tapped a finger on the date.

"Right." Alex scanned the screen, but the only name listed was her own. The order was real, the jacket had been dry cleaned, and the whole transaction had occurred—aboveboard. She said, "And who would have delivered it to my hotel?"

"Grosvenor, right, miss?" She tapped the screen and nodded. "That would have been Inga."

Inga was likely not a tall, handsome man. "Is she here?"

"Afraid not. She's off on delivery."

"When is she due back?" Alex glanced at her watch.

"She's off for holiday after her shift."

"She won't stop back here again today?"

"Not likely."

Not that it mattered. Edgar had somehow cached Alex's name and order into the Palace Gate system and had the suit delivered by someone else. He was more than a step ahead.

"Thanks for your time."

Alex walked out with no idea where to go next. With no leads, the only sensible move was to return to the hotel and try to pump the clerk for more information. That said, she hated retracing her moves. It wasn't just wasteful, it was tedious. Besides, her father had remained hidden from her for almost two decades. A professional among professionals, a legend in the days of the Cold War, the man had probably forgotten more tradecraft than she'd ever learned. A ditzy hotel desk clerk wasn't going to be his downfall.

Re-wrapping her neck scarf, Alex gave the street a requisite check. London was moving now, everyone with somewhere to go. There were no strangers smoking cigarettes on corners, no dog walkers traipsing the same corners, no interested faces peering at her from behind curtained windows.

An image popped into Alex's head just then. Edgar standing at her childhood bedside in the middle of the night, appearing so suddenly it was as if he'd been pulled from her somnolent consciousness. Disappearing again before she fully woke. Each time she'd wondered whether he'd really been there, and into her teens she'd convinced herself that he had. Instead of dying in an embassy bombing, she'd imagined he'd simply been on a long mission, and every once in a while he stole away—for a few hours, anything he had—and come home. Just to see her.

Alex cursed under her breath. Talk about pure fantasy. That Edgar Winter was a make-believe friend. That father had the imagined personality of a stuffed toy.

He'd *left* her.

Alex caught sight of a carriage-style London cab letting out a passenger across the street. Shortcuts were usually a bad idea, but she was tired and she was pissed. Her morning subterfuge had come to nothing, her emotions were up. She needed a moment to regroup. Besides, finding Edgar was going to be like finding a dime in a pool full of nickels. She knew that if he had his way she'd be headed to the airport now, enroute to D.C.

So she climbed into the cab and bluntly ordered the driver back to Grosvenor Square.

Staring out the side window as the taxi wound its way through the streets below Piccadilly, Alex's mind moved to thoughts about the bombing and all the people who had died. Each of them leaving behind unfinished business, incomplete tasks. Like a miniature version of 9/11, cars would be left in lots, ownerless; children would be left at home, parentless.

Anger crawled up her esophagus and into the back of her throat. She swallowed hard, but the hollowness felt like a bruise. It was all too familiar to Alex.

Forcing herself to breathe steadily, she put up a barrier between that feeling and this moment, and allowed the image of the briefcase popping open on the street to flash in her mind. Had all those people died because of a severed hand? She had absolutely no reference point on that—she'd been expecting to pick up documents or intelligence for the CIA, not human body parts. And what was Edgar's role in all of it?

In truth, there was no telling how many people he'd killed over the years. He disappeared for months at a time, even when she was young, and Alex had little doubt he was the type of specialist who got wet occasionally, but responsible for an attack that killed dozens of civilians?

She couldn't believe that.

The taxi veered onto a narrow side street, and began rocking over a patch of cobblestones. The block was empty but for a large truck, and just as they pulled around it, the driver yelled and slammed on the brakes. They spun to a stop on the curb, and the truck screeched to a halt behind them.

"What are you—" But a rumble drowned out her question and Alex lifted her head to find a man rocketing toward them. He was crouched over a BMW motorcycle, with a wool watch cap pulled low, and he was brandishing a thick and short-muzzled HK MP5 submachine gun. He roared past the driver's side window as a second masked cyclist swung behind the cab, pointing his MP5 at the back window.

The driver jerked the cab into Park and looked back and forth.

Alex yelled, "Get down!" Then she dove to the floor as a burst of flame shot from the front motorcyclist's gun, bullets shattering the windshield and hitting the driver in the side of the head. Gray matter and blood slapped glass as he slumped, and slid down onto the gas pedal, throttling the engine to a howl.

Another spray of bullets tore through the metal doors and thumped through the leather bench seat, grazing her head.

A half dozen options spired through her mind, none with a high chance of survival: kick open the door and run, try to overtake the rear motorcyclist, throw her jacket out one window as distraction and run the other way, or climb into the front seat and speed off. The last option was closest to what she did.

Before a full second had expired, Alex squeezed through the sliding window between the front and back seats, half expecting to be sprayed by bullets as she lunged for the gearshift and thrust it into Reverse.

A burst of gunfire erupted from both motorcyclists as she dived back behind the bulletproof barrier, and a crunch of flesh and metal and bone sounded as the cab crushed the rear cyclist against the truck.

Alex whirled to find the front shooter spinning his bike around and accelerating toward her, gun raised.

Ducking, she waited two full seconds, then kicked open the door.

The man swerved and slid on the snow-slicked cobblestones, the HK popping from his hands and skittering to the lip of a side-street stairwell.

Alex rolled from the taxi and drove a knee into the gunman's back as he lunged for the gun. They smacked the sidewalk together, his head striking the ground. He was shorter than Alex, but wiry and strong enough to roll atop her chest, his hands closing on her throat.

In a strange moment of acute awareness, Alex realized that both men looked exactly like each other. Twins. An equally acute and untimely observation: she'd never seen them before in her life. His grip tightening, Alex chose a human weakness and drove her thumb into the soft flesh between his ribs. The attacker grunted but kept hold of her windpipe. Twisting, she pushed back and let her head drop over the first step of the concrete stairwell, turning it to loosen his hold.

The man took two fistfuls of her hair and slammed her head into the concrete once, and then again. Blurry-eyed and dizzied, Alex fought to turn back over, but her bad shoulder prevented her from gaining leverage.

Kicking up with both legs, Alex catapulted backward, taking the man with her. They tumbled down the stairwell, end over end. Curling as they flipped, she locked the man's head between her knees. When they struck the bottom stair, she heard a double crack, like a wooden picture frame being snapped.

The man's body twitched and then fell limp with a dead stare.

Alex was pushing away when she noticed a tattoo peeking from beneath the black shirt. She tore back his sleeve to reveal a forearm inked with a golden eagle holding an anchor, a pitchfork, and a gun—the lower half of a Navy SEAL tattoo. Alex pulled up his shirt on the off-chance, but…no Talonstrike mark on his ribs. Her gaze moved toward his face, but stopped on a pool of blood glistening on his chest. A ton of it. A bullet must have ricocheted and caught him just right. She rubbed at her neck with her good hand. It certainly hadn't sapped his strength.

Alex looked back up the stairs, noting the trail of blood snaking from to the top just as her head began to throb and her hands tingled. There were suddenly three onlookers at the top of the stairs, and one of them said something she couldn't make out. Another pushed them aside from behind and broke through. Alex blinked, but figures began to blur. Blinking involuntarily, she tried to steady her breath, but surprised herself instead by falling to one knee.

A burning sensation pulsed from her shoulder and neck. She hurt her collarbone on the roll down the stairs, so she pressed against it to test if it was broken, but her hand slipped against her blouse. She held it up. A woman gasped from above. Alex blinked at the woman and the blood on her own hand. She looked down at her chest and pulled at her shirt. She was soaked in blood.

When Alex blinked again, she was on her back, staring up at the sky. London looked pretty, all gray like that in the morning. Snow was coming; she could feel it. She gulped for air and it hurt.

Alex blinked and a man was bent over her. He had his hands pressed to her shoulder and back. You'll ruin the scarf doing that, she thought. Blood is hard to get out of clothes. Alex tried to warn him, but her words were running together. He was telling Alex to breathe slow. It would be OK. Everything would be OK. It was the man who had stepped through the others.

The man who had stepped through all the others.

Alex blinked again. *How did you—?*

She took a gulp to ask him. And everything went black.

Seven

The drive from Tuzla up into the Dinaric Alps should have taken Lockard three hours tops, but with intermittent snow squalls and minimal road maintenance, it took almost seven. He didn't mind, though. His pack of Datrex food-ration bars, containing thirty-six-hundred calories each, ensured enough sustenance for seven *days*. While the bars were a bit grainy, they didn't require water. They gave him enough energy to carry a full rucksack up Kilimanjaro, and he liked the coconut flavor.

The drive was child's play.

Slowing the Jeep, the soft top flapping against the wind shears, Lockard chose a dark backstreet for his next order of business. It was lined with single-story gray concrete buildings that had padlocked, dented metal doors, and the sole signs of life in the narrow passage were two fat brown rats crawling on top of each other. If the rats were comfortable enough to fuck out in the open back there, then it was a good enough place for him to finish this.

He shut off the car's engine but left the lights on dim. Three full hours until his flight back to London. Lockard could complete this leg of the mission and be changed into his business-class suit in plenty of time.

He popped the trunk and retrieved the briefcase he'd repossessed from Josef, along with a long clear rubber hose the width of his thumb. He threaded one end of the hose into the Jeep's gas tank and took two steps to a small steel Dumpster, briefcase in hand. Avoiding a knee-high pile of twisted metal pushed against its side, he hefted open the Dumpster. It smelled like rodent death.

Stepping back and kneeling, Lockard unhitched the briefcase and stared for a moment at the choir of Ben Franklins, the man's pursed lips and sad eyes.

A million dollars.

It was more cash than most people ever saw in their lives, but for Lockard, it was a problem. He couldn't take the money on a commercial flight, and it wasn't worth chartering a private one from Sarajevo, one with a traceable manifest. Tuzla airbase had been tricky enough.

No, this pittance needed to disappear.

Lockard slipped a single bill from the top of a stack. Then, taking one long, hard suck on the hose and holding it below the level of the tank, he allowed the flow of petrol to douse the piles of money. Lockard lifted the briefcase to the edge and spilled the contents into the Dumpster. He held the hose to keep the gas in the tube, retrieved the rest of his winter gear, and tossed it inside as well, careful to cover the cash with the jacket. He tilted the tube and poured the remaining liquid onto the jacket and around the Dumpster's interior.

Using an orange disposable lighter, Lockard lit the bill he'd swiped. The flaming paper ignited the fuel-sopped jacket before it even floated to the pile. He stepped back and waited. No wisps of currency floated away to end up on some eager Interpol—or worse, CIA—agent's desk.

Lockard settled back into the Jeep, and smiled as he drove away.

"Not bad," Draganic said, as he walked the perimeter of the building's highest floor. "But you need more seating."

Randeep had set his lone desk, the half-circle composite piece of a Wall Street trading firm, in the center of the sprawling space. Hunkered before a dozen flat-screen monitors, he looked like the commander of a nuclear facility. There were no other seats in sight.

"I'd rather be on a lower floor, easier access," Randeep called from behind the screens.

"You wouldn't have this view." Draganic stopped and stared out the floor-to-ceiling window.

Located at 25 Marsh Wall in a development called Canary Wharf, the building was not restricted by the tight controls of the city, and was one of the tallest twenty buildings in all of London. The whole block sat atop the historic West India import-and-export docks, and Randeep's windows looked out to the still operable south dock, where two British naval ships sat idle.

"I don't look out the windows." Randeep waved a hand and continued staring at his monitors.

"Remember, Randeep. There is more to life than just models."

"Perhaps we both should take this advice."

Draganic glared back at the boy.

Sure, Draganic's recent escapades had been well covered by the news rags in the UK and Italy, but the paparazzi had gotten most of the details wrong; Draganic had not actually dated any of the models they'd snapped photos of him with. He'd met them in various nightclubs, ones he knew they frequented. He lured them close with champagne and vodka, and later promises of vacations to Geneva or Seychelles, though Draganic would never follow through. He knew the moment they fucked the fat man with a scar on his face, they'd be expecting a reward—perhaps a diamond-inlaid Chanel watch, or a Van Cleef & Arpels butterfly ring. He'd been right on the mark, too. Without a gift or a trip, even the youngest of them had not bothered to call him again.

Who cared? Those girls had a lifetime of disappointments from men ahead of them.

Tapping the Black Shark blade tucked below his waistband, Draganic wandered back around the desk and stopped behind Randeep. "When do you sleep?"

Randeep kept typing. "The window when Tokyo is quiet and London markets have not yet opened."

Four hours? "I need you alert, Randeep, a full night's—"

"Look. Do you see?" Randeep pointed at one screen, then the next, following a jagged line that rose then swooped and rose again, its tail littered with dots and adjacent lines. "Here." He tapped the screen on the last dot.

"I have no interest in this. It is why I have you." Draganic waved a hand.

"If you listened, you might."

Draganic rolled a hand in a signal for him to make it quick.

"It is called a neural network. It learns from the market itself, using historical values and indicators, then it predicts movements and prices."

"How?"

"I teach it, of course."

"It sounds like science fiction. Fantasy."

"You think?" Randeep swung his chair around and stared up at Draganic with a silly grin. "Give me your hand."

Draganic gave him a deadpan look.

"Please." Randeep held out a hand. "Shake."

Tempted to slice the damned thing off, Draganic shook the man's limp hand.

"OK." Randeep sat back down, folding his own hands in his lap. "Now, tell me how you did that."

"I just did it."

"Yes, but *how?* What did your brain tell your hand to make it do that? What nerve receptors did you activate to flex and relax which muscles, and when did you tell those nerve receptors to open and close in order to time the handshake to meet mine?"

"I have no idea."

Randeep grinned. "Now you understand." He spun in the chair, typed again, and the screen changed to show a large and elongated map of sorts. Lines interconnected like a tangle of barbed wire, each point of connection labeled with terms like GDP, ten-year rate, and Libor.

"Meet JONAH."

"Jonah." Draganic frowned. Draganic leaned closer again, this time trying to understand the numbers and data. "And you created this."

"Well, I created the fields, the algorithms. I told it what was most important and what wasn't, et cetera."

"Randeep, I ask that you begin speaking a language I understand. French, Italian, English. Pick one. But stop this algorithm nonsense. What in the fuck is this doing?"

Randeep paused for a second and said, "It is predicting the future."

"Is it accurate?"

"Highly." He held up a hand. "But before you start getting too excited. Only for currencies. Not stock markets, commodities, or anything like that."

"Why?"

"Because currencies are huge liquid instruments that take massive amounts of inertia to move one way or another. If equities are like speedboats, then currencies are like aircraft carriers. It makes them easier to predict."

"More science fiction."

"No. All the major banks use models like this on their currency trading desks. They each program their own proprietary version."

"So this JONAH is not special?" Draganic folded his arms above his belly.

"No, it is not special."

Draganic began to shake his head and laugh, but was cut off by Randeep in a frustrated tone.

"JONAH is one of a kind."

Still chuckling, Draganic asked, "Why?"

"Because this model is three dimensional compared to theirs. All the banks know is which currency is most likely to go in what direction. They may have an idea how powerful the signal is, but not how to play it."

"What are you saying?"

"I'm saying that JONAH can not only tell us what to buy and when, but which financial instruments to use when you do it."

"And what is this JONAH telling us, then?"

Randeep banged the keys, changing the screens again. The original line came back to the center. "Swiss francs. We need to buy enough to move the currency over the tipping point, where the overall momentum cannot be halted by intraday trading."

This time Draganic laughed so hard that spittle flew from his mouth and caught on his beard. Wiping it away with the inside of an elbow, he said, "Randeep, I may not know as much as you about trading, but I know the Swiss franc is one of the most liquid currencies in the world. We couldn't move it if we were the queen of England."

"And do you know what is happening in Zurich?" Randeep asked, frowning.

"I am certain you are to tell me."

"It has been revealed that the finance minister has been selling their own francs. Hundreds of millions of them."

"Why would they do that?"

"Because of the problems with European countries. People have been fleeing the euro to buy Swiss francs for safety. The currency's rise has made Swiss products too expensive for foreigners to buy, so the government is manipulating the currency to keep it artificially low. It is just like the UK did to sterling, remember?"

Of course Draganic remembered. Black Wednesday. When a hedge-fund titan named George Soros took on the British Empire and won. Draganic laughed again. "We can't compete with the Swiss government. That is ridiculous. We have one billion, not a hundred."

Randeep said, "Interventions do not work."

Draganic studied Randeep for a moment. The little man was dead serious. "Go on."

"JONAH's signal is so powerful, it suggests that we should not only buy the francs, but we should use offsetting options to pay for it. We could borrow unlimited amounts of money."

"Leverage."

"A hundred times."

Draganic turned and walked to the windows again. "And what does JONAH calculate as the likelihood of this trade's success?"

"Ninety-nine-point-nine-five percent."

Draganic stood tall and gazed at the view. Beyond the docks, the Isle of Dogs —once a stretch of marshlands known as the killing fields, where cows were slaughtered daily back in the mid-seventeen hundreds—was bordered on three sides by the meandering River Thames. A fact he'd read on the placard in the lobby.

A different kind of slaughtering goes on around here now, thought Draganic, tapping the Sea Shark again as he peered across the south dock at the Morgan Stanley and Citibank buildings. And why shouldn't he share the same successes? His partners would be livid if they found out, but they wouldn't. They would have their share of the original capital, and Draganic would keep the rest. He deserved it.

Draganic turned, met Randeep's eager eyes, and said, "Do it."

Eight

Blinking her eyes open then squeezing them closed, Alex tried to clear her vision. It was like looking at a dampened watercolor, everything blurry and distorted. A person stood above her, but a bright light high above prevented her from staring too long, so she closed her eyes again. Alex slipped back into the darkness.

The next time, Alex woke for good. The person standing over her was an older woman. With silvery black hair pulled into a low ponytail, she wore pink scrubs and blue latex gloves.

"Who are you?" Alex managed. "Where am I?" The room was the size of a typical hospital room, though the walls were painted a gentle gray, and trimmed in crown molding. The furniture, contemporary and expensive looking, also didn't fit a hospital setting. A Company safehouse?

"You...are lucky to be alive." She tapped a tube, then removed a piece of thick tape and a needle from Alex's arm. An IV. "But I bet you're well aware of that, aren't you?"

"You didn't answer either of my questions."

"Let's be sure all your faculties are in order first, shall we?"

"I'm guessing you insist."

"I do." She stared at a machine by the bed as she said, "Do you know your name, what day it is, the year?"

"Sarah Connor. The year is 1985, and a cyborg Terminator from the future just tried to kill me."

"Still have your sense of humor, I see."

"OK, so it's not 1985." Alex moved to sit up.

"And your wit."

Perhaps, but Alex still had no idea what the hell was going on. Navy SEALs. As good as she'd like to think she was, they didn't miss their targets. So, how the hell had Alex gotten out of there, and who the hell were they? She'd need to make a discreet inquiry from contacts on this side of the pond. Her head throbbed with questions, and her shoulder screamed. Alex grimaced as the woman helped her up.

"That shoulder will be a bit sore for a spell, but you're quite fortunate. The bullet passed between the scalenus medius and levator scapulae, missing all major arteries and both the clavicle and the spinal column." She reached up and pinched the soft flesh between her shoulder and neck. "Right through here."

"What about nerve damage? I never felt the bullet."

Shaking her head, she said, "You were in shock. Bottom line is, you've lost a fair amount of blood and received a transfusion. Other than that, you've about forty stitches, front and back."

"Lovely." Alex was thankful it was her right arm. Being lefty turned out to be a good thing once again.

Alex rotated her arm and the woman stopped her.

"Give it a bit. We don't want to tear it back open now, do we?" Then she smiled over Alex's shoulder as she gazed at the doorway. "Ah, there you are."

The woman left without another word as Alex turned and stared.

Lying out there in the street, she thought she'd been seeing things—the charcoal Harrington jacket, jeans, and boots. But she couldn't hallucinate the musky spice of the Guerlain cologne they'd picked out together in Monte Carlo last year. Or the warmth of his skin as he neared.

"Jack." He was lucky she'd had a bullet through her shoulder. Even so, she had to check her impulse to lunge at him. He had hurt her. Seeing him now hurt her again.

"I see you've made the acquaintance of Hanna." Was he intentionally laying on the British accent? He knew damn well what that did to her.

"She's a gem."

"I'd say a saint." Jack reached over and touched Alex's face with a warm palm. Those hands. "You're all but new."

She edged away from his touch, the message unspoken. *I'll let you know when I want you to touch me.* "Where am I?"

"You've been sleeping the better part of a day." Jack turned and reached for something on the desk a few feet away. "Hanna's a friend. She was an A&E surgeon at the St. Thomas Hospital for over two decades. Does her own thing now." *A&E* meant Accident and Emergency, the equivalent of an American ER.

"Uh-huh." That wasn't the question. "So where the hell I am?"

"Eaton Square. Three blocks from Victoria."

Victoria Station. "High-rent, even for a surgeon, no?"

"Suffice to say her husband left behind a small fortune. Hanna doesn't work for the money."

"And how did I get here?"

"Do you not recall?"

She gave him a look, and he countered with that smile. The one that melted her.

Bastard.

He continued, "You threatened to phone the police if I laid a finger on you."

"And you ignored that."

"I assured you the police were on their way. They would no doubt want to talk to you."

"I see."

"Yes, you came around in your thinking. Quite quickly I might add."

Right. And now it was time to address the elephant waiting patiently at the edge of the bed. Alex leaned forward and said, "Jack. Why were you even there?"

"I woke this morning to this. On my front step." He handed her the item he'd taken off the desk. A newspaper in French, something called *La Direct Metropolitaine*. A photograph stretched across the entire top half of the front page, showing flames rising and smoke billowing from the Café Martin. Above the photograph, the headline: 'Une Explosion Mystérieuse Détruit un Café à Londres. *Mystery Explosion Destroys Café in London.*

"And how does—"

"Here." He pointed to the corner of the photograph, at the image of a woman walking away from the smoking building, wearing a black dress with a satchel over one shoulder.

No shoes.

Alex must have just taken the keys from the valet stand and was leaving the wreckage. The image made her sick. All those people burning inside. Her, strolling calmly away like nothing out of the ordinary had happened. Much less a bombing that killed over fifty people, according to the photo's caption.

"Naturally, I was shocked. I took the first Chunnel in."

"And found me on a random street?"

He gave her a look of confusion. "You do recall that I sell microchips for a living. To mobile phone companies."

"You tracked me with cell-tower triangulation? What are you, the NSA?"

"I asked a favor of a friend. Nothing sinister about that."

She eyed him. "And when did you move to Paris?"

He glanced away and back again. "First of the month. I was transferred to Mainland Europe division."

"No reason to tell me, I suppose."

"I'm telling you now." He sat at the edge of the bed and took her hand, and with sudden seriousness in his voice, he said, "Alex. I was worried you may disappear forever."

Alex looked into his eyes, the ones she wanted to trust—or had at one time—and said, "I'd already accepted you had."

"I can't say I blame you."

She traced her gaze to his square jaw and strong neck. A day's reddish-blond stubble peppered his skin, like sand on a schoolboy. He looked goddamned delicious and he knew it.

"And you won't have to." She pushed up further and moved her feet off the edge of the bed. "Thanks for getting me here and the doctor and everything."

"What do you think you're doing?" He looked surprised as she stood up.

"My job."

"You've been shot. Surely your employer will understand."

"You don't know my employer."

Alex walked to the chair in the corner and held up a pair of jeans, a long-sleeve black shirt, and a black overcoat.

"I purchased them while you were resting. As well as those." He pointed to a pair of low-heeled boots.

She was getting tired of thanking the man who'd left her, so Alex just started dressing instead.

"Can I help you?"

"Sure. Gin, splash of soda? I'm sure you remember how I like it."

He'd remembered everything else. The boots were a perfect fit.

"I meant with your job."

She glanced back at him. "You can't."

"Why not?" He folded his arms across his chest.

Because her tolerance for disappearing acts had just expired.

"Look. Jack." She walked over and placed a hand on his arm. "I appreciate you coming, taking care of me. You probably saved my life. Thanks. Goodbye."

He took a step closer, raised his eyebrows. "I'm not leaving you."

"You already did."

"And it was a mistake."

"Damned straight."

"Alex—"

"Jack."

His voice edged with a hint of sternness. "You'd be well-advised to take the help. Physically."

There it was, the classic male argument. They'd been over it more than a few times in their passionate run-ins. Once, he had walked in on Alex practicing Muay Thai in his Paris apartment. She had just delivered a sweeping head-kick, knock-back combination to his life-size silicone dummy, leaving a swipe of white powder across the figure's head from the chalk on her feet.

He said something smart like, *You look adorable beating up on a dummy like that.*

And the next thing he knew, Alex was on him, throwing every punch and kick in the book, plus a few f-bombs. She wasn't trying to hurt him, just give him a little lesson, so he was able to fend off each blow but stay close enough to take her down. Pinning her from behind like that pissed Alex off for real, and she bucked hard enough to flip over in his grip, forcing him to keep his full body weight on her.

That's bullshit, I went soft on you and you know it, she said.

He smiled, *Alex, I'm a good deal heavier than you—I'd say eighty pounds—and I boxed in University, remember?* He stared back and continued, *But I must admit, you're a better match than over half the lads I've sparred with.*

Fuming for a few more seconds, she began to loosen her grip on his wrists. *Don't patronize me.*

Breathing hard, he said, *I wouldn't dream of it.*

After a moment, Alex stopped huffing and returned the look of hunger in his eyes. Then she said, *I'm too sweaty.*

He smoothed one of those wonderful hands over her ribs and said, *I was rather hoping you would be.*

And they made love right there on the blue-tiled floor of his workout room with the silicone dummy as a voyeur.

Bringing her back to the moment, he asked, "What exactly are you're tasked to do?"

Alex narrowed her eyes. She was, for all intents and purposes, one-armed for the time being, and on the run. She'd killed two men, after all, even if it was in self-defense. A partner—another set of eyes and ears—could help. Jack had demonstrated his intelligence and physical competence to her more than once. If he wanted in so badly, it would be his own doing.

So Alex blurted it out.

"Your father?" was the first of a long stream of questions from Jack.

Alex answered them all honestly, if not completely. She told him about the reception and her assignment and the briefcase and the hand and Edgar. Jack looked as surprised as she'd been about her father's resurrection. She also told him as much as she could remember about the twin motorcyclists and the Navy SEAL tattoo, but for the life of her, Alex still couldn't come up with a connection to them anywhere.

The one large detail she left out was her true employer. She let Jack assume her company employed those with highly specialized services. Hell, he already knew she was some sort of spy. It was probably why he'd left her in the first place. Admitting that she was CIA now would just aggravate that sore spot.

"Let me see that newspaper," Alex said, and scanned the article. It was written in French, which she hadn't used much lately but could understand well enough to get the main points.

"What are these?" he asked, holding up her sketchbook.

"Drawings, you've seen some of them before."

"Not this one." He lifted the book and turned the page. "Nor this." He stopped at the sketch of Geneva, Jack on the bridge. "Did you sketch this from a photograph? I don't remember you taking one."

"I didn't."

"How then?"

He had seen Alex draw, of course, but he'd never seen her do it from memory. There's something about recalling images from one's mind and transferring them to the page that seems impossible to most people. For Alex, it was as natural as practicing yoga—once she started, she slipped into a something akin to deep meditation. The end result was an extremely accurate, detailed drawing.

She said, "It's hard to explain."

Eying her, he said, "Do try."

Alex had thought about how to tell him before, of course, but there was never really a good or appropriate opportunity to bring it up in conversation. There never was with something like this. It would seem like a hoax, a trick, or just plain odd.

That said, he'd discovered it, and she knew it would be better to have the talk now. Exhaling, she said, "You've heard of an eidetic memory?"

"You mean photographic?"

"That's a subset of eidetic memory. Some people hear a piece of music once and are able to replicate it entirely on a piano. Others can read a series of numbers and regurgitate them. You've read about those people who can recite pi to, like, a hundred thousand decimals? Or people who can learn an entirely new language in a week?"

"Savants," he said.

"Right. Most of them are high-functioning autistics."

He raised his brows. "Are you telling me you're a prodigy?"

Taking the book back, Alex said, "Far from it. I've just got this quirky thing where I can draw what I've seen. From memory."

He pointed at the book. "Those. Are from…memory?"

"Most. See?" She flipped through the book and stopped on a page that showed Jack standing at the balcony of a hotel room, overlooking the Prague skyline. "This was the first city we visited together. And…"

She stopped on a page that showed a street scene in the heart of Milan. Nothing beautiful or remarkable about it; Jack was not even in the drawing. But he had just left and Alex could still still smell his musk on her body.

"Or this." She flipped to another page, this one showing a homeless family in Rio de Janeiro. "This one stayed with me for weeks."

"Alright, then…what's the key?"

"It usually has to be a powerful moment for me to remember the details well enough to draw them. The more powerful the emotion, the sharper the image."

"You're a regular Hannibal Lecter, that scene he drew of Florence."

And just like that, she was sorry she'd told him. "A lovely image of me. Thank you."

He laughed. "Will you draw me someday? I mean, while I'm there, watching."

"Not likely."

"I'll consider that a *perhaps*."

Alex didn't respond, and Jack took the hint that she was ready to move on. He glanced at the book in her hand and then back to her. "So, your father. Where would you like to begin?"

"Does Hanna have a computer I can borrow? And a printer?"

"Yes, of course. And then what?"

Thinking about the article and the drawings she would make, she said, "And then there's a certain chef I'd like to have a word with."

Nine

Shivering as they stared at the glossy black Porsche Cayenne Turbo in the underground garage, Alex recalled an ad she'd seen for the SUV in the British Airlines magazine a few days earlier. It boasted of over five hundred horsepower and zero to sixty in under four-point-five seconds. It was a land rocket.

She said, "Hanna lets you borrow this?"

Jack shrugged. "This vehicle was her husband's. She prefers her Mercedes, I believe."

"Right, this one's the spare." Leaning forward, Alex studied the inside of the car. "Damn, it's a standard." She questioned her driving ability with one arm numbed by whatever Hanna had injected into it. She'd be able to shift with her left hand, the good one, but steering would be sketchy until the meds wore off.

Jack stepped past her. "You navigate. I'll drive."

"I can probably do OK." She rolled her shoulder.

"Alex, you're at it again."

Alex tilted her head. "I get around just fine without a man to coddle me."

"Yes, well. Considering you have that hole in your shoulder." He pressed the remote, unlocking the doors. Then he paused and eyed her, gave her a wink. "You can think of me as your very own chauffeur. How's that?"

"That may work." She gave a mock frown and climbed in the passenger side.

About twenty minutes and a few less-than-professional traffic weaves later, Jack and Alex pulled up to the Continental Plaza hotel off of Hyde Park. The front of the glass-and-steel tower was lit with Christmas bulbs, and a huge tree surrounded by silver and gold presents shined through the lobby's glass. Flanking the revolving doors, six giant ball ornaments glittered with reflections of the driveway and street.

They told the valet they were there for dinner at The Wallard, and he guided them to a separate entrance off the side of the lobby. With no Christmas decorations, the restaurant had a traditional upscale setting, including dark wood paneling, chandeliers, and plenty of flowers. Though Chef Guy Martin didn't own this restaurant, it was where he'd made a name for himself. Still, that name was not on display anywhere in the foyer or on the matchbooks. His ego must have been burning at the lack of recognition.

Enough so, that he started his *own* restaurant, Café Martin, a few miles away.

Waiting for the hostess to return to her station, Alex scanned The Wallard menu. Tuna Salad Nicoîse, Duo Rack of Lamb, Buffalo Ribeye au Poîvre. No prices were shown, but the dining room was full of patrons, so revenues weren't hurting for the hotel-owned operation.

She said, "As popular as he is here, you'd never know the Chef was going bankrupt."

"Bankrupt?"

Alex tapped the article in her pocket. "The reason we're here."

"I thought you were keen to ask about the bombing at Café Martin."

"We'll get to that," She said, still thinking of the piano and that strange smell.

The hostess approached. With legs up to her ears, she had the bubbly, yet empty expression of a girl who'd relied on nothing more than her looks all her life. The type to ruin all credibility for the thinking women of this world.

"Reservations?" she asked, beaming with fake enthusiasm.

"Actually, we're just here to visit Chef Guy." Alex had read that the chef liked to be called by his first name, using the French pronunciation, as in Ghee. He also liked his last name pronounced Martán. But after minimal Web research, she also knew he had been born as Guy, rhymes with die, in South London, to Walter and Janet Martin. Last name rhymes with…Martin. Both Walter and Anne were schoolteachers, and they'd all lived in London all their lives.

Bottom line, he was about as Parisian as a French fry.

The hostess raised her chin and said, "Chef Guy is quite busy just before dinner. Why don't you schedule an appointment for the daytime, perhaps next week?" Her British accent had been tainted a bit French.

With her best British accent, Alex said, "Tell him that Inspectors Alex Winter and Jack Pope are here on an unannounced visit. From the MLHU."

She glanced between them and frowned at Alex. "The what?"

Jack said, "The Middlesex-London Health Unit."

She stiffened. "I don't care if you are from Scotland Yard. Without an appointment, I cannot help you."

Alex leaned forward and whispered, "We are being kind enough to not draw attention to the matter, see?"

She didn't see. She stared, wordless, wheels turning in the hamster cages upstairs.

"Look," Jack said, "we've reports a customer discovered a spot of unusual hair in one of your dishes."

The hostess crossed her arms. "That's hardly a health offense."

Alex said in a voice loud enough to carry past the hostess, "Ah, yes. But it is when the tests come back as raccoon."

The couple seated closest to the station turned to have a look.

The hostess's eyes widened as Alex leaned back and said, loud enough for it to bounce off the dining room ceiling now, "We believe it was the lamb."

Putting a hand to her mouth, the hostess said, "I'll get him straight away."

The couple stood, dropped their napkins on their menus, and left the restaurant.

"Alex," Jack said, glancing at them as they exited.

She gave him a *what?* look and he rolled his eyes.

The hostess returned with Chef Extraordinaire two minutes later. An enormous man, tall *and* wide, the chef looked behind them, as if seeing if Jack and Alex were alone or the front line of a paparazzi crew.

"What is the meaning of this?" he asked in a French accent.

Alex raised her eyebrows at Jack. *See?* Then she said, "Chef Martin, I'm Inspector Alex Winter and this is Chief Inspector Jack Pope. We're with the Metropolitan Police and we'd appreciate a moment."

"I thought you said you were with the health unit." He turned to the hostess, who held up both palms. He continued, "I have already spoken with the police twice. Why again?"

"I assure you, it will take but a few minutes," Alex said.

He glanced away and then back at them, wringing his hands as he said, "You are here about the accident, yes?"

"We work with Commander Lampard." She loved the news media. They told you everything you needed to know to bullshit your way into a situation. Nothing like responsible reporting. To knock Guy off balance and seal the deal, Alex leaned forward and said in a low voice, "And yes, it's about the *bombing*."

He stiffened and his face flushed to the color of eggplant. "Follow me."

Walking far ahead, he led them through the loud dining room and down a long hallway. Alex smiled at a nice older couple who caught her eyeing their plates. "That looks lovely."

Leaning toward her, Jack whispered, "Chief Inspector?"

"You look a lot older than me."

"Brilliant," he said in a sullen voice.

Guy ushered them into a windowless office no larger than a telemarketer's cubicle, with a thick wood desk and two chairs. The walls were draped with awards, plaques, and framed magazine articles, all starring the chef.

Impressive.

Alex and Jack each settled into a chair as the chef squeezed behind the desk. With his belly pressed against the edge of the wood and the chair pressed up and around his shoulders, he looked like a clove of garlic stuffed into a black olive.

Folding his hands before him and then unfolding them twice, he finally settled on letting them dangle to the sides. "Please. Call me Chef Guy." Ghee.

Sure thing, for now, Alex thought. "Chef Guy, we just have a few more minor questions, mostly to fill in the blanks on reports. Okay?"

"I suppose."

"Good. First…" Alex reached into the inside pocket of her overcoat and slipped out two pages with drawings she'd made at Hanna's. She showed the chef the top page, on which she'd drawn a three-quarter profile of her father. The sketch was from memory of the moment he had stood over Alex in the street, and she'd adjusted the background to look out of focus, softened the shading of his features. She'd also added a sharp border to the frame, leaving a white edge and making it look like a grainy black and white photograph taken with a telephoto lens.

Alex turned the sketch toward the chef. "What can you tell me about this man?"

Chef Guy leaned forward, inspected the page. "Not a thing. I have never before seen this man in my life."

"Are you sure? You may have seen him here or in Café Martin sometime in the last few weeks." If she knew anything about her father, it was that he was thorough and would have cased the location of the drop and maybe the proprietor of the restaurant. That said, he would have been ultra circumspect.

Confirming this, the chef shook his head. "I am certain." Not even a hint of reaction in his body language.

Alex eyed Jack and he nodded for her to show the next image.

She flipped to the second sketch. Smaller than the one of her father, this one had the look of a headshot taken for a passport photo. Again, not perfect in detail but she'd added some flat drapery behind him for effect. Close enough for the average eye. "How about this man? What can you tell me about him?"

The chef took the sketch and studied it. Then he slid it back to her. "Same. I have never seen him before. Who is he?"

Alex felt Jack peering over her shoulder as she said, "His name was Angus. He happened to be the guest of honor at your restaurant the other night."

Guy shrugged. "So? I don't always meet my guests."

"But you are usually there, at Café Martin, yes? At least on the nights you aren't working here."

"Like I've already said, it was just good luck."

"Right." Alex glanced at Jack. Thinking about the moment of the blast, the pianist playing off-key, she flipped the sketchbook to a blank page, then took out her pencil as if she were about to take notes. "And what about the piano? Where did you get it?"

"Holworths. Again, you have already asked these things." He kept looking at the door, as if he hoped they would soon exit or someone else would enter, saving him.

"Yes, it was not recorded. I apologize."

"It is difficult to keep talking about, you understand."

"I do, but there are some details we must confirm."

"Go on."

"Was the piano new or have you had it worked on recently?"

"It is the same one as always. Why? Shouldn't you be focused on the piping, the gas lines, and things of this matter?"

"This was no gas explosion."

He glanced away.

"You said the same as always." Jack sat forward. "So, what, you rent the piano —is that it?"

"Of course we lease. It is too expensive to buy an entire grand piano for one performance a month."

"Tell us about the piano shop."

He shrugged. "Holworths is the old family shop on Oxford. It is quite reputable."

"When was it delivered?"

"That afternoon."

Jack said, "You weren't present to oversee delivery?"

He glanced away for a second time. "My maître d' takes care of these things."

Alex had to admit, the French accent was pretty good. He must have worked on it for a while, and maybe even believed his own tale of being native.

"And by your account, she was there," Jack said.

"But of course." His bottom lip quivered. "She, too, died this night."

Not wanting to miss the opportunity of weakness, Alex reached into the overcoat's inside pocket and unfolded the articles she'd printed at Hanna's. There wasn't much information about the bombing itself, but there was plenty about Guy and his restaurants. "Chef Guy, I have reports that Café Martin was insured for over three million pounds. By you, the primary owner."

His face flushed. "And what of it?"

"And according to public records, the restaurant has been losing over seven hundred thousand pounds per year. For the last three years."

Guy stood and puffed out his chest. "What is it you are accusing me of?"

Alex just said, "The riverfront building was too expensive, you knew it going in, but you did it anyway. Anything to have a restaurant with your name on it, because The Wallard refuses to let you use it here. But then the business began to kill you, bleed you dry. You couldn't charge enough per plate to make up the cost of rent, could you? People didn't come in droves like you expected, did they? And soon you were dying, the business was dying." Her English accent may have faded a bit at the end there, but he didn't seem to notice.

"No. You are wrong. People love my restaurant!"

"But not enough. And so you killed them. You killed them all." Alex threw the papers at his chest. "Who assembled it for you? Who set the bomb?" She was provoking him, but that was OK. He needed to feel victory when she gave him an out in a few moments.

"I don't know what you're talking about! Leave! Leave this office right now! I want my lawyers." Guy stumbled around the desk and stood over Alex.

"Alright, alright. Hold it." Jack stepped forward between them and waved a hand to the seat behind her. "Please."

Keeping her gaze on the chef, Alex sat back down.

Jack said, "Chef Guy, I do apologize for my colleague's tactics. All of us are out of sorts here. Many people died last night. Please, have a seat."

"I won't answer any more questions. I won't do it."

Jack stared up at the man, who stood a good three inches taller than him. He said, "Mr. Martin, you are in grave trouble. I believe it to be in your best interests now to tell us what happened. What really happened that night."

He stared down at Jack, huffing.

Jack continued, "If we can prove who did this to you, to your restaurant, then the pressure's off. Do you understand?"

Guy glanced away. His eyes fogged over and he turned. Then, pacing between the desk and the wall, he started to babble—incoherent, nervous, almost twitching babble.

Jack raised his eyebrows to Alex.

"Come again?" he said to Guy.

Guy shook his head.

"No," he said. "*No!*" Taking his head in both hands, he muttered, "I didn't know. I didn't, I didn't, I didn't!" He flung his hands outward.

"Didn't know *what?*" Alex asked.

Guy glanced up at her with a look of dread.

Alex stood. "Chef, if you don't speak up soon, the only thing I can guarantee is that the Metropolitan Police will soon charge you murder."

Eyes widening, he pushed against the desk, making it slide back a few inches. "What are you—"

Calling him by his name was a good tactic that Jack had begun. Bring him down to size, so to speak. So Alex followed it. "This is bigger than you, Mr. Martin."

The chef slumped deep into his chair. He had the look of a man caught soliciting an undercover John—a mix of horror and shame. "I, I…want a lawyer."

Leaning forward, Alex squinted as she said, "If you hide behind a lawyer, it will only confirm guilt. You'll enjoy a quick path to prison, but the only dish you'll serve there is your own arse."

The chef stared at Alex and his hands began to shake. "But if I tell you?"

"Then we leave," Alex said. "And the police will have nothing to charge you with." That was a lie, the man would get what he deserved either way. It wasn't up to her to decide.

"It will be okay, then, yes? Will it?" He looked back and forth between Alex and Jack.

Jack nodded, sealing the deal with, "You have our word."

Guy nodded fast and hard and began to sob, softly at first, then loudly. Finally, he managed, "I, I, I…he…he said it would happen after the event. And it would be just fine. Then everyone would be better off. It would all go away and I would stop losing. It would stop the bleeding." He sobbed hard for a minute. He looked like a confused bull, snot stringing from his nose as he shook his head.

"Who said it?" Jack asked.

The chef wept into his hands.

"Chef." Jack walked around the desk, and with his wide-eyed gaze at Alex, he asked, "Who said it?" He calmly placed a hand on the chef's shoulder. "If you can tell us, we'll be on our way. No further questions from the police." He was good, damned good.

After a few moments, Guy nodded. "It was Aaron. Aaron Gebhart. He's the one who set it up. I am sure of it."

Alex had to time her question so he could answer between sobs. "And who is Aaron?"

The chef raised his face only high enough for her to see his eyes as he said, "The one who delivered the piano."

Alex and Jack sat there in near silence for a moment, digesting what they'd just learned. They got what they wanted and the chef now needed a minute to sort out his situation by himself. Alex nodded, Jack stood, and she followed.

Then, as they reached the door, Alex stopped, turned back to the chef and said, "One last question, Chef Martin, a simple one."

The chef looked up, and she said, "Was there anything on the menu last night that contained almonds?"

Moss hated Gatwick Airport. A mere ten miles farther from the city than Heathrow, yet the hired car had to wind its way through neighborhoods and backstreets to get to London, adding a good thirty minutes to the trip. Moss had traveled under his wealthy businessman identity and taken a privately chartered G550. It could only be tied to a third-party LLC, operated through a network of entities far removed from the CIA. A skilled forensic accountant might be able to trace the company's ties back to the government, but even then it would take months of digging to get anywhere near the Company.

The bottom line: other than the director of MI6 himself, the UK would have no idea the CIA's director of National Clandestine Service was in London.

Conveniently located in Grosvenor Square, five blocks from Victoria Station, the safe house was known to the two directors as Flat Six. The bottom two floors were occupied by CIA lamplighters, Company employees whose sole purpose was to keep house and act as a buffer zone for the workings on the third floor.

Moss crossed the flat's great room and pulled back the thick linen drapes. The bulletproof glass was barely noticeable even up this close. Set into steel-reinforced, Victorian-style windows, the special glass couldn't be detected from the street. He tapped his foot on the hardwood. The steel-cabled concrete floors and ceilings were bombproof, as were the walls, and a by-product of that treatment was the soundproofing of the entire flat. Twenty-seven million dollars had gone into this place, and this was only the third time it had ever been used. Extravagance? Maybe. Moss and his predecessors would argue it was necessity —Winston Churchill would have been lucky to have a safe house like this. The best he could do in World War II was the Dorchester Hotel.

Moss let the curtain drop and walked to the wet bar behind the blue-striped, French sofa. After fishing a few cubes from the small ice machine, he poured himself three fingers of scotch as he contemplated the impending events. The possibility of them had lain dormant for decades, and he thought it had disappeared for good. But life takes funny twists and turns sometimes, and this little problem had proven to be as winding as a man's lower intestine.

Moss took a long draw of the scotch and savored the burn as he swallowed. Then he did it again. He was still standing in the same spot twenty minutes later and on his second glass when the door buzzed.

He walked to the panel at the entry and touched a small screen embedded in the wall. The retina display showed a man at least ten years Moss's elder, wearing a long black overcoat, a bowler hat, and leaning on a cane. Of course, Moss and half the intelligence community would recognize Peter Grant in an instant. He'd been the head of MI6 for the last twelve years.

Moss pressed the button, unlocking the doors with a simple click.

Grant entered the short lobby, and the door automatically closed behind him.

After confirming Grant had come alone, Moss clicked him through the second set of doors, and waited for footsteps in the foyer before calling out, "Drink, Peter?" From the corner of his vision, he could see Grant hanging his overcoat and hat and leaning the cane—more of a prop than an aid—against the wall.

"That bad, is it?" Grant entered the den with a frown.

"Worse."

"Then I'll have what you're having."

Moss poured a double for Grant and a third helping for himself, then handed the other man the glass. "Not the occasion for a toast."

"I picked up on that."

"Who knows you're here?"

Standing before the huge stone fireplace, a pair of swords on the wall framing him in an ominous snapshot, Grant frowned. "Not a soul."

"What about Anne?" Moss said, referring to Grant's secretary.

"She thinks I'm Christmas shopping." Grant took a healthy sip.

"And your detail?" Like the CIA, MI6 security kept tight eyes on their chief.

Grant winked. "They think I'm with Anne."

"Clever."

"I thought so."

"You need to know, Peter." Moss swirled his drink, careful not to let it spill over the lip. "I'm on my own on this one, off the reservation for a few days."

"And on your side of the pond? Who knows about it?"

Moss tipped the glass up to the lights gleaming from a chandelier. "You and me, and the President makes three."

A pause, and then Grant said, "Well, the irony of the situation would no doubt be lost on that man. What can I do to help?"

"For starters, I need copies of every aspect of the café bombing. And I'll need the same on today's shooting in Piccadilly."

"I was afraid those were linked. What else?"

"Serial numbers." Moss drained his scotch and placed the empty glass on the bar. Then, without looking back, he exited the room and descended the tight spiral staircase into the basement. The strong room. Encased in three feet of the steel-cable-reinforced concrete, the vault could survive a bunker buster.

Grant began to descend the stairs, saying, "What on Earth does that mean?"

Moss placed his thumb on the biometric scanner and waited for the steel door to slide open. The lights blinked on and he entered the cool vault. A few seconds later, Grant followed Moss inside and stood there with his mouth open, like a teenage boy who'd just gotten his first peek at a centerfold's bush.

Moss had to admit it was breathtaking.

On the face of it, the swollen shrink-wrapped package would have looked like any ordinary shipment, with maybe boxes underneath holding toasters or books. But the translucent blue cellophane on this shipment had been torn open to expose the contents, letting the package's girth spill out.

Its obscenity.

There, stacked in dozens of tall, tight piles atop a standard wooden shipping pallet, three feet wide and four feet high, were not thousands, tens of thousands, or even hundreds of thousands of them. There were more.

"My God." Grant took a step forward and leaned in to have a closer look. "Just how many are there?"

"One-point-three million."

Grant licked a finger and stuck it to a bill, drawing it from the top of one stack. "All hundreds?"

"Every damn one of 'em."

"So that's…"

"One hundred and thirty million US dollars." The math was simple, but so boggling it tripped the human mind.

"God save the queen." Grant stood still as he soaked in the implications, gaping like a full-blown idiot at more money than all but a few human beings in the history of the world had ever been in the presence of.

After almost a minute, he tilted his head to Moss and said with more than a hint of incredulousness, "And your CIA has lost one of these? A whole damned pallet?"

"No, Peter," Moss scoffed, then lowered his eyes, feeling as though he may float sheer out of his body.

"We lost eight of them."

Ten

Before dusk turned to night, they stopped at a convenience store that advertised prepaid cell phones and Alex bought one. Then Jack decided he was hungry enough to eat an also advertised Pukka minced steak and onion pie. *Not all bad for a pound seventy*, he said, buying two of them.

The pies looked like something you would find in a pet store, so Alex opted for a bag of sea salt and vinegar chips and a Red Bull.

As they drove through South London, where Aaron Gebhart lived, Alex squinted at a lineup of decrepit storefronts and said, "Lovely."

"Not exactly a bankers' community, is it?" Jack shrugged. "Katy B was born here, though. Oh, and Rio Ferdinand."

"Rio who?"

He laughed. "Fullback, played for Manchester United?"

"I'm not surprised you know the soccer player." She reached across to the knob on the heater and switched it off. "But Katy B.?"

Turning the car onto a street about as wide as a motel hallway, Jack said, "Saw it on The Box, you know, our own version of MTV. Though we still play music, not reality rubbish."

"Novel." Alex had to admit she was annoyed that Jack knew more about contemporary media than she did—even if it was British trivia—he was a good ten years older than her. She'd have to brush up on her knowledge base there.

They eased down the narrow road, past yellowed picket fences and snow-dusted bags of trash lining the curbs. Aaron's house sat at the end of the street, next to a single-story mattress outlet. With simple square windows bracketed by decaying sills and peeling paint, the two-story structure looked like it could be in Ward 8 of DC. Lovely.

"Pull up there." Alex pointed to a house a couple of doors down and across the street. "And kill the lights."

Jack did, and Alex turned on her phone for a quick search in Google photos for Aaron.

"Have you found anything?" he asked.

"He's not a pro." She held up the phone. "Keeps a whole, unprotected profile on Facebook."

Two minutes later, as Alex was scrolling through his page, Jack nudged her.

A man with an Adam's apple the size of an ostrich egg had exited the house.

"That's him." She pocketed the phone.

Aaron was approaching a small Vauxhall hatchback, carrying the same type of aluminum Zero Halliburton briefcase that her father had.

"Shall we follow or have a look inside?" Jack asked.

Still feeling a bit confrontational after their visit with Chef Martin, Alex pointed ahead. "Let's follow."

They crossed back over the river and headed east on Victoria Embankment. Aaron drove fast, weaving in and out of cars, as if he were rushing to catch a flight. Jack navigated well, staying far enough back to prevent him from seeing them, yet keeping pace.

As they drove along the river, Alex wondered what was in the briefcase Aaron was carrying, and a vivid image of the severed hand flashed in her mind. The mere thought of losing a hand, her drawing hand, sent a cold chill up her spine and into the back of her neck. She tried to come up with a solid reason for a hand to be passed around, but for the life of her she couldn't. Was it proof of torture or maybe someone's penalty for stealing? Weak at best. As Alex contemplated this, Jack stayed laser focused on the cars around them and the traffic ahead. She was impressed.

About twenty minutes later, they reached a dark stretch near the waters of Canary Wharf. Aaron pulled between two tall office buildings, both half-lit in the evening, and stopped as a car pulled from the underground garage of one of the buildings. Alex signaled for Jack to ease to the curb and they waited until Aaron drove forward again, but then lost sight of him as he rounded the corner.

They exited the causeway between buildings and Alex glanced left and right. Aaron's Vauxhall was pulling into a construction site, the chain-link gate propped open just wide enough for his car to squeeze through.

"Now what?" Jack asked.

She looked around, then pointed to a small lot next to a Barclay's ATM machine, where an overhang shadowed one of the spaces. "Let's duck in there."

"Surveillance?"

"No. I'm going in."

"Surely not on your own."

"Easier to hide a single shadow." Alex got out, shutting the door on Jack's protest of *for God's sake*. Concern for his safety would only distract her from the task at hand.

Keeping tight to the plastic-wrapped chain-link fence as she approached the entrance, Alex heard a clank and then a whirring sound come from inside the construction area. She leaned back to see an exposed elevator climbing the building's exterior. Aaron's meeting, or drop, was up there.

Alex considered looking for an alternative entry, but the fence extended to the edge of the water, and unless she wanted to go for a cold dip without a dry suit she would have to take the front entrance ahead. So, staying low to the ground, she made her way to the entrance and stopped.

The tower reached high but with no glass and only beams and crossbeams extending into the sky, it had the looks of the beginnings of a sketch—if Alex were to draw a building, these would be the first few marks she'd make on the page. A large poster at the entrance of the worksite listed various permit numbers. Another one boasted the finest flats in all of London, and showed an artist's rendering of a finished residence, views of the city beyond.

The finished product looked ritzy.

Alex thought about ascending the crane at the building's corner but dismissed it, as she would have to climb all the way to the crane's cab and lower herself onto the roof. From where she stood, she couldn't see what kind of drop that was. Plus, then she'd have to go down about ten floors to get to the one where Aaron stopped, which looked to be floor twenty. And she'd have to do it all in silence.

Instead, Alex located the building's main stairwell, opposite the construction elevator, and stayed in the shadows as much as possible as she made her way across the site. The stairwell, like the elevator, was exposed to the outside, but separated from the rest of the building by a thick concrete firewall. Taking the stairs three steps at a time, she was thankful that Jack had bought her the low-heeled boots; their rubbery soles were almost silent against the concrete. When she reached the tenth floor, her heart began to beat faster. This was the body's way of prepping for a vital situation, surging adrenaline to one's synapses to make them hyper-alert. The instructors at Talonstrike called it *plugging in*, as if you'd just been attached to an electrical current, energized. Truth was, all soldiers felt it at the moment of engagement, which was why the Marines had a saying: "stay groovy." In other words, manage your adrenaline and don't freak out.

Well, they had their own saying out there in Corona del Mar, and it was a reference to enduring the Pacific Ocean's average temp of about fifty-five degrees Fahrenheit. Sans wetsuit. So, with the wind swirling, Alex toed up the stairs and steadied her breathing as she silently repeated to herself.

The water's toasty.

Still, by the time she made it to the fifteenth floor her hands were damp with sweat. Alex stopped. Listened. Heard nothing.

As she took another step, a rumble sounded from behind and below. A motorcycle rounded the corner and paused at the entrance of the construction site. The bike was identical to the BMWs from that morning. The driver—she assumed it was a man—wore a dark hooded sweatshirt. He looked in the direction of Barclay's and stared for a few moments. The nose of Hanna's SUV, with a tiny gold shield, was barely visible and she couldn't see if Jack had stayed put. The hooded man then took a long look around and up at the building.

Alex stood stone still at the edge of the stairs, hidden in the shadow cast by the firewall.

He kicked the bike forward and entered the construction area.

The motorcycle's engine quieted, and a few seconds later, a clank sounded. The whir of the elevator descending then re-ascending echoed throughout the site. Alex continued up after it, as quietly as she could. When she reached the twentieth floor, she crept up the last flight and pictured herself as a stalking puma, movements slow and fluid—nothing to cause a glance or a start. Then she lay, chest to the cold concrete floor, feet extended down the stairs, and watched the exchange.

High above the city, and in a district that effectively shut down at the end of the business day, the two men's voices echoed loudly throughout the concrete and metal structure. The second man said something that sounded like a quip, Aaron answered, then held out the briefcase. He stood a good half a foot taller than the hooded man.

Alex couldn't see well enough from where she was, so she crept forward while watching for obstructions, anything that would make a scraping sound under her.

The hooded man took the briefcase and motioned Aaron away.

When Aaron had moved back far enough, the hooded man opened the briefcase with four audible clicks.

Alex eased closer and stopped at a gaping hole in the floor before her where the wind twisted upward like a funnel. Looking down, she squinted to see another hole through the next floor and the next. A metal frame with two rails extended down the sides of the openings, but they otherwise gaped open. An unfinished elevator shaft.

Inching her way around the hole, Alex found herself deeper in the shadows but farther from the exchange. She kept crawling until she could see both men clearly again.

The hooded man's back was to her now, as he bent over the case and counted out loud.

She inched closer and stopped when Aaron looked up and around.

Any closer and they'd be able to hear her breathe.

The hooded man cursed and Alex almost flinched. "Where's the rest?"

The English was American, not British.

"I...I..." Aaron pushed against a metal beam, exposing his face to the lights from the building across the street, showing his wide-eyed expression.

"I told you not to spend any yet. Aaron..." The hooded man snapped the case closed. "That's failure number two."

"I'll pay you back," Aaron said in a pleading voice.

"It's already done."

Aaron stood there, his face long and sullen. "Look, I tried to get it, I really did. It's just he got to it first."

"Shut up," the hooded man said, standing again, looking away as if in thought.

Aaron rambled on. "I did half the job, the delivery part, so I should get to keep half, shouldn't I? That would be the fairest thing, and I'd like you to be fair about it."

The hooded man turned back to Aaron. "The deal was all or nothing. That means you accomplished nil." He reached back, came out with a pistol, and pointed it at Aaron's chest.

Aaron took a step backward and looked behind him at the open air, the ledge on which he had just put himself. Taking a quick step to the side, he said, "Why do you...?" He looked at the gun and then at the hooded man.

"Relax. I thought I heard something." The man lowered the gun.

"Why...why did we meet all the way up here?" Aaron had begun to stutter.

"Privacy." He swung his gun arm and scanned the floor.

Alex held her breath. Not moving. Watching.

"Anyway." The hooded man turned back. "I brought you something."

"What?" Aaron looked around.

The hooded man patted Aaron on the shoulder and handed him a folded piece of paper. "Read it."

Aaron took the paper and unfolded it. "Where did you get this? It's in my handwriting."

"Of course it is. You wrote it."

"Rubbish." Aaron gripped the paper.

The hooded man snatched the paper from him, folded it, and stuffed it into Aaron's chest pocket.

Aaron said, "What are you—"

The other man shoved him off the edge of the building. Aaron's scream echoed through the rafters, and grew fainter until it was silenced by a thud.

The hooded man spun, fired the pistol in Alex's direction, and ducked behind a half-finished wall.

She rolled to the side, heart pounding, and a thrum of blood rushing through her ears. The whoosh of the cold wind whipped at her through the upper floors of the structure. She had to keep moving. She had no gun, no weapon at all. Easing forward to see past a metal beam, she took a long stride. Her boot settled on a large, loose bolt on the floor, causing it to scrape against the smooth concrete.

Another gunshot clanked against the metal to her left.

Alex darted back behind the beam and searched the floor for a pipe, scrap metal, anything she could use as a weapon. There was nothing but the bolt she had stepped on. As she peeked around the edge of the beam, a single, soft footstep fell behind her.

Alex dove to the ground as a gunshot boomed and the bullet ricocheted off metal. She rolled away from the elevator shaft and behind the beam. Listening for another footstep, she pulled into a crouch. She felt around the floor until she found the bolt. She waited one full second and tossed it to the left.

The moment the next gunshot sounded, Alex jumped out from behind the beam and charged in the last direction he'd expect her to go—straight toward the muzzle flash. The hooded man wheeled toward her, but she swung a single kick straight up into his arm.

The man grunted as the gun sailed from his grip and across the floor, then tumbled off the edge. Before she could spin to ready position, Alex felt the smack of the metal briefcase against her back and she fell to the floor.

The man's face remained hidden in the shadows and under the hood. Still gripping the suitcase, he darted forward and swiveled his hips to deliver a kick, but Alex saw it coming and turned just enough to dodge the blow.

She grabbed his ankle—he was shorter than her, but thicker—and with a forearm lock, managed to twist him to the ground, wincing as the stitches tore from her shoulder.

The briefcase banged against the concrete and he dropped it. Then, ultra fast, he was up on his feet again.

Alex stayed low, delivering a sweeping kick to his legs, but he shifted his weight to deflect with one calf, and countered with a snapping kick, catching her kneecap and sending her stumbling backward.

She answered him with a spinning heel kick in the other direction and caught him in the abdomen, winning an *oof*, but he responded fast, with a quick punch that she partially deflected with a forearm block. Ready for his response, Alex let him get closer, and, with the agonizing pain of using her right arm to deflect the second blow, she shifted and thrust a solid uppercut to his jaw.

Nobody expected a lefty.

The hood slipped off a bit as the man stumbled backwards, exposing a thick, square chin and a drop of blood trickling to his neck. As Alex planted herself for another counter, a clank sounded from behind the man.

He spun, and she caught Jack ducking behind a pillar ten feet back.

Damn.

The hooded man took three efficient steps toward Jack and moved in for a volley of kicks and punches, each of which were easily turned away by Jack. Then Jack spun and delivered a solid high kick aimed at the hooded man's head, and the man barely deflected it with a forearm.

Alex darted forward to attack from behind.

Jack moved to deliver another blow.

But the hooded man dropped and rolled, knocking the briefcase into the empty elevator shaft.

And then he followed it.

Alex crouched forward to see him sliding down the elevator beam, like a fireman. Passing the floor below, he almost slipped off, but he wrapped his legs around the beam and slid lower.

No way could she do the same with one arm—

"Take the stairs!" Jack yelled, as he climbed down the shaft after the hooded man.

Alex sprinted to the stairwell and bounded down, four steps at a time, but it wasn't fast enough. The man had three floors on her and reached the bottom while she was still on floor two. Jack was not even in sight.

Alex rocketed from the stairwell, sprinting across the frozen dirt.

Holding the suitcase to his chest, the man kick-started his motorcycle and spun forward.

"Alex, wait!" Jack called from behind.

She darted to cut him off at the entrance. As she leapt toward the man's back, he jerked the bike with one arm, almost wiping out but avoiding impact. Her fingertips brushed his shoulders as she tumbled over the back of the bike and into the chain-link fence. As he exited, Alex caught the slightest glimpse of his profile in the harsh lighting from across the street. But it wasn't enough. She wouldn't be able draw him.

A moment later, Jack was bent over and heaving for air next to her.

And the hooded man was gone.

Eleven

Staring out at the ocean—teal blue as far as the eye could see—Draganic heard the landing gear kick into place. He turned his attention to the other side of the plane, where he could see Providenciales, the central city of the sprawling Turks and Caicos Islands. The descent had been so smooth that he hadn't realized they were about to land.

One of the many reasons he loved this plane.

Smooth and sleek as a Bentley limousine, the Boeing Business Jet boasted details like teakwood tables and Italian leather seats, plus a fully stocked wet bar, a king-sized bedroom, a mosaic-tiled shower, and a drop-down, eighty-inch movie screen.

It was considered the private sector's version of Air Force One.

His wife, Natasha, had chosen to sit in the living room at the rear of the jet and ignore him. With dark leather recliners, walnut furnishings, and Afghan rugs, it was the area Draganic liked best. By sitting in his favorite recliner, Natasha was showing her unending defiance.

Some sort of payback for the recent tabloid exposé, he figured.

After a quick deplaning on the tarmac at Providenciales International Airport, and while the pilots took care of the Customs nonsense, Draganic and Natasha were seated in the rented SUV to take them to their respective destinations. Natasha would be dropped at the docks then whisked off to the resort by boat, while Draganic would continue on in the SUV to meet with his bankers at the Royal Turks Bank, a few safe miles away.

While they were on Leeward Highway, the ocean scent hit full blast and filled Draganic's veins like a narcotic. Closing his eyes, he inhaled deeply.

Natasha said, "I would like you to close the windows and use the air coolers."

"You like the ocean," Draganic said.

"This land is ugly."

He had to admit, if he hadn't been to the Parrot Cay resort himself once before, he would have thought the same. They passed a large building with a sign that read TOWN CENTER MALL. The blocky concrete structure held smaller signs that bled dark orange and brown rust down the lighthouse's sides. They looked like shit stains.

"Buy some jewelry," he said. "It will make you feel better."

She crossed her arms, tightened her brows to match her pouting lips, and turned her gaze to the window.

When the car slid to a stop in a gravel parking lot in front of a one-room building, the waiting house for guests taking a private boat shuttle to the resort, Natasha opened the door and exited without a word.

Ten minutes later, the driver navigated Draganic to his meeting.

The headquarters for the Royal Turks Bank, with its white stucco walls, pale green shutters, and red clay roof, was less impressive than those in the Caymans that boasted tall steel structures with black tinted glass and armed guards. The Turks Bank place looked like a daily workforce building. But Draganic knew better; inside was one of the richest banks in all the region.

As Draganic exited the SUV, a black man in a dark suit hustled from the building to receive him. Inside, Harold Knell, a small man with patches of freckles and red hair, escorted Draganic to a long glass conference room with a view of smaller buildings and white-sand beaches. Closing the door, Knell said, "We have missed you here at the Royal Turks Bank, Mr. Draganic. We are glad to have you back."

Draganic looked past the man. "Yes. Yes, I am glad, too."

"We have reviewed all the documents and everything should be in perfect order. We'll just need some signatures for finalization." Translation: no red tape to trip over or choke you.

They completed the paperwork before finishing a single cup of black coffee, and Draganic couldn't help but remark at how easy it had become to move money around the world.

Once it had been entered into the virtual banking system, that was.

"One more thing," Draganic said. He explained a proposal for the bank. A deposit, of sorts.

Knell stared back at him. "We have done this for you before, of course."

"Yes, I'd like to do it for a separate account. Private."

He meant hidden. Contrary to Hollywood depiction, discreet banks didn't do numbered accounts anymore. They did something called virtual banking. Like a black market for banking, the virtual system kept money hidden from governments and officials. No taxes, no extra fees, no sanctions for improper accounting, or declaration of assets. A necessity for a man like Draganic.

"There would be a fee. How much are you planning to move?"

"About five times the amount of last time."

Knell fell back in his seat. It wasn't often that one could surprise a banker with the size of a deposit, so Draganic smiled.

"That would be a one-time charge of about ten million."

Draganic stood. "You'll have the deposits by Christmas."

"Three days?"

"Perhaps sooner."

Knell gave him a handshake that was so warm, Draganic thought the man would crawl right into his lap.

Draganic returned to the waiting SUV, and directed the driver back to the airport.

"Don't you wish to go to Parrot Cay?"

"Not this time."

Ten minutes later, when Draganic boarded the plane, he was pleasantly surprised to see Lulia, the Romanian flight attendant who had all but avoided him on the flight out.

"You are still here," he said.

She stood and smiled. "I am hoping this is of your agreement."

He shrugged out of his suit coat, letting it fall into her hands. "And the pilot?"

"He should soon be returning." She hung the jacket near the galley.

Draganic corrected, "He should *return soon*." Then he walked to her and stopped, inches from her modest chest. She smelled like body powder and boiled kolbász, and she moved like a ballerina with fluid and wide footsteps. A true Eastern Euro. "How old are you," he asked.

She stood a little taller as she said, "Twenty."

Draganic looked her over. Lulia was too old to continue in the Romanian ballet companies, but still quite delectable. He raised his brow and gave her a knowing smirk. "And the truth?"

Lulia blushed, turned her eyes away. "Eighteen."

"Even better," he said. Taking her by the hand, he led her to the office.

As they stepped inside, she reached up and touched his face, let her hand linger behind his ear, and down his neck. And with a finger, she traced the long rope of a scar.

Draganic froze.

She whispered, "Not to worry. I like it."

Draganic eyed her.

She said, "For real. It shows you are of strength. You have suffered through the battles. I respect this in a man."

He said, "And you have kept your skin white and pure. I like this in a girl."

She smiled. "Tell me, how did you get this one?" She cupped the scar with her hand now.

Draganic stared down at her. Contemplated his answer and decided on the truth. Why not?

He said, "I was a boy. Seven and one half years old. A lesson I would keep with me for eternity."

Lulia's eyebrows creased and she tilted her head. "An accident?"

Draganic said, "I was teasing my brother, placing the poker in the fire and then jabbing at him with it. And I accidentally hit him, in the arm. It gave him a small burn, but one he would carry forever. A scar. My mother immediately saw what had happened. She took the poker from me, placed it in the fire until it glowed red."

Lulia stiffened.

"And then she struck me across the head with it."

Lulia put her hand to her mouth and then back on Draganic's face. "I am so sorry. You were just a child, you didn't—"

"After she treated me with the oils and the wrapping, she patted my head and told me to go play."

Lulia stood still, mouth open. Perhaps it was too much of a story for her.

Draganic patted Lulia's hands and said, "It is OK. This happened many years ago."

Finally, she said. "Show me how I can make it feel better."

Draganic smiled. That was more like it. "Come."

He walked to the desk and picked up the phone. Dialing the cell number, he sat down in the chair.

Lulia shut the door and walked over to him.

Draganic took her hand, lowering her. She turned to sit in his lap, but he shook his head and pulled her down further until she was kneeling before him.

As the phone began to ring, he took Lulia's hand and guided it to his zipper.

She tugged it open as he said, "Natasha?"

Draganic listened to the nonsense coming from his wife's mouth as he filled

Lulia's. All he said was, "I will go to Gstaad in two days and send the plane back for you."

He dropped the phone on the desk, and ignored it as it immediately began to buzz. Instead, he took Lulia's small head in both his hands and helped her make it better.

Lockard pulled the motorcycle into the private garage, switched it off, and sat in the darkness.

Alex-fucking-Winter.

Rubbing the lump on his jawbone, Lockard laughed. Who knew she was a lefty?

Lockard shook his head at the irony of it all. The first time he'd seen her was at the funeral, and like her, he'd been just a child. They'd both mourned the loss of parents that day while Moss stood with a wall of intelligence officers, pretending he was worthy of honor. The memory had faded, though, along with the pain. Lockard had tucked it away deep inside and let it sit alone ever since.

Memories were like that. They resided in a vast forest, and you had to locate them regularly in order to remember their locations. The more you accessed, the easier they were to find. Like trampled paths in forest brush, the trails to their bedding became automatic, rote. And the ones you didn't access? Well, they eventually became lost in a tangle of growth. Still there, but almost impossible to find.

He should have anticipated Alex Winter being smart enough to track down Aaron. Winter came from a family of spies and knew damn well what she was doing. Maybe she was even working with Edgar. Lockard should have killed her tonight.

Pushed her right off the lip, like Aaron.

But then the other man had appeared. Unable to get a solid look at his face in the shadows, Lockard only caught a glimpse. Not enough to identify him.

Both of them had obviously taken more than the typical Company training of tae kwon do and muay Thai, and had clearly learned some sort of judo or maybe kung fu, as well. Between the two of them, they'd used just about every technique in just a few quick exchanges.

The woman had also caused him to lose one of his favorite pistols, an HK45

Tactical; good thing he had two more just like it inside the house. The best news was that they had most likely not identified him, so Lockard still had the edge. He could stay in the shadows for now. Maybe she would even lead him to Edgar. And because Aaron had royally fucked up the simplest of handoffs, Edgar still had the key.

Lockard needed that key.

He knew exactly who would lead him back to Alex Winter, and maybe Edgar. Like small grease fires, they were threatening and would be messy to clean up, but he couldn't let them smolder. They could take the whole house down. Sure, there was a bounty waiting for Lockard—large enough to be more than a mere distraction—but right now, he needed to focus on the battle. He couldn't let anything get in the way of that.

Not even the money.

He stood, unstrapped the briefcase, and unlocked the door leading to his flat. Speaking of money, he had some more to burn.

Literally.

Twelve

Alex needed a drink.

She convinced Jack to stop at a pub located in Canning Town, a small neighborhood wedged between the docks and an urban hospital. The place was called the Nag's Loaf Tavern, and sat across the street from a building labeled *South Canning Town Detached Youth Project*. With black steel bars covering the first and second-floor windows, and roll-down, dented steel doors, the building looked more like a prison than a youth center.

Considering that, and the three other patrons, two of whom had more chins than teeth, Alex figured the bartender had seen people in worse shape than her in his tenure. Still, she'd torn the surgical stitches from her shoulder in the fight with the hooded man, and it looked like she'd been shot.

Again.

Jack convinced the bartender to give them a few of his extra towels, which he tied tight against the wound to stem the bleeding.

The sole waitress approached their table and tossed a couple of cardboard coasters in front of them. Probably younger than Alex, but living hard enough to look decades older. She stared Alex up and down as she said, "You can order yourself a pint of ale, but that's all."

The other patrons all stood and yelled at the soccer game on a television above the bar. Two of them pushed each other, and one of them fell into the table, almost spilling his beer.

"It's a replay, you plonkers!" the waitress yelled back at them. "You already know how it ends."

One of the men waved her off and stumbled back into the booth.

"How about a pint of bitter?" Jack asked.

She turned back, saying, "Aye, we can do that." She pointed at Alex's shoulder. "What I'm sayin' is, she needs to stay where she is. I don't need no

John Thomases going off and bleeding all over the loo. Just gave it a bish bash bosh."

"Bish bash?"

"Wash," Jack said, leaning toward Alex.

The waitress stood there with a smirk.

Of course, she was speaking Cockney. Alex said, "It looks worse than it is."

"Wouldn't give a Kate Moss if you were dying. Just don't up 'n do it in there. Understand?"

Couldn't give a toss, couldn't give a damn. Right.

"Toss," Jack whispered.

"Shut up," Alex whispered back. She scanned the bar and brightened to see her favored small-batch gin on the shelf. "Hendricks with a splash of soda."

The waitress nodded and walked off.

Jack squinted at her. "How is it, really?"

"Kind of feels like I've been stabbed with an ice pick."

He sat back. "I should have gone in earlier."

"You shouldn't have come up at all."

"You've escaped a bombing, been shot at, then attacked in high-rise construction site. By my count you've only six lives left."

"Are you comparing me to a house cat?"

"More like a snow leopard, I'd say."

"A powerful, highly intelligent hunter. I'll take that as a compliment."

"Don't forget stunning to look at. Those grey-blue eyes." He placed his hand over hers and left it there. The warmth felt good. She had missed him and was glad he was with her now.

She said, "So where did you learn the kickboxing? Or was it muay Thai? Fairly impressive."

He winced. "It's actually a technique known as Savate. A martial art devised by the French."

She raised her eyebrows for more. From what she'd heard, Savate was a gritty technique born from French street-fighting that used violent kicks as the basis for both offense and defense.

He continued, "I've joined something of a club in Paris. When in Rome and all that..."

She considered the answer and almost remarked at just how good he'd gotten so quickly, but decided she didn't need to feed his ego any more after she'd asked him to stay put and he'd ignored her.

After a minute of silence, he finally said, "So you know, I spoke with Hanna. She's taking a holiday and has offered use of her flat while she's away."

Alex gave him a sidelong glance and said, "Okay." Then she watched the TV soccer game absentmindedly as she thought about Aaron and the briefcase, then wondered how the hooded man was connected to Edgar. Obviously, they both wanted the case. Aaron had said 'he' had gotten to it first. Was the hooded man an agent, too?

I'll pay you back, Aaron had said. *I tried to get it.*

As if reading her thoughts, Jack said, "The man with the hood stuffed the piano with explosives for Chef Guy. Aaron delivered it."

Not bad, but Jack didn't have to know about her father or her job with the CIA…not that being an insider had given Alex any sort of edge. She wondered if she should find a way to check in with Deputy Director Moss. She doubted he knew all this was going on, and if he did, Alex was pissed he hadn't clued her in a little better. Compartmentalization of information was sometimes necessary to protect the agent but this time it could get her killed.

Spinning the coaster on its edge, she said, "So the first million, the case of cash there tonight—that was half the payoff for planting the explosives."

"My thoughts exactly."

Alex leaned back in the booth. "That's a hell of a large sum for that kind of job."

"Makes you wonder about the end game."

Right. "And so Aaron was to pick up the second suitcase the night of the explosion and give it to the man with the hood."

"But your father beat him to it."

But why? If Alex knew who the hell he was working for, then she could have a handle on that answer.

"Any idea where he could be living?" Jack asked.

She squeezed her eyes closed. "Jack, I didn't even know he was alive until yesterday."

Before he could respond, the waitress brought their drinks. Cold and satisfying, the Hendricks unfolded with rose petals, a hit of cucumber, and a bite at the end. It felt like home. She held the cold glass to her head.

Standing over them but glaring out the window, the waitress said, "It's taters in the mold outside, ain't it?"

Jack nodded, then whispered to her, "Rhymes with --"

"Cold," she said, taking a good gulp of her drink. "I got it."

One Tooth called out to the waitress. "Hey, Mona, fancy you bringing us another round a Sammy Oaties."

She nodded back at them. "Right up your arse if you keep on with the yelling!" She turned to them. "They think Bart'll give 'em tickets if they keep coming here. They got another think coming."

"Bart?"

"The keeper." She nodded at the bartender. "His brother works in the ticket office for Arsenal. Bart's right popular around here. Attracts a lot of battle cruisers." She nodded back at the three buffoons and walked off.

Alex was at a loss on that one. "Cruisers?"

"Boozers," Jack said.

She shook her head.

They drank in silence until the game entered halftime and the Sky News broadcast came on. The announcer, a well-spoken woman, dived into a report about a murder-suicide in the Isle of Man.

A murder-suicide that involved the Treasury minister.

Alex sat forward.

Jack whispered, "The passport you saw in your father's briefcase."

She nodded, still staring at the screen. "Isle of Man."

The Isle of Man, otherwise known as just Mann, was a self-governing British Crown dependency located in the Irish Sea between Great Britain and Ireland. Populated by only about eighty thousand people, Mann was famous for motorcycle racing, its tailless Manx cats, and that was about it. Alex wondered what business her father could possibly have in Mann.

The picture switched to a reporter interviewing a Metropolitan Police inspector in what looked to be Scotland Yard's press office. "At this point, we are focusing on the lengthy relationship between the two men. If anyone has seen them together recently or would like to assist with knowledge, we ask you to call this number."

A UK telephone number flashed on the screen below her, all fives and ones, before the picture returned to the anchor, who said, "No clues at this time, at least none that the police are willing to share publicly, however inside sources have suggested that one of the bodies was mutilated, perhaps missing a limb."

"Son of a—" Alex fished the newly bought disposable cell phone from her pocket and began dialing fives and ones.

Someone picked up on the second ring. "Good evening, Metropolitan Police. How may I direct your call?"

Matching the man's British accent, Alex said, "Yes, I'm looking for Inspector Valerie Wainscott. She's lead on the Mann murders."

"Please hold the line."

A few seconds later, Alex was directed to another line that began to ring with the deep buzzing sound of old English phones. A man answered this time, "Special Investigation. How may I be of assist?"

"I'm looking for Inspector Wainscott. Can you please transfer me?"

"She's a bit tied up at the moment. Can I be of assist?"

"Tell her it's a friend from Legoland." Legoland was the current nickname for 85 Vauxhall Cross, the new building that housed the bulk of MI6. Off the Thames and stacked with multiple levels, cylindrical bay towers, and green glass, it looked like it was made of giant plastic bricks.

"Right, then. I'll advise."

Jack gave her a skeptical look. "Your accent sounds off."

She placed a hand over the microphone. "How so?"

"It's a little like a Brit trying to be an American."

"Very helpful, thank you."

A woman came on the line. "Inspector Wainscott. Who's speaking?"

"As your colleague informed you, I'm a friend." She raised her eyebrows to Jack. *Better?*

He wobbled a flat palm in the air. *Not really.*

"And are you going to tell me your name?"

"I'm afraid I can't on this one."

"Then how do I know you're authentic?"

"Call Director Grant's secretary, Anne. She's just moved across the hall to a new half-oval desk made of sleek white composite. On it, she has a photo of her sons, Cameron and Charles, both dressed in their Oxford Day School uniforms. If I'm correct, call me back at this number." I gave her the cell number and hung up.

Jack looked at Alex with his eyebrows raised.

She shrugged. "I met Grant last month through a client."

"Uh-huh."

Less than a minute later, the disposable cell phone buzzed on the table. Alex answered.

Wainscott said, "So she does. Now, what can you tell me?"

"Not here. We'll have to meet." And as Alex considered options for a meeting place, a schedule of upcoming games flashed on the TV. It gave her an idea.

"First tell me what it's all about."

Damn inspectors didn't get the cloak-and-dagger workbook. They had no patience. Alex said, "It's about the murder-suicide in Isle of Man, the investigation I believe you are heading up."

She stayed silent for a bit, then said, "Unless you can give me more, I'm sorry."

On a hunch, but with confidence, Alex said, "I can connect this to your other case."

"What other—"

"The bombing at Café Martin."

Silence, then, "How?"

"The victim in Mann, he was missing a hand."

She cleared her throat. "Tell me where you are. I can come to you."

"Not now." Glancing up at the television, Alex said, "Tomorrow, noon, at Ashburton Grove, Emirates. There will be a ticket in your name at the Match Day window."

"A football game?" She snorted. "Anything else?"

"Yes." Alex nodded at Jack as she said, "I'll need a mobile number for you."

After memorizing the number, Alex told her she'd call with instructions and hung up.

Jack said, "Good luck finding tickets to that match, it's been sold out for weeks I'm sure."

"We'll see about that." Alex stood and walked to the bar. "Bart?"

"Aye, yeah? Can I do for you?" He kept wiping glasses with a dirty rag and never looked up.

"I hear you can get tickets to football games."

He stopped. Still didn't look up. "Mona tell you that?"

"She did."

He sucked something from his top tooth and said, "Not any game, just Arsenal. And home only." Then he turned and started placing glasses on the long shelf behind him. "It'll cost you, though. What game you hoping for?"

"Liverpool."

"Tomorrow? You're right crazy, love."

Alex took out her wallet and unfolded five hundred-pound notes out of view of the other patrons. "I'll pay a premium."

"Don't care what you're willing. The match is tomorrow, you're bloody bonkers if you—"

Jack walked up next to her and leaned against the bar, nodded to the man's cell phone near the bottles. "That your mobile?" He asked.

Bart eyed him, and said, "Aye, what's it to ya?"

Jack reached into his pocket and drew out what looked to be the latest model Samsung *Ultra-Whatever* phone. It was still covered with a thick wrap of cellophane. He placed it on the bar.

Alex tried to give him a look that told him she was doing just fine without Jack and his sexy boy toys, but it seemed that Jack and Bart were having a moment.

Bart said, "That the latest model?"

"Hasn't even hit the market."

"That right?" Bart reached over and picked it up, turned it with a look of amazement and wonder. "Stolen?"

"Not like that. I work for Samsung, yeah?" Jack showed him a card. "That there's set to retail at over four-hundred pound next month. I'm hearing pre-orders have the first lot sold out already."

"How do I—"

And Jack cut him off. "No problem, see? Just put the SIM card from your current phone into the Samsung, it won't know the difference."

Bart looked back and forth between Jack and the cash in Alex's hand. Then he glanced around, slipped the new Samsung into his pocket, and sucked the tooth again. "How many tickets you need?"

Okay, so maybe Jack sped things up a bit.

"Four," Alex said, "but only two together."

Thirteen

By the time Alex showered back at Hanna's, Jack had crashed in the second bedroom. Exhausted and with no interest in relationship noise at the moment, she slipped into the den and onto a nailhead leather sofa. She curled under a grey, soft wool blanket and slept like a slab of granite.

Almost.

She's nine, and playing barefoot soccer with her best friend Roberto. She does this when she stays out in Fairfax with Ginger, her grandmother, whenever her mom goes to spend time with her dad in Europe somewhere. They usually spend a solid two weeks together and then apart again for months. Other people ask how she does it, but it's her normal, so she never thinks about it.

As for that day, Robbie and Alex had met up after school, kicked off their shoes, and popped the ball around the street all afternoon as usual. The first time Robbie had goaded her into playing barefoot with him, she'd ended up with blisters from her heels to her toes. Now she had a thick pad of callus on each foot, same as Robbie, along with some Argentinian style soccer skills.

The two of them are lying on the sidewalk, oblivious to the passing cars and everyone else in the world, and debating the best soccer player in history. Alex insists it's Pelé, and he counters with Maradona. A baloney argument, and he knows it, but who else can he pick against Pelé?

The day hasn't been perfect, just typical. School. Robbie. Dinner soon. Then homework. An average spring day in Northern Virginia, where the sun peeks at you with hints but no promises. Nothing special. So when Alex hears Ginger swing open that screen door and call her name, she's not surprised. Dinnertime, is all.

Her mom is coming back tomorrow, so she's a little disappointed to have to say good-bye to Robbie early. Though he lives right across the street from Ginger, she never knows when she'll be back to see him.

He says, "I wish you could stay with Ginger all the time."

"Yeah, but then I'd have to school you in soccer every day."

"Whatever, Allejandra." He kicks the ball at her and misses, and his mom tells him to come on in, let Alex go home now.

Alex walks up to the porch where Ginger is waiting alongside a tall man in a dark suit. She hadn't noticed him arrive. And as she strolls that length of grass, she slowly gets a funny feeling deep in her stomach, a flutter, a tightening. Then she notices that Ginger's face looks sad, her eyes are swollen and red. The man stands tall and silent, hat in his hand.

She smiles, but it's a lie.

"Hey there, darling. Having fun with Roberto?"

"Yeah." Alex's heart is in her stomach, and she has no idea why.

"That's good." She holds out her arms.

Alex looks back at Robbie, who has just collected the ball in his yard. He shrugs and waves, then dribbles the ball in a zigzag toward his own mom, who stands at their front door.

Ginger looks out that way and gives Robbie's mom a modest wave.

Robbie's mom waves back, then puts her hand to her mouth, hustles Robbie to her, and holds him. Tight.

"What's going on?" Alex asks.

The man glances away.

Ginger gets down on one knee, taking Alex's hands in hers. She smiles again. But this time it wavers and spills. "Honey, there was accident last night. An explosion at a restaurant in Spain..."

And there it was. The stomach never lies.

Alex swallows. Hard. "Where Mom went to see Dad?"

Ginger nods as the tears begin to fill her eyes, but she blinks hard, as though she's willing them away. "Yes. They were there. A lot of people from the government were there."

Alex stares at her as her knees buckle. She swallows, and Ginger holds her up.

A solid lump forms in Alex's throat, like a peach pit, and she fights it down to say, "How bad of an explosion?"

Ginger stares right into her eyes, the strongest woman in the world, and says, "As bad as it could be." With a long blink, she nods.

Alex stares past her into the living room, at the funny little clock shaped like a crystal heart. It's never worked, but Ginger refuses to fix it or throw it away. Alex lets Ginger hold her so she doesn't have to stand on her own, and Ginger whispers again, "As bad as it could be."

Numb and scared and confused and suddenly so wobbly that she can fall back into the threadbare grass, Alex looks back across the street at Robbie's house. Poor Robbie, with his tangled curly hair and crooked smile. Robbie has gotten his wish. But he's crying, too.

Because Robbie would have never wished for this.

"Been awake for long?"

Alex startled when Jack entered the room. He wore a long, black robe that accented his broad shoulders, but hid the sculpted body that she knew was beneath. She didn't know how he did it, but he was always attuned to her biorhythms. When she woke, when she slept. She remembered she couldn't turn over in bed without at least one of his limbs snaking out to find her in his twilight sleep.

Sitting up straight at one end of the sofa, she said, "A few minutes."

"How's your shoulder?"

"Sore." Alex stretched it a bit. "Like a bad bruise."

"It's a hole from a bullet."

"Right. Today it feels like a bruise."

"Right." He walked to the windows, pulled aside the sheers, and looked out at London's version of a hazy sunrise. Keeping his back to her, he said, "I'm curious. Why didn't you…join me last night?"

Alex imagined the powerful legs underneath that robe and asked herself the same question. "Didn't want to wake you."

He looked at her. "Would've been nice to be woken by you again."

Alex answered with a nearly audible gulp.

He peered at her for a moment and said, "Have you had a look outside?"

"Not yet."

"Eerie with the cloud cover low as it is."

"May be a white Christmas after all," she said. "History in the making."

He turned, eyes flicking to her sketchbook on the coffee table. "You should draw it."

"If they cancel the soccer match, I'll have nothing better to do."

"They'll only cancel on account of a blizzard." He walked over to the sofa and stood above Alex. Looked at the sketchbook in her hands. "How about you draw me?"

"Now?"

He looked her over and said, "We have the time."

Keeping her gaze on his, Alex said, "You're overdressed."

"Am I?" Jack took hold of a length of the robe's belt, gave her a mischievous look, but didn't pull it. "Perhaps you could use your imagination."

Biting her lip, Alex said, "Perhaps."

He smiled and turned to the sofa as she gathered her sketchbook and pencils and walked over to the desk. She chose a few harder leads suitable for detailed work. Then she wheeled the chair to the front of the desk and balanced the sketchbook on her thighs.

Jack had already stretched the length of the sofa, hands locked behind his head. Alex had drawn plenty of live models in her study, but this time she'd have to improvise a bit.

Alex sat back, closed her eyes for a few moments and took in the image she would create. Then, using long, slow strokes, she outlined Jack's figure. His legs and chest and neck and head.

He had the form and physical balance of a swimmer or a triathlete, muscular but not bulging. The drawing came easy, lines formed shapes and shapes became defined. Each stroke brought certainty and strength to the image. A sensual exercise of perception meeting veracity. An artist's essence of pleasure.

"What is it?" Jack asked.

He'd caught Alex smiling as she worked. "Nothing."

He gave her a crooked, almost evil little smirk.

Alex let her mind wander until her subconscious took over and created from within its own vault. She caught the muted sunlight stretching through the glass French doors, reaching across the striped sofa and up the wall to add contrast and depth. She modulated the light and shadows of his body, the strength of his arms and the surety of his hands. Then she continued with his neckline. The muscles there were defined but not overwhelming, and at that moment he'd held them just taut enough.

As she moved to his face and searching eyes, Jack drew Alex from her trance, asking, "I believe you were dreaming this morning."

"Why do you say that?"

"I heard you make ... a noise."

Alex kept her hand moving without making any defining marks.

"You know, it's really alright to talk about yourself."

"Thanks."

"Alex," he said quietly. "Tell me more about what happened to your parents."

She stopped for a moment, but kept her gaze on the page. "The bombing in Spain. I told you before. It happened in a restaurant outside Madrid. Eighty-two people died, eleven…well, ten were Americans. They were said to be the targets."

"And now you're thinking maybe it was only nine people?"

"No." She looked up at him, blinked once. "My mother was selfless. She would have never left me."

"That doesn't necessarily mean—"

"I know exactly what it means." Alex turned back to the drawing, where she started detailing Jack's eyes, keeping them pure and not inquisitive, like they were now.

"Sorry, I should never have implied…"

She shrugged the conversation away.

They stayed quiet for a long time. Long enough for Alex to finish the first layer of details, the ones that made the scene, and finish a second. Then she started that third layer of work, filling in the smallest and most intimate of details, and Jack's next question almost knocked her from the chair.

"Are you happy you followed the same path as your father?"

Alex had to work to steady her hand while she continued with the details the eyes that now looked challenging. "What do you mean?"

"The CIA."

Alex stopped drawing.

Upon receiving her assignment into Clandestine Service, she'd signed a standard CIA nondisclosure agreement that precluded Alex from sharing her position—much less assignment details, classified or not—with anyone other than her husband, of which she had none, and direct family members, also nil. So, during her seven years as an agent, Alex had told exactly no one. She'd been meticulous with her cover and always gave simple explanations for every move she made around Jack.

Then Alex realized it. When he had found her lying in the street, she was wearing the suit her father had left for her. When she awoke at Hanna's, she was wearing different clothes. Jack must have seen the passport, the one with Alex's photo and the name Amanda Carr. She was so groggy, she hadn't noticed. Still, Alex could easily explain it away, saying it was given to her by her contractor to gain entry to some facility or something.

If Alex confirmed his knowledge, it would not only be a direct and severe violation of her signed agreement, it would also put him in danger … more danger. He'd been seen with her in public. On the other hand, Alex had been left out in the cold. Moss knew she was here and some of what had happened, but still hadn't initiated contact. She had been effectively orphaned by the CIA while Jack had saved her life.

Alex was still tempted to weave an explanation. She had plenty of rabbit trails to send him on, tangle him up in.

She eased her gaze back up to Jack's and held his stare.

He didn't blink.

She said, "It's what I was built to do."

He nodded, held the stare for a while, and then looked away.

Alex waited for the onslaught of questions.

"When did you learn you could draw?"

Exhaling slowly, she resumed detailing. "The same year my parents died— or...when they were gone—my best friend moved, and I spent a lot of hours alone. Drawing became a kind of therapy for me."

"The sketches of the river."

"The first of hundreds of that day, yes."

Alex concentrated on the drawing. If not for that, she wasn't sure she could have this conversation at all. Yet by the time she finished the last of the details, she was still calm, and she leaned back to inspect her work.

"May I have a look now?" he asked.

"Not yet."

Alex worked for a few more minutes in silence and he said, "Now?"

She made a face as she reviewed her work.

"That's it, I'm having a look." He hopped to his feet and hurried across the office, leaned over her. He stopped and pulled back. "What on earth?"

She turned just enough to see his face above hers.

He glanced around the room, then pointed at the sketch. "That's not—"

She raised her eyebrows, tilted up her chin as she watched him study the scene, Jack leaning to Alex, their reflections in the glass of the French doors, the sea-aged building beyond them, across the canal.

He said, "Venice."

They'd made love for days.

He leaned further as he studied the details and textures. "It's magnificent. Just like yesterday."

"Sometimes it feels that way."

"Incredible." Jack pulled back, turned his attention to Alex. He held her gaze as he then leaned forward. His kiss met Alex right in the middle. She wavered, then rose and they joined hands, ending up back at the sofa. He pulled away and stroked his strong fingers along her body as he moved lower, slipping off her panties and tasting her breasts. Just long enough to tease Alex. She tugged the robe open, ready to make new memories.

Slowly, traced his fingers over the eagles on her ribs. "Will you tell me about this now?"

Alex gave him a look of *you've got to be fucking kidding me.*

He smiled. "Right, then. Later it is."

Then he hooked an arm around her lower back, and careful of her shoulder, eased Alex onto the sofa. When he leaned in to kiss her this time, she kissed him back, hard and full, and pressed up against him from below. Then Jack's legs widening hers and he took Alex whole, for all she really was, somehow making her a little more of who she wanted to be.

She cried out again, and this time, it was from pleasure.

Fourteen

Draganic woke to raindrops pattering against the bedroom window. Typical weather for Dubrovnik this time of year. It kept the tourists away, all but clearing the restaurants and shops for the residents' benefit.

Climbing from the bed as quietly as he could, so as to not wake Lulia, he grabbed his cell phone and checked for messages, but there were none. Mildly irritating, as he should have heard from Lockard by now. Draganic noticed Lulia's phone on the side table, next to the empty bottle of Russian Standard Imperia vodka.

Had she taken photos of them last night, having sex?

He tried to search the phone but it was locked with a code, so he set it back down.

Pulling his robe tight over his belly, Draganic slipped the sheathed Sea Shark into his robe pocket—one could never be too paranoid, even in one's own house. Then he walked down the limestone stairs, across the house, and into the sprawling kitchen that was equipped with enough wares to service a Michelin-starred restaurant.

Too bad Natasha could only cook cabbage soup.

After pouring himself a triple espresso, Draganic continued down the hall to the office. With a view of the red clay rooftops to the right and the blue-green ocean to the left, the desk had been named by the *Robb Report* as "one of the single best office seats in all of Croatia." But Draganic had no interest in views today, only news. He had half-heard something on the radio while riding home in the limousine last night, and was curious about the report.

Settling into the tall leatherback seat, Draganic slid the Sea Shark onto the desk and pulled the keyboard to him. He logged into his RSS newsfeed and read the headlines. Nothing about it in the international news, so he clicked on his UK feed.

His heart rate jumped and he had to put the espresso down.

The headline from the *Financial Times* read, "Treasury Minister and Banker Found Dead in Isle of Man." Draganic clicked open the article and read about the suspected murder-suicide, and the possible romantic relationship between the banker and the Treasury minister. He didn't care about that. He cared only about the banker's name.

Sid Oban.

Draganic's banker.

He opened and read as many of the stories as he could, skimming the content, though they all said essentially the same thing—both men were found dead at the bottom of a cliff of the Treasury minister's estate, a few meters from the ocean. The last one, though, added another detail that made Draganic's heart race even faster. The journalist reported a rumor: The police had cordoned off the area because they were looking for a missing body part.

Realizing he was holding his breath, Draganic opened another browser window and picked up the espresso. His hand shook as he brought the now lukewarm drink to his lips. He quickly keyed in the search and scrolled down, looking for news rags like the *Sun* or the *Daily Mail*. When he found one, he clicked it open and read as fast as he could. Halfway through the article, Draganic saw it.

Oban was found with *one hand missing*.

He gasped and dropped the espresso onto the keyboard, spilling it all over the new white computer and his robe.

"Yebeni kuchkin sin!" he yelled, and in an involuntary reaction, he unsheathed the Sea Shark and drove the knife into the center of the keyboard, splintering it in half and sending keys and plastic shrapnel across the stone floor.

Leaving the knife embedded in the huge wooden desk, Draganic pushed from his seat and paced the room, window to wall, wall to window.

How the hell did he do that?

Why the hell did he do that?

And the answers to both were obvious.

How? Lockard could steal the goddamn queen's tiara diamond ring right off her goddamn finger. In her bed, with the guards watching, for goddamn sakes!

And *why?* Greed, pure and simple. To cut Draganic out. Lockard had the key and Draganic had to find him. He needed to get that key back.

But locating Lockard would be problematic at best. Draganic could finance a search, but money wasn't enough to get this job done.

Calming as he paced, Draganic realized something that made him feel better.

No, it made him feel *good*. Because any way you sliced it, and one could take that literally in this case, Lockard only had half of the key.

Draganic held the other half.

Smiling, he eased back into the seat and pried the Sea Shark from the desk. He was thankful he had instructed Randeep to initiate the trading, essentially firing the first shot. And then the second, initiating the secret transfer of capital to the new account in Turks & Caicos. Shrewd moves in the face of conflict. Because with money—especially money like this—a battle always ensued.

And this battle, he thought, spinning the knife in his hands, had just escalated to war.

Moss woke to the buzzing of his cell phone on the side table. His first thought was, *Where the hell am I?* And his second, after figuring it out, *Did I remember to close the strong room?*

With a jet-lag headache brewing, he reached over and picked up the phone.

Grant.

"A bit early," Moss answered.

"News for you, old boy. Not sure if it's good or bad."

"Go on." Moss sat up and rubbed his neck.

"Just received word from a friend at Five."

MI5, the domestic branch of British intelligence, equivalent to the FBI. Moss eased his legs over the bed and stood.

Grant continued, "Seems a few of your Benjamin Franklins have landed right here in London. They were in the flat owned by the man we found at the Canary Wharf construction site."

Damn. Moss cradled the phone to his ear with one shoulder while he slipped into a robe. The same exact robe as those found in The Peninsula Hotels across the world, save the emblem.

"You still there, Bill?"

"When?" Moss asked.

"An hour ago. But that's not the finest point. The man found in the wharf was connected to our own café bombing. He delivered the damn piano. I'd say there's a storm brewing your way, ol' boy."

More like a tsunami, Moss thought. "How much?"

"One sleeve, ten thousand. We found it in the chap's sports locker. Seems he was a weekend cricketer. Not half bad, from what I hear."

"Do you have the cash?"

"I'm staring at it."

Holding the back of his head—maybe too much scotch last night, if that was even possible—Moss said, "And the containment?"

"Don't worry, it's under wraps. I've had Five place a mum order all the way down to the shields." Grant meant even the police were to keep it quiet. That would hold off the press. For now.

"I owe you, Peter."

"So you're letting me keep the stash?"

"I'll come for it this afternoon."

"Sore sport. See you then." He hung up.

What a damn mess, Moss thought, as he tightened his robe and headed downstairs. With all the noise this was causing, he could soon find himself on the wrong side of a Congressional panel.

If he ever ventured back into the United States, that was.

After rounding the corner of the oak stairwell on the main floor, Moss took a single step into the great room and almost screamed.

"Jesus H," Moss said, glancing at the alarm panel on the wall. The red light was shining solid, the alarm still armed. Yet sitting in the tall Elizabethan armchair in the far corner of the room, hands folded in his lap, wearing a suit with no tie, was Evan Lockard. "How the hell—?"

"You overpaid for the system."

Straightening his robe, Moss said, "What are you doing here?"

Lockard squinted at Moss.

Moss's stomach tightened, and he wished he had his Beretta Cougar on him, but why would he? He was in the goddamned *safe* house. His heart began to thump so loudly he thought Lockard would hear it.

Then Moss pulled it the fuck together.

He was a deputy director of the CIA, for God's sake. The mere idea of feeling threatened by one of his own foot soldiers was absurd. Besides, Moss was bigger than Lockard by a solid twenty pounds, he'd say. Taking a step forward, he thrust out his chin. "I asked what you are doing here."

Lockard raised his own chin. "Why did you intervene?"

Mind spinning to catch up to the thought—he hadn't had a cup of coffee yet —Moss stood there, puzzled. "With what?"

"The Winters. You told them about the delivery. The handoff, so to speak." He smiled at his elementary joke. "Why?"

About to cross his arms, Moss stopped himself. That would be a physical display of uneasiness, of insecurity. He dropped his hands into the robe's pockets and leaned against the tall stone fireplace mantel instead. He shrugged. "Insurance."

Lockard nodded, nice and slow. "So now *you* have the key?"

Half true. Edgar had the key, but Moss was working on that. "I do."

"You're lying."

Staring him down, Moss decided to put Lockard on the defensive instead. "And the bombing? I would say nice touch, except it was idiotic."

Lockard frowned while nodding. "Or maybe it kept the Yard off our trail, looking at dignitaries and motives for assassination, rather than the pedestrian killing of a Royal Air Force pilot."

Lockard half turned away.

Then, in an almost superhuman move, so fast Moss couldn't even get his hands out of his pockets, Lockard was on him—stripping off the robe's belt, winding it around Moss's neck, over the iron sconce, pulling him up, off the floor. Hanging him.

With his robe gaping open, his willy dangling free, Moss flailed at the makeshift noose.

"You sonofa—"

Eyes wide, his body twisting against the wall, gulping for air, Moss watched Lockard climb up the mantel and take a sword off the wall.

"I'll kill—" Moss's head slammed against the stone. "Help."

Standing before him, Lockard unsheathed the sword. He held it out, inches from Moss's groin.

Moss twisted, turning against the wall, but that only made the noose tighter. "Help," he tried to yell, but all that came was a raspy whisper.

Lockard reached up and took hold of Moss's right hand. He placed it on the mantel.

"Tell me where Edgar's safe house is."

"I don't know—" Moss tried to pull away but it was futile.

Lockard pressed Moss's hand tighter and raised the sword. "Then I'll make my own key."

"Wait. Wait." Moss blinked, his eyes tearing up.

Lockard paused, sword high over his head. "Yes?"

Staring at the blade, so dull it would probably shatter the bones right up to his elbow, Moss opened his mouth. His arms had begun to tingle and his head felt like a balloon full of blood. A few more seconds and it would pop. He managed to wheeze the address from his throat.

Nodding, Lockard raised the sword a few inches higher.

Moss's sphincter clenched.

Lockard swung, slicing through the terry belt and dropping Moss to the floor.

Gasping, Moss rubbed his throat and watched Lockard re-sheath the sword, exit the room. Moss felt the warmth spread from his groin as Lockard tripped the deafening alarm on the way out.

Fifteen

The Tube ride on the Victoria line to Kings Cross and then the Piccadilly line to Arsenal took about twenty minutes. It had begun to snow, but only flurries, and when Alex and Jack crossed white-railed bridge aboveground, they fell into a growing crowd of fans. Tits-up blitzed before the first kick, Alex thought, being jostled by fans yelling and singing, an entire drunken chorus making their way into the stadium.

Jack pressed close to Alex in the growing chaos, scanning the left side as she studied the right. The silence between them was knowing, they were both satisfied by their morning interlude, but also smart enough not to take it for more than it was. Not this time. Still, she couldn't help wondering what was going through his mind. Whether he was thriving on the adrenaline of all this or really trying to get close to her again.

Nothing like a near-death experience to make someone realize how much they'd missed you.

Funneling between two life-size cannons in the street's median, they entered the fan shop called The Armoury and bought sweatshirts, hats, and scarves, all in bright red Arsenal colors. They kept the sweatshirts under their buttoned coats, and the hats and scarves tucked into their pockets. The last item Alex bought was a rayon Arsenal flag. This little number would come in handy when the meeting was finished.

For now, they looked like soccer fans with no affiliation, exactly what she wanted.

Enormous murals of heroic players, locked arm in arm, adorned the outside of the stadium, wide and tall, all glittering glass and steel. Alex showed the Amanda Carr ID at the Match Day window, and then they entered the stadium in a river of fans rushing through floor-to-ceiling turnstiles. Inhaling deeply the scent of beer, minced beef, and sausage—footballer's pheromones—she nodded at the tenth yellow-jacketed policeman in about as many feet.

"All set?" she asked Jack.

It wasn't too complicated. They had four tickets: two separate singles and one set of seats together. Alex and Jack would start out in the single seats a few sections apart from each other, watching and waiting. Then Jack would go take one of the paired seats, where Wainscott would be waiting. Alex figured Wainscott also would have bought a couple of extra seats and scoped out the scene before halftime. Only question was who she'd bring as backup.

Jack winked. "At the ready."

Alex said, "Just remember, wait until three minutes into the second half to switch seats. And only if Wainscott is already there."

Looking around, he said, "Got it."

"And leave immediately after I signal."

"Right."

"Don't hesitate."

He stopped looking around, put a hand on her shoulder, and stared down at her. "Alex. I'm quite capable, trust me."

"Okay."

He turned and casually weaved his way into the stream of fans entering the stands. Just another fan at a football game.

Microchip salesman, my ass, Alex thought, narrowing her eyes.

Alex headed in the opposite direction to enter the stands directly across from the pair of seats waiting for Wainscott and Jack. A dusting of snow covered the field, but was being trampled away by the practicing players. Alex's section had broken into a slurred version of "The Greatest Team," Arsenal's song. She settled into her seat and located Jack with a glance. He, too, was surrounded by Arsenal fans, some dressed in the team's red jerseys, and some in coats. His charcoal jacket blended in fine.

Angled so that it appeared she was watching the players on the field, Alex took out the binoculars and began scanning the crowd for Wainscott.

Alex's choice of tickets had given the Inspector only two strong vantage points to view the seat she'd saved for her, and she scanned those for a woman looking in that direction or just above. It took less than five minutes. Wainscott's chosen seats were close to the tunnel—easy exit, Alex thought. Smart—and as predicted she did not come alone. A tall man dressed in a tan trench coat sat with her, scanning the crowd like a nervous gull. He wore black Lennon-style sunglasses, and as Alex watched him tap the back of his gloved hand with the palm of the other, "Lonely Hearts Club Band," chorused through her head.

Sergeant Pepper leaned over and whispered something to Wainscott, who nodded. Then the two of them stared directly above Alex. She resisted the urge to turn, that would have been a tell, and kept the binoculars pointed straight ahead. Wainscott whispered something to Sergeant Pepper and they looked back to the field.

The seat Alex had left for her still sat empty.

Pressing her cell phone's call button, Alex placed an earbud in one ear and leaned to the microphone clipped to her lapel. When Wainscott answered, Alex said, "One minute after halftime, be in the seat I left for you."

"And where will you be?"

"Where I am now. Watching." Alex hung up.

The match started with a roar, fans immediately on their feet, singing and cheering and yelling at good or bad plays. Arsenal took it to Liverpool, scoring twice in the first twenty minutes, sending the home fans into an absolute frenzy.

Playing the part, Alex stood and swayed with the crowd as they sang, while keeping her eyes on Wainscott and Sergeant Pepper, and glancing at Jack every now and then.

Standing and cheering with the best of them, Jack could've passed for an Arsenal lifer. Then, four minutes before halftime, as planned, Jack left his initial spot and exited the tunnel.

Two minutes before halftime, Wainscott followed.

Sergeant Pepper stayed put. So did Alex.

At the three-minute mark of the second half, Wainscott climbed the five rows to her appointed seat. Jack followed one minute later. Wainscott made a move to get back up to allow Jack to continue down the row, but he took her forearm, and guided her back down into her seat. He whispered the words Alex had told him, and Wainscott unhooked her necklace. Jack inspected it, ground it under his foot, then kicked the debris beneath the seats in front of him before settling next to the Inspector.

Alex smiled.

Leaving Wainscott looking appropriately sullen next to Jack, Alex went up to visit her friend.

Sixteen

"Don't get up. Don't turn your head." Alex settled next to Sergeant Pepper, eyes trained on the yellow-jacketed policeman at the bottom of the section looking up at their area. "Your partner believes my partner has strapped a bomb to the bottom of her seat."

The Sergeant jerked his head across the pitch at Jack sitting next to Inspector Wainscott.

"Seven pounds of it. What do you think—Section Five would probably disappear, yes?" A bomb threat was a dirty trick, but they had a scarcity of options here. "I'm going to reach into my pocket now. Don't panic."

"Righto, love."

Alex took a laminated, blue-bordered ID card from her wallet. Reserved for diplomatic officers, the card granted full criminal immunity. The revered Get Out of *any* Jail *anytime* Free card. It meant she either worked for the State Department or that other little agency in DC.

She let it sink in for a moment. "Do you understand?"

"You're CIA."

She settled back into her seat now that that was out of the way. It didn't matter if he was the top of his division, a Company agent outranked him in political and military cover. "Tell me your role in the investigation of the Isle of Man murders."

Incredulous, he looked at her. "I'm the JTAC Lead Intelligence Officer on the case. I answer to the Director General himself." *Joint Terrorism Analysis Center.* Alex had been right; he was MI5 and the head of the investigation. Wainscott was basically in charge of arrests and detainment, nothing more.

This was good.

"You have your warrant card?" Like a badge, it would show his name and division, as well as his warrant number. MI5 personnel were required to have it on them in street clothes.

Grunting, he reached into his breast pocket and pulled out a leather billfold. After flipping it open, he showed Alex the ID with his photo, overlaid with a gold and blue holograph. Sergeant Pepper's real name was Rogan Burke, not that she cared. She just wanted to see where he put the card.

He flipped it closed after Alex nodded, slipped it back into his chest pocket, and closed his coat.

"Okay, Agent Burke. Open your mobile phone, call your assistant, and tell her to e-mail the digital files you've compiled on the Isle of Mann case to an address I give you." Before he refused, she added, "You'll do this to save your own ass, and avoid public humiliation not just for your unit, but all of British intelligence."

"Rubbish," he scoffed.

"Or else WebLeaks will print a fascinating story about the Café Martin bombing."

Tightening his lips, Burke shrugged, as if to say, *What story?* He'd also kept his shades on, which made Alex want to put her fist through the black lenses and split open his unibrow. Instead, she hit him with, "You know that story, right? The one about British military explosives being stuffed into a piano and killing over fifty civilians, two foreign diplomats, and a decorated Royal Air Force intelligence agent."

He laughed. "Preposterous. How would you even—"

"I was there."

His face drained of color.

"Despite what you have released to the papers, you and I both know it wasn't C-4."

Only blackness through the depths of his sunglasses, but Alex sensed the poor man's pucker factor had skyrocket to about frog's-anus level.

"All C-4 is primarily composed of cyclotrimethylene trinitramine, also known as RDX, grade B; and pentaerythritol dioleate, or PEDO." Alex was pleased she'd paid attention during explosives month in training. That shit was confusing as hell, and you had to know it inside and out if you were to ever use or defuse it. She had been on the defusing side twice in her career thus far and was compelled to keep brushing up on the latest as well as the basics.

"But you probably already know all that." She doubted he did, but flattered him anyway. What was the saying? It's easier to win over someone with sugar than vinegar? Maybe Alex was only dissolving a pinch of sugar in the vinegar, but what the hell. "Here's where it gets interesting. Most developed countries use C-4 or some variation thereof for military purposes. Developers and private enterprises use Semtex, somewhat of a variation of C-4. Either way, both compounds have high amounts of plasticizer for malleability. This makes them smell like...?"

"Plastic," Burke said, looking dumbfounded. Alex took that to mean he'd guessed where she was going with this.

"Right. But an early type of explosive used by the military was composed of something entirely different. The Brits tried to assassinate Hitler with it, in fact."

Burke's pucker tightened a couple more notches, to about gnat's-ass level now. "Nobel 808."

Alex nodded. "Made of primarily nitroglycerine and nitrocellulose, it's cheap and easy to manufacture. Perfect for hard times. Eight-oh-eight, as you know, also has a distinctive scent, doesn't it?"

He stared at her, unmoving.

Alex continued, "So, when I was standing there at the party, leaning on the edge of the piano, I thought I smelled almonds. Not roasted, not bitter, just strong. Almost overwhelming. But there wasn't an almond in sight. Not a bowl, not a plate, nothing. The chef confirmed, not a single hors d'oeuvre or dish served that night contained almonds. Yet the piano reeked of it."

He smiled. "808 has been out of production for half a century, love."

"Officially." Patting his leg, *love*, Alex leaned closer. "But you and I know different, don't we? The British military manufactured over three tons of the explosive for the war in Iraq. Easy, quick, cheap. Perfect for a bottom of the barrel war."

"Doesn't mean British military was involved."

"Stolen, then. What's worse, involvement or incompetence?" Smiling, she sat back just as Arsenal scored a third goal The crowd erupted, singing "God Save the Queen" while waving scarves and spreading them wide, showering the stadium in white and red stripes. "You have five minutes to send the files."

"We don't keep them on digital," he tried. "They're recorded on paper first, then scanned later."

"Bullshit. Now you have four."

He stared Alex down and finally said, "Bollocks."

He stood and reached for his phone. Alex listened from her seat. When he asked for an e-mail address, she gave him a Hushmail reserved for a digital drop she'd never used. She could tap into it anywhere fast, and it was secure from message recalls or tampering. Even MI5 would need a warrant for access, and that would take days at least.

"It'll be there in three. A zip file. It's rather large."

"I expect so."

They waited about two minutes as she watched Jack. Using his cell, he checked the account. No signal from him meant nothing yet.

Three minutes.

Jack checked again. Still nothing.

Alex looked at Burke. His ridiculous hippie shades. "You are cutting it awfully close."

"It's on its way, I assure you."

Narrowing her eyes, Alex glanced to the bottom of their seating section. Two policemen had suddenly appeared, one whispering to the other, both looking up their way. When a third policeman joined them, she looked back at Jack to find he'd stood and shrugged off his jacket, showing his Arsenal colors.

He had received the file.

A fourth policeman sidestepped the front of the stands, and began making his way over to the gathering artillery.

Alex looked back at Burke, who wore an *I just ate a shit-stuffed crumpet* grin.

Turning, she saw more officers hurrying down the stairs toward them, hands on their batons. Then another one on the other side. All headed her way.

Alex pulled the Arsenal flag from her coat and fished around her pocket for the lighter.

"What are you—"

Before he could finish, she lit the flag, thrust it into his hands, and yelled in a throaty cry, "Die Arsenal!" as she let her coat drop.

Burke held the flaming flag high and away from his body, a natural reaction, as Alex ducked and bumped him under the immediate swell of fans around them. Dressed in Arsenal red now, she pushed past Burke, up through the chaos, and into the far aisle as she sneaked a look back at the riot erupting below her.

Police charged the stairs on both sides, batons out and swinging, pushing through the gathering fans in the aisles.

On the other side of the stadium from the melee, Wainscott was hurrying up the stairs. Jack was gone. Burke was buried by the masses.

An Arsenal fan powered through the crowd and pushed past Alex with a knife, his eyes like lasers on Burke. "Die, Arsenal? Die, Liverpool! Die, *you*!"

She turned and twisted his arm until she heard a pop and he dropped the knife. Then she pushed him in the path two officers bounding down the stairs toward the melee.

The entire section Alex had been sitting in turned into a full-fledged riot before she reached the tunnel, consuming every effort of the police to contain the crowd. She felt a momentary regret, but then noted two policemen had already reached the center of the action and were pulling rabid fans backward. Burke would be fine.

Whistling "Helter Skelter," Alex exited the tunnel, headed straight down the stairs, two at a time, and out through stadium's turnstiles. By the time she reached the mouth of the Tube a block and a half away, Jack was already there. He looked winded.

"I got something for you." Alex slipped the leather billfold from her pocket, flipped it open, and showed him Burke's MI5 warrant card. "Now you have some cover."

"Yeah?" Jack slipped a hand in his jacket and came out with another card, this one labeled *Metropolitan Police* and sheathed in a clear plastic and nylon case. Wainscott's ID.

"How did you…?"

"You should know." He winked at Alex. "You're not the only one with skilled hands."

Seventeen

Randeep paced in front of the screens, watching the trade signals, ticking off each purchase of Swiss francs as JONAH automatically sent the orders to the futures exchange and they were completed.

Bending to the keyboard, Randeep typed the shortcuts to bring up the Prince Alexander Capital accounts. He had spent over two billion dollars that morning, and it was having no effect on the price of the franc. The trades were not only *not* making a dent, they were effectively being swallowed by the markets.

It was as if JONAH wasn't in the markets at all.

Randeep had underestimated the Swiss National Bank's resolve. It was selling as many francs as Randeep was buying, and more. Perhaps it was willing to make unlimited trades to keep the currency below the 1.20 level.

Randeep slammed a hand on the keyboard. "Impossible!"

Running his hands through his hair, he stepped away from the computers. He needed a minute to breathe. He needed a moment to think. He walked to the glass wall at the front door and picked up his blue canvas backpack. Found the Nestlé chocolate bars.

Swiss chocolate. Fitting.

He stripped off a wrapper and ate half the bar in two chomps.

Pacing around the half-circle control station, Randeep formulated a strategy. As the steps solidified in his mind, he let the trades play out in his imagination, visualizing his success, reveling in his genius. Not like Newton or da Vinci. More like Sachin Tendulkar seeing the cricket pitch and the players and all their positions on the field, visualizing the bat slapping the ball into the open space. Seeing the score hit the board.

And just like that, within one minute, Randeep had organized the list, cross-weighing the rankings of the most influential with the wealthiest with the most trustworthy of his colleagues. He saw them make their trades. He saw the franc spike in value, breaking through the Swiss National Bank's resistance level, forcing it into submission.

He paused for a moment.

Draganic would be infuriated if he discovered the plan. He'd made it clear that the trades needed to be *discreet*, that *Prince Alexander needed to stay hidden this time around*. But what Draganic didn't understand was that there was an ocean of money sloshing back and forth throughout the markets these days. Heaves of movement no longer created opportunity at the fringes. No, this day and age had brought sloppiness and danger with the movements. Instead of traders picking off inefficiencies caused by the money ocean, they were being swallowed by it.

But not Randeep. He would ensure that never happened. And this plan, as angry as it may make Draganic, was necessary. Randeep had to enlist financial heavyweights to help take on the Swiss National Bank.

First on the list would be Paul Gott, Connecticut's original hedge fund manager. Worth seventeen billion, he could pile onto this trade without mercy. Then Randeep would call Xin Cheng in Hong Kong, the animal FX trader for Shanghai Trust. The man had control of almost a trillion dollars in assets, if you included fixed income. Then Randeep's double contact in Chicago, the Craig twins, owed him for his last tip to them, the mortgage trade that netted their derivatives fund almost four hundred million in profits. In a single day. Finally, he'd call Ivan. Awash in over thirty billion dollars of Russian oil assets, the man was struggling to put his money to work. This trade would solve that and make him a killing at the same time. Ivan would owe Randeep after this tip.

All in, these five could source over one hundred billion dollars.

Before leverage.

Randeep settled back into his seat and slipped on the headset. He swallowed the last of the Nestlé bar. Then he started dialing.

Bern, Switzerland
The Federal Palace

The seven members of the Swiss Federal Council entered the private meeting room in a single file. Paneled in dark walnut, with seven matching walnut desks and a maple floor, the room exuded the opulence one would expect for the presiding entity over Swiss government and affairs. The overhead lamps humming overhead was loudest noise in the room as the six heads of each federal department—nicknamed ministers—waited for Karl von Zeller to read the agenda.

As president of the Federal Council, von Zeller was in charge of the weekly meetings but not the governing. There was no single president or prime minister in Switzerland. Members were elected to four-year terms by the Swiss Federal Assembly, and the council itself was the governing body.

The minister of finance, Stefan Lory, anticipated a grilling of his recommended policies. The other five ministers sat silent, like a pack of lionesses waiting for the signal to feed.

Von Zeller picked up the agenda from his desk, crumpled the single sheet of paper into a ball, and tossed it into the wastebasket below. A significant physical statement in this non-confrontational state.

All six ministers stared as it bounced within the metal can.

Von Zeller raised his brows as he looked around. All three native languages of Switzerland were represented in the room—German, French, and Italian—so it was up to von Zeller to decide which one to use. To facilitate easy communication, he chose English, as usual. "We shall discuss the franc situation, yes?"

Shifting in his seat, Lory said, "The intervention is still working."

"Selling our own currency? Nonsense!" von Zeller snapped back. "People are buying francs in droves. Tell me, what is the average amount of currency we have sold monthly since you convinced the council to take this course of action?"

Lory glanced at the notes on his desk, though he knew the answer down to the decimal. "Sixteen-point-nine billion francs per month. On average."

Shaking his head, von Zeller asked, "And this month?"

After a long pause, Lory said, "Thirty-five billion."

"Quite a spike, yes? One that significantly raises our exposure to the spendthrifts around us." Von Zeller turned to Greta, the minister of foreign affairs. "What is the likelihood that Italy defaults?"

Greta leaned back in her chair. "After Greece, it is a matter of when."

"And *when* Italy defaults?" Von Zeller removed his glasses and pinched the bridge of his nose.

Greta said, "Spain goes, too. Maybe France."

"Regardless," Klaus, the minister of home affairs, said, "exports comprise fifty percent of our gross national product. We need to have a cheap currency for people to buy our goods. I am still with Minister Lory on this."

"We have little choice," Fuhr, the minister of economics, added. "We must keep our currency attainable, whether the euro crumbles or not. Minister Klaus is correct."

"And if there is no euro anymore?" Von Zeller tightened his brows.

"Then Americans will buy our products. They account for almost forty percent of all pharmaceutical sales alone, and all Americans like Swiss watches," Klaus answered. "Those two goods represent over half of our exports."

Turning back to Lory, von Zeller pursed his lips. "By selling our franc, precisely how many euros do we own now?"

Lory said, "Three-hundred and seventy-nine billion euros, sir."

"Do we have any idea who is trading against us? Is it the US government? China? Who is so eager to make our franc so expensive?"

The room fell silent. One by one, they turned to face the minister of justice and police. Von Zeller followed their gazes and settled on her, too.

Eyes darting around, the minister raised her chin and said, "We have received reports that the Serbian Whale has entered the markets again."

Von Zeller sat forward. "Draganic?"

"How is that possible? He is banned," Klaus said.

Lory tapped his desk with a pen. "The ban is only as strong as the securities and exchange commission of any country."

"Where is he?" von Zeller asked.

The minister of police said, "We have heard he is in the Isle of Man. With purchases also coming from the Caribbean somewhere. Bahamas, maybe the Cayman Islands."

"We can prevail over him," Klaus said, looking at Lory.

"I am not so sure," Greta said. "He is most likely using leverage, and could have a hundred billion at his disposal, maybe more. Remember what Soros did to pound sterling? We could suffer losses of a quarter of a trillion euros. Not to mention worldwide humiliation."

"I agree," said the minister of defense with a stern nod.

Sitting as tall as the high, leather-backed seat would allow, von Zeller swept his gaze across the room. He had their support; he could sense it. This would be over in a matter of minutes. "Then we put it back to a vote. A show of hands of those who would like to continue this nonsense of intervention. Shall we risk bankrupting our national bank? Destroy Switzerland's unrivaled reputation in banking forever?"

Put that way and only two types of people would raise a hand—an idiot or a fool.

One by one, Lory, Klaus, and Fuhr raised their hands. Three of seven.

But the others looked away.

The intervention would be abandoned, and Draganic would win. But so be it. This insanity would end.

Lory began to drop his hand, but then Janowitz, the minister of transportation and communications, the man who had yet to utter a single word in the meeting, cleared his throat. All six ministers turned to him.

"I would rather go down fighting," he said, raising his hand and giving the fourth and deciding vote.

It turned out there could be a third type of supporter—the madman.

Flopping back into his seat, von Zeller said, "Then we keep pace with the Whale. God help us all."

Eighteen

"Nothing here." Alex took a sip of coffee hot enough to use as a weapon, then placed it by the keyboard.

"Nothing new, or at all?" Jack stood behind her as she scanned Agent Burke's files in the basement floor of an Internet coffee shop called the Sacred Café. A Buddha statue wore a Santa cap across from her.

They were on Ganton Street back near Hyde Park, Alex and Jack were one of two pairs of patrons in the basement; the other was huddled together on a leather double lounger and sharing a bowl-sized cup of tea. They looked cozy. They looked happy. Like Christmas was coming and they were worry free.

Alex wondered what that felt like.

"New," she said. "MI5 is looking into it as a double murder, not a murder-suicide, no surprise. But the missing hand is confirmed."

"Do you reckon it was Edgar who killed them?"

"No." A knee-jerk answer, and one Alex truly believed, though she couldn't say why.

Scrolling down the fifty-page document, she paused on the listed biographies of the deceased. The governor of the Isle of Man appeared to have had a solid marriage, though that could be faked. Yet there was no evidence of any impropriety going back the last five years.

No evidence that the second man, Sid Oban, was anything more than a playboy, either. In fact, though he was a banker at IMB Securities in Douglas, Isle of Man's capital, he was reportedly keeping multiple girlfriends in separate cities.

For a politician and a banker, these guys were squeaky clean. The half-naked photo of them together was a plant, some sort of a cover-up staged by the murderer and most likely digitally fabricated. If this work had been done by an intelligence agent or agency, it would've included background evidence, plants of impropriety to cement the tale before it could be picked apart.

Perhaps the plant was a last minute decision, a plan that hadn't been fully contemplated or prepped?

Alex turned to Jack. "How much do you know about the inner workings of the UK police and MI5?"

He gave her a sidelong look. "As much as the average bloke, why?"

"For one," Alex said, glancing at the other couple and leaning closer to Jack, "why is Five overseeing this investigation? As I understand it, the Isle of Man maintains its own police and investigative forces."

"Perhaps they believed royal investigators were in order, on account of the involvement of a governor and all."

"But Burke is head of the terrorist unit at Five. This does not appear to be an act of terrorism."

"You have a point." He pulled a seat over and sat next to her. Then he picked up her coffee, and Alex eyed him as he took a defiant sip.

She turned back to the montage of crime scene photos, zeroing in on the banker's arm with no hand. She thought of being unable to draw, unable to create. Her own hands began to tingle.

"Have they surmised a connection to the café bombing?" Jack asked. "That would no doubt be overseen by the terrorism unit."

"Nothing in here on the café." Alex scrolled down the screen again until she reached a list of Oban's clients. She scanned each name, searching for any that stood out. She didn't recognize anyone from her work with the Company, nor, racking her brain, any she could connect to her father or Moss.

Leaning back, Alex placed her hands behind her head and closed her eyes. The pain from the shoulder wound throbbed, but not as much as her head.

"Maybe you're chasing the wrong rabbits." Jack leaned in front of Alex and took her hand off the mouse. "Let me have a go."

She kept her eyes closed and heard him scrolling the wheel up and down, but kept her eyes closed. After about a minute, he said, "Here's something of interest."

Alex blinked her eyes open. Jack had his finger pressed to a name.

"Zoran Draganic," she said. "Sounds vaguely familiar. Who is he?"

"Serbian money launderer who teamed with his brother during the war in Bosnia."

"And you know this, how?"

"Article in *The Economist* a few months back."

"You read that magazine?"

"I like the political cartoons." He mocked her incredulity with a fake scowl. "Anyway, Draganic's also known as the Serbian Whale. You may have heard of him."

"First time," Alex muttered, picturing the suitcase of money Aaron had. "So … this is about hiding money?"

"Serious business," Jack pointed out, raiding her coffee again.

"Would you like your own?" Alex said pointedly.

Jack grinned. "I'm quite happy to share yours."

Alex took the coffee back before it was shared away to nothing. Tilting the cup toward Jack, she said, "Let's say Draganic uses the Isle of Man banker to launder cash from some illicit business or businesses. He then has the banker killed to keep him quiet, but why the governor?"

"Perhaps he was also cut in on the deal."

"Still doesn't connect him directly to the bombing." She leaned back again and glanced at Jack. "What else do you know about this Draganic guy?"

He grimaced. "The Economist article tied him to human trafficking. Apparently he liked to take payment in the form of girls under the age of sixteen."

"Fucker." No question where the two brothers would find their human goods for trade. It was well documented that Serbian war criminals used women and children as collateral damage in their terrorizing tactics of Bosnian villages in Yugoslavia. "And exactly how is Draganic out and about now?"

"You can thank the Hague for that. The ICC dismissed all charges against him after his brother, a Serbian warlord in Bosnia, died in their custody under suspicious circumstances." ICC stood for International Criminal Court, the justice system for war crimes.

"Suspicious?"

"With a wire around his neck."

"Lucky bastard." Hanging by a wire was getting off easy for that guy. "And now Draganic is, what, free and clear?"

"He's apparently banned from trading securities, but still…the man's not exactly penniless. Word has it, he shares his time between a mansion outside Gstaad and another in Dubrovnik."

Alex felt her pulse quicken and her neck become hot. Why the hell did these men always get away with treating women like possessions? Forget objectification, they were one goddamned step above slavery in most countries. In some, a significant step below.

Jack sensed Alex's building fury. He placed a hand on her arm and said, "Hold on now, one battle at a time, yes?"

She took a deep breath, then another. She exhaled loudly, then turned back to the screen and redirected. She punched in a search for information about the shooting in Piccadilly yesterday with the twin motorcyclists. A dozen stories appeared, all with the same strange core storyline: a taxi robbery gone bad. A career spy, Alex understood the importance of controlling sensitive information. It wasn't necessarily conspiracy, but the public didn't need to know every damned thing, especially if it would compromise a mission.

Yet cover-ups were difficult, expensive, and required a directive from very high up to tighten the dissemination of information.

This one was *above the atmosphere, U2 bomber* airtight.

Jack reached for her coffee again, and she grabbed his wrist without looking up. "One more sip and you'll be the next one missing a hand."

Jack, a smart man, placed his palms up and stood. "You could have just said as much."

Alex smiled as he walked away, but continued studying the same wide-angle, long-range photo of the crime scene, and same square photo of the murdered taxi driver appeared in each paper. Furthermore, neither of the felled motorcyclists were identified—not as being American, or being Navy SEALs. And, of course, no mention of the passenger—Alex—at all.

Not one eyewitness, even though she'd noticed at least three before passing out.

So who'd hushed the story, the US, the UK, or both?

After returning to Alex's side, Jack stood silent, drinking his coffee as she explained what she'd found—or not found. He frowned. "I don't suppose there's a possibility of cross-referencing Oban's list of clients with the names of Navy SEALs."

"Nope." Alex cleared the cache and shut down the computer. "Let's walk. Sometimes it helps shake something loose."

As they left the Sacred Café and walked down the block together, Alex wondered if she should just forget about the bombing and refocus on finding her father. Because *that* would be easy, she thought, shoving her hands deep into her pockets. Edgar had been gone for almost two decades, far away from DC, and likely in Europe, as this is where he'd popped up.

He'd have various aliases, underground financial arrangements, and likely remained socially isolated to keep all of this safe. He'd want to be near an airport, too, for easy access and travel. A major metro would allow him to blend. But what else?

No physical ailment or scar to compromise that, plain features. Exceptional intelligence. "The perfect deep spy," she muttered to herself, thinking back to that last day with him and staring at the storefront ahead.

Fishing is not something I do. It's something I am.

Jack turned, noting she had stopped. He raised a brow when he noted she was smiling as well. "Alex?"

"I have an idea."

"How on earth is a fly-fishing shop to help us?"

"Humor me," Alex said, nodding for him to follow. The shop was called Fielders. It had a tobacco-stained wooden façade, cast-iron lettering, and store hours listed on the glass door. Dark inside, the shop was empty of customers. The air was hot but damp, and smelled like a mix of Earl Grey tea and gear oil. A small space, the entire store consisted of two aisles, one holding rods and the other displaying flies, lines, and other smaller items. An ancient, steel cash register the size of a outboard motor and littered with yellow sticky notes sat on a glass case full of antique and new fly reels.

"Hello?" Alex called out.

A petite, elderly woman emerged from the rear of the shop, holding nail-clipper-sized hackle pliers, used for tying flies. She walked with her head tilted to one side, her body the other. "Good evening. May I help you?"

"I was wondering if you could give me some advice, help me find a fishing spot."

She eyed Alex. "What sort of spot?"

Alex glanced back at Jack, who raised his eyebrows at her as she said, "I've been there before, but it was a long time ago."

"Very well." Frowning, she walked to the counter and placed the tool on the glass. "What can you tell me about it?"

Alex thought about the day they'd spent there, the atmosphere, the feelings, as she searched for any details that would distinguish the place. She remembered they had stayed in a hotel in the city, and had wandered a bit then stopped for lunch on their way to the stream.

This is why trout get caught, Alex. They have patterns.

"I believe it was an hour's drive from the city on a weekday, but that was a number of years ago. Anyway, the small stream ran clear as gin, with white rocks at the bottom and tall grass on the banks."

"Obviously a chalk stream," she said, "so west of London, maybe Berkshire or Dorset, but I'll need a bit more than that."

"Why don't you show the picture, love?" Jack called from the front.

"You have a photo, then?"

"Of sorts." Alex took out her sketchbook and flipped through the first pages until she came to it. The setting she had drawn over a hundred times from every thinkable angle. This was her favorite, though, the clear stream with milky bottom winding between fields of tall grass and off into the distance. It was a peaceful, good memory. Until this week.

Turning the book for the shop owner to see, Alex watched her eyes.

Jack walked closer and peered over Alex's shoulder at the drawing.

"Well, this could be anywhere in the country," the woman said, bending to study the drawing. "Was there anything else about? Special houses, or maybe bridges?"

"There was a mill, red brick, just behind a bridge. Here." Alex pointed to the front part of the drawing.

Waving a hand, the woman said, "I'll need more than that. Must be dozens of mills along the chalk streams. And bridges—could be hundreds."

"Perhaps you should draw her another view," Jack said.

"This is a drawing?" The woman snatched the book. "I thought it was a photograph."

Flipping the pages, she said, "My God, it's fantastic. You drew all of these?"

"I did."

Jack winked at Alex as the woman continued, "Well, I wouldn't have taken you for an artist. You look nothing like one."

"No?"

"You're much too healthy and have beautiful skin." The woman continued leafing through the book. Obviously not the starving type."

"Thanks, I think."

Jack pointed at the sketches. "Do you have some paper? A large sheet, maybe?"

"In fact, I do. I'd love to see you have a go at it," the woman said enthusiastically. She held out a hand. "I'm Rebecca, by the by." She pointed a crooked finger at the front door. "Fielder, that is."

"Great little shop," Alex said, reaching to shake her hand but stopping, noticing a tiny fly, a nymph, hooked into Rebecca's thumb. She pointed at it. "Did you realize…?"

Rebecca gave a throaty laugh. "Happens all the time. Not as nimble as I once was. Come on."

Rebecca showed them to the back room, where she cleared off the fly-tying station and laid down a large piece of paper. "It's only packing paper, but the sheets are quite large."

"It's perfect," Alex said, choosing some pencils from her satchel and then settling onto the stool across from a wall of edge-to-edge Polaroids of fishermen proudly posing with catch. She closed her eyes and began to block out the sights and sounds around her, replacing them with the stimuli of that day—the last time she went fishing with her father. The process was easier than it otherwise may have been since she'd already created the drawing so many times, even with Rebecca the complete stranger standing behind as Alex worked her pencil across the page.

The first lines, the most daring and sweeping, flowed from her like simple sentences, long and curving and fluid, just like the chalk stream they would soon represent. Alex remembered the emotion of her father's words, his hand on her shoulder, the sparkle of the water's surface, and the glitter of the trout below. The blue-gray sky stretched to the horizon behind the fields, and the small stone bridge joining the two sides. The scent of the tall grass mixed with wildflowers and the rust, the aging metal of the waterwheel at the side of the mill.

She couldn't smell rust that day, but the image—the imprint burned into her mind—gave Alex the lasting memory of the feeling of the wheel, the shape of the curve in the bank, the smell of the tall grass along it, and the water. The clear, cold water of the chalk stream.

The mill, with a steep-pitched roof and walls of aged red brick, stretched along the stream's edge. Almost out of place in such a calm and peaceful setting, the building emerged from the grass as a solid structure, one that could not be negotiated, one that would always remain at the stream's edge. Yet the bridge, made of brick and cement, had forfeited the fight to span the water in one solid piece, and had crumbled in spots where it met the stream, leaving hiding places—small nooks for grass animals, and larger underwater caves for trout.

The clouds stretched above in gray smoke, hiding a good portion of the sun and keeping the water cool from the midday burn. The shadows on all the structures, all the shapes, all the images remained soft and true to the muted light.

"My goodness." Rebecca stirred Alex from her drawing trance. "You are quite a talent."

Studying the work, Alex decided she was almost finished. Just a few more details. Not photographic quality, but close enough for today.

Jack stood above and behind her still, and Alex could feel him studying the image, studying her perhaps.

Rebecca walked behind and leaned into the page. She stared hard at the drawing. Then she turned her head and stared into Alex's eyes. "Truly amazing."

"Thank you."

"Are you a prodigy?"

Jack said, "I assure you, she's not."

Alex elbowed him in the gut.

Rebecca snapped her fingers, sending the fly stuck in her thumb high into the air and then onto the floor. "Blimey, that's the Century Mill off the River Kennet in Marlborough. A historic landmark."

"This drawing looks more of a stream," Jack said.

Rebecca said, "The Kennet's considered a river, but it's hardly rushing. Wide, yes, but more of a trickler, really."

Alex said, "Do you know where it is?"

"Of course, but it's off the path, love. A good bit west of here." She gestured for the pencil, and then began jotting down the directions. Alex rose and stretched, and wandered to the wall of Polaroids while she waited. There must have been over a hundred of them, but she scanned each one quickly, for the hell of it. After a few minutes, she'd been through all of them with no luck.

Of course he wouldn't allow his photograph to be hanging in a store. Or anywhere else for that matter.

She said, "Rebecca, is this the most popular shop for fly fishermen in the city?"

Rebecca smiled, "Not to bluster about, but it's known as the enthusiasts shop. People come from all over the UK to visit. Men and women alike."

"Do they?" Alex pulled the sketchbook out and flipped it open to the drawing she'd made of Edgar's three-quarter profile the night of the bombing. Pointing to the sketch, she said, "Tell me. Has this man even been in?"

"Of course! That's old ... well, I don't know his name, but he's been in the shop numerous times. Though it has been a while."

"Really?" To hide her nerves, Alex bent down to pick up the nymph that had fallen from Rebecca's thumb, and said, "Has he been in recently, by chance?"

"I'm afraid not." Rebecca nodded a *thanks* to Alex as she handed it to her.

"But I remember him because he always paid cash. I admire that in a person."

No chance of snagging an alias from the credit card records, then. "Did he say where he lived, or maybe where he liked to fish?"

"Not that I recall, no. But I reckon he was looking for fly patterns that would work west of here. Why?"

West. Like the River Kennet.

"Because in that case..." Alex turned back to Jack, who was already nodding to her as she said, "We're going to need Hanna's car again."

Nineteen

"This man," Natasha Draganic said, her hand shaking cigarette ash onto the floor while she circled the living room of the two-bedroom villa. Dragging on the last of the butt, she flicked it out the door toward the powdered white sand and endless blue ocean.

She turned and picked up the case of Sobranie Cocktail cigarettes. They came in five different colors and with a gold band on each of them, but none fit her mood. She chose red—it was the closest she could get—lit up, and took a long suck.

Better.

At least there was Swastikman, she thought, as its club hit "Basstards" vibrated from the bedroom sound system.

The violent electronica matched her state perfectly.

"This man."

She picked up her phone and stared at the image one more time. Zoran, his head tilted in a way that showed that hideous scar, and the child-stewardess naked in his lap. Her face was contorted in a twisted show of pleasure with her arm outstretched.

A god-damned *selfie*.

Natasha flung the phone across the room, where it got tangled in the mosquito netting of the poster bed and slid to the floor. She picked up the sweating Mai Tai from the sideboard and downed the last of it.

What a *basstard*.

She wondered how the man who had forwarded it to Natasha had tricked the stewardess into giving him the image. And why he had sent it on to Natasha. He claimed to be a partner of Zoran's, someone who could help her get what she wanted, if she would help him.

Perhaps he just wanted to fuck Natasha. Didn't they all?

So maybe she would do that to get back at Zoran. Plus, she appreciated the gesture and needed to pay the man back accordingly. After all, with this photograph, Natasha could get quite a nice settlement from a divorce court in Switzerland.

It would make him pay for the grievance.

Taking a drag from the Sobranie, Natasha picked up the phone. She rang for her appointed butler. It took almost seven minutes for the lazy island man to find his way to the villa. And he was sweating when he arrived.

She opened the door a little wider than a crack, and appraised him fully. Tall, dark and shiny skin, healthy, an attractive smile. Perhaps a little young, but she wouldn't ask about that.

Studying his jacket, she said, "Where is it you are coming from…Ano?"

"From?" His eyes widened.

"Your country."

"Oh." He smiled with a bright white grin. "Mo'orea, Ms. Draganic."

"I am Natasha, please."

He nodded. "Yes, ma'am."

"Where is this Mo'orea?" She looked him over again, this time tilting her head when she got to his groin.

Shifting his feet, he said, "It is near Bora Bora."

"Mmm…" She licked her lips, feeling the first of the Mai Tai's effects. "Perhaps I should…see this soon, yes?" She blinked up at him.

If his skin could show it, Natasha would have guessed he'd blushed.

"Mrs…Natasha…I should tell you that there is no smoking in these villas. There will be a charge for this."

"I don't care." She waved a hand, then extinguished the butt in an empty glass.

"Are you ready for these?" He held up the tray with two more Mai Tais.

"Of course. Please, I am being rude. Come." She opened the door wide, and let her robe fall open just enough as he passed her for him to get a good look between her breasts. After spending the day at the pool yesterday, she'd decided her breasts were the finest set on the whole resort. Even better than those belonging to the American actress staying in the neighboring villa.

Turning to watch him pass, Natasha bent her head a bit to check out his ass in those white trousers. Yes. Unlike the troll she was married to, this man stayed in shape. Very good shape. She could imagine bending over for this man.

She shut the door.

Smiling back at her, Ano placed the drinks on the table and glanced at the bedroom as he handed her the folder with the tab. Perhaps the music was not to his taste.

"Why is it you are rushing? Sit for a moment, please, I beg of you…" She checked the name tag again. "Ano?"

"I really must—"

"You are seeing me for two days now. I am no stranger. Do you not like me?"

"You're very nice, Mrs. Natasha. Yes."

"And I ordered two drinks. This is for reason." She walked a few steps and stood before him. "Plus, you are my butler, and I insist you are staying with me for a while. Just a little while, yes?"

Sensing his urgency to flee, Natasha knew she had to pin him with an offer he couldn't refuse. In other words, give him a taste of what would come, so to speak, if he did stay with her. She turned to pick up her drink, and let her wrist and hand brush against the front of his trousers.

To her pleasure, she found his interest in her had begun to solidify.

He glanced at the door.

She picked up the drink and held it high to him.

He tilted his head. "Mrs. Natasha."

"Please. No more of this Mrs. On this island, I am not married, *da?*"

Natasha's phone buzzed on the table, making the second drink vibrate, its sweat pooling to the bottom of the glass.

She read the caller ID. It was him, Zoran's partner.

Ano, thinking he was saved by the bell, made a move to leave.

But Natasha caught his wrist and said, "Please, one moment. I must answer this." She pulled him to the chair in the corner of the villa and urged him into the seat.

"Natasha," she answered.

Ano looked uncomfortable.

The partner said, "Are you ready to make a deal?"

"More than ready," she said, easing down to her knees before Ano. "What is it you are needing?" She licked her lips and stared at the beautiful black man before her as she said it. He looked away as she placed one hand on his belt buckle. She took that as a yes.

The partner said, "I'll need the use of Zoran's jet."

"This will not be a problem," she said, Ano arching as she freed him from restriction. "When will you be…riding it?"

"In two days, three at most. I will let you know."

Natasha's mouth watered when she saw the sheer size of Ano as he grew to her touch. He must have been twice as large as her husband. "Perfect," she said.

"You'll want to help me with one other minor thing."

"More? I'm not sure I can do any more than this." Her mind had become clouded for a moment and she fought to focus again. Ano had pushed deeper into the seat and his eyes were closed. Natasha stood and slid her panties down.

"I am sending you a new phone for Zoran. This will help record conversations he is having with these women. Do you understand?"

"I understand." She turned, widened her stance, and eased back until Ano's large hands were on her hips to guide her. "He will be in Gstaad tomorrow. There, I will do this thing."

"Good."

Natasha waited a moment, her eyes sleepy with anticipation of Ano. She said, almost slurring, "Maybe I can join you on the jet, yes?" then glanced back at Ano. "We could have some fun."

"I'll be in touch," the partner said.

"Yes," she answered, easing herself onto Ano, and dropping the phone to the floor.

You most certainly will.

Twenty

They bought Alex a new disposable phone to replace the phone she'd used with Wainscott. Alex bent that phone's SIM card in half, crushed the phone's body under a boot heel, and tossed it in three separate trash bins. Then they returned to Hanna's.

"I have a couple of calls to make before we leave," she told Jack.

Smart enough to know she was asking for space, Jack muttered an excuse about needing to call into work himself, and disappeared into the home office in the back of Hanna's flat.

After changing her shirt, Alex dialed the number to Legoland and asked for Denise, an MI6 counterpart who had worked multiple cases with her on this side of the pond and could be trusted. Maintaining a strong network of female relationships in this business had proven beneficial in her young career, and helped offset some of the *Boy's Club* attitude that was prevalent in certain divisions of the agencies.

No surprise that Denise sounded happy to hear from her.

Alex gave her the quick rundown of her blackout situation with the Company. "I'd appreciate your discreteness on this one."

"Seems to me I owe you for that little tip you'd given me in Copenhagen last year. What do you need?"

"A check on major cash purchases in the UK over the last ten years—houses, cars, land. The purchaser will be Caucasian, mid-fifties, and a UK resident. See if you can isolate or track the purchases back to the Marlborough area specifically."

"What are we looking at here, a launderer? A drug op?"

"It's more like a...rogue agent."

"Bloody hell, Alex, I'm sorry I asked. One of yours?"

"Yes."

"We'll keep it on the down low all around, then," she said. "Give me a bit and I'll ring you back. Until then, keep smart."

And toasty, Alex thought, as she hung up.

Twenty-One

When they'd arrived at the townhouse, Jack told Alex he needed to make a phone call to work, explain that he would be out for the rest of the week and back after Christmas.

With no reason to expect otherwise, she bought it.

Jack peeked back into the living area once more before closing the office door to be sure Alex was occupied. Or at least that's what he told himself.

Yet when he caught sight of her, he let his gaze linger, watching Alex's movements as she changed her shirt. Even without knowing he was watching, she moved with the fluid efficiency of a leopard. Pair that with the analytical intelligence and that insane drawing ability and you had the makings of a Renaissance woman. Perfectly imperfect.

Jack took a deep breath, eased the door closed, and bolted it.

"Pull it together, lad," he muttered to himself. If he didn't his employer might yank him back off the case. Jack retrieved the cell phone from his pocket, considered his options for a moment, and then exhaled as he dialed the number.

A man answered in the middle of the second ring. "Yes?"

"She's even better than we expected."

"I was afraid of that." The man clicked his tongue. "And now?"

"We're in the nest, but you should know—there was an incident yesterday."

"I heard. How bad?"

"Not that, Hanna fixed her all up. But then we had a run-in, evening last. The man escaped."

"Who?"

"No idea." He peeled back the rug to expose the floor safe. "I'll see if I can get her to draw a sketch."

"Yes, do that." He paused for a while and then said, "Can you stay at

Hanna's?"

Jack placed his fingertips to the biosensory lock guarding the weapons beneath. "Doubtful. She's quite determined."

"Fine." For a moment, Jack thought he heard a smile through the response. "Then let's see how far she gets."

And Edgar hung up.

Lockard sat in the tan Range Rover, parked in a street space around the corner from Hereford Square with a clear view of the front of the building between the trees. Edgar wouldn't likely just stroll up to the front gate, so Lockard had pointed a simple surveillance device at the underground garage in the back of the townhouse. The device broadcast images, twenty-two per second, to a similarly modified smartphone in his hand.

Having sat in the cold for almost five hours—couldn't have a car running in this weather, its exhaust too obvious, and had to keep the windows cracked open to prevent them from fogging up—Lockard had spied no activity in the house all day. Drinking a thick, green protein shake, he held the binoculars steady, then glanced at the screen. He drained the drink, looked again, and froze.

Two people, a man in a faded black jacket and a woman in a long overcoat, had stopped at the front gate. The man, as blond and handsome as an Aryan son, looked mildly familiar but Lockard couldn't place him without better seeing his face. The woman, however, was none other than Alex Winter, the woman he'd fought the other night.

So Alex had joined Edgar's little operation. Interesting, though not shocking. The Aryan man was likely Edgar's go-between, taking her in from the exposure of the last few days.

Smart operator, that Edgar.

But now Lockard had a dilemma. Should he enter the house, layout unknown, and try to take on the two, possibly three, of them? Or he could wait. His gut told him Edgar wasn't there yet, and if they were there for a meet, Lockard could take him before he ever entered the house. Because, though he'd like to see this Aryan man up close, Edgar was who Lockard really needed.

Fuck it. He'd waited long enough. The snow was increasing, decreasing the probability of Edgar traveling the streets by foot, anyway. Besides, he wanted a closer look at Alex Winter, the adult, too. One without her fists or feet in his face.

Lockard watched Winter and the man enter the house, but waited until the seven-minute mark to exit his vehicle and head in the opposite direction of the house. But after only six steps, he heard a rumble and saw a car, a Porsche SUV, exiting the easement. The man drove, Winter in the passenger seat. No Edgar.

Lockard slipped back into the Range Rover and watched them pull to the corner. As the Porsche rolled to a stop, its taillights glowing back at Lockard, he tapped the wheel, looked up at the building, and contemplated his options.

Take them both now. Follow them and take the daughter. Stay and wait for Edgar.

Curiosity.

It may have killed the cat, but it'd fed plenty a lion.

The Porsche turned and accelerated, and Lockard finally got a full shot of the Aryan man. His breath hitched with surprise, and he found his hands caressing the steering wheel. Though he hadn't seen him in a good two years, he knew exactly who he was.

Jack Pope.

And one of Lockard's questions was answered for him.

Twenty-Two

They had a saying in the CIA. A tired spy was a dangerous spy. After sleeping half a night in the front seat of a stolen car, and another half on a sofa that couldn't fit an Olsen twin, Alex was on edge. Add to that near-death by bombing, being shot at —twice—and sparring with a man on the twentieth floor of an open-construction building, all within two days, Alex felt about as composed as an injured bobcat.

So when Jack offered to drive, Alex took the opportunity to rest her eyes. She would let her mind wander to see if there were any clues to her father buried in deep in the subconscious. Or maybe just get some sleep.

As she laid her head back, her thoughts drifted to the memory of a day not long after her parents had supposedly died. Ginger, standing in the kitchen, leaned against the counter while cradling a cup of tea. Standing quietly as Alex did her homework at the table.

"It will get easier," Ginger said, startling Alex and making her realize that she in fact hadn't been working. She had been staring ahead. And then she felt it, the involuntary tear rolling down her cheek.

Alex wiped it away and nodded.

Ginger said, "Like a person who has lost a limb. They say there's sometimes an itch there, as if the limb were not gone at all." She tilted her head and walked over to Alex, placed a hand on her shoulder. "Eventually the mind realizes that the limb is gone. It doesn't forget it, but it closes off the nerves to it, numbs the sensation. I imagine that's what this will be like for you."

Alex bit her lip. She took in a breath and said, "I feel like he's still around."

"Like that, yes."

"No," Alex turned and said, "Not like that at all. Because I don't feel like Mom is here. Just him. Like he's watching over me. Why?" She slapped the table with an open palm. "He was never around when he was alive, so, what? He's making up for it now, when he's gone?"

"It's normal."

Her throat burned as she said, "I'd rather have Mom with me. I'd rather have her spirit here."

"Maybe they're both here." She smiled and looked around the kitchen.

"I don't feel like *they* are."

"It will pass, I promise." Ginger softened her brow and squeezed Alex's shoulder. "It will get easier. That feeling will eventually just...fade."

But it hadn't.

Ever since that day, Alex had felt it. There had been no concrete proof, not a single thread of evidence that he was still alive. There'd been nothing that gave her hope or even pause from that day forward. Nothing that unseated the belief that her parents had indeed been in that restaurant, had both been taken, had both died. Up until two days ago, there'd been nothing but silence from either of them.

And with the same burning anger in her throat, Alex closed her eyes and tried to forget.

By the time they pulled into Marlborough, the temperature had dropped a good ten to fifteen degrees, and the snow clouds hung above them like wet gauze. The head of the storm had finally moved inland, and was about to pound the countryside and then London.

Alex looked outside and took stock of the scene before them.

Few people were on the streets of the traditional English market town, and those who were out shuffled from one heated shop to the next, bundled in wool overcoats and hats. Straight ahead was what she figured to be the town hall, a Dutch-style, red brick and light stucco building with prominent steps behind it. The rest of the buildings were from the sixteenth century or so. Looming above and beyond all of them, a castle-like tower displayed a huge clock that read six thirty.

She checked the phone again to make sure she still had a signal. If Alex didn't hear back from Denise soon, they'd miss their chance to find Edgar today.

"No word yet?" Jack asked.

Shaking her head, Alex squeezed the cell phone. She felt like a super computer that had just analyzed a thousand points of data, eliminating scenario after scenario and settling on the one with the highest probability. The answer had burrowed into the core of her being the moment the fly-shop owner had confirmed Edgar had been in the UK.

Edgar would need a major city for convenient meetings, access to banks, access to materials or drops. The city would have to be international, a place with many nationalities represented, many languages spoken, and what was more international than London?

But if Alex knew anything at all about her father, a shred of his personal wants and needs, then she knew he would be near a chalk stream. But not just any chalk stream. If in Britain, if he was still working, he would live near the River Kennet.

Her phone rang, interrupting her thoughts. A central London number that Alex didn't recognize, but she answered it.

Denise said, "I didn't find exactly what you were looking for, but I did have some luck."

"Tell me."

"Well, there were no houses or cars bought by individuals in cash that would fit your make. A few footballers and a US stock picker, but none were Caucasian. At least none that led back to Marlborough, and not in the last ten years."

"Maybe we need to go further back, fifteen or even twenty-five years."

"That would require access to the archives and could take days," Denise said. "But we may not need to, anyway. I have a property that has been paying its municipal land levies in cash every year for the last nineteen."

Alex sat up a bit straighter. "The owner's name?"

"Not exactly. The property is listed as a reference number and the owner is a limited liability corporation."

An LLC. "A holding company?"

"Right, and the owner is another LLC listed only as a Cayman entity."

"Offshore, so the owner or owners are hidden."

"Yup, and the address is at Ugland House."

Just about every hedge fund in the world had an address in the Caymans, and the building that acted as the local address was Ugland House. It represented thousands of addressees.

"So either you found a rogue trader, or my rogue pretending to be a hedge fund trader."

"That's what I'm thinking. I have calls in, but they won't be back until tomorrow."

"I need it sooner," Alex said.

"Best I can do, Alex."

"What's the entity's name?"

"RiverRock Ventures."

Not an obvious connection to Edgar, but still, if he were hiding out here on these rivers, it sounded right. Staring up the street at Marlborough Town Hall, Alex realized she may have the answer right in front of her. "Denise, did you say you have a reference number on those tax transactions?"

"I did."

Alex drew Agent Wainscott's ID card from her pocket. "Give it to me."

Pulling the white cape tight around his body, Edgar Winter eased from one uneven shadow to the next, as he made his way down the snow-draped Bishops Avenue in the posh London district of East Finchley.

This particular street would have video surveillance devices triggered by movement, audio triggered by sound, and MI6 personnel on standby, reviewing footage, listening to conversations, ready to react to a threat in mere seconds. If caught by the eye in the sky, Edgar figured he would have less than a full minute before the British ghosts descended.

After all, Bishops Avenue housed the most important figure in MI6.

Edgar stopped twenty-two yards from the front entrance of the townhouse, studying the second floor through the windows. Not much to go on from here, but he'd seen schematics of the place and was confident he could make his way through the dark. Still, the four-story, white stone structure looked more like a federal bank than a house. Grant, old boy, lived like royalty. Noting seven cameras and four motion detectors on the structure, Edgar slipped past one street camera and between the next set of bushes and into a shadow cast by a pillar. He checked his watch.

He slowed his breathing and willed himself not to rub his hands together against the cold. Keeping the white exhale of each breath to a minimum by breathing through his nose, he stood as still as the pillar he leaned against, and waited.

The truck arrived two minutes later, a full minute early. Light gray and with the words Paulson's Spirits scripted on the sides, it paused at the entrance as the iron gates began to swing open.

Predictability, Grant. You've gotten soft, old boy.

After turning the cap inside out to a gray matching the shade on the truck, Edgar dashed to the far side of the entry, an angle out of view of the gate-top camera, and stepped up onto the bumper without a bounce as the driver drove forward. With one hand, Edgar swiveled the cape around, gray side out, and hid against the vehicle before passing the next camera.

The truck stopped ten seconds later.

Ears on full alert, Edgar waited as the driver exited the cab and crunched in the snow to the back. The moment he heard the words, "What the—" Edgar dove off the bumper and tackled the man in the snow.

Edgar had the easy advantage, size and surprise. He had the driver in a choke hold within two seconds, and after twenty—and a series of kicks and a single grunt—the man slumped into the snow.

Edgar hurried, swinging the doors open and yanking the driver by the collar up and into the back of the truck.

Too many cases of wine. The man's legs wouldn't fit.

Once Grant's crate was placed on the ground, Edgar was able to stuff the driver in all the way. He strapped the man's ankles and hands together with silver duct tape, hog style, then wrapped his mouth tight. Patting him on a leg, Edgar apologized.

He removed the cape and took the man's hat, then closed the truck and carried Grant's delivery to the front door.

As expected, the butler greeted him. "You're new," he said.

Edgar tipped the hat to hide his face from the entry camera. "Just for the evening, Thomas. Not to worry. Harold will return next week."

Turning away, the butler said, "They're supposed to advise us. We don't like surprises around here."

"Right. Sorry about that."

"Let's get on with it." The butler walked through the foyer and stopped at an arched door halfway down the first hall. He opened it and began down the stairs.

Edgar put down the crate and followed.

At the bottom of the stairs, the butler turned. "Where did you put—"

Edgar had him choked out faster than the driver. No need for tape on this one.

He ascended the stairs, grabbed the crate, and carried it up two floors of the curved grand staircase. Classical music echoed from the library, Chopin's nocturnes. He walked straight down the hall and stopped in the doorway.

Grant sat in a maroon paisley silk robe with his head down, reading. A fire flickered under the stone mantel behind him. A peaceful evening about to end badly.

Edgar knocked on the doorframe.

Looking up, Grant called past him, "Thomas! What the hell is the delivery boy doing up here? Thomas!"

Edgar dropped the crate, shattering the contents and exploding red wine and glass across the floor.

"Good *God*!" Grant leapt from the chair and backed away.

Taking off his cap, Edgar said, "Evening, Grant. Long time."

"What are you—Edgar!"

"We need to talk." Edgar took a step forward, his flat black SIG Sauer P229 drawn to the side.

"I...I..." Grant backed to the fireplace, burned himself, and stumbled forward.

Edgar said, "It's about Moss."

"What about him?" Grant rubbed his arm. "What the hell are you doing here?"

"There are some things happening in Virginia that you may or may not know about. That doesn't matter to me." Edgar waved the SIG.

Grant waited, like a good schoolboy, staring at Edgar.

Edgar continued, "And it's come together for me, all of it, except for one piece."

"What's that?" Grant asked in a sullen voice.

"I'm going to ask you to think back, way back, to a night in 1995. April 12, to be exact. Remember that day?"

Grant's eyes widened, like a fawn seeing headlamps for the very first time. Paralyzed by the oncoming lights.

"Edgar said. "So do I."

"Look, I don't know what you think you're doing in here, but I assure you, I had nothing to do with any bombing. Not here, not in Spain. Not ever."

"I believe that," Edgar said, taking another step forward. "But here's the problem. I've uncovered the archives from the Centro Nacional de Inteligencia. Spanish Intelligence, if you don't remember."

"Fuck off. What of it?" Grant asked.

"Records have a call being placed from the Madrid office on April 11. And then another on the twelfth. Two hours before the bombing."

Grant blushed. The man actually blushed. Forget being out of the field for a while. This guy had lost all his skills sitting behind a desk.

Edgar shook his head. "You know who those calls went to."

Grant opened and shut his mouth three times, like a fish in the grass.

Edgar waited, letting the silence build. Until he said, "Tell me about Moss."

Twenty-Three

Tearing Edgar's profile drawing from her sketchbook, Alex told Jack to park on the far side of the town hall, away from the front entrance. God knew what kind of network of eyes her father had out here. The last thing she wanted to do was tip him off minutes before they found him.

As she rolled the drawing and placed it in her pocket, Alex felt Jack staring at her. He was holding something, and she did a double take.

"Jack?"

He flipped the flat black SIG Sauer P229 pistol around and handed it to Alex. "To look authentic," he said, nodding at the town hall. "Oh, and this." He pulled a shoulder holster from the middle glove box.

She stared at him, then held up the gun. "Where...or should I say, *how* did you get this?" Personal ownership of firearms were illegal on the mainland of UK. Other than specially permitted shotguns and muzzle loaders, pistols were virtually impossible to attain.

He gave a small shrug. "Hanna purchased it a few months after her husband died. I didn't ask where."

"She lives in a safe neighborhood. Why would she risk having this?"

"Right, but she does all that medical work for charity. Some tough blokes come her way, yeah? And she's a single woman, all alone in a house like that."

"Seems excessive." Alex turned the SIG over, playing along. A P229, it was—conveniently—the same model she carried in the field, and it felt comfortable in her grip. Accurate, reliable, and small enough to be concealed, yet powerful enough to stop a large man, it was the ideal weapon for her. "And...she just lent it to you?"

Jack tilted his head. "You can say I took it on loan. She hides it away in her office."

"Not well enough," Alex muttered, checking the magazine—full—then the slide. One round chambered.

She wasn't sure what concerned her most: Jack claiming Hanna owned a gun or saying that he'd *borrowed* it from her. Was he trying to blow his cover with Alex—did he no longer care? Either way, Alex was thankful to have some protection again. She had felt naked all week. Jack's lies could wait.

The SIG has a double-action trigger with no manual safety, so she uncocked the hammer with the lever to be sure she didn't shoot herself, then slipped the holster on as she followed Jack into the hall. Since it was Christmas week, the place was open, but dead. The long marble hallway was barely lit, and their footsteps echoed like a death march all the way to the tax office. There, behind a black steel desk that looked to have been built before the war, sat a woman named Miss Pinkerton.

Alex had to announce their names to her three times. Then Miss Pinkerton stared so hard at the Metro Pol ID card, Alex was initially concerned she was memorizing it. But when she said Wainscott's name aloud to herself, Alex wondered if Miss Pinkerton had been around as long as the building itself.

Finally, she said, "You're the first visitors I've had all day."

Shocking.

Alex said, "We won't take up much of your time, but we're conducting an investigation and we just need to see the records room. We're looking for the address of a person of interest."

Miss Pinkerton studied them for a long five seconds and frowned. "We can't have you rummaging about. There's a system in employ here, of filing and the like."

"I assure you that we will leave everything exactly as we find it."

"Afraid not, Mrs. Wainscott. You'll need special permission for that, and I'm neither able nor willing to give it."

Seriously? What the hell was she protecting back there anyway? Alex was afraid she'd have to shoot the old bird to get past, when Jack said, "And what if we have the reference number, and all we need is the owner's address?"

Miss Pinkerton folded her arms. "That's not the way it works. You've got it all backwards. Transactions are filed by address, then you can look up the reference number."

Alex said, "What if we know the owner's name?"

Miss Pinkerton shook her head. "Still no good."

"Then how about this?" As a last-ditch effort, before Alex kicked in the records room door and started rifling through the files herself, she took out the drawing of Edgar and showed it to Miss Pinkerton. "This is the man we are looking for. Have you noticed him in here paying his taxes in cash? Or maybe seen him around town before?"

Staring at it, she lifted her chin, squinted, held it as far as she could from her face, tilted her head, and said, "Nope. Never seen him in my life."

She dropped the drawing on her desk.

Alex moved to explain to the old woman that her job was on the line just as a voice from behind them said, "Visitors?" It sounded like an echo of Miss Pinkerton's voice.

Alex turned to see a woman, who continued, "I'm Miss Pinkerton."

Feeling like they'd entered some sort of time continuum, a parallel universe or something, Alex looked back and forth between the two women and then at Jack.

The first Pinkerton said, "Not just that. These two want to go rummaging about the filings."

"Do they?" Pinkerton Two said. "What seems to be the problem?"

Alex explained the situation to her, in full this time, telling her about the offshore LLC and the name of RiverRock, yet she too stared at Alex, expressionless. Finally, she said, "Can't help you there, I'm afraid. It would take days to locate a reference number or owner name in the files. Perhaps weeks."

Alex was about to insist they let them try when Pinkerton Two added, "Is that a mug shot?"

"A police sketch is more like it," Pinkerton One said.

"Well, I'll be mogadored!" Pinkerton Two picked up the drawing and studied it about an inch from her face.

"What?" Pinkerton One said.

"What?" said Alex.

Pinkerton Two tapped the drawing and held it out. "This chap's my neighbor!"

The white sky descended, swallowing the horizon, and dumping endless shreds of white on the landscape. Reduced to a faint glow like a dying flashlight, the afternoon sun settled low and threatened to disappear altogether. Even though the address was only twelve miles from town center, the small roads leading to it were difficult to differentiate. It had taken them a full hour to find it.

A long, wordless hour in the gathering blizzard.

Having ditched the holster and tucked the SIG into the small of her back, Alex sat forward and scanned the property. The mound of a thatched cottage lay under a thicket of tall oaks far away from the other houses, and a wire fence bordered a thicker and taller iron fence at the home's back. A small wooden barn edged the fence, near the shallow stream that cut through the field like a wide footpath. Overgrown grass reached through the snow and up the fence posts, suggesting a small amount of neglect or maybe recent absence of the owner.

The whole scene reminded her of a series of winter landscapes she'd studied in college by Dutch painter Andreas Schelfhout. In short, the dull, dusky, and white-washed scene was no Thomas Kinkade.

"See anything?" Jack asked.

Scanning the windows, Alex shook her head. "Not a hint of light anywhere."

"Maybe he saw us on the approach."

"Maybe." She turned and stared out the back window. "Did you notice that SUV before? The white one?" She pointed back up the road, where it forked to the north. The red glow of taillights turned and moved away.

"I didn't."

Alex stared at the lights as they disappeared, wondering if it was her father.

Jack said, "Another neighbor?"

"Maybe." She kept her eyes on the blank horizon. "Let's keep moving."

Jack spun back around and eased the Porsche forward again, parking a few feet from the cottage's front entry.

Alex popped open the door and shrugged into her overcoat as she got out. Her ears perked up in hyper-attention as they walked through the flakes on the stone walkway. The chalk stream slurped behind the house. No other sounds.

Stopping next to her, Jack nodded at the front door.

Alex stepped forward and, feeling her heart rate rise at the sudden thought of seeing her father again, she knocked. Nothing. Tempted to yell, *open the damn door!* She stopped and called, "Edgar?" Then, knocking harder, she called out to the second-floor windows, "Anyone home?"

Jack said, "Stay here." He trotted off into the yard and disappeared behind the corner of the house.

Alex banged again, and tried the door just in case, but it was locked. Peeking through the window over a thick, snow-covered bush, she could make out a long wooden table and metal chairs in what looked to be a dining area off a kitchen. As she was looking around for a rock or something to break a window with, she heard a loud crack and a thump from behind the house.

"Shit." Alex hopped into the snowy grass and leaned low, one hand on the SIG, edging to the corner for a look. But the front door opened.

"Here, love," Jack called. "The back door was…open."

Dropping her aim, Alex spun back around. "Open?"

"Well. It is now." He smiled.

"Two felonies in a day, Jack." Shaking her head, Alex walked past him and into the house. "I'm impressed."

As Alex had imagined, the cottage was furnished with Old World items and classic European pieces, like the French pine table and black cast iron stove. A stone fireplace dominated the living area, with a pair of club chairs sharing a view of the snowy stream. She imagined her father sitting fireside, reading Dickens or Tolstoy, and drinking a few fingers of Scotch, neat. In her image he was lonely, regretful.

Alex and Jack split up to look around, and a few minutes later he called from the kitchen, "It's quite evident that he lives alone."

"Agreed." Among the paintings, there was not a single personal photograph, framed or otherwise, anywhere in the house. She wandered into the kitchen.

"He's not exactly a gourmet." He leaned back from the cabinets.

Inside sat two boxes of the same type of Dorset muesli, two boxes of Carr's whole wheat crackers, and two jars of Nutella. Nothing else. It made her sad for the man.

"Or a connoisseur." He opened the refrigerator. Two bottles of the same no-name Bordeaux were tucked into the bottom shelf. No perishable items, either, only ketchup, mustard, and some jellies. He nodded to the counter, where, sitting on a towel next to the sink, were a single fork, knife, dinner plate, and wine glass. The glass was spotted. Hand-washed and air dried, Alex thought.

"Maybe he's on a starvation diet," Alex said.

She opened a drawer. Empty. Then another. Silverware and napkins. Working her way through the kitchen and into the living area, she scoured for a clue, any verification that Edgar was the one who lived there.

Jack searched the rest of the kitchen as Alex made her way around the house and upstairs. A long bed sat undisturbed, along with a thick quilt and one large pillow propped to the wrought iron headboard. Returning from the bedroom, she stopped at the top of the stairs and looked back. The room overlooked the front of the house, but seemed too small to be the only room upstairs. So what about the space looking out to the stream? She returned to the bedroom and looked for doors to an attic or eaves, but there was nothing.

Alex descended the stairs and glanced at Jack as he flipped through every page of every book on the shelves at the back of the kitchen. A fine job of turning the place over. Interesting that he had that skill, too. She filed the information away for later. Behind him, a sliver of a doorway opened to a mudroom, where a set of waders hung in the corner, a fishing rod propped against them.

"Strange," she said.

"You're just now having that thought?" He was leafing through a thick cookbook. As he held it up, Alex noticed the binding hadn't been creased.

She looked to the ceiling. "I think there's a hidden room up there, but I can't figure out how to get to it."

He smiled for a second, glancing at Alex as he set the book down. "Ahh."

"What?"

"It seems the art of intelligence runs in the family."

"Not flattering." She walked behind Jack and into the tiny mudroom. The ceiling reached no higher than in the rest of the house. There was nothing in the little mudroom but boots and coats and fishing gear. A small wooden bench was pushed against the back door to prop it closed since Jack's kick to the lock had split the wooden frame.

Alex knocked on the walls, listening for hollowing or echoes, but every wall sounded the same. She tried again, slower this time, and paused when she heard a deeper thump on the wall facing the kitchen. Knocking harder, she put her ear against the wall.

"What are you doing?" Jack asked, standing in the doorway.

"There's something here."

"It's probably just insulation or an old stone wall behind the sheetrock."

"Then why doesn't the wall on the other side of the doorway sound the same?"

"That's where the water and gas pipes run?"

Peeking behind the waders—no closet, nothing—Alex said, "And did you notice that this is the only room with wainscoting?"

"I hadn't."

"I think it's an odd decorative choice for a mudroom, don't you?" She moved the bench from the door and stepped outside. Sure enough, a small round window peered back from the second floor, and it was the only window in the house with stained glass. Alex frowned. She was wiry, but even her nine-year-old self wouldn't have fit through that.

She returned inside and moved the waders, then stepped back and compared that wall to the one on the other side of the door. With one hand flat against the wood, she inspected it from the ceiling to the floor.

And noticed that one notch of wainscoting was thicker than the rest. Alex pressed on the thick panel, felt it give and come back, unhitching itself.

"Well, well," Jack said, as she pulled back the hinged panel.

Tucked behind the door, a narrow spiral staircase extended up to the second floor. Just wide enough for a single person.

"Why do I feel like I'm entering a Berlin safehouse?" Leaning in, Alex found a single bulb and pulled the string to switch it on.

She ascended the stairs to the top, and looked over the lip of the ceiling and across the wood floor of the secret alcove. Smaller than most modern-day American bathrooms, the recess held a makeshift desk made of a thick slab of pine suspended by two file cabinets, a steel swivel stool, a corkboard wall stuck with papers and photos, and a box under the desk. Squinting, she continued higher to get a better look at the box.

And stopped cold.

Even in the dim light, she could see the item was not a box after all. It was a large metal briefcase, a Zero-Halliburton. And inside, spilling over the edges, were stacks and stacks of one-hundred-dollar bills.

Twenty-Four

Lockard was right. They'd led him straight to Edgar. Too bad the super spy himself wasn't home.

Nothing came easy these days, did it?

That said, it had taken Lockard a mere seventeen minutes to traverse the stream, stash the Range Rover, and trudge back across the water back to the cottage. He hadn't planned on a slop-op and was drenched from the waist down, his legs numbed by the cold water. He knew he had ten, fifteen minutes tops before frostbite set in, or worse, hypothermia. Still, he needed to be patient, to act with surgical precision. Lockard had the element of surprise on his side, but there were two of them.

Standing at the edge of the iron fence and behind a bent oak, Lockard watched for movement inside the house. Of course it would have been easy for him to snipe them from this vantage. Just wait for them to move to separate areas of the home, shoot the first target near a window, wait for the second to investigate, and finish the job. With nobody within half a mile of the home, it would be undetected, too. About ten times easier than Baghdad.

Baghdad.

Ironic if you thought about it. The place was so damned poor, devoid of the world's luxuries, yet that was where Lockard had found riches beyond a king's ransom, a fortune worthy of a god. He'd orchestrated the grandest heist of all history. It made *Oceans Eleven* look like an ATM withdrawal.

The memory of it warmed him while he waited.

Najaf, Iraq
One hundred sixty-eight kilometers from Baghdad

Evan Lockard felt at home in the Blackhawk helicopter, surrounded by eight Navy SEALs dressed and painted in so much black that only their eyeballs showed in the moonlight. Having led three of them on a SEAL team dubbed Red Cell, Lockard trusted the other five to go along with today's effort without question. People said marines were like brothers, but SEAL teams were more than that. SEALs were one unit, with one mind, focused on one mission. Having been weeded and sorted and chiseled into the finest of soldiers through BUD/S training, relentless testing and prep missions, these men were assembled not only by particular skills, but by their ability to become one consciousness together. An organism, as his own leader had liked to refer to Lockard's first team. Normally, the mere presence of a CIA intelligence officer would be seen as an intrusion by the others. Their minds had been programmed to think one thought:

Unless you were a SEAL, you could not be trusted.

Good programming. Which was why Lockard, having been a SEAL, was critical to the success of the mission. He had handpicked this team. Gregory Pierce and the O'Doyle twins, Mark and Mike, had all served under him on Red Cell, and because today's mission was a CIA directive, Lockard was in charge of the overall operation. Pierce trusted Lockard and the team trusted Pierce.

A perfect chain.

The Blackhawk descended to the brown grass and circled the half-toppled Baghdad palace —the former residence of one of the Hussein sons—as brown dust kicked up from the chopper's blades, enveloping the men in a cloud. The O'Doyle twins stared at the playing cards displaying a photo of the supposed target's mug shot. A nice trick by the CIA, putting the fifty-two highest value Middle Eastern terrorist targets on a deck of cards and assigning values accordingly. Of course bin Laden had been the ace of spades. Though now a member of what was known as ISIS, the Islamic State, today's target was Akbar Say Naat Muhleen, Ak-Snot for short, the jack of clubs.

In succession, the twins folded the playing cards back into their breast pockets and buttoned them closed. They were ready.

They should be, Lockard thought. The team had planned the mission to the millisecond for almost three weeks. According to CIA (read: Lockard's) intelligence, there would be eleven insurgents inside the palace, ten of whom would die for their leader, Muhleen, who was holed up in the basement. Of course Lockard was the only one who knew this was all untrue.

The SEALs tipped forward to the edges of their seats, and Pierce stood and moved to the door. The twins followed, securing the rope and crouching on each side as the dust and wind whipped into the cavity. Then, like high-wire acrobats, the other men assembled and dropped out the door one by one until each of them, Pierce being the last to go, disappeared into the predawn haze. The pilot lowered the helicopter to the ground and stood ready to evac at the exact moment Pierce instructed.

Earphones secured, Lockard waited, listening to the pop-pop of gunfire coming from inside the palace, picturing the men entering the compound and killing their way into the basement. They would not find what they were looking for, so they would clear the entirety of the palace first. When they were sure the mission had failed—at least in their minds—they would signal Lockard.

So he waited.

Less than three minutes later, he got the signal. "Secure, sir."

Removing the headphones, he nodded at the pilot, drew his HK45 Compact Tactical pistol from a concealed hip holster, and shot the man in the side of the head, sending a splat of blood and brains across the windshield. Then, Lockard exited the Blackhawk into the darkness and strode across the crumpled grass. His heart beat fast, but unlike the others, it was not because of adrenaline for the unknown.

His heart thumped in anticipation.

After reaching a pair of towering and splintered doors, Lockard stepped into the gun smoke. Two bodies, both men's faces torn open by point-blank shots, lay beside the entry, their arms and legs bent at awkward angles.

Lockard stepped over one of the legs and entered the cavernous foyer. Lit by a single lamp from the corner, the gold-trimmed walls that remained intact from past bombings glittered. Following the path he'd suggested to the SEALs, and past two more fallen men, Lockard found a fifth body at the top of the basement stairwell with a single hole in the forehead. Clean and industrious. Lockard stepped around the body, and was taking the first step down when Pierce appeared at the bottom of the stairs.

"Down here, sir." Pierce disappeared again.

Willing himself not to bound down the stairs, Lockard descended to the bottom, entered the basement, and stopped before the men. Pierce stood at the front, with the other seven fanned out with their MP5s held at their sides. As planned by Lockard, one twin stood at each end. An oil lamp flickered behind the stoic silhouettes, making them look like an Orwellian nightmare.

Looking around, Lockard said, "Where's Ak-Snot?"

Pierce glanced at his men and then at Lockard. "Target absent, sir."

"Absent or escaped?" Lockard asked, staring back at him.

One of the twins stepped forward. Lockard thought it was Mark but he couldn't tell in the dark. "There's no evidence he was ever here, sir."

Lockard frowned. "Have you notified Camp Victory yet?"

"No, sir, wanted you to hear it first." Pierce paused. "Plus…there's something else we

think you ought to see."

"*Something else?*" *Lockard feigned surprise as he fingered the trigger of his HK.*

"*In there, sir. You, um...*"—*Pierce looked around*—"*need to see it for yourself.*" *He tilted his head toward a doorway in the corner opposite the lamp. The door was half open but Lockard couldn't see inside from where he stood.*

Still, he knew what they had found.

Lockard nodded at one twin, then the other. "*You did the right thing, soldiers.*"

Then he raised his HK and shot Pierce in the forehead.

The twins stepped from each end of the room and both fired double-tap shots as Lockard fired his second. Six shots, six dead, three seconds. The quickest of the men managed to get a single round off with his MP5, errant but impressive even for a SEAL.

As they checked the bodies, Mike lit a flare and dropped it near the doorway. "*It's here,*" *he said.*

Closing his eyes, Mark wiped sweat across his black-painted face. "*What about our exit strategy?*" *He kept glancing at the bodies of the SEALs, as if he felt guilty.*

Lockard said, "*Truck is at the back. And if my intelligence is correct, I'd say we need to load up. It'll take us all night.*"

Mike walked to the stairs and glanced up. "*As in a semi?*"

Lockard smiled. "*Consider it a present from the CIA.*"

"*Jes-us.*"

"*Let's have a look,*" *Lockard said, taking a few choice items from Pierce's person: AN/PVS-15 binocular night vision goggles—very nice, a Glock 19, and matches. Passing by Mark, Lockard took the oil lamp and pushed open the door. The twins hovered behind him as he walked inside and surveyed the find.*

Cool and damp and lined with hundreds and hundreds of bottles, the room was large enough to park five pickup trucks side by side, and this wasn't just a storage space. It was a giant wine cellar.

Sneaky little Hussein boys.

Preach the Quran and oppress your people by the words of Muhammad, damning the Americans and their hedonistic ways, yet live like the very people you have reviled all your life, drinking wine, smoking tobacco and other things, and enjoying pop music on your iPods and Hollywood movies on your flat-screen televisions. Not to mention skin flicks and prostitutes.

A fraud at the cellular level.

But Lockard didn't care about that. He couldn't give a roach's dick about Saddam Hussein or his shit-ass sons. He only cared about what was pushed up against all those wine bottles and into the corners of the cellar, bulging to the point of spilling over and onto the floor and into the shelves.

The scent of it was overwhelming, the world's dirtiest and most intoxicating perfume. The sight alone was enough to take your breath away.

There, at the bottom of this bombed-out and bullet-ridden palace, stacked on a cluster of wooden pallets, all swelling with the bulk of the load—half a person wide and chest high— were stacks and stacks, piles and piles, loads and loads of US bills. Not thousands of them. Millions.

All one-hundred-dollar bills, shrink-wrapped to keep them from falling over.

"Whoa," one of the twins whispered from behind.

Lockard took a step forward and peeled back a corner of the shrink-wrap, then unhinged a packet of bills and flipped through them.

"As much as we expected?" one of them asked.

Lockard tucked the stack back inside and turned to them. "More."

"How much, do you think?"

Lockard tilted his head and stared.

Eight standard shipping pallets, three feet wide on all sides by five feet high, each tiny packet containing ten thousand dollars. He closed his eyes, added the stacks, made the calculations. Then he nodded three times and opened his eyes.

After turning back to the twins, Lockard could see them clearly in the lamplight, but neither man looked at him. They simply stood dumbfounded in the presence of the hoard.

"Fuck me," Mark finally said, standing in an awkward position with his face flush. He had sprung a hard-on.

Mike stepped forward and asked, "What's that?" while pointing at the corner of the cellar.

Staring at the mini-pallet draped in a white plastic covering, Lockard frowned. "I'll be damned."

He squeezed between two pallets and bent lower to inspect the load.

Sure enough, the smell gave it away. Roasted almonds with a hint of tar. Lockard knew exactly what was hidden below. Not American, though—British. Weird—it really reeked of almonds.

"Leave it," he said. "We'll take that last."

"So we get it on the truck, then what? A CIA Gulfstream can't handle this much money. It'd be too heavy."

"Now you know why we need Draganic. His Boeing Business Jet is sitting at an abandoned airstrip, forty-seven miles from here."

"Is that Brit, Angus, still piloting?"

"He's already there," Lockard said. "Better hurry now. We're supposed to be dead." After ripping open the first package, he hauled about a hundred pounds of bills up the stairs, and the two brothers followed with stacks of their own.

It took two full hours to haul the endless piles of cash up and into the truck. Without ceremony, Lockard, drenched in sweat, doused the compound with the insurgent's stash of kerosene and dropped a single match, incinerating the palace, the helicopter, and the bodies inside. As far as the CIA and navy knew, they'd all perished in the failed mission.

Two hours later, after driving the forty-seven-mile stretch by moonlight alone, the men transferred the hoard of cash to the waiting jet and disappeared. The three of them sat in the aft, wide awake and wordless, for the rest of the night. Staring at the bounty of the greatest heist in the history of the world.

One-point-three billion dollars.

Lockard opened his eyes and zeroed in on Alex Winter and Jack Pope rooting around in the house of the man who now stood between Lockard and his money.

Up against that, neither of them stood a chance.

Twenty-Five

Evan Lockard.

Alex stared at the photo on the CIA dossier, known as a 201 file. She remembered the name. She had met the boy, now a man, at Langley back in 1995. Both their fathers had earned the honor of having stars forever etched in white marble on the Memorial Wall at Langley. Both were also listed in the Moroccan goatskin-bound Book of Honor after dying in the El Descanso restaurant bombing in Spain. Squinting at the photo, she was sure of it. Lockard who had killed Aaron. Then he had tried to kill Alex.

Why?

She thumbed to the next page of the 201 and read about Lockard's background as a Navy SEAL. Lockard had commanded a team called Red Cell, a unit that acted as Russian terrorists to test the defenses of various US military bases and stations around the world. A highly secretive operation, Red Cell had been able to penetrate dozens of sensitive locations, even overtaking a whole naval base along with a nuclear submarine.

Right in Groton, Connecticut.

Shaking her head, Alex read on.

After retiring from the SEALs, Lockard joined the CIA's Clandestine Service. Where he graduated into the elite operative training program dubbed—wouldn't you know it—Talonstrike.

Well fuck me.

Lockard was then sent to the Middle East, where he was stationed in Islamabad and then Baghdad, all the way up until three weeks ago. That's when, according to the dossier, Lockard was killed, along with an entire team of Navy SEALs, in a high-value-target, blast-and-grab mission in western Iraq.

So how was it that Alex had just fought him—hand to hand—in a half-finished high-rise in London?

She placed the folder down and picked up another. Inside were the dossiers of two brothers, the O'Doyles. Seeing the photos of them, she slumped onto the metal stool. Also Navy SEALs, these two had served in Red Cell along with Lockard before joining an elite SEAL team named Striper. The same team that was killed along with Lockard in the Iraqi mission three weeks ago. These men had not died that day, either.

They died when they tried to kill her on their motorcycles two days ago.

How did Edgar have all of this?

Alex dropped the dossiers onto the desk and leafed through the pile of papers along the edge. This stack contained articles and white papers about banking, money laundering, and offshore havens including the Caymans, Bahamas, and other island locales. On the bottom of the stack sat a legal pad with notes about banking governance and formation laws in the Isle of Man.

In Edgar's handwriting.

After picking up the last folder on the desk, she studied the photo clipped to the papers. An older man in a large BMW sedan. A thick, fleshy scar extended from the man's ear down his neck and into his shirt. No date on the photo, but a piece of tape with the words *Serbian Whale* was stuck to the bottom. The reviled child molesting money launderer.

Alex wondered if Draganic was suddenly doing some bill bleaching in the Isle of Man.

Reading through his file, she saw that Draganic had been banned from financial investment activities by seventeen securities enforcement agencies around the world, just as Jack had thought, and Interpol-compiled list of Draganic's assets showed the mansions he'd told her about in Dubrovnik and Gstaad, plus another in Seychelles...along with fourteen cars, *and* a new Boeing Business Jet.

Un-fucking-real.

The last sheet in Draganic's folder showed a photo of a man named Pachai Randeep, along with a list of hedge fund experience beneath. Most of the positions he held were in derivatives and structured instruments.

Mr. Randeep was no bucket-shop broker.

Stuck to the back of the folder, a piece of paper was covered in bubbles and names and lines, again in Edgar's handwriting, connecting Evan Lockard to Draganic, and then the O'Doyle twins, and Draganic to the Isle of Man, and then a company called Prince Alexander Capital. The words *UK* and *Canary Wharf* were scribbled under the Prince Alexander bubble. All three of the SEALs' names were listed in a bubble labeled *Iraq CIA mission*, and the bubble was arrowed to *Sarajevo* then to *Isle of Man*. A simple dollar sign was drawn into the two long arrows.

Just then, Jack called to her from the bottom of the stairs. "Alex?"

"Yes?" She said, staring at the map of connections.

"Perhaps you ought to have a look at this."

"What is it?" She called without full attention.

"I've found something in the icebox."

Lockard watched Winter in the kitchen for a good ten minutes. He told himself he was just making sure Edgar was not inside, that Pope and Alex were the only ones there.

But that was a lie.

Truth was, this was no ordinary woman. She would not come easily. She would put up a fight. Lockard had seen her perform savate, a kicking-intensive martial art that originated from French street fighting. She had used the form to escape a brawl inside a nightclub in Tangier, after a few men had hit the firewater a bit too hard that night, and like a testosterone cliché, had started pawing her.

Idiots. After splitting open the soft tissue of the first man's eye with her bare heel, she'd fended off three others with a bottle and a glass. Lockard, tucked in the corner and sitting alone that night, was almost tempted to help the fellow spy, but decided to sit back and watch as she dismantled three more. He'd then followed her for several blocks before she shook him off.

It might have been the closest thing he'd ever felt to love.

He'd felt a shadow of the emotion again, after their brawl in the London high-rise. And here she was now, as if preordained.

Lockard reached into his jacket pocket and retrieved the pouch with the meds. A simple, albeit strong dose of benzodiazepine, known as Benzo in Company circles, would sedate a person, but keep them mobile.

Lockard prepped the needle and drew the clear liquid from the bottle into the syringe. Tucking the device into the palm of his hand, he watched her move for another moment and then disappear up a stairwell. So smooth and easy and strong. It was a shame she had chosen the other side on this one.

War was war.

The hand.

That was all Alex could think of as Jack called up the stairs from the kitchen.

The briefcase that Edgar had intercepted. It was here.

With a picture of it clear in her mind, she hustled the papers back together into a stack and placed them on the desk.

"Don't touch it," she called down.

But Jack didn't answer.

Pope called out to Winter from the kitchen just as Lockard stepped through the splintered door into the small entryway. Winter answered from the stairway that was now behind him, and he turned and peered up the spiral staircase. Must have been some sort of attic or eaves up there.

He didn't see a way to close it off without making noise, but was satisfied enough that Winter and Pope were separated. That made things infinitely easier for him.

Crouched low, he hurried into the corner and reflexively touched the hip holster of his HK45. Footsteps sounded from the kitchen, Pope coming straight to him.

"I've found something in the icebox," he said, stepping into the entry.

Lockard pounced from behind, taking Pope in a quick chokehold while keeping his right hand loose with the syringe. Tightening his forearm, he thrust the tip of the needle into the thick jugular vein in Pope's neck.

"Don't touch it," Winter called down.

Pope tried to yell, but paralyzed vocal cords rendered him mute.

"Stay calm," Lockard said, pulling the needle back out just as quickly.

"Bloody bastard," Pope slurred as he stumbled forward.

"No blood at all, yet." Feeling Pope slump, Lockard dragged him toward the door.

Then the bastard elbowed him in the jaw.

The man swung his arm free, then gave a guttural *boof* as he thrust a shin to the back of Lockard's leg, but his strength had been sapped and the blow landed errant and weak. Lockard pushed him forward, out the door, and into the snow.

Alex heard a scuffle and then a throaty *boof* from Jack in the mudroom below her.

She didn't want to call out again; it would be easy for an attacker to shoot blindly through the floor, and she had nowhere to hide in the tiny room.

Drawing the SIG, she moved away from the stairwell and pressed flat against the wall, minimizing exposure to possible gunshots. After hearing the door kicked open, she counted to five and bounded downstairs, three steps at a time.

Hugging the wall, Alex peered outside into the muted afternoon sunlight and driving snow.

A man held Jack in a headlock, pulling him toward the stream's edge.

If she shot from here, she'd have as much chance of hitting Jack as she did the man. So Alex bolted into the snow, staying low and arcing wide around the yard to keep them from hearing or seeing her. Though she still couldn't get enough of a bead on the man to fire, she could now see his face.

And Lockard saw her, too.

Grabbing Jack by the hair, he ducked low, using him as a shield as he dragged him through the slushy water. *Damn.* As tough as Jack was, he had no chance with Lockard—not with that man's training. Jack looked hurt, too, somehow disabled.

Instead of firing wildly from that distance, Alex sprinted back through the snowy field and to the front of the house. She jumped into the Porsche, jammed the keys into the ignition, and thrust the SUV into reverse. She steeled her mind against the throb in her shoulder and pounded the gas to swing the car around. Slamming the clutch, she switched from first to fourth in less than three seconds, and rocketed toward the fence at the back of her father's yard.

She shielded her face with a forearm as the nose of the Porsche crashed through the railings, the splintered fence popping up and over the car.

Bounding on the open field alongside the stream, she saw Lockard—now a solid fifty yards ahead and on the far bank—forcing Jack into the passenger side of a Range Rover. He spun silt, then took off, barreling along the opposite side of the stream. Alex figured he would cut out into the field and away, but then saw the mangled wire-and-wood fence laying twisted in the high grass, and stretching as far as she could see. If Lockard drove through it, he risked a blowout or, worse, a tangle of wire around his car's axles.

Yet the Rover chewed through the high grass along the stream bank with ease. Alex gunned the engine, racing down the opposite side of the stream, a good thirty yards behind Lockard but gaining ground.

A cluster of trees and brush signaled a fence line on her side of the stream up ahead. The row was too thick to drive over, even in the SUV. She could try to break through, or veer a hard right and hope she didn't lose too much ground in the maneuver.

Instead, Alex slammed her foot on the brake and downshifted, causing the engine to scream and the vehicle to go from a hundred kilometers per hour to thirty. Then she jerked the wheel left and punched the accelerator, aiming the Porsche's nose at the stream.

The stream was too wide to leap across with no incline, so she slammed into the water then turned to drive upriver, the shallow water splashing up onto the windshield as she shifted and hammered the accelerator again.

Lockard wasted no time, barreling forward on the soft earth and snow, gaining ground as Alex bounced along the chalky bottom and rocks. Spotting the gradual incline on the bank ahead, Alex pulled the wheel left and climbed the bank as she tipped the Porsche to forty-five degrees. The windshield wipers couldn't keep up, smearing thick wet snowflakes across the glass as she upshifted to four and then five, but she got the Porsche up to a hundred again.

The Rover might be a machine, but this bitch was a rocket.

Lockard must have realized then he'd lose the race, because he slammed on the brakes and spun the vehicle one hundred and eighty degrees. Then he jammed the accelerator again, and headed back along the stream bank. Straight toward Alex.

Unblinking, Alex stared at the man behind the wheel as the Rover raced toward her. He was little more than a silhouette behind the falling snow, but he still looked insane: face forward, shoulders high, both hands gripping the wheel. Jack was unmoving next to him, his head slumped against the passenger seat, body bouncing with the movement of the vehicle.

The sight pushed her to rage, but Alex focused it. He couldn't have killed him yet; that would make no sense. He'd have done that back at the house and then riddled the ceiling with bullets to kill Alex. No, he wanted Jack alive for some reason.

Yet he kept coming. Fifty feet. Thirty.

Alex downshifted to third and then second, and jerked the wheel to the left again, avoiding the Rover's bumper by maybe a foot. The other SUV screamed past her and she kept veering until she made a wide arc, driving into the wet snowy field. She hammered the accelerator and pushed the engine as hard as it would go. All the way to sixth gear and a hundred and thirty kilometers per hour.

She turned back toward Lockard and the Rover and steered the nose, directing it at the driver's side.

Fifty feet. Thirty feet. Ten.

Holding the wheel with one hand and the hand stabilizer with the other, Alex slammed the front of the Porsche into the side of the Rover, sending both SUVs catapulting into the water and activating both vehicle's airbags. Hers exploded from the steering wheel, a stiff, white, nylon pillow punching Alex in the face and deflating in under a second.

The Rover launched upward and plowed into the far edge with the force of a tank, and the Porsche pounded into the stream's bottom with a jarring crash and loud crack.

Alex looked up to find the Rover jammed into the muddy bank, Lockard already flinging open the driver's door.

She slammed on the accelerator, intent on running the bastard over, but the back wheels just spun, sending a spray of water high into the snowfall and driving the limp Porsche deeper into the streambed. The SUV was all-wheel drive, but all the wheels were dead.

Shaking his head as he walked toward Alex, Lockard took aim.

Jack willed his eyes to open, his arms to move. His limbs felt heavy and numb, as if their circulation had been cut off in a poor sleeping position. Whatever Lockard had drugged him with was pulling him under. Edgar had warned Jack about this man, saying he was as ruthless as any Edgar'd ever met.

Blinking and flopping his head to the side, Jack saw the driver-side door open, the airbags hanging limp from the doorframe, and a blurry vision of Lockard tromping into the water.

This would be his last chance.

Jack fumbled the phone from his pocket. The numbers on the keypad swirled and doubled, then tripled. He blinked hard. Focused. He had to enter the code.

Staring at the keys with all the concentration he had left, Jack pressed the first number and the second and the third. He heard a gunshot, and another, and pressed the last two numbers with his eyes closed, hoping he'd hit the proper ones.

Then the phone dropped from his grip and the world fell black.

Ducking, Alex heard the bullets ricochet off the windshield. She turned her head to see three small dents in the glass. Nothing else. The glass was bulletproof; the vehicle was armored.

Jack and Hanna were just full of surprises.

Alex jerked the slide of her SIG, kicked open the passenger door, and took aim, but Lockard had already retreated and was climbing into the Rover as he yelled, "Tell your father I'll trade." He slipped inside.

As Lockard pulled the Rover free of the bank, Alex stumbled through the freezing water, gun aimed at the driver's side as she fired.

Two chips off the back corner of the vehicle, but nothing more.

The fucking Rover was armored, too.

Water and mud sprayed from the back of the vehicle as the Rover climbed the bank in victory. In a matter of seconds, it disappeared over the lip, leaving Alex breathless and knee deep in the frigid water.

She bent forward and looked under the front of the Porsche. The wheels lay in awkward positions, unconnected and unmoving. The front skid plate had dented, causing the axle to collide with a single boulder in the middle of the stream, breaking the axle and chipping the boulder. Moving the Porsche from the stream would be like trying to push a field plow through rocks.

Standing there, still out of breath and somewhat dazed, Alex heard the trill of a phone ring. "What the hell?"

She hurried back to the Porsche and peered under the driver's seat. Nothing. Then the passenger side. There, strapped to the leather bottom, a small cell phone was plugged into an alternative power source. She unplugged it and checked the caller ID. Blocked. No surprise.

Alex answered anyway. She expected to hear Lockard's voice, demanding. Or maybe even Jack's, begging. This was neither.

"Alex," her father said.

And suddenly it all made sense. Jack, Edgar, Lockard. And the briefcase with the hand.

Tell your father I'll trade.

"Where's Jack?"

Twenty-Six

Walking along the stream, soaked and freezing in a wind that swept the icy snow sideways, Alex's hands shook as she said, "Who is he, Dad? And who the fuck are you?"

"Calm down."

"How did you even know to call me?" She glanced around, half-expecting to see Edgar peering at her from a distance.

"Jack activated the kill code. It sends an SOS and destroys the phone."

"So he works for you? Through CIA, MI6…what?"

"Officially? Neither. But yes, he was there to watch over you. For me."

Alex pushed through the thicket of brush and trees that she'd avoided a few minutes earlier, and stepped over the Porsche tracks leading into the stream.

"Gee, Dad. I don't know if I should feel heartened by that or offended."

"Darling…"

"Don't. Don't you dare call me that. You gave up that right a long time ago."

He stayed quiet.

She started walking again.

"We need to get him back," he finally said, "He's valuable to me."

"It must feel like having the son you never had. The son you always wanted."

"Alex."

"Tell you what. He's yours, he works for you, he's loyal to you. So go find him yourself." She hung up.

Alex squeezed her eyes with a free hand, as her shoulder wound burned. She knew the jab at her father about feeling more attached to Jack than her was untrue. In reality, he didn't care about either of them. All but void of emotion, the man spoke of Jack as if he were an object, something that belonged to him. A mere item on a balance sheet. If removed, if abandoned, it would simply free up space for other ventures, different assets, new interests. The man was not tied to anything in this world but himself.

A serial narcissist to the end.

That meant Alex was all on her own for this one. Again.

Standing there, in the wet, cold air, Alex shook with a mix of anger and frustration. She'd allowed herself to let emotions interfere with judgment. Only a fool would have ignored the clues that Jack was more than he'd claimed. Like a silly schoolgirl, though, she'd allowed herself to believe he really liked her. For what? Her bristling personality and propensity to keep everyone at arms-length? Oh yes, she was about as charming as an injured bobcat.

Alex laughed sarcastically and the chalk stream trickled coldly in reply.

She stood still for a few moments, both hands on her hips, staring up at the shreds of snow leaking from the grey clouds like nuclear fallout. And then she remembered. Jack said he had found something in the freezer a few minutes ago. It probably wasn't more money; that would not have produced a reaction like that. *You ought to have a look at this.*

Was it the hand?

She trudged through the thick, frozen grass and, stopping at the barn, she peered inside. The walls were lined with various tools for gardening and house maintenance, nothing electric. Quite a contrast to what sat in the center of the dusty concrete floor. Black cobalt, sleek, and looking brand-new. She'd never even seen one before.

The Mansory BMW 760Li. "Freakin' land-jet."

Not exactly low profile, she added silently, but at least she had a ride back to the city.

Returning to the house, Alex entered where Jack had broken the back door and headed straight to the kitchen where she pulled the cold SIG from the small of her back and placed it on the table next to the package he'd found.

It wasn't a briefcase, and there was no hand.

The thick wrap of tin foil was thoroughly wrinkled and torn at the edges, as though it had been opened and re-closed many times. The package lay peeled open now, and the contents—dozens of photographs; color, black-and-white, large and small—spilled over the sides.

Alex in high school, being handed a blue and yellow jacket by the track coach after being named as a member of the varsity team. In a cap and gown, walking across the stage at high school graduation. With Ginger, unloading a few suitcases and a trunk in front of a dormitory, her first day at Yale. Four years later, another cap and gown. Alex's graduation at Langley, no ceremony, but a sit-down meeting in the office of the DDO—deputy director of operations—

now known as the director of the National Clandestine Service, or DNCS. This photo looked to have been taken through the office's windows. *How the hell did he get that shot?* And lastly, Alex dressed in a wetsuit during training with the Talonstrike class. This was taken from out in the Pacific somewhere, with the Naval Amphibious Base Coronado in the background.

Alex stood still, numb, wondering about the man who'd chosen the life of secrecy and travel over a lifetime with his daughter. Gritting her teeth, she shook her head, though she was alone in the room. He'd abandoned her, no other way to put it.

But as she stood there, staring at the moments before her, a small wave of comprehension moved through her. Like a curator trying to extrapolate and interpret an artist's message, it was impossible to do with just one piece of work, from one angle of view. She needed to pull back, see the gallery of works, the layers of individual interpretations and conveyances of the artist. The mere existence of these photos forced her to see more than before. Allowed her to see the whole of it and not just the part that she'd been obsessing over: herself.

In that moment, in some strange way, she understood why he'd done it. Was it reasonable to expect the super spy to switch to a desk position just because he had a kid? Leave the field and become an operator? Or what, leave the Company altogether, work nine-to-five somewhere? *Please.*

Alex herself had vowed never to be faced with the same choice herself.

As she placed the photos in a neat pile at the center of the wrinkled foil, tucking the memories back away, she spotted one last photo. Different, more recent, and one that raised a new set of questions. Alex was leaning up and kissing a man good-bye at the airport in Geneva. He was tall, broad of shoulder, with short blond hair, striking in jeans and that charcoal Harrington jacket.

She took the photo and stared at it for a while, wondering who Jack really was. Why Edgar had used him to watch over her. Whoever he was, Jack was the real deal. He was as good as either one of them.

And he was in deep trouble.

Alex drew the cell phone from her pocket and held it out for a moment. Then she pressed the numbers and waited.

Her father answered on the second ring.

Alex said, "Where do we meet?"

Twenty-Seven

Bern, Switzerland

Swiss Federal Council President Karl von Zeller stood before his window and stared at the snow-dusted cobblestones below. Many people braved the cold this time of year, running from shop to shop, buying trinkets and perfumes, perhaps even jewelry. Definitely toys.

Zeller turned to the minister of finance, Stefan Lory, who was seated in a tall leather-backed chair, legs crossed, hands resting on a folder in his lap. Seemingly at ease.

Not for long.

Zeller asked in German, "Have you finished your Christkind shopping? The children all ready for baby Jesus?"

"Mostly," Lory answered. "But my twins want the latest gaming system for the television. A Nintendo or X-something. I don't know. They're impossible to find."

"Yes, yes. I remember those days. Except my boys wanted a Rubik's cube. They were sold out, across the city, the whole country. And this was before that wonderful eBay." He smiled. "But you can always count on ringli in my house." He loved those huge doughnuts his wife made each year. The savory sweet taste of potatoes and honey.

Lory nodded without emotion. He was clearly on edge, despite his relaxed posture.

Von Zeller switched to French, a tactic to put the other man at ease, show him von Zeller was working with Geneva's interest on this one. "And how is Mrs. Lory? Enjoying life as the finance minister's wife?"

"It is more stressful than either of us expected."

"Ah, yes." Von Zeller squeezed under a low-hanging painting of himself and sat down, pulling his chair to the desk. "With responsibility comes pressure."

Lory stayed quiet, and von Zeller decided to get right to it.

"Do you have the reports?"

Lory held up the folder. "I do." He handed them to von Zeller.

"Don't make me read all this. Just give me the highlights...or lowlights, as they may be."

Lory said, "The program has accelerated. The Treasury is struggling to keep up."

"How bad?"

"We've spent thirty-seven billion so far." Lory glanced away. "This week."

Von Zeller sat stunned. "The Serbian Whale?"

"It seems he has a syndicate, a consortium of players. Hedge funds, I'd say, with deep pockets."

"How deep?"

"Our estimates say they could have borrowing power of up to a trillion francs."

Von Zeller placed a hand to his forehead and fell back into his chair with all his weight, causing it to roll backward a foot. "That could break us."

"It could."

"It would be Black Wednesday all over again. Except the British would be the ones laughing to the bank on this one."

"Not necessarily."

"How?" Von Zeller tightened his brow.

"We don't have to act. We just need to threaten action, if you know what I mean."

"I don't."

"The Euro." Lory was stoic, staring back at von Zeller, taking a good three seconds between blinks.

Von Zeller sat forward. "Are you suggesting we say that we are joining the European Union? Abandoning our own currency? They would have our heads!"

"Not joining, of course not. That is ridiculous."

"Then what?"

"Considering."

Von Zeller pushed from the desk, the chair rolling back and smacking the bottom of the painting. "It is our duty to consider all options."

"That is all we have to say."

"And what, the consortium backs down? They walk away from the trades?"

"The bulk of the trades were made through options."

Von Zeller slapped the desk and said, "They'll expire!"

"Worthless."

Von Zeller felt the flush of a smile burn into his face. If Lory weren't a man, he would kiss him.

Instead, he rounded the desk and slapped the man's shoulder, a hearty thump. "Arrange a press conference. Right here at Bundeshaus." The Federal Palace. "That will get people's attention before the announcement. Then, Stefan, I would start looking for a new house. A larger one."

"Why's that?" Lory asked.

"Because, my dear friend, with your genius…" Von Zeller slapped his hands together and then held them wide. "You will be president one day."

Randeep refreshed the screens, which showed the chart of that day's move in the Swiss franc.

Brilliant.

Not only had he stemmed the losses from earlier, but with several key phone calls, he'd turned the entire market. All in mere hours. It was like that within his circle of colleagues. People thought hedge funds were some sort of fellowship or brotherhood, something born out of the Ivy League like Skull and Bones, but that wasn't quite true. Hedge funds were the purest of meritocracies in the working world. Each hedge fund's allegiance was to itself. Eat what you kill.

Yet hedge-fund managers were also the smartest investors in the world, and they knew that power came with size, and that working together could often be the difference between a successful trade and a failure.

The self-allegiance becomes an alliance.

Still, the franc had not moved as much as Randeep had anticipated. It needed to rise another three percent for most of his trades to be in the money. He expected the momentum to build and the trades to work, but he may have to give the market a push at the end of the day.

Randeep tapped the keyboard again. He had a choice to make. Because the futures and options would expire in two days, the leverage he'd assumed—the loans he'd taken on the cash in the bank—would be outstanding for less than seventy-two hours. A lot of money, but not a long time.

He could stomach even more.

Staring at the price on the screen, Randeep took a deep breath. What was another billion? When his colleagues saw the trade print, they would follow. He was sure of it. In twelve more hours, they would break the Swiss National Bank.

He pressed the button and made the trade.

Ten seconds later, he saw the announcement.

Sitting in the corner of Le Bar du Grill of the Gstaad Palace Hotel, Draganic waved the white-coated waiter to him and ordered a Russian Standard Imperia martini, straight up, three olives.

"I apologize, but we do not carry Russian Standard." The waiter gave a smirky frown with his perfect English. "Perhaps Belvedere or Chopin would do?"

"Give me Belvedere." Draganic waved the man away.

The drink took almost five minutes to serve, ridiculous considering Draganic was one of only three other customers that morning. He took a sip—it tasted as boring as ice water, no bite at all—just as Greta Muller arrived.

Pausing at the high backed chair next to him, she scowled. "I thought we were having tea."

"I needed something stronger today. Perhaps you do, too."

"I'm the minister of foreign affairs. I can't be seen drinking alcohol during council hours, and certainly not with the likes of you."

Draganic took a long drink of the martini, held it in his mouth for a few seconds, swallowed, and then glared up at her. "Sit."

She stared back, then with tight lips, she glanced around and sat. "I'm not staying."

Ignoring that, he said, "You were supposed to feed me information on the program. That is what I am paying you for."

She whispered, "Keep your money. I don't want it anymore. It has become too risky."

"Tell me about the Swiss Federal Council's announcement planned for tomorrow."

She leaned forward and whispered, "You are crossing the line here."

Draganic tapped the metal of the Sea Shark blade that was sheathed against his hip. "Is it about the Swiss franc intervention?"

"I'm not playing this game."

He stopped tapping and snarled, "I've already wired the money to your account, and I have clear records of the transaction…start to finish. What we are playing, minister, is not a game."

Greta stared back, contemplating her situation, and finding no solution. Once inside, there was no way out of Draganic's den.

The waiter approached again and asked Greta if she wanted a beverage as well.

"Get her one of these." Draganic pointed at his martini.

"No, no!" Greta said. "Just…bring me breakfast tea, please."

"Very well." The waiter nodded and strode off.

Greta crossed her arms and looked away. "I told you it is foolish to take on the Swiss government."

"Stop with the lecture and tell me what the hell is going on in Bern!"

She hissed. "They are fighting dirty. They will crush you."

"How?"

"Think, Zoran. What would wipe out the gains in the Swiss franc in one minute? A single stupid proposal by a reckless president and an eager finance minister?"

Draganic fell back in his seat, stared at the crystal chandelier above the bar. He imagined the chain snapping and the chandelier crashing down. Shards of glass exploding onto this woman's head.

He shook his. "They wouldn't."

"They *are!*"

"The people would never allow it. The mere thought is absurd."

"They don't have to join. They only have to say they are thinking about it."

Draganic traced the thick scar up his neck and to his ear, then pulled his hand away. "Then you will stop the announcement."

"This is not possible. It is already set for tomorrow at the Federal Palace, three p.m. There is no stopping it."

Tempted to stab the useless hag in the face, Draganic stood. "Find a way."

He exited the hotel and climbed into his BMW. Now, his own foot soldier had double-crossed him, his inside source at the Council had failed him, and his currency genius was set to fuck him good. Because of Randeep's idea—one that would enable the greedy little man to have his own payday—Draganic was to be left with nothing.

Taking one, long and deep breath, he drew out his cell phone and dialed the number to the trading floor.

Randeep picked up on the first ring. "I know, Zoran. I am trying to unwind them, but nobody will take the other side! They know about the announcement, and the currency has already fallen below our strike. What do you want me to do?"

"Pachai. I am going to tell you a story."

"Zoran, I—"

"Shut up and listen."

The line went quiet.

"I once accepted unique payment for a special financial service I provided a man in the northern hills of what is now known as Macedonia. He did not have cash money, but he had other assets. Three daughters, aged eleven to fourteen."

Randeep sighed and Draganic continued, "The smallest of them was too young, even for me. So I accepted the middle child. She was old enough to know certain things, how to do them. With proper instruction, how to do them well."

"Zoran, this is not—"

"This good man showed me to the girl's bedroom, he put her to her knees, and he shut the door as he left."

"Being a patient man myself, I removed my jacket and gave the girl detailed instruction. I told her exactly what to do and how. I let her know that if she performed well that her father would earn great rewards. And in turn, so would she."

Randeep gulped audibly.

Draganic continued, "Truth be told, she was surprisingly proficient in her service. It was clear I was not her first. In fact, she was to be one of the best payments I had ever received. But then she did a thing that not only spoiled the release, but it ruined the entire experience."

Draganic sat quiet, waited for Pachai to ask. They always did. He said, in a sullen but curious voice, "What did she do, Zoran?"

Draganic said, "At the moment of ejaculation, she tightened her mouth and pinched the shaft so hard that I fell off the bed. Then, not only did she spit my seed out, she dumped it onto my brand new suit jacket."

Pachai coughed, though it almost sounded like a laugh.

Draganic said, "She apologized, but the damage was done. I took her hand, dragged her back down the hallway and told her father of the horror of her actions. The humiliation she had caused him."

"This good man asked what he needed to do to set things right for us and I gave him two clear options. One would be financial ruin for his family. Then I unsheathed my blade and handed it to the man. Gave him a single nod, as he would know what to do next. The girl, screaming and begging as he poured a full inch of cooking oil into the iron skillet. After turning the gas on high, he commanded her two sisters to hold her arm steady on the butcher block. Lucky for the girl, I keep a sharp knife."

Randeep remained quiet, and Draganic thought he heard him gag.

He continued, "A single slice removed the disobedient thumb. Right through the soft flesh and cartilage of the joint. The father, being a compassionate man, immediately cauterized the wound in the smoking oil and saved the rest of the girl's hand. But she would never pinch another man in that place again. Do you see?"

Randeep vomited on the other end of the line.

When he was through, Draganic said, "Pachai?"

The man coughed and then he came back onto the line. "Yes, Zoran."

"I tell you this story for two reasons. First, don't ever pinch me."

"Yes, Zoran."

"And second, because if you do, it won't be your thumb that succumbs to the blade."

Twenty-Eight

Jack woke feeling cold and sluggish, a migraine throbbing from the base of his skull all the way to his face. He felt sharp pains in his wrists and ankles, and realized his arms were pulled above his head. His legs, too, were spread wide with restraints, and he lay naked in a cold pool of water within a cast iron bathtub.

Evan Lockard stood over the tub, staring into Jack's eyes. He had a cut across his nose that was scabbing over, making him look like a boxer after a solid bout.

"There we are," he said. "That's a good boy. Wake up."

The words echoed off the tall ceiling of the small bathroom. No windows, so Jack guessed it was at the center of the house or apartment—wherever he was —well insulated from sounds echoing into other flats or apartments.

Lockard, the stalker-agent from Tangier. The same bloody psychotic bastard who had followed Winter for nearly a mile before she'd shaken him off. The madman was so brazen that he'd tipped off Alex to his presence before she'd even left the bar. It'd also forced Jack to take the most aggressive of approaches and actually meet Alex during her next operation. After that night in Tangier, she'd become hyper-aware of anyone within a thousand feet of her. No way Jack could stay in those shadows for long. It'd pissed off Edgar, but he got over it, requesting only that Jack keep his feelings in check on the assignment.

Something he'd been unable to do.

And now here was psycho-macho-SEAL boy Lockard, and the bastard was smiling.

Lockard said, "I've administered a dose of Flumazenil. It is a benzodiazepine receptor antagonist. An antidote to what you received before." He tilted his head from side to side. "This will wake you for a bit, but when it wears off, you'll go back to sleep. And I can do whatever I like to you again."

He leaned close to Jack's face and said, "So I suggest you cooperate."

Jack tried to gather enough saliva to respond, but his throat and mouth were kiln dry. He pulled at the restraints, but with his wrists wrapped tight in thick black nylon straps, his fingers were already purple.

Lockard followed his gaze. He said, "I'll loosen those after you help me."

"Fuck off," he managed.

"I'm not that kind of boy." He tilted his head to look between Jack's legs. His ankles were held out of the water and anchored to the tub's feet, forcing his hips to tilt up. "But I might make an exception for such a specimen."

Jack tightened his jaw but stayed quiet.

"Yes, maybe later. But first." Lockard held up a device. Jack's phone.

He turned it in his hand as he said, "You've made it difficult for both of us, see? When you destroyed this."

Jack stared straight ahead. Destroying the phone was simple protocol for an agent in his situation. He had to close all avenues, erase any information that could lead to Edgar. Lockard would threaten Jack, but he knew that torture was an ineffective way to get information from someone, as the subject often gave up any answer, even a wrong one, to make the pain stop. So the most effective way to get the right answer was to use the threat of torture instead. Bend the subject just enough. Make the person just uncomfortable enough. Give the captive just enough pain.

"You are in a very bad position, Jack."

"I see." Jack glanced around. "It's not exactly The Dorchester, is it?"

Lockard frowned and looked from wall to wall. "It serves its purpose."

"What purpose is that?"

"Well that depends on you, doesn't it? Your attitude."

Jack continued staring straight ahead. It was coming, the threat. Maybe some pain. The start of it, anyway.

"All you need to do is tell me where Edgar is."

"I've no idea," Jack said in a flat voice.

"Tough boy. Or should I say man?" He circled the tub, stopped, and leaned down to whisper in Jack's ear, "Either way, you are a beautiful one."

Jack turned away slightly and then slammed the side of his head into Lockard's cheek.

Lockard stumbled back and then darted forward like a cobra and struck Jack with the back of a hand across the mouth.

Jack felt the trickle of blood form at the corner of his lips.

"Bad little boy," Lockard said, then he smiled.

"You like that, role-play? Or perhaps you like real schoolboys."

"I'll like it better if you tell me what I want to know."

"I already told you, I don't know."

"Then where is the briefcase?"

"You're a fool if you think Edgar would tell anyone."

"He would tell you." The snarl turned into a growl.

Jack gave his best shrug within the restraints.

"Have it your way." Lockard tossed the phone into the tub. It swirled then clanked at the bottom.

He walked forward and loosened the lead above Jack's head. This gave him a longer tether, but Jack's hands remained cuffed tight by the nylon.

Jack sat forward, gathering his energy as fast as he could, readying to dig his fingers into Lockard's eye sockets the moment he got near enough.

But the man took three quick strides to the end of the tub and grabbed Jack's ankles. And now Jack knew why he'd lengthened the tether.

Lockard said, "This little technique is called The Slide. And I'm proud to say that I invented it." He yanked Jack's feet toward him, pulling his hips out of the water and his head into it.

Jack gasped for a single breath before he went under, and took in half a mouthful of water.

Jack pulled at the tether on his wrists. He tried to fight him, haul himself back up and out of the water, but Lockard was too strong and with both feet anchored against the tub, his entire weight leaned back, Lockard had all the leverage. He pulled Jack further under.

Eyes bulging and lungs tightening, a rush of blood surged through Jack, making him lightheaded. He willed himself not to breathe, not to give in. Then, unable to take any more, he pulled with his arms as hard as he could, forcing his head up and mouth out of the water. Fighting for a single breath.

He took a gulp of air, and Lockard yanked him under again.

This was no threat. A single breath underwater would fill Jack's lungs. Another would drown him. The son of a bitch would kill him.

No.

Jack pulled back against him, but Lockard wouldn't give. Jack's elbows banged against the tub, echoing in the water.

He fought back as hard as he could, pulling as the nylon dug into his wrists, so hard that he risked dislocating a hand. Still, Lockard didn't move an inch. Jack thrashed and pulled and yanked and willed himself.

Do not breathe.

Jack's vision blurred and the light above squeezed into a pinpoint and then blackness as he lost the last gasp, the last energy, the last ounce of oxygen in his lungs. His chest tightened and the needles spread from his feet and hands up his legs and down his arms and across his torso and numbed him. He had nothing, no more. He needed another breath. One more.

So he fought for it.

Jack pulled and yanked and thrashed, hauling himself against the weight and force of Lockard, and just as he was about to give, Lockard dropped Jack's feet.

Jack raised his head above the water and gasped for air. He coughed and sucked water into his mouth and nose as he breathed. He found the oxygen. He gave his body life again.

Lockard circled the tub and stopped above Jack. Palming the top of his head, he pushed Jack back under again. Lockard gripped Jack's hair and held him down as Jack pushed back and yelled underwater. Lockard yanked his head back out and he breathed, and he thrust Jack back under, yelling back at him, "You will submit!"

Out of the water. Thrust back below. Out of the water.

"You will submit to me!"

Out of the water and back below.

"You will submit!"

And then he dropped Jack's head, banging it against the side of the iron tub. He reached between Jack's legs, into the water, and groped deeper until he pulled the plug, draining the tub in *glug glug glug*s, as Jack gasped and leaned backward. Away from Lockard and into the empty cold air.

Shivering, exhausted, Jack watched as Lockard pull the straps of his arms tight again, and left him there, in the cold tub. As he walked out the door, he said, "You will tell me."

But they both knew. Jack had just won the first round.

Moss stared at the snow-dusted trees in St. James's Park from the backseat of his SUV. Dusk had come earlier than normal with the storm, and few pedestrians braved the cold. The park was almost empty, and those who ventured out walked with one hand fisting their overcoats closed over their faces, leaving the mood of the streets sullen.

As for Moss, he was royally pissed off, but he'd gotten himself into this mess and could only blame himself. Though he hated that bastard Lockard, Moss would have done the same thing. After all, the question wasn't: What would you do for a billion dollars?

It was: What *wouldn't* you do?

His phone chirped and Moss checked the ID.

Damn.

He tapped on the driver's shoulder and pointed to the curb, then snapped his fingers once. This call required privacy.

The driver exited the vehicle and walked to the front bumper.

"Mr. President."

A millisecond of hang time, the tiniest clue that the signal had just traveled across the Atlantic. Moss hoped the man didn't notice.

"Director Moss, it took my gal almost a full minute to reach you. Are you not on our fertile shores?"

Moment of truth. Or not. "I'm at the ranch, sir. You know what Jackson is like this time of year. We're buried in snow." Moss winced as he said it, and watched a lone man walking a little white dog wearing a sweater enter the park. The damn dog turned in circles, sniffing the snow and snorting it from its nose. Stupid animal couldn't hunt down a bowl of kibbles in its own kitchen.

"Yes, we all need a break once in a while, don't we?"

Moss knew why the president was calling, but he wasn't going to bring it up. That would just make it easier for the ivory tower to scold him. He said, "I suppose, Mr. President."

"Yet now's not the time for a holiday, is it?"

Well, well. The slick bastard knew he was in London. That's why he used the word *holiday* and not *vacation*. "Yes, Mr. President."

"Good. Now, I'm up for reelection this year. Do you know what that means?"

"Sir?"

"It means you're up for reelection too."

"I suppose it does, sir."

"Damn well right, it does. And that means we can't have another CIA scandal. Not with all these people out of work and looking for handouts. We've come too far, done too much with this cabinet of mine. We can't be seen as poor stewards of the Treasury, can we?"

Moss was smart enough to shut up and just regurgitate. "No, sir. We've come too far."

"That's right." He stopped for a moment and Moss let the silence sit between them, the pause between lightning and thunder. "The bottom line, Director, is that we cannot have you and your spies settling old scores at the expense of my administration."

Tempted to set the record straight with the ignorant fool, Moss bit his tongue and said, "Yes, sir."

"Good. I trust this will no longer be a problem, then?"

Not for me, Moss thought, but maybe for you. He said, "Not at all, sir. It'll be resolved by Christmas."

"Ah, yes. That'd be a nice present for you, wouldn't it?"

"Yes, sir."

"Now, go find that money. Let's get reelected."

Twenty-Nine

Pulling her overcoat tight, Alex entered the designated meeting spot called The Queen's Ransom pub and was surprised to see it packed. She supposed the storm gave people a reason to forgo a commute in favor of a pint or two, or—from the late hour and sound of the crowd—maybe three or four. Not expecting Edgar to show himself, Alex scanned the crowd for signs of a contact, someone to either tell her where he was or take her to him. Nobody stood out to her.

She weaved through the suits and tucked herself at the corner of the server's station, resting an elbow on the rubber mat atop the bar. A middle-aged waiter wearing a suit one full size too big looked at her elbow then the bar and back to the elbow.

Perhaps Alex was in his way. She placed her other elbow next to the first and clasped her hands together as she blinked back at him a few times.

He rolled his eyes and barked an order at the bartender, filled his tray with frothy pints, and strode off.

Guess he wasn't Edgar's contact.

Leaning into the bar, Alex ordered a Hendricks gin, splash of soda. The bartender nodded with a frown.

She watched him pour her drink, the photos from her father's house flashing in her mind. She imagined Edgar standing to the side in each of them, hidden from Alex, maybe even cheering her on in silence.

She wished she'd known he was there.

Alex shook the images from her head and took a drink the moment the bartender set down the glass.

Better.

Done with the sudden onset of daddy issues, Alex pulled out her sketchbook and a few pencils then focused her mind as she worked on the likeness of Evan

Lockard. The image of him standing beside the Range Rover, knee deep in the freezing water, came quickly and in vivid detail. The deep-set dark eyes, the wide and flat nose, the square jaw. The man's intelligence was hidden behind that hard facade. So was his hatred. But her goal was to give the sketch no bias. She could not infect the image with her own emotions or knowledge of the man. The portrait would only be useful if it was accurate and untarnished.

She finished the details of the shoulders and the man's stance, but left out the background, kept it blank. As she modulated the final shadows of the man's features, the bartender leaned over and said, "Well done. That's talent."

"Thanks."

While shaking a cocktail strainer, he said, "Deep Cover is playing downstairs." He paused in making the drink and stared up at her. "The lead is not half bad. You may want to have a look."

Alex peered over the crowd and the bartender tilted his head. "In the corner."

She looked back at him. He nodded and moved off.

Her cue?

Alex paid for the drink and weaved through the suits, which had somehow multiplied. In the far corner of the pub, a line of people had formed at a doorway with a neon sign saying *The Drop-In* above it. At the edge of the doorway, behind a red silk rope, stood an enormous bald man. He looked like an albino bull.

Figuring Edgar would have arranged for her to bypass the line, Alex approached the bull.

"Name?" he asked without moving his mouth a centimeter.

She started to say *Alex* but quickly corrected herself. "Amanda Carr."

The bull eyed her and then looked at his curved smartphone. It was so small in his hand, it looked like a potato chip. He scrolled the screen with the tip of a pinky, a delicate move for the bull, and then puckered. "Welcome to The Drop-In, Ms. Carr. Enjoy yourself." He moved aside, unclipped the rope, and let her through.

A few groans sounded from a trio of girls near the middle of the line but the bouncer ignored them, as did Alex.

Leaving the sounds of the pub, Alex entered the thump of electronica, slugging the Hendricks before she reached the bottom of the stairs.

The Drop-In had blue and pink neon lights behind the bottles, gothic mirrors on the walls, and a stage big enough for a one-man comedy act, all stuffed into a basement studio apartment. No sign of Edgar anywhere. The rest of the patrons were middle-aged and looked like successful businesspeople.

Alex made her way to the bar, and before she could order, a tall bartender dressed in a shiny black button-up shirt reached for the Hendricks bottle and poured a double over ice, splash of soda. Without a word, he handed it to her.

Interesting. Though still no sign of Edgar or her contact.

Alex took the drink, left ten pounds on the bar for him, and watched behind her through the mirrors. The crowd grew as the bull let more people in, and after a while the electronic thump stopped. A few minutes later, a band, which she figured was Deep Cover, made its way onto the stage to the loud cheers of the crowd. The band members were all dressed in black jeans and nondescript T-shirts, except for the lead singer. She was in a gray T-shirt dress and platform shoes. No bra, from what Alex could tell.

She had low hopes for the music getting any better than the techno thump.

But then Deep Cover broke into a pretty damned good rendition of Siouxsie and the Banshees' "Peek-A-Boo." Not that Alex was a big Siouxsie fan as a kid or anything—not many non-rebel teens were—but it brought her right back to the nineties. The band proceeded to play other covers, ranging from the Pretenders' "Brass In Pocket" to No Doubt's "Don't Speak."

With the music and another Hendricks, she was almost in a better mood, but then Deep Cover slid into a tribute of The Cure's "Pictures of You." And Alex checked her watch.

Edgar's contact was over an hour late. Her father had either chickened out or decided he didn't need Alex after all.

Though he'd made that decision long ago, hadn't he?

Alex downed the last of the drink and set it down on the bar, then turned to go back upstairs. As she turned, the bartender grabbed her wrist. In no mood, Alex slipped out of his grasp and reversed the move so that the bartender was in her grasp.

"I paid," She said, nodding at the pile of notes on the edge of the bar.

He shook his head slightly and eyed the lead singer.

"It's rude to leave in the middle of an act, yea?"

Alex looked at the band. The lead had been working so hard that sweat soaked through the front of her dress. She could see way more than she'd paid for already. Her contact?

"Right." She released the bartender, walked to the end of the bar, and took a seat. The singer ended the song, told the crowd she'd be back for another set in a few minutes, and walked off the stage.

Alex watched her saunter around the room, giving clusters of people attention. Some more than others, some only a wave and a smile. Popular gal.

As the girl neared, Alex watched for a signal, but saw none.

Maybe she wasn't Alex's contact after all. Alex could have been confused after the day she'd had. She waited another moment anyway.

The singer walked in full stride, smiling at people as she passed them. When she finally reached Alex's seat, she stopped right next to her and leaned over the bar to order a drink. Close enough that Alex smelled her perfume. Peach and sandalwood—unmistakably Bois de Iles by Chanel. The same scent Jack had given her last year.

A flash of heat spread across Alex's back as her mind blinked with what could be happening to him right now. She steadied her thoughts, steering them back to the present moment. She had to focus if she was going to help him.

After the bartender handed the singer her drink, she turned with it in her hand, leaned close, whispered, "What are waiting you for?" and brushed past Alex.

About damned time.

Alex followed her to the back hallway, where the walls were lined with more baroque mirrors. After passing both loos, she stopped in front of a tall, thin black door at the end of the hall. You almost couldn't see it with the dismal lighting. She unbolted the door and slid the long steel rod aside. Then she turned and smiled, as she walked past Alex without a word.

The door opened, and a blast of cold air hit her in the face. Standing outside, at the bottom of an external stairwell, was her father.

Starting up the stairs, he said, "Let's go. We need to hurry."

"Where is he?" Lockard stalked across the floor, staring at the stupid Indian man surrounded by computer monitors. The screens flickered with red and green, echoing the city's Christmas lights flashing through the windows from far below.

Irony at its best.

"How did you get in? There is security for this," Randeep said. He looked like a brown mushroom with his thick head and tiny neck. Lockard wanted to split the man's face open with a fist.

"Where. Is. Draganic?" Lockard repeated.

"I am not knowing this," Randeep said, nerves thickening his accent. He wrung his hands and spun back around to look at his screens. He began typing furiously.

Lockard walked up behind him and slapped his head so hard that Randeep's face smacked the monitor before him, causing his nose to bleed.

"Stop! Stop this now! Are you a madman?" Randeep cried.

"Worse." Lockard spun him around by a shoulder and stared him down. "I want answers."

With blood trickling to his upper lip, Randeep began to shake. "I'm telling you, I do not know."

"Find him."

"You don't understand. We will lose it. We will lose all the money if I don't hurry."

Lockard picked up a stack of papers next to Randeep, scanned them. "How much are we in for?"

"Of what? The franc?"

Lockard blinked once. *Idiot.* "Yes, the franc, Pachai."

"A great amount."

Lockard focused his breathing to calm himself so he wouldn't tear the man's face from his skull. "Define 'great.'"

Randeep turned his gaze to the floor, nodded like a four-year-old caught with the proverbial cookie. "All of it."

"Christ." Lockard walked away, paced the room. "When's the Swiss council speaking?"

"Tomorrow. At Bundeshaus in Bern. It will cause a flood against the currency. This is why I must act."

"Can you unwind the trades by then?"

"I'm not having luck, no. Everyone is going against me. They know about the announcement." He pointed to a television screen above the computers. Though the sound was muted, subtitles scrolled on the bottom detailing the intent of the Swiss Federal Council to announce its consideration of joining the European Union.

Lockard nodded. That made it easy. A binary event. Either the council would make the announcement and they lose the billion dollars, or it wouldn't and they keep the billion.

Randeep said, "What should we do?"

"For now?" Lockard turned back around to him, walked closer, drew out his HK45, and shot Randeep in the face. "Nothing."

Her father drove fast as he spoke. "We had to be sure you weren't followed, you understand."

Sitting in the passenger seat of the Mercedes SUV, Alex glanced at Edgar as he sped them across the city. She paid close attention to where he was taking her, in case they had some sort of disagreement or separation. They had already bypassed Hyde Park and were traveling west of Victoria.

"We." She nodded. "The CIA owns the pub, then?"

"No affiliation to The Company. The owner is a personal…ally. He lets me use it for meet-ups from time to time."

"I see." So, her father had his own network of agents, cleanrooms, and safehouses. A completely separate *cell system*. Impressive. And she bet quite expensive.

He glanced at her. "You have good tradecraft. No tails for the last two days."

"Except you."

"I employ eyes."

"You mean Jack."

"Alex, what was the first damn thing they taught you at the Farm, long before Talonstrike?"

"Relax, father. I'll quarantine my emotion. I'm just making observations, analyzing the situation, *my* situation."

"Are you ready or not?"

"I am."

"Good. We're almost there."

They drove in silence for a few more minutes along the Thames, the city's echoes dampened by a thickening layer of snow. Alex gave up reflecting on her father for the time being, in favor of focusing on the task at hand. She still had not been briefed.

He pulled the Mercedes into a dark lot and shut off the engine. "We'll walk from here." Alex looked out the window. The local streets were all but empty of pedestrians, and Christmas lights flickered on storefronts and apartments across the river, giving a powerful atmosphere to the night. More pre-apocalyptic than romantic.

"How much time do we have?" She asked.

"Three hours, if it's on."

Giving him a sidelong glance, she said, "We're a bit early."

"We're late. I like to set up at least four hours in advance of a meet."

Alex felt as if Kim Philby and the Cambridge Five would emerge from the shadows any moment. Either that, or a meteor would hit the Earth, wiping out both her and the T-Rex behind the wheel.

"Edgar, they have technology these days allowing spies to bypass hours of field waiting. You know, satellites and listening devices? Even remote cameras. London is littered with CCTV."

"Technology is unreliable. Never underestimate traditional methods."

Right.

"Are you hungry?" he asked. "I brought some fruit. It's in a bag in the back."

"I'm touched."

He stopped, turned, eyed her. "Alex."

"Edgar."

"Honey, I've thought about this moment for many years, not sure it would ever even come. And I know that whatever I say right now will sound trite."

Alex stared at him for a while, not moving. She imagined his face disappearing on a page and then reappearing line by line. Stroke by stroke. She wondered which of the lines were created purely by living and which were the result of living a life of lies. The deep-set eyes darkened in her image and the face became drawn, pulled by the force of gravity.

She said, "Trite, like calling me honey?"

He sighed. "There're two steel containers of coffee on the floor." He thumbed the backseat. "And some gloves. You'll need them."

Alex grabbed the gloves and thermoses and handed him one. "Tell me the plan."

"First, I want to brief you on the background." Edgar reached into his jacket and pulled out a fold of papers, then clicked on the overhead light. "You need to know the basis for all of this."

He sipped his coffee as Alex read a printout of an Associated Press newspaper article titled "Cash Vanishes in Iraq." The photo in the article showed a US Marine, about eighteen, maybe twenty years old, grinning as he leaned against a shipping pallet. Atop the pallet were stacks and stacks of shrink-wrapped packages of money.

A veritable shit ton of it.

"How much is there?" She asked.

"Each pallet is over a hundred million. Records show that we sent fifty of them, straight from the coffers of the US Treasury."

"For what purpose, exactly?"

"To pay the Iraqi government, their soldiers, and our own independent contractors."

"In cash? Brilliant. And that's what this is about? They lost a pallet?" Alex pictured the briefcase in Edgar's research room back at his house, the money spilling over the edge. It was a pittance compared to that pallet of cash.

"According to the Pentagon and a Congress-appointed independent auditor, they've all been located and accounted for."

"But you think they're lying."

"My sources tell me that eight are still missing." He stared at her. "Over a billion dollars in cash. Vanished."

Sitting back, Alex stared out the windshield as a few more lines of this operation's landscape appeared to her. Big ones. Foundation lines.

"The bombing. It wasn't about the briefcase, was it? It was about the pilot."

Edgar nodded. "He was stationed as an American ally for the Royal Air Force in Iraq. He went on leave the same day that Lockard and the SEALs supposedly died."

"He flew the money out for them," she said.

"Just another loose end to Lockard." The man who now had Jack.

Alex shuddered.

People killed each other just for money in a wallet. Imagine what they'd do for a billion dollars. *Cash.* That was enough money to spend a million dollars a year for a *thousand* years. If you invested it and made only five percent interest annually, you would make fifty million. Per year. *Forever.*

Holy shit.

Edgar said, "Money will make people do strange things. Often evil things."

Alex glanced at him and away. Thinking of the house near the river, the townhouse in London, and the hundred-thousand-dollar cars. "Was that it for you? An offer you couldn't refuse?"

"This isn't about me."

"Then what?" She turned her gaze to him.

He started to respond, but stopped a couple of times. Then he said, "Look, Alex, I knew I wasn't a very good father. I knew Ginger would be a better parent for you than I ever could. That's why I chose this path."

"You could have tried."

"I missed the first five years of your life. Don't you remember?"

"I remember seeing you when you came home."

"That wasn't very often."

"It was more often than never."

He nodded and looked out the side window. "That wasn't an option for me. Not in this line of work. I had the advantage of being dead. It allowed me to do things I could never do as a regular agent. It was a chance of a lifetime. And not just for me. For the United States."

"You could have assumed an alias like the rest of us do."

"And you know how that's recorded in The Company. All the way up the line. Too many eyes, even on SCI folders."

He was talking about Sensitive Compartmented Information. Special clearance granted to only a handful of CIA agents or members of Congress. "You did this for internal anonymity?"

"That was a major part of it."

Alex thought about that for a moment. "So...you, what? Spy on our own spies?"

"Mainly, yes."

She shook her head. "Then who the hell is your handler?"

"Moss." He tapped the wheel. "It was Tippet before that. And Flint before him."

"The Director of Clandestine, whoever it is at the time, then."

Edgar nodded. "It's all passed through a verbal handoff. It's not on the books, it's not triple classified or top secret, it's not locked away in some safe somewhere for untrustworthy eyes to see. I am eternally persona non grata." He leaned back and took a swig of his coffee. "No record of me in Langley or even the DNI's office."

Ever since 9/11, the director of the CIA reported to the director of national intelligence. The DNI, well, he was appointed by and reported to only one individual. "What about the president?"

"Plausible deniability." Edgar shrugged.

A total black op. For two decades. Longer, if there were others before him.

"And Jack?"

"He's former MI6."

"But he's one of yours now."

He nodded, and with the barest hint of emotion, said, "And he's in trouble, Alex. We all are."

"Then what's our plan?"

"I have a source I need to meet with. He may lead us to Jack. But I need you to stay in the background." He looked out the windshield. "You need to know more. You need to know everything. That's what traditionalists like me call deep intelligence. And it starts with knowing yourself, particularly knowing what you *don't* know. It won't only save your career, it will save your life."

Perhaps realizing he was being cryptic, he turned away and opened the door. "Unless it goes terribly wrong."

As Alex watched him exit the car, she thought, *Hasn't it already?*

Jack lay exposed in the iron tub, his mouth still dry, his head aching, and his stomach and chest slick with sweat.

Lockard had turned up the heat.

He didn't know how long he'd been there. Most of a day and maybe part of a night, he figured, though he kept slipping in and out of consciousness with fatigue and dehydration and whatever Lockard had drugged him with.

About to nod off again, he heard a clack and the door swing open behind him.

The blade came into view before Lockard's face did. Serrated and with a black rubber handle, it looked like a navy-issue MK3, maybe the one Lockard had used as a SEAL. A hard plastic sheath was hooked to the waist of his pants.

Lockard stood over Jack and turned the blade in his hand, the sharp silver edge flickering in the dim light. He watched Lockard with the anticipation of a patient waiting for his doctor to reveal the diagnosis. How bad was it going to be? Just painful, or fatal?

Lockard pressed the tip to Jack's belly and Jack held his breath, tightened his abs as Lockard traced around his belly button and down to his pubic bone. Barely breaking the skin, he left a thin white line that slowly turned to bright red.

Jack closed his eyes in relief. If Lockard was going to gut him, he'd already have done it.

"Have you reconsidered?" Lockard asked.

"Reconsidered what?"

"Helping me. Helping yourself."

"The sort of help you need requires a clinical psychologist."

Lockard pressed the tip of the knife into the center of Jack's bellybutton, and Jack felt a searing pain as the blade sliced into the unbearably soft flesh. After a moment, blood pooled into the bellybutton. Lockard said, "Be careful. I'm not in the mood."

"Then what do you want?"

"The briefcase."

"For God's sake, I told you. I've no idea where it is."

"Bullshit!" He grabbed the back of Jack's head and pulled him forward, pressing the blade to Jack's neck.

Jack gritted his teeth and stared at Lockard's face from the corners of his eyes. "Even if I am lying, you shouldn't kill me."

"You don't seem to understand the severity of your situation. You don't know what you are fucking with. Who you are fucking with." Lockard moved his grip to Jack's neck, and tightened his fingers like an industrial vise.

As Jack's breath left him, he realized what Lockard was doing. With a wide, steely grip, he pressed a thumb on one carotid and his middle finger on the other. He tried to turn away, loosen Lockard's hold, but the man overpowered him like a machine. Jack twisted and groaned, but the image of Lockard over him turned to black as Jack's vision began to fade.

Jack tightened his abs, pushed his torso forward, but it was no use. With Jack's arms still restrained above him, Lockard had him in an impossible position.

Jack twisted and pushed, Lockard gripped tighter. Tighter.

Seconds later, the room abruptly fell to blackness.

When Jack came to again, Lockard was on top of him. Jack's naked back was pressed to the floor, and his numbed hands were secured underneath him and bound with duct tape. One knee on each side of Jack, Lockard had him pinned tight. He had moved Jack from the bathroom to a small room with lacquered hardwood floors, tall ceilings, and rich baroque detailing. It was cold and damp and empty of furniture.

Jack could feel Lockard's breath on his face. It smelled bitter, like stale coffee.

Lockard moved his hand and a cold plate of steel pressed against Jack's cheek. The barrel of his HK45.

"Jack," he said, "your position just got worse."

Jack laughed—maybe he was losing his mind, but he couldn't help it—and then decided he should cool it. He didn't need this psycho too pissed off. Not yet. Jack had to figure out how to get him irritated enough to make a mistake, first. Then Jack could take him.

"You find it funny?" Lockard pressed the barrel of the pistol to Jack's forehead.

Jack watched as Lockard stared into his face before letting his gaze move to his body. He said, "I like the little blonde hairs on your body. The way they glisten with your sweat."

Jack reminded himself that this was part of the game. The purpose of keeping him naked was to make Jack feel self-conscious, vulnerable. Undressed, literally, by another man, he was supposed to feel humiliated.

So why was Jack starting to get the feeling that Lockard was serious?

The man leaned back and looked at Jack's groin then licked his lips. "Yes, you are a specimen to the last hair."

Okay. If he was serious, Jack could use that to his advantage. Sexual attraction or desire was the sort of emotion that made an opponent slip up.

Jack clenched his jaw to keep from smiling. He'd endured worse tests in military intelligence training. He could still take this psycho. Even from here. Even naked.

Jack centered his energy, prepared himself for the coming fight.

"Tell me where it is. Now."

"Or?" Jack knew it would provoke him, but he needed to change his position, to adjust the leverage.

"Or this."

Lockard widened Jack's legs with his feet, opening him up. Threatening him.

Jack stayed centered, coiled his energy rather than fighting that first move.

But Jack needed Lockard to lean forward just a bit more, enough to give him room for a reversal. Jack whispered, "I said fuck off," and Lockard took the bait.

Leaning forward, he whispered, "How about I fuck you?"

Jack timed it to the fraction of a second and the window of an inch. As Lockard leaned, Jack bucked, tipping the center of their collective weight from his lower back to his shoulders and gaining the necessary momentum to throw Lockard forward.

Lockard rolled off Jack with a thud and spun to a knee, pistol raised and pointed at his chest as Jack thrust his hands below his feet, bringing them to his front, then sprang upright.

He wouldn't shoot him, Jack told himself, and took the risk.

Spinning low, Jack drew a lunge from Lockard's punching hand, allowing Jack to kick the pistol from the other hand and causing it to tumble across the floor. Then Jack spun left and raised a right heel high, arching all the way back and hammering Lockard's skull with a crack.

Lockard tumbled forward just as Jack finished his momentum, and before he could regain his balance, Lockard punched his stabilizing leg.

Jumping upon impact, Jack avoided falling back. Then he countered, leveling a leg parallel to the floor, and thrusting forward with his heel aimed at Lockard's stomach.

Lockard grasped Jack's foot as he fell backward, pinning it between his forearms. Using his weight and strength, he took Jack with him, twisting and pulling him down.

In a single body roll, Lockard spun Jack and fell atop him on the floor.

Damnit.

Lockard slammed Jack's face on the ground and drove a knee in his spine.

"That was a mistake, Pope."

No, the mistake would be to stop now. But before he could try again, Lockard choked Jack with his forearm, pulling his neck up and back. Jack wedged a row of fingers underneath and managed a quarter of an inch of breathing room. He wouldn't submit. He wouldn't give in. Jack pulled at the psycho-SEAL's grip as the oxygen escaped him, and Lockard tightened, digging the knee into Jack back, pulling Jack's head and neck up further.

"Tell me!"

The white of the sun faded as Jack's vision began to turn gray. Then black.

He bucked, and Lockard drove the butt of the pistol into the back of Jack's skull. "You will tell me." He released the chokehold and slammed Jack's cheek against the wood floor again, blasting a bright yellow and black star in his vision.

But Lockard was off him.

Jack said, "You're losing this fight."

Jack moved to roll over, and Lockard said, "Am I?"

Then Jack felt Lockard drag him backward across the room. His genitals scraped across the waxy floor, burning the skin. Jack pushed up with his bound fists, but Lockard kicked him down again.

Jack tried to spin, to look back, but Lockard stopped dragging then speared Jack's spine with a knee.

And then Jack felt him, Lockard's cold fingers between Jack's legs. "Then how can I do this?"

Jack twisted his head to see. *His pants. Are they off? Is this still a humiliation game? Or is he—?*

Then Jack felt it. Lockard was separating his buttocks.

It was too late.

Lockard pressed against Jack's entry and he felt it was cold. Lockard pushed. And Jack froze. Unable to move a millimeter. Unable to breathe.

It was the barrel of his gun. Between his legs. At the edge of his anus.

And Lockard pressed it further, into him.

It hurt and Jack tightened against it, but in this position, bound and face down, he was defenseless. A man at the mercy of the brute strength of another.

Lockard left it there. Made Jack feel it inside him.

Bile rose in Jack's throat to match the burn he felt from the barrel of the pistol. He swallowed it down. Tried not to move a single millimeter as his mind swarmed. He'd read countless times about how some women just lay there as they are being raped, paralyzed with fear, gripped with the thought that they just wanted it to end. They just wanted to make it all disappear. For the life of him, he could never understand that feeling.

Until now.

But he couldn't just lay there. He had to fight back. Even if it was fatal.

Then Lockard shifted positions. He'd leaned close enough that Jack could feel his breath on his neck as he said, "It looks as though you like this."

And Jack realized that he must be looking halfway back behind him. And if so, he had finally fucked up.

With the last of his will, the final ounces of his energy, Jack thrust his hands straight back over his head, pounding the back of his fists into Lockard's temple, and twisted to the side. Releasing himself from the violation.

The pistol fired with a loud *bang*, sending a bullet into the floor.

Lockard rolled along with Jack as he spun, but Jack moved his arms as fast as he could, as far as they would go. As they rolled over again, Jack grabbed the knife from the rubber sheath.

Lockard forced Jack onto his back and pressed a forearm to his neck. Then Jack thrust the knife down, spearing Lockard's other hand into the floor.

Lockard yelled and Jack slipped from beneath him.

Lockard yelled again, leveling a flat-footed blow to Jack's chest. Jack was hurtled across the room, and his back and head slammed into the corner of the wall.

Blinking and gasping for a breath, the wind blown out of him, Jack watched Lockard place the Glock down and pry the knife from the floor, from the flesh between his bones.

Breathing hard and shaking his head, Lockard looked at the hole in his hand, blood streaming down his elbow onto the floor. He raised the Glock, pointed it at Jack's head.

He stood stone still as Lockard let his aim lower to Jack's abdomen, then a few inches further.

A boom echoed in the small room.

Jack waited for the searing pain of a gunshot in his groin, but it didn't come.

Lockard had shot between his legs.

Lockard stepped forward and thrust a heel into Jack's stomach, driving him to the floor. "You will soon wish I'd killed you."

Then Lockard turned and left the room, locking Jack inside.

Jack thinking, *Unless I kill you first.*

Thirty

As expected, her father had devised a meet straight out of a Cold War spy novel, complete with lookouts, listening devices, and a bridge. All he had to do was make a call to set it in motion. Alex restrained herself from pointing out that he'd have to use a cell phone, modern-day technology, to do that.

Edgar's contact could lead them to Lockard and Jack, but it was someone he obviously didn't fully trust. Alex knew he couldn't let on to that, though. He had to act like it was as normal as the sunset to see this person alone. The nuance could be the difference between getting information or not. Between life or death.

Taking a circuitous route along the side streets, they made their way to the walkway parallel to the Thames, the predawn sounds of nearby traffic muted by the accumulation of snow, snowflakes melting on their faces as they followed the path. Her father said, "Settle in and just listen, unless I give the signal." He would use the word *retribution* if he needed backup or sensed something was wrong.

"I've done this before, Dad."

"Prague, last winter."

"Wait. How'd you—"

"Who do you think was waiting for your signal?" He pulled his trench coat closed and belted it.

Alex stared at him for a moment and decided not to even respond.

She reached to her back and touched the butt of the SIG. She had thirteen rounds left after engaging Lockard earlier. On a battlefield that would be minuscule; in a spy meet it was nearly infinite. Edgar hadn't told her yet whom he was meeting, and she knew better than to ask. This business was built on information compartmentalization. He had a reason for keeping that to himself and she had to respect that reason. When Alex was a rookie agent, this kind of secrecy had driven her crazy. Later, once she was in the position of compartmentalizing herself, she understood.

"That's the meeting site." Halting behind a lamppost, her father stared out at the Millennium Bridge. The footbridge's long steel piping, steel foot grates, and steel cables, caused it to resemble a giant creature's spinal column. Green plates of glass capped off stairwells at each end, and every corner of the structure held a pocket of snow.

As Alex studied the meet's entries and exits, a man approached from the darkness to their right. Hunched over and carrying a bag full of oranges, he had thick dreadlocks that grew right into a tangle of a beard. He looked cold and his face was drawn to his cheekbones, as if he had been eating nothing but scraps for years.

Her father stepped deeper into the shadows.

Alex stepped forward and met the man's gaze as she reached into her jeans. She handed him a twenty-pound note, folding away the queen and her jeweled crown.

With the tiniest watery eyes, the man stared at the bill and merely smiled as he stuffed it into his own pocket. Then he turned and walked down the stairs beside the footbridge, shivering with his oranges.

"That was kind," her father said.

"Least I could do."

"And reckless. He could be eyes for someone."

Alex watched the man disappear around the bend of the stairwell. "He didn't look like he was pretending to be starving."

"Let's get to work." Her father pointed east, to the far side of the bridge. "I expect my contact will be coming from there. The best place for you will be at the bottom of the stairs on this side." He pointed to where the concrete support plates came together and formed a small dark wedge at ground level.

"Fine," Alex said, peering at a cardboard box and blanket jutting from the opposite nook.

Her father held out a hand. "Got that drawing?"

She pulled the sketchbook from her overcoat pocket and tore out the page with Lockard's half profile. Handing it to Edgar, Alex thought of Jack with that man and what he could be doing to get what he wanted.

She said, "About Jack."

"He wasn't supposed to fall for you." Her father pocketed the drawing and stared at her. "That wasn't the plan."

Alex nodded, believing that Jack was not a *raven*—the male version of a female spy known as a *swallow*. She'd have caught onto him if he'd seen her as a target. If he were using sex to pry secrets from her. She hoped.

She said, "It was you who told him to back off."

"Yes."

Alex blinked once. "You were right to do what you did."

"I know."

Looking out to the icy water, she shrugged. "I mean, this was your calling. Not fatherhood." Alex turned to walk to her hiding spot.

Her father touched her shoulder and stopped her.

"Alex, I lived in a world of mistrust, spies, and double spies. I didn't know how to be a father. I didn't know how to live in that world. I meant to protect you from mine."

"And yet..." she gestured around them with a small laugh. "Like father, like daughter, I suppose."

"Let's hope not."

They stood there, the flakes drifting to the path around them, silent, until a siren sounded nearby.

"One more thing." Her father leaned to her and with his face down, almost on Alex's shoulder, he whispered, "If something happens here—you wind up back in the middle—you don't know where the briefcase is. Period."

"Dad, I don't know."

He stared at her, a confused look on his face. "Just tell them that." He turned and walked away.

Did she?

Alex pulled on her gloves then made her way under the bridge and settled into the shadow, noting the blanket from around the corner had been tugged from view. Glancing at her watch, she counted just under three hours until the appointed time for Edgar's source to arrive. That gave her plenty of time to think, and with nothing but the city sounds and river flowing near her, she let the events of the last few days flow with them. Lockard, Draganic, the SEALs.

Alex rubbed her hands together in the damp cold, breathing into them and watching the walkway above. Few people were wandering around at this hour, though a drunk couple staggered near her and up the stairwell then across the bridge, their laughs muted by the snowfall, their footfalls traced in it.

One thing Alex had a hard time wrapping her brain around was the billion-dollar bounty. Not only the value, but the sheer size and weight, the physicality of it. Yet as she tried to picture the cash, a few more aspects of the operation's landscape formed for her. The mental sketch she had created filled in and the corners of the drawing appeared, began to take shape.

First, Draganic. According to Interpol, the Serbian Whale was the most cunning money launderer in all of Europe. As a CIA man stationed in Eastern Europe before the Middle East, Lockard would have known this. Maybe he'd even crossed paths with Draganic a time or two. He would have found a way to cut the man a deal for his participation. A billion dollars is a whole lot easier to move once it's in the banking system and Draganic was the key to that. So was the Isle of Man.

But what had gone wrong between Draganic and Lockard? Someone had clearly betrayed the other. Or maybe they both did. Like her father said, money made people do strange things. And a billion dollars? Well, that could turn someone bat-shit crazy, couldn't it?

In any case, if Alex found Draganic, she'd find Lockard.

With thirty minutes until the meet, Alex placed the listening device in her left ear. Paired with a device inside Edgar's trench coat, the earbud allowed her to hear everything in real time.

Alex wondered what deep intelligence Edgar was looking to gain with this meet and how it would it lead to Jack. How would it help fill in the rest of the drawing?

And as she sat there, the minutes ticking off, the last half hour scrolling by, an epiphany hit, the kind that shifts the ground below you, changing your world forever. Like finding out you weren't really an orphan. Like finding out your lover was spying on you for your father.

For the third time in as many days, the Earth's plates moved beneath Alex.

Lockard was not involved by chance. He was connected to her, to her father. He was connected so deeply in this that there was only one way he could have the inside intelligence to pull off one of the greatest thefts in history.

It's why her father didn't tell Alex who he was meeting with, why he had kept her in the shadows but nearby. To believe it, she'd have to hear it for herself.

A set of footfalls echoed across the bridge and stopped. Her father said, "I'm in position and my contact is nearing. Stay alert."

Alex didn't bother answering. Edgar was not wearing an earpiece.

Another set of footfalls clanked on the metal grates of the bridge, and by the time they stopped, Alex was shaking. A searing, throbbing anger started in her chest and gripped her throat. She felt foolish, vulnerable, enraged, and ready to kill, all at the same time.

How could she have not seen it before? It had been right in front of her the whole time.

The answer came: her father had been protecting her from it.

And then the man spoke, and Alex's life as she knew was over.

"You Winters just keep getting in the way," Deputy Director William Moss said.

"No protection? The DDO came alone? Why, Bill?" A scuffing noise, like thumping static, sounded in the microphone; her father shifting his arms as he spoke.

"Christ, Edgar...just give me the briefcase. Finish this mission and get back in the field." Moss's voice was loud and clear. He was facing her father. Probably had his hands in his long gray overcoat, like he did when walking into the offices on cold winter days at Langley.

"Not yet."

"Where is it? Tell me you brought the goddamn thing."

"We need to talk, Bill."

"About what?"

"Alex."

"What about her?"

"Not what. *Why*...her?"

A few moments of silence passed and then Moss laughed. "C'mon Edgar, it's in the genes. Of course I'd use her to track my most skilled—and therefore most dangerous—asset. She was my insurance against you."

"You knew I'd burn myself, blow my cover for your tracker. Otherwise my own daughter would be left in that restaurant with the others. A bomb, one keystroke away."

And there it was. The bastard Moss had placed Alex right in the middle of a war zone. Used her not as much as a pawn, more like bait. And if the target didn't take the bait, then she would have died.

"Don't tell me you're getting sentimental in your years, Edgar. She may be related to you, but you said yourself, you don't even know her."

"You went too far this time."

"Think about it Edgar. A billion dollars. It would have been so easy to cut you in on a slice."

"I don't want a penny of your blood money."

"Which is how I knew you couldn't be trusted in the first place."

"I can't say I'm shocked. Nothing you do could surprise me anymore."

"Good. Business is business. Now—"A flash of static, then, "—is that it? Can we get down to today's business?"

"Not quite yet. See, I've been thinking about it all, and there's something that I just can't reconcile. Like a timeline that doesn't quite match up when a spouse is out of town. Or a cash register that's a few dollars short one night. A simple discrepancy, but an important one. One that nags at you. Tells you there's something larger behind it. An affair, a dishonest employee. A lie."

"Our lives are built on lies."

"Our lives are also destroyed by them."

"What the hell's your point?"

"That night. When—" a loud scraping noise and then the hollow echo of Edgar's voice "—at El Descanso."

Then a massive pop blared in Alex's eardrum and she tore the listening device out.

She leaned forward and caught the glimpse of a foot—Edgar's boot—using a toe to crush something into the walkway. The microphone.

Damn it. Don't shut me out again. *Not now.*

Alex hurried from the shadows, stalked to the end of the footbridge, and pulled off the gloves. Then she drew out the SIG and bent back down as she listened to the soft echo of the two men's voices. The metal slide felt cold against her bare hand but couldn't make out a word they were saying.

Until Moss yelled, "Give me the goddamn briefcase!"

A loud shuffling noise sounded, and then the sound of two slides being jerked back—rounds being loaded into pistol chambers.

Alex moved to the top of the stairs, careful to stay hidden below the top stair but in a spot she could hear them without echo.

Moss said, "What? Are we going to shoot one another over something that happened decades ago?"

"We all should have died that day, Bill. Starting with you."

A boom sounded and then another.

Shit. Alex crested the top stair, SIG drawn. Trying to make out the figures, blurry through the green glass.

Both men staggered back. Moss, hand raised, gun pointed at her father. Another shot blazed from Moss's pistol. Alex fired through the green glass before her, causing Moss to turn his head.

Stumbling backwards, her father shot Moss again and then toppled over the railing, into the icy water below.

Alex sprinted up the last of the stairs and across the walkway. Moss lay crumpled against the wires below the railing. His Beretta had fallen from his hand and a pool of blood bloomed in the snow below him. His eyes were open and he was gasping for breath, blood seeping between his gloved hands. He turned his head, looked at Alex, and said, "Help."

Darting across the footpath, Alex yanked off her overcoat and kicked off her boots. She climbed onto the steel railing and searched the river below. Nothing. The blocks of ice were almost stagnant, so he couldn't have gone far. She took a deep breath. Told herself she could do it. She'd hesitated once and regretted it. Besides, her father would do it for her.

Right?

Alex willed the thought away, closed her eyes, took another deep breath, and dove.

Forget the training in the cold Pacific. Fuck *the water's toasty* bullshit.

This was agony.

Alex's body immediately began to shake as she peered deep into the inky water, swimming furiously, reaching out her arms, searching for her father right below the surface. Blackness spread below her and sparkling white ice floated above. She spun and searched and swam and spun again, and again. Then, knowing she'd kill herself if she stayed under any longer, Alex surfaced.

Her muscles began to lock up and she gasped frigid air as she fought her way through the slushy water to the edge of the river. Spasming, Alex hauled herself up onto a concrete piling. Blinking and shaking, the cold overtaking her body, she tried to sit up but couldn't move. Her feet and hands were numb, her strength annihilated by the dive. Her internal temperature had dropped to severe levels; her nervous system was shutting down. Alex was going to black out. If she didn't warm up soon, she was going to die. And just as she had the thought, her vision blurring, Alex saw him. Wandering toward her and hauling his blanket over a shoulder.

Right before her vision faded, the homeless man took the blanket off his back and wrapped it around her.

Thirty-One

Natasha paced in the kitchen, holding a coffee cup. She hadn't had a sip in over twenty minutes. Still, she cradled the cup like it was a Fabergé egg. She supposed it was her nervousness that kept her from drinking any more caffeine that morning.

Her mind was occupied with the task at hand.

She wanted nothing more than to leave this prison of boredom in Gstaad. There was nothing to do up here if one didn't like to ski, and she hated it. The cold, the snow, the drunken celebrities, obnoxious and entitled. Boring beyond belief. But the good thing was that the house, a new construction with solid floors, was quiet and didn't creak.

This would help her succeed in the small exchange. The tiny betrayal was dwarfed by Zoran's offenses, but still, if he caught her, who knew what he would do.

Natasha stopped pacing and stared at the snow-draped trees outside the kitchen window, listening for sounds in the room above her. Zoran had been camped in that office for over four hours. He had made phone calls, turned the television louder, then softer, then changed the channel. He opened the safe and closed it, then opened it again. He'd left the office only once, stomping across the house to the bedroom and retrieving a black duffel bag, one she didn't even know he had. Strange things, this man did. Maybe he was filling it up with toys for his next escapade. His next romp with the runway sluts.

Finally, Natasha had all but given up, retreating to the kitchen to wait him out. After dumping the coffee into the sink, she retrieved the phone from her purse.

A small Blackberry, the same make and model as Zoran's, the phone was also scratched along the side and at the corner of the display. A perfect replica that the man named Evan Lockard had left in the glove compartment of her Jaguar.

How had he done that?

She had left her vehicle parked in the Gstaad house garage while she was in the Turks, and when she returned, *voilà*. The phone was sitting there. Lockard had bypassed the house's security system, somehow entered the garage without disturbing any doors or windows, and slipped into her vehicle to hide it for her.

He was like some sort of spirit, this man.

Thinking about this, Natasha finally heard Zoran's clumsy footsteps in the hall above her. He was walking away from the office and to the bedroom.

Still holding the replica, she hurried across the kitchen and, kicking off her heels, toed her way up the stairs and into the hall. She stopped there and listened. Zoran was speaking to someone; he must have been on his precious phone.

If that damn thing had tits, he'd marry it.

Leaning against the wall, wondering if she should sneak back downstairs, Natasha closed her eyes. This was very stressful, this part. All to catch this man doing something wrong, something illegal. Something that would put the bastard back into prison and free her from him for good. The listening device that Lockard had placed in the replica phone would solve everything for Natasha.

She would soon be free.

Then she heard it. The water running in the master bathroom.

Finally, her chance. Zoran was stepping into the shower. Surely he couldn't take his little electronic lover inside there with him. Maybe he left it on the bed.

Listening closely, Natasha tiptoed closer to the bedroom. From what she could tell, Zoran was fumbling in the walk-in closet for clothes. Natasha peered around the doorway, but pulled back just as Zoran exited the closet, carrying a dark suit and a pair of black dress shoes.

Holding her breath, Natasha listened from the edge of the doorway.

She could do this, she told herself. She must do this. Someone had to stop this despicable man. This animal. This grotesque beast. He had to be caught doing his illegal things.

Natasha would be the one to do it.

His footfalls slapped against the tile floor of the bathroom, the glass shower door creaked open, then clicked closed.

Taking a deep breath, Natasha gathered her resolve and darted into the bedroom.

The charcoal suit lay spread across the bed, stark against the white, pure down duvet and soft, purple cashmere throw Natasha had bought for the bed last year. She wondered how many whores he had fucked on this bed. Her bed.

Her cashmere throw was probably crusted with fluids.

Natasha banished the thought as she hurried to the other side of the bed and searched the side table, under the jacket, in the closet. Where was the phone? Where had he left the damn thing? He was just talking on it!

After checking the side-table drawers and the top drawers in the closet dressers, she found nothing.

Dammit.

Tiptoeing back across the bedroom carpet, she peeked from the doorway of the bathroom and, sure enough, there it was sitting at the edge of the sink, his sink. His precious Blackberry.

Three feet from the shower.

This was it, though. He was obviously leaving after the shower. This was Natasha's last chance.

Palming the replica in her hand, she now wished she weren't wearing this damn skin-tight dress. If she'd been wearing pants, she could have hidden it in a pocket. But pants made her thighs look puffy. In contrast, the dresses accented her boobs. Her boobs were fantastic, too, the best part of her.

She stepped into the bathroom, careful to keep the replica against her left leg, out of view of Zoran, and heard him startle in the shower.

"What do you want?"

"I am needing something."

"What?" He stood behind the water-speckled glass, facing her with his hands on both hips, no shame, giving her a full display of his swollen gut, with gray and black hairs covering his body up to his chest and over his shoulders. A bushel of it over his shriveled *kolbasa*.

Natasha kept walking forward, straight to the counter, and said, "I am looking for my lip gloss. I think I left it in here."

"Right now?"

"Yes, I am going outside of the house."

"Good. Go." He turned around and poured a glop of shampoo in one hand and rubbed his almost bald head with it. What did he need so much shampoo for? This man had more hair on his ass than his head.

Thankful he had turned, though, Natasha opened the cabinet and watched him from the corner of her eye as she reached across to pick up his phone. Just as her arm extended across his sink and her fingers touched the device, he yelled, "Shut that door. It's cold in here!"

Natasha jerked, knocking Zoran's phone off the counter and onto the floor, its battery case popping open and the battery skittering across the tile and under the toilet.

"You idiot! Get it and fix it! And make sure your hands aren't wet!"

Breathing hard, her heart pounding against her chest, Natasha felt her face turn as red as borscht. "Why are you insisting on placing it so close to the edge? It is the fault of your own!" she yelled back as she bent over, still hiding the replica phone in her left hand.

"The battery—don't forget to put that back in!" Zoran was wiping shampoo off his face with one hand and pointing with the other, watching Natasha.

"I know, I know!" she said, placing the replica phone on the tile next to her foot.

She picked up the battery and replaced it as fast as she could. She snapped the back cover on as Zoran mumbled "idiot" again. Watching him from the corner of her eye, she quickly picked up the replica and switched it with the other phone.

"What is that?" he called, pressing his face and finger against the glass.

"What is what?" Natasha said, kneeling over Zoran's phone, not sure how he could have seen it.

"That! Right there! Did you move my razor? Leave it where it was!"

"I have never touched that razor," she said, relieved, but wondering if she should stand or wait until he turned again.

"Put the phone back and leave me in peace in here."

"Whatever." Natasha stood, placing the replica next to the razor while gripping his phone against her leg.

"Good girl," he called from the shower.

Natasha felt his stare on her as she walked out of the bathroom, covering the real phone under her hand at her side the best she could, hoping it would not ring as she fled.

When she made it into the bedroom, Natasha finally exhaled, ran down the stairs and into the kitchen while thinking, *Who is the idiot now, Zoran?*

Thirty-Two

Still damp and shaking under her overcoat, Alex had used most of her remaining strength to trudge along Victoria Embankment and down Strand to the Savoy Hotel. Convincing the front desk clerk to give her a room at three a.m. consumed the rest of her depleted energy. Money talks, though, and with the Amanda Carr credit card as security, the clerk found it within himself to let her pay with cash a full night's fee for the eight hours she needed.

What a gentleman.

In the shower, hands still blue and stiff, Alex contemplated losing her father again. She found it difficult to grieve for him a second time. Alex figured she was suppressing her true feelings about the situation. In a sense, lying to herself. Or maybe she had just shifted into pure survival mode.

Alex checked her phone, but there were no messages from Jack or Lockard. So, after finishing her shower, she dried her clothes with an iron and lay on the bed to collect a couple hours of fitful sleep, enough to be able to think again.

But all her mind did was spin. She climbed back out of bed, slipped the passport case out of her overcoat, and looked at the *pocket litter* Edgar had given her. Cash, passport, and a Barclay's ATM card, along with a stash of receipts, as if she'd been actively using the cards and identity.

If something happens here…you don't know where the briefcase is.

Her first thought was that the Barclay's card was not just for cash. Maybe her father had also rented a safe deposit box under the Amanda Carr name. But British banks had all but given up on maintaining safe deposit boxes, and Barclay's was no exception. A quick phone call to the branch nearest the hotel confirmed the bank had not accepted new safe deposit box clients in over two years.

Alex slid the archaic phone book from under the night table and opened to the Security section. She scanned the page, looking for any identifier, any detail at all, and stopped on a firm called Hatton Garden Safe Deposit, Ltd.

Hatton Garden.

Alex fingered the receipts one by one: a few restaurants, a clothing receipt from Debenhams, Starbucks, Prêt A Manger, and then the one she was looking for, Hatton Garden Jewelers. A receipt for watch repair. *Son of a bitch*—the address was 90 Hatton Garden. Right next door to Hatton Garden Safe Deposit at 88 Hatton Garden.

It took Alex just enough time to walk the fifteen blocks to reach Hatton Garden at opening time, where she was buzzed into a small, marble-walled receiving area. The entrance was lined with thick black iron bars behind a glass plate. After another buzz, Alex was received by a tall, humorless English man in a thick-knotted tie and hard-creased suit.

In the administrative area, a place that could double as a Customs and Immigration center, the man verified her identity as Amanda Carr. Then, with the same skepticism that a Royal Guard might use on a palace visitor, he said, "Follow me."

He led Alex down a double staircase into the basement, where another man used a key and a retina scanner to unlock a large, thick vault door. The humorless man ignored the security guard stationed next to the vault door as he led her into the chamber. They walked along the wall of numbered safe drawers, and he stopped when they reached a line of vault doors.

"There is a viewing room located behind us, if you require privacy in your review." He pointed to an open door and walked away.

Standing before the six-foot-tall door, Alex stared at the keypad. It was electronic and required five numbers. Her father wouldn't just lead her to this spot to allow Alex to fumble around with birthdays or phone numbers or other significant sequences in her life. That would draw attention from the security guard watching from the small, purple-glassed ceiling dome. No, her father would have laid it out for Alex, clear and concise.

She opened her passport case and fished out the Hatton Garden Jewelers receipt. The ticket had an identifier number at the top, but it was only four numbers and a dash, then a letter. No good. But there, at the bottom, the cost of the watch repair was 112.97 pounds. She placed the receipt back into her wallet, pressed 1-1-2-9-7, and a moment later, the vault lock clicked.

Smiling up at the eye in the sky, Alex pulled open the door.

Sure enough, the only item inside, sitting on the floor in the center of the safe, was an aluminum Zero Halliburton attaché. She took it to the viewing room, and closed the door.

Heart thumping a bit harder than it'd been a few minutes earlier, Alex flipped up the thin panel under the attaché's handle and looked at the three-number combination. It was set to all zeros. She pressed the button and two more buttons popped up along the front of the attaché's seam. No guesswork here. Alex was the only one who could have gotten this far.

She pressed those two buttons and the case eased open.

Staring at the contents, she realized she'd been holding her breath the entire time inside this little room, an absolute violation of standard operations—a good way to become lightheaded or weak in a life or death situation, and a bad habit otherwise. So Alex forced herself to breathe easily. Not that anything was easy about looking at a dead man's severed, and strangely hairless, hand.

Logistically and medically, it didn't make sense. The briefcase was not refrigerated. And what she had taken to be some sort of cryogenic preservation packaging, when the hand fell from the attaché the night of the bombing, was nothing more than a thick, vacuum-sealed, translucent plastic sack. A medical version of a Ziploc baggie.

Alex sniffed around it. Nothing but the scent of plastic.

Why was it not decaying?

She touched the hand with a single finger. The skin had a hardness to it, unlike either bone or frozen tissue. It was like a plastic of some sort, with a bit of give.

Alex pried it from the foam casing and turned it over.

The hand, she realized, was not human at all. It was some sort of replication of a human limb. A Hollywood special effect or something. The consistency was like a hardened silicone.

Quite impressive. It even had fingerprints.

Leaving the hand in the bag, Alex wedged it back into the foam casing and shut the briefcase. She closed her eyes and pressed both thumbs into her aching eyes.

This was the Isle of Man banker's hand. Draganic's banker. It didn't really matter who'd killed him—though her money was on Lockard—but this was why Lockard and Moss were desperate for this attaché. This hand was literally the key to a hidden a billion dollars of US cash currency.

How else could Draganic have started a new hedge fund? Trades required collateral. The chart in Edgar's office connected Draganic to a fund in the UK, managed by superstar trader Pachai Randeep. But after being sentenced at The Hague and banned from securities activity in Europe, that would be all but impossible for Draganic. Unless that fund was *domiciled* offshore. Maybe the Caymans or Bermuda.

Either way, it would have been created with—collateralized by—the money stolen in Iraq.

Alex gathered the briefcase and deposited it back into the safe, then pressed the exit button to be released from the vault. She needed to hurry. An offshore account would have to be handled by a prime bank—the hedge fund's bank—that housed the collateral in order to make trades. There was no other way. So… locate the prime bank, locate the money. That was the only way to help Jack.

Alex knew how to do it, too. She just needed a drawing to help her get inside.

Lockard stared out the window at the street below. Muddied from passing cars, and with cobblestones breaking to the surface, the snow looked more like shit-stains than winter wonder.

And the crap kept spewing from the sky.

He raised his hand before him and tried to flex it against the duct tape he'd used as a makeshift bandage. He had loosened the wrapping twice, but still no give. Unable to close his hand more than half an inch, Lockard couldn't grip a plastic cup, much less his HK45. He certainly couldn't pilot a plane. The whole goddamn hand was numb.

Still, that wasn't the worst of it.

The bastard had fucked him up something good. Pope must have hit the median nerve that ran up the center of the wrist. Severing that would prove problematic in more ways than one. It would require surgery to fix, and that meant finding discreet medical care. That was not about to happen any time soon. Nor was getting into the damn vault.

Well, that was a bridge to cross later, so to speak.

As for now, he was lucky he had learned to shoot equally well with his left hand. No, that was bullshit. It wasn't luck. It was a calculated decision to enhance that skill. Plus, the HK45 Tactical came with an ambidextrous mag release. Good planning on Lockard's part. You never knew when you may need to be ambidextrous. He glanced back at the closed door.

Pope hadn't made a sound since their last "interaction." Fucking blond wolverine was what he was. He hadn't dreamed pretty boy would fight back like that. And it downright turned him on. Gave him a fucking boner just thinking about it.

Before he could take that thought further, his phone buzzed in his pocket.

Pulling it out, he checked the caller ID. About damn time.

"Lockard," he answered.

"I suppose you haven't had the pleasure of viewing the morning's media as of yet?" Grant's British accent seemed thicker today.

"No telly here."

"Well, suffice to say that there was a murder last night on the Millennium footbridge. It's been reported that an unidentified American businessman died from a single gunshot wound. I've had the site cleaned, and the police have classified the event as a mugging gone wrong."

"Moss?"

"You are a smart one, indeed."

"What about Edgar Winter?"

"Reports tell me that he won't be giving us any more troubles."

Lockard believed that like he believed a fat old man with a white beard was going to bring him a sack of presents tomorrow night. No, he'd have to find his own sack of presents. Like always.

"I'm assuming we didn't recover the attaché, then." Why else would he call?

Grant said, "Just sit tight. I'm telling you, this Alex Winter is smarter than you realize. She'll fall right into it. And when she does, we'll be there. We have many eyes in the city."

"Where is she now?"

"Not quite sure, but she'll turn up."

Translated to American English: *Not enough eyes.*

Lockard said, "You understand this is all over by tomorrow."

Either the announcement about the Swiss franc will have collapsed the franc by then, destroying Draganic's trades and causing the collateral to be seized, or the announcement was prevented, the franc emboldened, and the trades would go through. In that case the collateral would disappear into the vault of some Third World bank to be retrieved later by Draganic.

Either way, Lockard would be left with nothing.

"Don't worry, old boy, we'll lock down the entire block if we must. We'll get the money."

An absolute last resort for them. Things were always better accomplished from the inside out. No witnesses, no additional heat from authorities. As for Draganic, Lockard had to assume the man was desperate to disrupt the Swiss council's announcement. But it was difficult to enjoy your earnings when you were on the run. Guys like Draganic never understood this. He did things the hard way.

Fool.

With a little help from the inside, that battle would be over before it ever began.

Grant said, "We'd better clear the line, then. Relax and remember, I've been at this a lot longer than you have, son."

"Don't call me that," Lockard said and hung up.

Then he dialed the number to his key contact in these final tactics.

She answered on the third ring. "Evan?"

"No names, remember?"

No apology from this one. She said, "Yes, yes."

"Did you replace the phone?"

"This morning. He is already gone to Bern."

"Good. And the jet?"

"It is on the way. Unless delayed by the snowing, it should arrive any minute."

"You did the right thing. I will contact you soon."

"Don't keep me waiting." She hung up.

Lockard stared back out the window. All the idiocies and failures around him still paled in comparison to a billion dollars. Sure, some things had occurred that he hadn't orchestrated, hadn't expected, but it was like that with any mission.

Shit happens.

Lockard raised his arm and tried to flex his hand again.

Nothing.

Shifting only his eyes, Lockard stared back at the door where Pope still waited. People would die in the next few hours—people always did in war—but Pope, he would suffer.

And Lockard would soak up his blood with a billion dollars in cold, hard cash.

Thirty-Three

Alex stared up through the snowflakes at the monstrous steel office tower, its mirrored glass reflecting the buildings and concrete sky around her. At the edge of the reflection sat the half-finished high-rise where she'd fought Lockard only two days ago.

It'd been a long week.

She glanced back at the construction site, noting there wasn't a crime scene cordoned off where Aaron had fallen. The police would normally conduct an on-site investigation, suicide or not. Unless the body had become buried in a snowdrift before anyone noticed.

But this body had disappeared long before that. Cleaned up and covered up.

Turning her attention back to the matter at hand, Alex skirted around a white Bentley parked in front of her. A small man sat in the driver's seat, talking on a cell phone. She couldn't hear him, but he looked pretty heated. Not recognizing him, and confident he was not surveilling her, Alex moved along the narrow stone plaza then entered the building.

Black marble floors stretched from corner to corner in the gaping lobby, and a curved black marble desk blockaded six elevator banks. Computer screens embedded the front of the desk, a uniformed guard standing behind it, and Alex tried to decide if it looked more like the *USS Enterprise* or the Death Star.

Alex approached the guard. About the size of a UPS truck and with a chin as wide as a ski lift, he wore a small brass badge that read Gabriel.

Blinking once, and without the hint of a smile, Gabriel raised the ski lift and said, "Business?" His voice echoed in the cavernous space.

"I'm here to visit Prince Alexander Capital."

"Do you have an appointment?" He reached for the phone and readied himself to dial.

Alex drew out her—Agent Wainscott's—wallet, and showed him the Metro

Police ID card. "I have this."

"Do you have a written warrant?" Gabriel asked, folding his giant hands across his chest.

"I'm here for unofficial questioning." Alex tilted her head like she was on the same team as he, the good guys keeping the peace. Casual.

He smirked and raised a coil of an eyebrow. "Strict orders from the penthouse. No official business, no access."

"Look, Gabriel," she said, reaching into her jacket and taking out a fold of papers. "I believe a man named Zoran Draganic is upstairs and I'd like to see him." Alex flashed the first drawing she'd made from memory of the CIA file she'd seen in Edgar's house. To enhance authenticity, she had forged the drawing with stencil-type Metropolitan Police letterhead and fax codes.

"You can believe he's there all day, you're still not going up."

Alex deadpanned him. "Have you seen him entering or leaving the Prince Alexander offices in the last two or three days?"

Gabriel glanced at the drawing and said, "I can't say."

The door opened before she responded, and the man who had been on the phone in the Bentley entered the building and strode across the lobby. He was wearing a light blue and white striped scarf and a camel-colored overcoat, and his lips were pursed tight, like he'd just tasted a turd.

Ignoring Alex, he walked right up to Gabriel. "Well?"

Gabriel bent behind the desk and came up with a solid, leather-bound, tan briefcase, the kind Wall Street types carry in movies.

The man flared his nose. "You left it out all day? Are you some sort of nitwit?" Then he looked Alex up and down. "Stop staring."

Willing herself to not bury a boot heel in his mouth, Alex smiled. And kept staring.

He huffed and turned back to Gabriel. "Well? Did you?"

Gabriel said, "I never left my post. It was safe, I assure you."

Looking behind Gabriel, he said, "Back there?."

"You have it, right?" Gabriel crossed his forearms that were like two Christmas hams. Not a snowball's chance that Alex would win a physical confrontation with this guy. She'd need a bazooka to get past him.

"Perhaps you should have used your brain." The guy tapped his own forehead to emphasize his important point while jutting out his chin toward Gabriel. He was lucky the big guy didn't wrap the little man's lower jaw up over his forehead.

Instead, Gabriel calmly replied, "I said I've been here all day. And it was safe."

"Well, you're lucky. My son's gift is in this." He raised the briefcase chest high. "And he won't have a proper Christmas without it."

"Maybe you shouldn't have left it in the elevator, then." Gabriel said.

"Are you getting cheeky? I'm a part owner of this building!"

Gabriel stood tall and quiet.

Shit.

"Damn idiot." The man shook his phone in the air. "You'll be out of a job by day's end." He tightened his scarf and stomped off. "Happy fucking Christmas."

Watching the man fumble with a pair of gloves at the doors, Alex shook her head. "Was he being serious?"

"I hope not." Gabriel shuffled behind the reception desk.

"Ok, a couple more questions and I'll be on my way, promise." Alex pulled another drawing from her stack, this one of Lockard. "What about this man? Seen him here?"

Gabriel shrugged. "Still can't say."

"Can't or won't?" She asked.

He sighed and said, "Both."

OK. Alex was getting nowhere and didn't have the time or patience for Gabriel's stonewalling. She was about to show him the drawing of Pachai Randeep when Gabriel's phone rang.

He said to Alex, "I better do my job, while I still have one," and turned around to answer it.

Meanwhile, the pin-prick behind her had finally managed to get both gloves over his fingers and was exiting the building.

Fine. We'll do this the messy way today.

Alex took long but unhurried strides to the same exit and followed the man out. He walked straight to the Bentley and, unlocking it remotely, pulled open the driver's door a moment before she caught up.

Alex glanced around, hastened her last few steps, and moved directly behind him, snow dampening her footfalls into silence.

Alex grabbed the back of his head and slammed it against the frame of the door. Striking above the temple but not crushing it, the blow knocked him out. His body slumped into her arms and she dished him into the passenger seat, tossing his briefcase in his lap. Picking the keys off the ground, she shook the snow off them. She climbed into the driver's seat, started the Bentley, and drove the first leg of a K-turn, lining up the car so it was perpendicular to the curb and facing the plaza.

Alex looked around again, climbed out, pulled the man to the driver's seat, and buckled him in. Then she wedged his briefcase between the seat and the gas pedal. The engine roared and whined in a squeal, like it was caged and fighting, ready to explode with unbridled energy.

The poor guy was about to wake up to an air bag exploding in his face. A bad day for Mr. Wall Street.

Alex reached across and—careful to keep her injured shoulder clear— jammed the gearshift into Drive. She jumped back as the Bentley lunged.

The thick white car ripped across the courtyard and crashed into the double glass doors, glass and metal exploding to spray over the stone plaza. Gabriel dove aside as the car tore across the lobby and pummeled the security desk in a cloud of crushed marble. The air bags swallowed the unconscious man whole.

Alarms sounded, the sprinklers activated, and people flooded into the lobby. Alex entered the building through the handy new entrance and walked straight to the elevators.

Alex rode the lift to the penthouse on the fiftieth floor and exited into a narrow entrance hall with commercial-style carpeting and beige walls. Draganic had done little to alter the appearance of the space. A frosted glass door with a black magnetic card reader stood at one end, and a dark gray steel door sat at the other.

She'd learned in Talonstrike training that most security systems were flawed in predictable ways. For instance, civilian house systems might have sensors to signal when a door or window was opened, yet no glass-break sensors to indicate if the glass has been removed or shattered. Break the glass, or cut a hole, and one could slip through undetected. Another common deficiency: motion sensors arranged to monitor entries and exits and stairwells, but nothing else. Avoiding those spots allows one to roam a space without detection.

In an office setting, the security system would most likely be set to detect a breach from the main entrance, but not the exit. The back door, then, would be locked but not alarmed. Especially if the door had no magnetic sensor pad.

A guess, of course, but one she would bet money on.

Ignoring the frosted-glass entry, Alex tested the handle of the metal door, just in case. As ridiculous as it sounds, she'd found unlocked exits during operations before. Human error is the most common of all security system flaws.

Not this time, though, so Alex listened to the hollow sounds echoing from the other side of the door. A television played loudly, but there were no voices. She also noticed that the door was significantly colder than the lobby.

Damn.

Alex knocked on the door, drew the SIG, then stepped aside and waited. Maybe Randeep would think it was the cleaning crew and stick his head out to check. An easy entry for her. After a minute, she knocked again, louder this time.

Nothing. But she wasn't expecting an answer by now, anyway.

Alex looked around, double-checking for cameras, then took a deep breath and shot the deadbolt mechanism twice. Louder than she'd hoped in the small space. She lowered the aim and shot the handle lock twice as well. Not perfect hits on either, but when she yanked the handle, the door wrenched open, pieces of metal falling to the carpet. Frigid air from the penthouse mixed with sulfurous gun smoke from the lobby as Alex pulled the door open wide.

It must have been forty degrees in there.

Alex stepped inside and moved nice and slow—no mad rush like in the movies. She crept close to the wall, SIG trained on the unlit space ahead of her. One beige hallway turned into another, and then she was in the floor's main room.

The space was enormous and housed one area for work, and one incredible view.

A television tuned to BBC News blared from a ceiling mount at the center of the room, and a half-moon, trading-style desk sat underneath it. There must have been a dozen computer monitors, one on top of another in a semicircle, facing away.

The rest of the space sat empty. No other offices, no other furniture.

Keeping low, Alex called out, "Mr. Randeep? Are you here?" But no one responded. Nothing moved at all.

She eased across the room, keeping the main entrance hall in her view, and paused behind the monitors. The flat-screen wires were all pulled together into a huge, twisted rope and entered the floor under the desk. Beyond them was a pair of legs, bony knees in blue jeans and a pair of green suede running shoes.

Alex also made out a faint, and familiar, odor. She stood up and took a step to the side.

Sure enough, a man sat slumped in his seat. He had clearly taken a shot to the head, as half of it was on the floor next to him. Even so, Alex could tell from the undamaged features that it was Randeep. Behind him, snow swirled into the office through a shattered window, dusting the floor.

Not too worried about disturbing the crime scene, she turned off the television, walked to the body, and picked up the wrist. Rigid and unyielding. It appeared he had been dead for at least a day, probably not longer, though it was hard to tell with the cold air keeping decomposition at bay.

Anyone with enough experience or even simple deterrence training could have had the peace of mind to leave the television blaring and set the air to the lowest temperature—or opening a window, in this case. Still, it appeared Randeep had been sitting in his seat when he was shot, not moved there afterward. The front entry had not been disturbed, the shattered window was the top pane, and the hole was too small for an adult to fit through. So, whoever had been there was either cleared to enter the offices or let inside by Randeep. Her guess was Lockard or Draganic.

The things people will do for money.

Alex turned her attention to the computers, and noticed every screen was in save mode. When she touched the mouse, the computers all woke, as if startled. Half the screens showed charts, and the other half had scrolling news headlines, mostly reports on the Swiss franc.

But one showed a financial model labeled JONAH, and that screen was filled with a list of market trades.

Alex studied the numbers and charts, ignoring the faint odor behind her. It took a little while to figure out what it all meant. First, all the trades were in options, and in Swiss francs. And all long calls or short puts. In other words, Randeep was expecting the Swiss franc to go up, to get stronger against the euro. He had used options and futures to create leverage on his trades and make huge money bets. After calculating the foreign exchange rates, she figured the trades were well over a billion dollars' worth.

And they all expired tomorrow.

Jesus.

Alex picked up a stack of papers, articles Randeep had printed and piled on the desk before him. Each of the articles was about the Swiss franc. All but one of them. That one was about the Swiss finance minister, Stefan Lory. He was making an announcement later today about the Swiss Federal Council's program to keep the franc "affordable" for EU-based consumers. The correspondent went on to speculate that the special press conference was for the council to announce it was contemplating joining the Euro currency. A move that was, according to the correspondent, "a surefire way to make the franc fall in value by over twenty percent."

She turned back to the screens and looked at the trades. Specifically at the strike prices, or where they would make money if the franc went high enough. Then she looked at the current value of the franc and where the paper thought it would go. Alex checked, and double-checked. Then she set down the papers and took a step back.

Now she knew why someone had shot Randeep in the face. An emotional statement. She also concluded her hunch was right: Lockard and Draganic were not working together on this anymore. Because Draganic had bet every penny of the billion. Plus more.

And when that announcement was made today, he would lose all of it.

Looks like JONAH swallowed the Whale this time.

Alex looked back at the article. The press conference was set to take place this afternoon in Bern, Switzerland, where the Swiss council was headquartered.

And Draganic kept a house in Gstaad.

She reached for the mouse, pulled up the web browser, and searched for directions from Gstaad to Bern. Less than an hour on main roads or highways.

So, what? Tell the Swiss authorities, have them call off the announcement as a precaution against sabotage, and let the trades end up in the money? Draganic makes an extra billion dollars? Maybe more?

But there was no doubt in her mind. If she didn't tell them, people would die. No way could Alex get there in time to stop Dragonic.

Only one thing to do, thought Alex. Straightening, she pulled out her cell phone, turned it on, and dialed the number.

Denise answered on the third ring. Alex noted she did so in a whisper. "What's going on?"

"Bloody hell, Alex, you're in quite the mess now, aren't you?"

She pictured a billion dollars in a great big pile with bodies strewn around it. "You're telling me."

"I've heard your name two times in the past day and neither of them was in flattery."

"And yet I'm flattered."

"You took a Metro badge from someone named Wainscott? What on earth, Alex? You're lucky they haven't initiated a public sweep for you."

"Right. What else?"

Denise whispered louder, "The director. G himself."

Alex startled. What the hell did Peter Grant want with her? "In what context?"

"Well, I couldn't hear. The door was closing just as he brought you up. But it seems your own CIA is on the hunt for you."

Of course they were. Moss had been in bed with Lockard. God knew what he'd told the home office.

"Have they issued a sweep through MI, then? Going after me?"

"That's the oddity of it. I haven't heard peep otherwise, just your name."

"OK, listen, forget about all that. I'll deal with it. I have intelligence and it's urgent."

Alex told Denise about the hedge fund, the trades, and the Swiss finance minister. Then she told her about Lockard and Draganic, Randeep, and the stakes.

"My days, that is a problem. Look, we have plenty of eyes in Bern. It'll be taken care of straightaway."

"I think it'll be a bomb, something very large and likely disruptive to demonstrate violent protest to the idea of Switzerland joining the Euro. It will have to be big to save these trades. Maybe a straight assassination."

"Got it, Alex. Now let me go run it down."

Denise hung up and Alex switched off her phone, hoping that MI6 had enough Swiss assets to act within the next two hours.

In the meantime, she had to locate the money. That would lead her to Lockard and hopefully Jack, but her time was running out, too.

Alex turned back to the computer, clicked on the hard drive, and searched for legal documents, financing agreements, anything that showed how Prince Alexander was sourcing its capital. In other words, where the hell had the fund stashed all this cash? The Caymans? Serbia? It must have been laundered somehow and sent to a custodian, a name to back up the trades. Randeep's trading sheet listed a DTC—Depository Trust Company—number, but there was no name listed for the custodian itself. Every hedge fund had to have a custodian. If Alex found this one, she would find the offshore bank where the cash was stashed.

Alex clicked on folder after folder, looking at everything Randeep had been working on in the past month, searching for words like *Cayman* or phrases like *prime broker*. As she searched, she realized something basic about the whole theory was driving her mad. How the hell could a guy like Draganic still be operating in high finance? How could he have had an account with the banker from Isle of Man to even enter the money into the system in the first place? You don't just secretly deposit a billion dollars cash into a bank. It isn't possible with international disclosure laws. It didn't matter what country you operated in. Unless he was specially approved by the authorities.

No way.

Sure, the governor of Mann had been involved somehow, but he couldn't have hidden the deposit from international bodies of oversight. Not across multiple countries.

So where to start?

Draganic's offices were in the UK, but he couldn't be headquartered here. He had to be offshore somewhere and he needed a major bank, one with sufficient capital and trustworthiness, to back up his trades.

Alex stared at the screens and thought of the banking articles in her father's house. What if Draganic wasn't a *client* of the Mann banker, but they were *partners* instead? What if he didn't deposit the money into a bank…

What if?

Alex reached for the keyboard and entered the banker's name. Nothing came up. On the hunch, she entered the name of the Mann governor. Sure enough, a single document appeared in the search window, titled Isle of Man Bank Charter.

He didn't transfer the funds to a bank. Draganic opened a whole new one.

Alex clicked on the file and began to read. That's when she heard the rack of a pistol slide.

"Pity about Bill Moss," Director Grant said. Standing in the doorway to the office's back hall, where Alex had entered, he tapped his Walther P99 against the palm of his hand while aiming it at her.

"Which part?"

Grant met Alex's eye then waved the barrel of the Walther. "I've always liked you, Alex. Maybe even felt a sense of custodial duty to you, you know, since Edgar went offline, dedicated himself to the field. So I've been watching you. We all have."

"I'm flattered. Really."

"You should be proud. You've been quite an asset to the Company. I've seen your two-oh-one."

"Now I'm touched." Alex took a half step to move behind the computer monitors, away from his view. Maybe she could draw her SIG.

"Careful now," he said. "Come back out here."

This time he trained the gun on her chest.

She eased her way back out. Stood still. Stared at him.

"What do you want?" She asked, trying to stall and maybe distract him.

"Same as you."

"I don't care about the money."

He laughed, a good hearty laugh, and said, "But I do." He stopped and stared at her. "Now where's that damn attaché?"

Alex contemplated going for her SIG, knowing she could beat the old man to the trigger—but just as she had the thought, another person entered from the front hall.

Valerie Wainscott wore her police vest and a puffy, long Metropolitan Police jacket. She held a matching brown and black Walther P99, also pointed at Alex. She'd only seen Wainscott from afar before, but now could see Wainscott had a hard yet attractive face, like a former athlete who had joined the force. Maybe she ran triathlons or something.

"Nice to see you again, Inspector," Alex said, smiling.

"Remove your weapon with two fingers and lay it on the ground. You are under arrest by order of the Metropolitan Police."

Alex looked back and forth between them. "Funny, I thought Met agents didn't carry guns."

"They do to take a murderer," Grant said.

Alex glanced back at Randeep, and then at Wainscott. "This guy has been dead for a day. Don't be ridiculous."

"We're not talking about him," Wainscott said.

Grant finished for her. "You're on the hook for Moss."

"Bullshit," Alex said. "I wasn't even there."

"But someone's got to be pinned with it, and since your father has disappeared again, it'll have to be you. Unless…" He stepped forward and continued, "You cooperate. You give us the attaché. Then all charges will be… erased."

Right, along with Alex.

"Your gun," Wainscott said.

And there it was. Alex could shoot her way out of this, but she would wound or kill a Met inspector and the head of MI6.

Not exactly a career move.

Or she could cooperate, bide her time, and wait for the right opportunity to act. She still had to find Jack, and maybe they would lead her right to him.

So, Alex drew the SIG with two fingers from behind her, kneeled, and placed it on the floor. Inspector Wainscott put Alex in plastic zip cuffs, took her satchel, then she and Grant led her to the service elevator at the edge of the small lobby.

Inside, she caught Wainscott eyeing her. Smiling again, Alex nodded toward her chest pocket.

Wainscott took the badge from the pocket. "I should shoot you for that alone. Where's Burke's?"

Alex shrugged.

"On with it." Grant nodded to the hallway.

They took the lift to the garage, where they led Alex to a waiting car—a white

Range Rover that looked much like Lockard's—with MI5 Agent Burke behind the wheel, grinning beneath his Lennon shades.

Excellent. Three on one now. Alex's prospects were dimming along with the blackening sky. A Hendricks would have been good right about then. Maybe a double.

"Well, well, nowhere to run," Burke said out the open driver's window. "No riots to incite up here now, are there?" Wainscott turned away, as Alex realized Burke's English accent had suddenly disappeared and he sounded firmly American.

Son of a bitch. Not MI5, after all.

Alex climbed inside, and Wainscott sat next to her. Grant sat up front.

Wainscott flipped through Alex's sketchbook. "Not half bad. Where'd you get them?"

Alex ignored her, stared out the window.

Grant turned around. "Now, Alex. About that attaché."

Burke dialed his cell and, after a moment, said, "We're on the way to get the briefcase. If I don't call you in thirty minutes confirming possession, kill Pope."

Turning to look out the other window, Alex said, "I'll take you to it."

Thirty-Four

Draganic squinted against fat snowflakes that slapped at the windshield like dead moths. The damn storm threatened to push him right off the Schönriedstrasse pass. He was glad he'd left when he did. It had taken almost four hours to travel the seventy miles. If he'd waited until after sunrise to leave, he would have missed the shot at Finance Minister Lory.

Literally.

His throat ached with anger about the uncontrolled circumstances. Here he was, closer to more money than God—ten times more than he ever had before —and it was under threat of being royally fucked up by the government. Again. The goddamn institution. Play by the rules and all you got was a good solid bending over. Take it right there like everyone else, they'd say. He and Randeep would not only lose the money, though, they would be sent to prison for securities violations. Trading in the markets when Draganic had been banned.

Speaking of Randeep.

The little dothead was nowhere to be found. He was probably crying in the corner over his own monumental fuck-ups, refusing to answer his phone. If it weren't for Draganic stepping in to fix his problems, Randeep would be up there with Nick Leeson for worst trader in history. Still, Draganic wanted to speak with him one more time, be sure that the trades would work if he went through with this. If not, then Draganic would be forced to use Plan B. Find Lockard and take back the money by force. Unless.

Had Randeep already double-crossed him? Was he with Lockard now?

Goddamn all of them.

Draganic reached for his phone in the passenger seat. As he leaned over, he swerved into the other lane, where two bright oncoming lights blinded him. A deep, bellowing horn sounded and he jerked back upright.

Draganic spun the wheel right—the blaring horn fading behind him—but he overcompensated, causing the BMW's right bumper to scrape the snow and send a stream of powder up into the windshield. He turned the wheel left again and lost control of the car, spinning around three full times until the back end bounced off the railing, and the front end plowed into the snowbank, jerking him to a halt.

His heart racing, Draganic gripped the wheel with both hands and dropped his head.

He was getting sloppy, perhaps too anxious with the day ahead of him. He wasn't nervous about killing, of course—he'd done that plenty of times before. No, what concerned him was time. He hadn't had enough of it to plan this properly. Plus he was being fueled by emotion and he knew it.

Dangerous in this line of work. A dose of emotion could give someone an edge, but too much could blind them.

Easing the BMW out of the snowbank without spinning the wheels—thank God the 8-Series kept the rear-wheel drivetrain—Draganic pulled back onto the highway. Then his mind began to play tricks on him, making him smell almond butter. Strange. Perhaps the rush of adrenaline from the wipeout was making him hungry.

Having settled on this explanation, Draganic drove the rest of the way to Bern, trying to think of nothing at all.

By the time he arrived at the MetroBern Hotel, Draganic had calmed himself and felt steady again. After pulling into the valet line, he studied the Federal Palace across the street.

There would be no motorcade and though Councillors could use Army security detail if they wanted personal protection, they almost never did. Draganic had learned this on a segment of BBC's *Panorama* about Lory that aired last May. In televised special, Lory emphasized that even though he had been elected Swiss Financial Minister—a position that paid the equivalent of five hundred thousand US dollars per year—he was still like any ordinary Swiss citizen. He drove the same seventeen-year-old black Mercedes Benz, and he never used a driver. They even showed his shit-box car on television. Furthermore, Lory regularly used the Monte Rosa Suite to rest and prep the day of public appearances at the Palace. Right here at the MetroBern Hotel.

What were they thinking, these politicians?

Draganic exited the BMW and handed the keys to the valet.

"Name?" the man asked, his red puffy hood pulled over his brow.

"Lockard," Draganic said, handing over the keys.

The man reached in to take the duffel bag, but Draganic grabbed the bag himself. "I don't need assistance."

Draganic walked away from the valet, feeling the man's gaze burning into his back. He didn't care. He would never see that man or this hotel again. All he had to do was finish today's work and transfer the money by nightfall. Then it would be done.

He walked through the automatic, double glass doors. The lobby was a welcome sight. Designed in some sort of New Age contemporary style, with granite floors and light wood furnishings, it had an open and spacious feel.

"Good morning," a tall blonde behind the front desk greeted him. "Reservation?"

"Evan Lockard," Draganic said. "I have forgotten my wallet, though. I trust you will take cash?"

"Certainly, but we will need the credit card for a deposit."

"I am by myself, and will be gone first thing in the morning. You will never know I was here."

"I am afraid this is hotel policy." She flashed a magazine smile.

Draganic pulled ten US one-hundred-dollar bills from his pocket and handed her five of them. "This is for you." He handed her the other five. "And this is for a room number six-twelve."

Then, careful to keep the scar from her view, he turned his head slightly and flashed his own smile.

Three minutes later, Draganic stood at the double French doors to the opera balcony of room six-twelve. A boring courtyard view, but this did not matter because the door to the room sat directly across the hall from that of the Monte Rosa Suite. A perfect view from the peephole.

Now all Draganic had to do was wait.

He checked his watch and calculated the time until he expected Lory to arrive. It would be in one hour, at most. Lory would want to enter the building a good two-hours before the announcement to prepare, perhaps freshen up for the cameras.

Staring at the hands on his watch, Draganic remembered Natasha and his eyes suddenly glazed over.

She would have slept late after drinking a whole bottle of Bordeaux and would have a typical headache. She would wander into the kitchen, half naked and half asleep. While cursing Draganic for this or that, she would reach for her purse across the counter. He could see her, opening her purse, taking out the carton of ridiculous pink-and-gold cigarettes, maybe cursing him again, one more time.

"I'm sorry, Natasha." He actually said the words out loud. "But you can't have a divorce."

You can have this instead.

Natasha stood before the full-length mirror on her side of the walk-in closet, wearing nothing but a pair of spandex yoga shorts. She turned left and right. She sucked in her stomach and raised her chin. She picked up one magazine and then another. She flipped through the pages and compared herself to the women inside. She stopped on a full-page shot in *Vogue*. Her ass was not that different from Megan Fox's.

And Natasha was older.

She dropped the magazine and cupped her breasts. More than a handful each, they were fantastic and she knew it. It was important to know your assets as a woman—what you could use and what was tradable. How else would you get what you wanted in life?

All in all, she looked good. Not perfect yet, but good.

And very fuckable.

Yes, she was ready to be single again, and now that she had her evidence from Mr. Lockard, she would demand the divorce. Zoran would throw a fit when he heard what she wanted for alimony, but he'd get over it. He had come into a large sum of money doing whatever he was doing with that Evan Lockard, and they had hidden it away somewhere. Sure, she would get some from Lockard for helping him, but a hundred thousand would hardly last a few months.

She needed more.

She would have to double back on Lockard until either he or Zoran agreed to cut her in on the deal. It would be a small price to pay for her not to turn them in to the authorities. Zoran would do anything to stay out of The Hague. And Lockard? Well, he was not fit for prison, that man. Like a bison, he needed to roam free.

It would be painful, yes, all the yelling and the bitter battle of a divorce, but soon it would be over. And she would find herself a nice young boy toy to keep her company, someone to enjoy her newfound wealth with her. No one serious, but someone to play with, like a professional fùtbol player. Maybe a dark Italian boy. Yes, that would be it. She would go straight to Milan and shop for a new dress and a new boy.

Not bothering to put on clothes—she'd turned the heat up to eighty when Zoran left—Natasha walked down the stairs and went straight to the kitchen. All the talk about money and her future had made her tingle and she needed a cigarette.

Entering the kitchen, she wrinkled her nose. Something had soured in here. It smelled like rotten eggs. Holding her breath, she pushed the steel trash bin into the mudroom. Who knew what that ape ate this morning? Probably boiled eggs and kraut.

Once a Serbian, always a Serbian.

Natasha tapped out a pink pastel cigarette from the box of Sobranie Cocktails and held it to her nostrils.

That smelled delicious.

She strode over to the stovetop and put her hand on the dial. Nobody was here to scold her for the so-called filthy habit of lighting her cigarette with the open flame. And nobody would ever be able to tell her not to again.

As she smiled at that and twisted the dial past High, she heard a single click of the electric sparker—and saw the lower oven propped open with a wine cork. She tilted her head, thinking, *That is strange. How did that*…And then the burner clicked a second time.

The blue flame erupted from the stovetop, engulfing her and the oven for a single moment.

Then the entire room exploded.

Thirty-Five

Naked, Jack had pushed into the far corner of the empty room, using the internal walls as insulation. Still, he shivered like a starving dog. He'd slid in and out of consciousness and wasn't sure how long he'd been there. Two nights? Three? Was it early morning? Afternoon? At one point, he'd woken to the gurgling sound of birds and thought he was back in New Cross. The pigeons' coos had settled him back then, when he'd been locked in the eves of the crumbling townhome. When he'd disobeyed Papa.

His despot grandfather.

But like Alex, Jack wasn't damaged. He had been a different person then, living a separate life from this one. He'd found himself a little more isolated than others. Perhaps losing parents at a young age did that to you. He knew he hesitated before opening up, rarely forming any real personal bond—which was the main reason Edgar had tasked him with watching Alex. "Just get close enough to see if she's okay. She doesn't seem to have any close friends, any confidants. It think it's abnormal."

"No men?" Jack had asked, intrigued.

"Not too close," Edgar had warned him.

He wasn't sure if he'd purposefully disobeyed that warning or merely discarded it along the way, but he wasn't sorry he'd done it. A man would kill for that kind of woman.

At least Jack would.

As he had that thought, the door clanked with the deadbolt being disengaged from the other side.

Jack sat up, readied himself again. One last battle.

Lockard swung open the door. He wore black pants and a black field jacket. One hand was wrapped in silver duct tape up to the wrist, and a bag of ice was taped tight around the wound. The other hand held the HK45, aimed at Jack's chest.

"On your knees, face the wall. Hands over your head."

Shivering, Jack turned and complied, while gathering the last of his reserves for the final fight.

But Lockard just cut the tape from his wrists. Then he dragged a pile of clothes into the room with a foot. After kicking them across the floor, he pointed the pistol at them and then back at Jack.

"We're leaving in ten minutes."

Jack kept himself from looking back as he grabbed the clothes, and Lockard left the room.

He'd soon have the chance to deliver some payback of his own.

Thirty-Six

From British MI6, to Swiss Federal Intelligence Service, to Bern's newly formed Swiss Special Intervention Unit, reports of an imminent terrorist attack by a man named Zoran Draganic had traveled through the channels at light speed. It was most likely a bomb, but perhaps a direct affront to a member of the Swiss Council. Rolf Brunner, the lead tactical officer of the counterterrorism unit called Enzion, used the twelve-and-a-half-minute drive of the armored vehicle approach to the suspected location to prepare his team for the intervention.

Not enough, he worried. Not even for this team.

Rolf cursed President von Zeller. If the politico had half the sense of a military leader, he would call off the press conference. This would eliminate the problem.

Sure, they had trained in all sorts of environments and for all kinds of operations, but this was asking a bit much, even for Enzion. Rolf's team was charged with detonation intervention once Swiss Intelligence had located the suspected terrorist. Meanwhile, Stern, the hostage-rescue and VIP-protection unit, was designated for a bomb sweep and security lockdown of the Federal Palace. The problem was, on strict instructions from Intelligence, from here on out, there would be no contact between Enzion and Stern. Apparently, Intelligence was worried its own communication could somehow be intercepted and throw the whole intervention down the tubes.

So Enzion and Stern were both going in dark.

Rolf ascended the last half flight of stairs of the MetroBern Hotel and held up a hand, signaling his team to stop. The other six members, all dressed in black tactical outfits with their face shields lowered and holding their SIG 551 double-magazine assault rifles, halted with the abruptness of a salute.

Rolf pointed to the two officers with the battering ram and signaled them forward to his immediate right. He motioned for the officer holding the long-range laser microphone to flank his left.

Rolf nodded, and the mic man eased the dish out around the corner and pointed it at the door. He held up a finger. Listening.

He shook his head once. *Nothing.*

Rolf had to choose. Go forward and pounce, hoping to catch the suspect by surprise, or wait. Listen a bit longer and see if they could determine his approximate location in the room, if there were others with him, and whether he had his finger on the button of an explosive. Intelligence was certain this was Draganic's plan. Why else rent a room under an assumed name at a hotel located directly across from the palace entrance? Proximity was key. Draganic needed to be close enough to detonate whatever device was inside the federal building. A modified mobile phone detonator would be ineffective within those stone walls. It had to be some sort of RF signal. Unless Draganic had planted the explosive inside the suite across the hall, the one that Finance Minister Lory always used. No secret, that. But then, why not just step out and shoot Lory? Either way, Rolf and his men had to intercept Draganic before he acted on any plan.

Staring at the mic man, Rolf put a finger to his own ear. *Anything?*

The mic man shook his head again, but then he cocked it. Held up a hand. Something. He nodded vigorously. Something important. He held up one finger.

Draganic was alone.

He put his hand to his ear, fingers spread, like he was holding a device.

Draganic was on the phone.

He pointed to the sky.

A mobile phone.

Okay. Rolf adjusted the team again, bringing the officer with the full body shield in front. Then the battering-ram men. Three riflemen in a triangular formation behind him, Rolf at the front of those. He signaled that they would listen and be at the ready. From this corner, they were approximately seven and a half feet from Draganic's door. They could cover that and be in the room in three seconds flat. All Rolf had to do was give the signal.

Rolf glanced back at his team and raised his hand in a fist.

Be ready.

Draganic closed the drapes, walked back to the bed, unpacked the change of clothes from his duffel, and laid them out neatly on the coverlet. Then he placed two long bath sheets on the floor between the door and the bathroom. Finally, he kicked off his shoes and set them out of the way.

He drew the *Sea Shark* from the sheath and held it against his leg as he peered through the peephole toward the Monte Rosa Suite. Lory would approach the suite, perhaps with a day bag. Then he would hold the magnetic key to the doorplate, wait for it to click, and push the door open. At that moment, Draganic would yank open his own door and spring the man from behind, slitting his throat and pushing him into the suite in one fluid motion.

Draganic would then retreat back into his room. He would remove his own bloodied clothes, wrap them in the two towels, and stuff them into the duffel. Then a quick wash of his hands and maybe his face, and he would be on his way.

But as he stood there, waiting by the door, Draganic smelled the faint scent of almond butter, making him hungry again.

What the hell was wrong with him?

He felt a warmth surge through his body. Not a comforting warmth—quite the opposite. Like a feeling that something was up, something was wrong here. He turned his head and stared at the window to the courtyard. When was the last time he'd heard the elevator move? Had he heard the voice of any another human in the hotel yet?

Odd.

He walked to the bed, placed the knife on the pillow, and approached the window. He looked out to the courtyard.

Quieter than a church on Monday.

He walked back to the door and peered through the peephole. Nothing but a distorted view of the door to the Monte Rosa Suite.

Draganic eased open his own door and peeked out into the hallway. Not a single sound in the entire hotel.

Pondering that, Draganic jolted when his cell phone rang from inside the room. Jesus Christ. He'd forgotten to turn the damn thing off.

Shutting the door, he hurried over to the duffel bag, pulled out the phone, and checked the caller ID. Lockard. Draganic forced himself not to yell as he answered.

"Where the fuck are you?"

"Where the fuck are *you*?" Lockard asked. Staring out the window and across the street again, he began counting cobblestones that were peeking from below the snow.

One. Two. Three—

Draganic began to yell and Lockard struggled not to smile. Poor man had become unnerved. It happened to even the very best of them. Everyone had a breaking point. Better yet, everyone had a weak spot, useful for exploitation. For most, it was family. Threaten the safety of a beloved wife or child, and you could break most anyone. For others, it was more complex, like integrity. Threaten their reputation. Or freedom, their ability to make free choices.

Hell, Lockard had seen SEALs who'd never displayed a weakness in any exercise or mission break on the strangest things. One guy had no family—wife or children—to threaten. No obvious interests or needs. No habits or addictions. Yet this man broke because he'd lost a teammate in an operation. Blaming himself for the misstep, for having led the downed man into a firefight, the SEAL claimed he could no longer command. It was all his fault. So he stepped down and out, dropped off the face.

Strange.

Tuning back to the tongue-lashing that Draganic was giving him, Lockard heard him say, "…money has all been pledged. It will be seized by the authorities."

This moron didn't know the cash would disappear today anyway. What did Lockard care about the trades?

"And then I'll find you," Draganic said. "I will have two billion dollars at my disposal to hunt you down and give you exactly what you deserve."

Lockard would yawn, but he wasn't tired. He walked back to the window and put Draganic on speakerphone. "Zoran, are you listening? I want you to hear this."

"Hear what?"

Lockard typed the text message, then poised his finger above the send button.

The mic man nodded at Rolf and drew a circle with his finger.

Draganic was contained and not currently a threat.

Rolf pointed at the battering ram, drew a swift line with his hand to Draganic's door, and held up three fingers.

He dropped a finger. Two.

Then another.

One.

He nodded.

The two men moved silent and quick, like stags in a forest. They drew back the ram. Rolf and his team followed in formation, stopping just to the side of the door. The shield at the front, Rolf to his direct left, the others drawn and ready to fire.

And then the man at the very back coughed.

"Hear what?" Draganic yelled at Lockard. He felt his face burn and his vision turn blood red.

As he was about to throw the phone at the wall, he heard it. Muffled but distinct.

A cough.

Right outside the door.

He hurried across the room and looked through the peephole.

What in God's holy hell?

It was not Lory. It was an army of men, all dressed in black riot gear, at least ten of them standing there. The Swiss SWAT team. Two were drawing back a battering ram.

"You son of a bitch!" Draganic yelled into the phone.

The ram battered the door once.

Draganic backed away and yelled again. Then he smelled that stupid almond butter. Stronger than before. Like it was all over his hands. Like the goddamn phone had been dipped in it.

He was going crazy. Lockard had fucked him over so badly, he'd lost his mind!

He yelled, "I'll kill you, you son of a bitch! I will slit your throat!"

Lockard just whispered to himself as he sent the text. "Boom."

The two men with the battering ram looked to the back of the team, then to Rolf.

From inside the room, the suspect yelled, "I'll kill you, you son of a bitch! I'll slit your throat!"

The mic man nodded furiously while patting his hands in the air. *Movement inside the room.*

Son of a bitch is right!

An instant of hesitation, but it was enough. As Rolf rolled his hand, signaling for the men to continue, a blast sounded from inside the room, shattering glass and thumping the door.

"*Go! Go!*" Rolf yelled.

After swinging the ram and hitting the door one last time, the team rushed into the room in perfect formation, guns at the ready. But the man was on the floor. Not moving.

The team scanned the room, checking for booby traps but finding none. They finally eased their guard and flipped up their masks.

"Sir?" the mic man called to Rolf. "I believe I've found what hit the door."

He pointed to the floor. A flap of skin, a half-mangled ear, and the once pristine half of Draganic's skull.

Thirty-Seven

It took Alex and Burke eight and a half minutes to enter Hatton Garden Safe Deposit and retrieve the attaché.

As they were leaving the facility, the tall security guard glanced at them and Alex smiled as casual as a Sunday jogger, but then looked past his shoulder.

A television on the far wall was showing the news, and a reporter stood in front of what looked to be some sort of federal building. Scrolling on the bottom of the screen were the words *Breaking news: Explosion in hotel across the street from Federal Palace in Bern...One confirmed dead...*A photo of Zoran Draganic flashed on the screen.

The reporter said, "Police believe this man was plotting to assassinate a Swiss council member, perhaps the president, at today's press conference. Authorities have postponed the event until further notice, but indicate that it may take place in a secure location later today. That's all we have right now..."

"Let's go. We have work to do," Burke said.

Exiting the building and ducking under a long tail of Christmas garland that had come unhinged from the top of the entry, Alex thought of the trail of bodies this operation was leaving behind. The crossfire of all these spies, her included. Killing each other for the pot—no, the swimming pool full of gold at the end of the soiled rainbow.

Back in the Range Rover, Grant shook his head. "Took long enough."

Alex nodded back at Burke. "Sergeant Pepper here almost blew it, refusing to remove his shades for the guards."

"Shut it," Burke said, pushing her into the backseat.

With Inspector Wainscott behind the wheel now, Burke joined Alex in the back while Grant inspected the contents of the attaché. "This should do it," he said, then nodded at Burke. "Call Evan."

Burke made the phone call. "Package secure. ETA, one hour."

So Lockard and Jack were in the UK somewhere, not far from the city. It would take a good three or four hours—maybe more with the snow—to get anywhere like Manchester. Assuming they were driving, that was.

They wound their way out of downtown London and into East Finchley. Maybe Lockard and Jack were right there in London after all. But that would be nowhere near the money, which had been stashed in Draganic's bank in Isle of Man. That much Alex was certain of. But how did these three come into play? If she figured that out, maybe she could use the information to turn them against each other somehow, incite more infighting. There was clearly no shortage of greed around here, and that was enough to bring down a whole team.

Alex turned to Burke and said, "Military Intelligence, CIA—what are you?"

He tilted his head toward her. "Former Company man."

"Why former?"

"Are you kidding?" He snorted. "A billion, cold. Do the math."

Though the idea seemed foreign to her, Alex knew money could intensify an already simmering problem, drawing someone to the other side. But it wouldn't be the only reason. There had to be a trigger to make someone vulnerable for defection.

Perhaps sensing her skepticism and maybe a bit of disgust, he gave Alex an irritated look. "The first time the White House blamed the CIA for inciting violence in the Middle East with our interrogation tactics, I laughed." He laughed to emphasize the point before continuing. "Then the podium-jockey press secretary started talking about failed intelligence missions in Pakistan and Afghanistan. I brushed that off, too."

Burke's face darkened into a scowl. "But then the president himself blamed us. My team, for losing that drone in Iran. It was bullshit. We'd warned him against entering that airspace, but he didn't listen. Hell, POTUS didn't even have the respect to attend the goddamn intelligence briefing three days before it happened. The guy was too busy making his NCAA Final Four picks." Burke waved a hand and looked out the window. "And we were demoted."

After a minute or so, he said, "So now I work for myself."

Alex waited, then said, "The Arsenal game. You set me up, knew what you'd feed me all along, and what I would ask for."

He shrugged. "We needed to get you on Draganic's tail. Distract him while we took the cash from the vault."

She tipped her chin to Wainscott. "And what about her?"

Burke smiled and said, "Valerie? We're a team." He laughed again and looked at Alex like she was the last one in on the joke. Then he emphasized each word.

"She's my wife."

And there it was. Grant, Lockard, Burke, and Wainscott. The Dream Team. Alex let it drop and turned back to her window.

It all made sense. Rookie spies were taught that disillusion often led to defection. People worked for money, but labored for a sense of accomplishment; long-term loyalty to a job required it. Otherwise, the worker eventually left the position or betrayed his boss with embezzlement of money or secrets or even outright sabotage. It was the same for grade-school teachers and engineers and bankers. The pay might differ from profession to profession, but everyone needed to be treated fairly and with respect. Period.

Alex had to admit, the same held true for her.

Of course there are other reasons, too; money wasn't the *be all, end all*. Alex believed Lockard fell into the defect-for-revenge category. He wanted the CIA to pay for his own father dying in Spain, too. A billion to be exact. As Burke had said, *do the math*.

And Grant? Well, she figured he wanted his share of a billion, too. Maybe MI6 didn't pay well in retirement. Or maybe he was just sick of the endless red tape choking the agencies these days. A shame because, as they pulled into what she recognized as Grant's estate, it was clear that he already lived like a Fortune 500 CEO. What else did one man need?

"Go around back," Grant said. "There." He pointed at a white stable gate that sat half open.

They rounded the mansion, and the grounds came into view, acres and acres of it, stretching on in one long, billowing sheet of snow. The white was broken only at the center by an idle, bright-silver helicopter. As they neared, Alex noted the piano-gloss-black trim and tinted glass. An EC145s Eurocopter, interior like a Mercedes S class.

Damn.

The snow around the helicopter had been blown aside, showing sprouts of grass underneath and suggesting a recent arrival. Wainscott navigated the Range Rover to about ten yards from the helicopter, tires crunching over icy gravel as the SUV tilted and bounced on uneven terrain.

Alex looked around but didn't see anyone else, a good sign. If there were others waiting, the prospect of the Dream Team killing and leaving her for a cleanup crew was higher. That said, these people were acting with reckless abandon, ready to give up every ounce of life they had here in the UK for whatever life they expected to have with their new riches.

Alex could not assume rational thought.

When the vehicle stopped, Burke removed a Beretta M9 from his shoulder holster and pointed it at the door. "Get out."

Three on one. They all had guns.

Nodding, Alex simply shifted in her seat.

Burke turned to her. "I said get out."

And she acted.

Alex thrust an elbow into Burke's solar plexus then took hold of his wrist and forced the pistol up. A shot fired into the roof and she wrenched Burke's wrist, causing the gun to drop behind him. Then Alex wrapped her left hand around Grant's seatbelt. He yelped as she wound the nylon strap around his neck then yanked down and anchored it around the metal tines of the headrest. Meanwhile, Burke had found the gun, so she lunged to pull it from him.

Burke pushed into Alex and her door popped open. They tumbled out into the snow and gravel—both their hands wrapped around the pistol. She moved fast in order to immobilize him before Wainscott had a chance to round the car. Easily wrenching her leg around his—Burke had not taken his judo training seriously—Alex gained advantage and pressed the side of his face into the gravel with her shoulder.

His street fighting was sufficient, though, and he head-butted Alex in the cheek, causing her to fall to the side.

Right onto her bad shoulder.

Their hands shaking on the gun, the barrel pressed straight upward between their faces, Alex used all her strength to angle it back toward his chin.

Gritting his teeth and staring into her eyes, Burke did not give.

Neither did Alex. But, just as she was about to win the battle, forcing the barrel into the soft flesh of Burke's neck, she felt the cold metal of another pistol press into her skull, right behind the temple.

"Let it go," Wainscott said.

"Will someone detach this? I'm strangling here," called Grant from inside the Range Rover.

Poor execution on my part, Alex thought. *If he was strangling, he couldn't talk.*

She said, "I'm not afraid to die." And she wasn't. Pressing the barrel deeper into Burke's throat, Alex was ready to shut this operation down for good.

Burke squeezed his eyes closed and kept stone still.

"I'm certain of that," Wainscott said. She tilted her head and continued, "But give it up now. You need to save your energy. It's going to be a long day for you."

Staring into Burke's face, Alex considered pulling the trigger. Releasing one of them from their materialistic bondage for good. But then she thought of

Jack, held captive somewhere in a makeshift death row. And she thought of her father, considered what he would do. He would stay alive. He would finish the job.

Alex let go.

She was curious to see what these turncoats had planned for her anyway.

The Benz-outfitted Eurocopter lived up to the expectation of its luxury, with white leather seats, wood trim, and all the amenities, including a flat-screen television and a full wet bar, complete with tall crystal decanters and thick crystal highballs.

Alex half-expected someone to offer her a cocktail with her handcuffs.

Burke piloted while the rest of them sat in the back. Alex was the lone lady without a pistol to point at anyone, so she spent the time watching the landscape pass … and preparing herself for the battle of her life. Breathing slow and steady, she slipped into a near-meditative state and imagined drawing the scenery as they passed over it.

An ancient snow-draped cathedral edged London, its cross-shaped structure spread wide and its steeple spearing the sky, like a giant stingray half buried in bleached sand. A dormant horse farm at the edge of the city was marked with the thick line of a meandering stream slicing through the property, like the black ink of a child's angry scribble. Finally, the edge of the snow-covered UK isle drifting and disappearing into the Irish Sea, like a spoiled watercolor, the drawing's details dissolved by an errant spill.

They landed in the middle of a field somewhere south of Douglas, Mann's capital city, where another Range Rover awaited. The interior held the strong smell of new leather.

Luxury helicopters, luxury cars. Alex couldn't wait to see the safe house at the end of the line.

With Burke driving the Rover, they weaved their way through the mostly empty snow-covered streets of downtown Douglas. The city celebrated Christmas like the rest of the Western world, so it looked like any small European city at this time of year. Mr. B's Deli was strung with colored lights, and Lucinda's Hairstylists sported a small Christmas tree in the window.

Being Christmas Eve, both shops were closed.

Alex wondered what had happened in Bern and wished she could call Denise to get an update, but that wasn't possible with Wainscott pointing her gun at her. Alex was surprised they hadn't confiscated her cell phone yet. Too distracted, Alex thought. Visions of money plums dancing in their heads.

After navigating a few tight alleys, Burke parked the Rover at the back of a three-story brick building and next to a full-sized tractor trailer. Not Volvo or Mercedes. Alex was disappointed. Burke took out his phone, dialed, and waited. "Here," he said, and hung up.

"Hope you're rested," Grant said, opening his car door to let in the damp, cold air.

Climbing from the car, Alex spotted an orange and brown tabby with a stubbed tail darting from behind the truck and across the snow. A famous no-tailed Isle of Man Manx.

She took it as a sign of good luck.

Wainscott led them up a short flight of stairs to a green steel door and entered the building. They walked up another two gloss-painted, half-flights of stairs and through a second door. This led them into a large open space, the main floor of the building.

The main floor of the bank.

The detail was impressive. Tall ceilings, hand-painted in an intricate, gold-and-black design, and huge, bulbous light fixtures hanging by chains in the same colors. Yet the hardwood floors sat lonely, the only furniture a long, chest-high teller booth, devoid of any computers or papers. No rugs or desks.

It was a giant, gold-crusted cocoon.

At the very end of the space, on the floor, with his back against the wall, was Jack. Seeing Alex, he simply lifted his chin and nodded once. *I survived.*

Lockard sat on a chair across from Jack, with an HK45 on his knee, finger bent on the trigger and barrel pointed at Jack's chest. Lockard's other hand was wrapped in a huge makeshift bandage, like something a soldier might use in the outskirts of Kabul. It was leaking water and blood down the side of the chair, forming a small, reddish pool on the floor.

Lockard sat as still as a lion in waiting. No expression at all.

When the four of them entered—Wainscott in front, then Alex, then Burke, and Grant—Lockard stood and looked straight at Alex.

"This could have been easier," he said, his voice echoing in the chamber.

"Bloody hell, what happened to you?" Grant said, placing the attaché down.

Alex leaned over, eyed the wrapping, and said, "Playing with the pet wolf again?"

A corner of Jack's mouth turned up ever-so-slightly.

Well done. Alex took a step toward him but Lockard pointed his HK at her. "Stay there."

"Would you like me to fix that wrapping?" Wainscott approached Lockard.

"It's fine." Lockard pointed at the attaché at Grant's feet. "Let's have a look."

Cozy little group, this Dream Team. Like a nest of crocodiles.

Lockard nodded to Burke and Wainscott, and they pointed their pistols at Alex and Jack while he knelt at the attaché and opened it. After pulling out the synthetic hand, he inspected it while his own injured hand oozed red liquid on the floor.

Jack had gotten him good.

"Let's go." Lockard and Grant turned and crossed behind the teller desk to a set of open double doors at the back of the bank. Burke and Wainscott waved their pistols at Alex and Jack, and they followed.

Jack stood, wobbled up to Alex. His face looked drawn and he had a large bruise on his cheek. She hoped her worst fears for him had not come true, that Lockard had held him for leverage and negotiation in this situation alone. That he hadn't used Jack as an outlet for his own frustrations with the situation. Though, glancing at Lockard's elephantine hand, Alex didn't know why she was worried at all. Jack was a fighter to the end.

He stared at Alex and said, "I regret not telling you about Edgar."

Alex shook her head, took his hand for a moment. "We'll talk about that later, I'm just happy you're OK."

"That's sweet," Burke said, rolling his eyes to Wainscott.

Wainscott looked away, Alex ignored him, and they headed to the double doors at the back of the bank.

Lockard stood in a short but wide hallway next to a couple of flat pull carts, same as those used for materials at Home Depot. A bottle of water and a towel lay on one cart. Behind Lockard, an enormous steel door stretched six feet wide and to the ceiling. Alex tried to imagine the piles of cash behind there, or maybe they had traded it in for platinum bars or diamonds. A billion dollars was a hell of a load to sit on.

Lockard and Grant approached a metal-and-glass pocket in the wall that looked like a small document scanner. Alex had seen a biological hand scanner before, but never seen it used.

Lockard handed the silicone limb to Grant. "Try this first."

Grant took the replica, pressed a green button to the side of the scanner, and placed the hand on the glass. A set of green, laser-like lights emitted from all sides of the scanner and Grant gave Lockard a skeptical look. His mistrust was confirmed when the scanner emitted a harsh buzz, like a spaceship self-destruct alarm, and blinked bright red three times. A woman's voice with a Scottish accent said, "Initial scan fail. Please be sure to place your hand flush to the surface."

"It needs to read the prints," Lockard said. "And keep your own hand out of view."

Frowning, Grant tried again, manipulating and pressing the hand down this time. After the green lights scanned the hand for the second time, a blue light flashed from the glass and the voice said, "Initial scan complete. Please commence second scan."

"That's a tickle. It worked!" Wainscott said.

"Of course it did," Lockard said, looking at Jack. "Let's hope loverboy hasn't fucked it up for all of us."

Lockard peeled the corner of a strip of the duct tape from his wrist and unwrapped the slushy ice bag, letting the bloody sack fall to the floor. He then pulled the rest of the tape off his hand. The last strips stuck to the skin and the wound, causing Lockard to clench his jaw. He stared at Jack as he tugged off the final strip.

"Bloody hell, he butchered you," Wainscott said, glancing at Burke, who just shook his head.

And there was the rub. Lockard's hand was key number two. Jack had somehow mangled that key.

Not good … and awesome at the same time.

Lockard uncapped the water and rinsed the blood from his palm, drying it with the towel. With a large gash in the back of his hand and through his palm, it looked like he'd been crucified with a chef's knife.

Lockard looked at Jack. Jack shrugged. "Could've been worse."

Lockard stepped to the scanner, pressed the button, and placed his damaged hand on the glass. After a moment, the green lasers scanned his hand and flashed red. "Second scan fail," the electronic voice said.

Lockard exhaled loudly and tried again, cleaning the glass and re-rinsing his hand.

A triple flash of red and the voice said, "Second scan fail."

"Son of a bitch!"

Grabbing the pistol, he walked over to Jack and, standing inches from his face, stared at him. Before anyone could react, Lockard drove the butt of his pistol into Jack's stomach.

Alex lunged, but Burke was too fast, thrusting an elbow into her injured shoulder and tripping her to the ground.

Jack doubled over and heaved, as Alex crawled next to him.

"Fools," Alex said, looking back at Lockard. "The machine is scanning the shape of the hand to match a previously stored 3D image."

"No shit," Lockard said, "and your fucking honeypot destroyed the matching hand." He held up his palm. A long rope of mangled skin flapped to the side of the wound.

"We'll never get in with that," Burke said. "I should shoot him in the face." He turned and pointed his Beretta at Jack's forehead.

Jack looked up, but didn't blink.

Pacing back and forth, Lockard was unraveling. He stopped and tried to tuck the skin into the wound, causing it to bleed again. It reminded Alex of the stories of D-Day soldiers carrying their own arms around or trying to tuck their spilled guts back into their bellies.

The man was about to lose it, meaning Alex and Jack had minutes until the Dream Team killed them. She no longer cared if they got the money. She just wanted to maneuver them out of there alive.

Alex pushed to her feet. "Let me help."

"How?" Grant asked.

She held out a hand to Lockard.

Lockard stared at her with sleepy eyes. Then he held out his hand.

"And the other?" Alex said.

Lockard held up his good hand.

Sure, she wanted to dig her fingers into the wound, make him pay for all this, but that would be foolish. It was four on two here, and Alex's two were not armed.

She turned his good hand over and signaled for him to do the same with the injured one. Inspecting both, Alex said, "You've done well to keep the swelling down. That's good for the imaging. Also, there's no fingerprint damage, though the dried blood may be a problem."

"Then why isn't it working?" Grant asked.

"This." She turned the hands back over. "See this tendon? On your good hand?"

"What about it?" Lockard asked.

"Did you have a similar one here?" Alex traced a finger above the back of his wounded hand.

Glancing at Jack, he said, "I used to."

She nodded at the silicone replica of the hand. "Any chance you have some of that silicone left?"

"The materials?" Lockard asked, then looked at the others. "Across the street. Why?"

"Because I can recreate the tendon using this flap of skin and trick the scanner with a mold."

"You want to cut me." Lockard shook his head. "It won't heal in time to be molded. It'll bleed like hell."

"Not if I use duct tape."

They stared at Alex, the idea sinking in, perhaps.

She continued, "Then I'll smooth the mold to remove the impression of the tape. Should work fine."

Wainscott folded her arms. "I say we let her have a go at it."

"Easy, honey." Lockard looked at her and back to Alex. "Okay. But Burke here will have his gun buried in the back of your skull while you hold the knife."

"I would expect nothing less." Alex smiled.

"And another thing." Lockard pulled the knife from a sheath at his side. "If it doesn't work." He walked to Jack, who was sitting up again, and grabbed the back of his head, then held the knife to his throat. "I'll cut the whole goddamn head off while you watch."

No pressure there, Alex thought.

Lockard tossed a set of keys to Wainscott. "Go get the mixture."

"Why not just blow through the door with the explosives? You must have some of that Nobel 808 left." Jack looked back and forth between Grant and Lockard.

Alex didn't know if Jack was worried about her sculpting abilities or if he thought an explosion would cause enough mayhem to give them a chance to act.

"Because it's in the vault, genius." Lockard pointed at the door.

"It makes no matter. This building was the original Douglas post office." Grant waved a hand toward the ceiling. "A prewar construction, it held the kingdom's bearer bonds in this vault for a decade. It would require a tank to force your way inside. Literally. Explosives would merely bury the treasure."

Alex said, "Which is how Draganic convinced the Isle of Man to issue the bank charter in the first place. They knew you couldn't loot the vault without the banker being present."

"Or part of him, anyway," Grant said.

Lovely.

"That moron insisted on being one of the human keys," Burke pointed out. "It's his own doing."

"Enough. Let's get on with this," Lockard said. "We'll do it in the men's room."

Three minutes later, Lockard stood stone still while Alex examined his good hand versus his bad one. Burke hovered behind her but did not keep the barrel of his Beretta shoved into her neck as threatened.

"I need my sketchbook and pencils," Alex said.

"Why?" Lockard asked.

"Because I want to create the mirror image in a series of sketches before making any cuts. It will lessen the likelihood of error."

"Get them," Lockard said to Burke.

Alex considered jumping Lockard as Burke left, but the prospect of winning the blade from him, immobilizing him with it, then using his HK to beat three other agents—all without putting Jack at risk—seemed ridiculous. Besides, her best chance for escape would come when the Dream Team was distracted by the money.

So she examined Lockard's hands instead.

When Burke returned with her satchel and materials, Alex sketched Lockard's good hand from several angles. He had large knuckles, thick fingers, a series of bulbous veins, and wrists as wide as a cricket bat. The man was all testosterone, one link away from missing.

Anyway.

The defining feature was the thick ridge of tendon that stretched from wrist to pointer on his good hand. Jack had destroyed this on the other. That said, he had also made a clean stab, a through and through, leaving the bones and other tendons in place. She would need to cut away the lengths of skin that were swollen to the sides of the entry point, and secure one of the strips underneath the healthy skin, thus recreating the tendon.

"I can do it," she finally said, "But it's going to hurt like a bitch."

Oh, well.

"Try not to enjoy it too much." He gripped the side of the sink and closed his eyes as he handed her the knife. Unflinching and silent, he stood stock still as Alex carved his flesh and recreated the missing tendon. She worked for a full hour and Lockard never made a sound.

Fucking cyborg.

In lieu of stitches, Alex secured the long strand of skin under the wound with a thin strip of duct tape—the stuff was amazing in a pinch—then closed the wound on the palm with another thin strip. After placing a final strip around his wrist to secure the ends, she rinsed off Lockard's hand and her own, gave back the knife, and said, "Don't flex it."

"Don't worry." He stuffed the knife back into its holster. "I can't."

Good to know.

They stopped in front of Wainscott when they returned to the vault. She'd prepped all the materials for a new silicone mold. One large paint bucket was half full of water and another was half full of the white thickening powder.

"Ready." Lockard held up his injured hand.

Wainscott began mixing the mold as Burke poured the powder into the water. The mixture turned purple as she stirred. When there were no lumps or bubbles, she looked at Lockard and pointed at the bucket. "It'll harden in seven minutes. Go."

Lockard bent to a knee, then eased his hand into the purple ooze.

"Now, remember how we did the banker's hand. Your fingers must remain a full inch from the bottom," Wainscott said.

"I know." Lockard stopped plunging his hand and stayed rock still for nine minutes. The mixture hardened around his wrist and hand, and Lockard eased it back out.

Burke and Wainscott then mixed another set of powder and water. This time, the mixture turned flesh-colored when churned. Once smooth, it was poured into the mold.

"It'll be ready in twenty minutes."

So they sat there, two guns trained on Alex, two on Jack, and waited for the silicone hand to cure. Burke finally flipped the bucket and pried out the fixtures. He split the purple mold and worked the silicone hand free.

"Perfect," Wainscott said.

Lockard looked at Alex. "What do you think?"

She walked over and inspected the replica. Across the top of the hand and around the wrist, evidence of the duct tape showed and would have to be smoothed out. Also, the area where she had recreated the tendon was quite swollen and would have to be carved back a bit. Alex knew these biometric systems allowed for a certain degree of difference from the original scan to account for slight weight gain or daily fluctuation of water retention. She just had to adjust the replica while keeping original proportions. Still, it was a long shot. She said, "A few minor adjustments and it'll work great."

Lockard motioned for Burke to hand the replica to Alex.

"Knife?" She looked at Lockard.

"Right." He unsheathed and handed Alex the knife again.

Taking her time, Alex placed the silicone hand on one of the pull carts, and used Lockard's healthy hand and her mirror-image drawing as models for the replica. She scraped away the excess layer of silicone where the tape was and smoothed the area clean.

"Here," she said, handing the replica to Grant.

After reengaging the scanner with the banker's replica, Grant placed Lockard's replica on the glass. He pressed the button.

Almost immediately, the scanner buzzed and the voice said, "Second scan fail."

"Shit!" Lockard glared at Alex.

Jack gave her a look of concern.

Keeping calm, she said, "Let me see it again."

Grant handed the replica her.

Holding the silicone version up to Lockard's good hand, Alex said, "It's just swollen. Knife?"

He hesitated before holding out the blade to her.

Alex took it and again contemplated gutting him right then and there. Jack could jump Wainscott and get a gun, and she'd have Lockard's in a matter of seconds. Problem was, that left two others armed and ready. In those seconds, Alex and Jack would be killed.

Exhaling loudly, she placed the replica back on the cart and went to work, shaving and carving and smoothing all the edges and lines of the hand and the wrist to make it as close of a mirror image of Lockard's good hand as she could. When she was finished, all eyes on her, Alex said, "This should work."

"You'd better hope," Lockard said. He glanced at Jack as he took the hand and placed it back on the scanner.

Alex took a deep breath as he pressed the button again.

Nobody moved. Nobody uttered a sound.

The green lasers shined and swirled. The glass flashed blue and then green. A few moments later, the voice said, "Second scan complete. Access granted."

"Son of a bitch," Burke muttered.

Alex exhaled as the vault clanked open, echoing into the room behind them.

Nothing could prepare a person for the sight of that much cash in one place. Visit the Treasury or go to Fort Knox, and your heart rate would damn sure accelerate in the presence of piles of cash or mounds of gold bars. But with more Secret Service than the presidential detail around, and complex security vaulting systems, the sight of the money was just that. Here, the cash was loose. Unprotected. Free for the taking. Wall to wall, chest high, packed in tight cellophane wrapping, stacks and stacks of one-hundred-dollar bills beckoned them forward. Forget about rising heart rates. This could give someone a coronary.

Lockard pulled the vault door all the way open, and the smell of dirty money wafted out to hit them like the scent of an ex-lover. Powerful, exciting.

Carnal.

Some of the packs had been torn open—no doubt for someone to use a portion of the capital to move and hide it—leaving hundred-dollar bills spilling to the side and onto the floor. There was so much, it overflowed.

They all stood there staring for a good ten or fifteen seconds.

Jack said, "It's like all the world's evils are right here in this room."

Lockard rolled his eyes, then looked at his watch. "Let's go. The plane is waiting." He turned to Grant. "Your choice. Which end?"

"I'll watch the truck," he said, and walked out of the vault and down the long hallway.

Lockard turned to Burke. "You work with her." He nodded at Alex, then looked to Wainscott. "And you're with him." He nodded to Jack.

Jack said, "That's why you've brought us along? To help move this?"

Stepping to the edge of the vault, Lockard said, "There are new pallets in the truck. Move the cash from one pallet onto a pull cart. You and Burke load it, Jack and Wainscott pull it to the truck and re-stack it onto a new pallet inside, then these two start stacking the next cart. Then repeat. Let's get started."

Alex stepped forward and picked up a stack. It felt like forty or fifty pounds. "How much is each—"

"Two and a half million, each pack. There're fifty-two packs per pallet. Eight pallets is 416 packs total. I figure at two minutes per pack, a minute here and one in the truck, we can be done in just over three hours."

She did the math. A hundred thirty million per pallet, times eight pallets. "That's one-point-four billion dollars."

"And they say girls aren't good at math." Lockard waved the gun at her, but he stopped her just as she turned away. "And by the way, no. That's not the only reason you're here."

For the first time yet, she saw Lockard smile.

Lockard stood to the side, poised like a viper as Alex and Burke worked themselves into a sweat. It actually only took two hours to move it all. They'd have moved even more quickly, but Alex had to stop and stabilize her injured shoulder with duct tape. Then Wainscott complained, as it had begun to snow again and she was cold in the truck, so Alex and Burke switched ends with them.

The cold air made her shoulder feel better, and Alex didn't mind working in the darkness of the trailer. Grant smoked one cigarette after another, and sat in a chair under the back awning, gun trained on her as they worked. He held a walkie-talkie to report their progress to Lockard. Again, since Alex and Jack were separated, she didn't attempt anything heroic. They were valuable workhorses and safe ... at least until the plane was loaded.

The plane. Alex stared at the money. There was too much of it. She knew the weight limits of jets with full fuel tanks, and there was no way this would fit on a charter. She turned to Grant and said, "This is eleven tons of money. I hope you leased more than a G6."

"Don't worry yourself with that," he said, lighting up another Parliament Super Slim. He looked like an aging actor the way he held the cigarette in two extended fingers. Alex wanted to jam the lit end up his—

"Come on!" Burke said, moving another packet.

Right.

They loaded the last of the packets onto the truck and Grant said into the radio, "What about the rest of the Nobel?"

Lockard's voice came over in static. "We're leaving it."

Grant nodded, clicked off, and turned to them. "All right, then. Back in the vault. We'll need to brief you before we leave."

Alex was too damn tired to argue. They trudged down the hallway and into the vault, where Jack and Wainscott both sat in the corner drinking bottles of water. Burke wiped his forehead with the tail of his shirt and sat next to his wife. Jack held up a bottle for Alex.

"Before that," Lockard said, joining Grant. "A little housekeeping."

And suddenly facing Alex and Jack, they had their pistols drawn. Grant pointing at Alex, Lockard pointing at Jack.

Too late for heroics now, Alex reached for Jack's hand, closed her eyes, and braced for the impact.

But instead, she heard both Burke and Wainscott's screams match the staccato shots echoing through the vault.

Blood seeped from holes in the center of Burke's and Wainscott's foreheads as they slumped. Gray matter and bone splattered the wall behind them.

Lockard bent and picked up the bottle of water that had fallen from Jack's hand. He threw it to Alex. "Drink it on the way."

Thirty-Eight

Alex and Jack were locked in the trailer, backs pressed against a pallet of cash, while Lockard and Grant rode in the truck's cab. It was cold and damp and they were still drenched in sweat, so Jack pulled Alex close, giving them both some warmth. The low throttle of the diesel truck overshadowed any conversation Lockard and Grant were having.

Staring into the darkness, Alex tried to soften the question best she could. "So, what happened? To his hand."

Jack stayed silent for a few seconds and then said, "He broke the rules of engagement."

"You okay?"

He nodded. "I will be."

Knowing that meant torture of some sort, Alex let it drop for now.

They sat like that, holding each other in a heavy silence for a good twenty or thirty minutes. The weight of the last few days' events—the last year's—hanging between them like a cinderblock, threatening to drag them under a flood of of pent up emotions and fears. Even so, Alex felt no anger at Jack. Yes, he'd lied to her, but she'd lied to him, too. So he was a spy. So was she. There was one little difference between them, though, and if they were going to get out of this alive, they needed to mend their communication now. At least enough to keep going. To fight this battle together.

"About my father..."

Alex paused to clear her throat, and then told him about the confrontation with Moss on the bridge. She relayed what she'd learned about Moss, and kept her report level of emotion when describing how Edgar confronted him. How there was apparently more—much more—to that day her parents supposedly died in Spain. But she didn't find out what, because the next thing that happened was she'd lost her father in the icy river.

Jack squeezed her hand in a way that said he understood how Alex could be torn between anger and aching. Not really able to grieve the man again after all these years, but still somehow needing to.

"I know you believe I betrayed you," he finally said. His voice was rough with exhaustion, perhaps something more. "But in truth, if it were anyone I betrayed, it would be Edgar. He warned me not to cross the line with you, and was vexed when he discovered I had. Pulled me right off your surveillance."

And there it was. Alex thought he'd just left on his own will. "And London?"

"Edgar'd asked me to convince you to leave. To go anywhere with you, just get you the hell out of London. You were determined to find him, though. Goddamned stubborn. No different than him. Considering that, I told Edgar I'd stay and keep an eye on you." He shook his head. "But instead, I carried on helping you find him. I suppose it's my fault he's now gone for good."

"Jack. No one could have talked Edgar off *that* bridge. Stubborn, remember?"

And she felt better saying it. As the silence stretched, the truck thrumming on the wet streets, she thought maybe Jack did, too.

"So," she finally said. "MI6?"

"Seven years."

"And under Edgar?"

"Three more—but no official ties to your Langley."

"You going to tell me where you really learned Savate? You looked more than proficient."

"Edgar sent me to Lyon for six months. I progressed to silver glove level 2, which is similar to a second degree black belt in Karate, I believe."

Alex smiled in the dark. Intensive study and submersion. That was Edgar.

And it could make all the difference for them today. Lockard and Grant had guns and knives, but Jack had already injured one of them. Alex thought of the way Lockard had looked at her—before shooting a similarly oily look at Jack— and she couldn't say she liked their chances of winning this one. But she'd choose Jack in this fight over either of those backstabbing crooks.

She'd choose Jack, she suddenly realized, over anyone.

Jack squeezed her hand as the truck slowed for one last wide turn, and even as they pulled to a stop she managed a ghost of a smile. He chose her as well.

Alex and Jack climbed to their feet and waited until the doors were unlocked and the latches unhitched. A blast of cold air hit them along with the sight of Grant and Lockard, pistols already drawn. Behind them were the skeletal insides of an aircraft hangar, and the surreal gleam of a white Boeing Business Jet.

Sure, Alex thought. The largest heist in history practically required escape via the finest luxury jet known to man.

"Ever see one of those before?" she asked Jack.

"Not from the inside."

Neither had she. It was nearly the size of a 737, far larger than the Gulfstream she'd expected. This thing could swallow the billion dollars whole.

"Hurry up." Lockard motioned to them with the gun. "We leave in ninety minutes."

Alex glanced at Jack. Ninety minutes—was he kidding?

"We just lost half our workcrew to your trigger finger, Boss," Alex said, but before she could ask if he and Grant planned on chipping in with the manual labor, Lockard pointed to the forklift.

"You'll operate this while those two load the plane."

She said, "Let Jack run the forklift. I'll can move the packages with Grant."

Lockard shook his head. "You need to conserve your energy." Then he walked away.

It took ten minutes per pallet, from forking it in the truck, raising it, and for Jack and Grant to load it into the cargo hold. Most of it, that was. Even the enormous jet couldn't transport that much cash in its belly, and half the pallets had to be stuffed into the cabin. When finished, Lockard led Alex and Jack up the stairs to the plane, and sat them on a leather sofa facing a widescreen television.

Hundreds of millions of dollars scattered them. Under the seats and tables, around and above them. Alex felt like a modern-day pirate…one who was about to walk the plank. Lockard planned on killing them soon. She doubted he'd dump them in the hangar, though. That would raise too many alarms, questions as to where the plane had landed next.

"I need to call Customs," Grant said, as if reading her mind. "Get our final clearance straightened out."

And that was his value. Lockard got the cash out of Iraqi sandland via Draganic. Draganic used his money-laundering contacts and knowledge to open the bank in Isle of Man, entering the cash into the financial system. It was actually brilliant—until the greed kicked in. Now Lockard had to physically remove the cash from the system, and the only way to get it out of the UK was through someone who could bypass Customs and Immigration on the premise of a classified operation.

Grant headed to the cockpit to make his call while Lockard kept his HK pointed at Alex and Jack as he struggled with his own phone. Using his mangled hand, he speed-dialed a number, placed the call on speakerphone, and set it on top of a leather seat.

After a few odd-sounding rings, a man answered in Spanish, "First Security of Santiago. Agostin Herrera speaking."

"Agostin, es Evan Lockard."

"Good afternoon, sir. It is a pleasure to hear from you. When shall we expect you?"

Lockard answered in Spanish, a language Alex was familiar with in numerous dialects. "We arrive in three and a half hours."

"Excellent. We will have our trucks waiting for you at La Gomera Airport."

So Grant's contacts extended to the autonomous Canary Islands. Interesting, though Alex guessed that wasn't the last stop for Lockard. No, he'd take off for a far-away paradise once the cash was reentered into the world's banking system, he'd take off for a far-away paradise. Maybe Fiji or Easter Island.

Lockard suddenly switched to English, presumably to elevate his authority. "That's good, Agostin, but I'm reconsidering the price you quoted. Fifteen-point-six million seems steep for a transaction like this."

Agostin hesitated before saying, "One and one half percent of the total to be invested is standard for a transaction of this magnitude. In most other cases, it is two to three percent."

Lockard remained silent, a tried and true negotiation tactic.

The only thing that kept Alex from rolling her eyes was the HK pointed at her chest. A billion dollars in an illegal transfer of funds, one hidden from international banking disclosures, and this macho tool was negotiating for a lower fee.

Agostin finally broke the uncomfortable silence. "I tell you what, my friend. What do you say to us splitting the difference? A one-and-one-quarter-percent fee for thirteen million?"

"Done." Lockard hung up.

The testosterone-soaked billionaire had saved himself two-point-six million dollars.

Jack said, "Being Christmas and all, perhaps you should donate a portion of your savings to charity. Perhaps the Mental Health Foundation, seems a worthy cause."

"One more word, sweetheart," Lockard said, looked Jack up and down and continued, "and I'll finish what the two of us started yesterday. You can watch." He glanced at Alex.

Jack's jaw tightened and his back arched in response. *Jesus.*

Seeing it, Lockard puckered his lips and kept the pistol trained on Jack's face. Alex wanted to charge him. Fuck reason, she'd make an unholy mess of things if he shot Jack. What she didn't quite understand was why was he even keeping them around this long?

Grant exited the cockpit. "We're all set. Have you got that duct tape handy?"

Lockard pointed his pistol at the seat behind him, and nodded to Jack. "Close the cabin door."

Jack reached for the handle slowly, angled in a way that left only half his body exposed to the outside so that he couldn't be pushed out the door, away from Alex.

It was exactly what Lockard wanted. He grinned as he pointed his gun at Jack. "For this," he said, raising his wounded hand.

Then he shot him in the leg.

Alex had no recollection of reaching Jack. She had her palm pressed to his leg, but it was still flowering with blood. He was going to pass out if it kept up like this. Jack moaned as she pressed her other palm to the side of his thigh and tried to stem the bleeding.

Lockard said, "Relax. He'll live. I missed the femoral artery."

Grant grabbed the roll of black duct tape. "Right, then. Pants off, then lie back, put your foot up on the seat."

Alex helped Jack undress. The bullet had torn right across the upper thigh muscle, though not through the leg. Lockard hadn't only managed the perfect immobilizing shot, he'd made sure the bullet had continued out the door and into the hangar.

No damage to the aircraft.

Alex squeezed Jack's hand to keep him from passing out, as Grant used a towel to cleaned off the thigh so that the tape would stick. He applied a short strip across the wound, then wrapped the thigh so tight that he nearly cut off the circulation completely.

Gritting his teeth, Jack said to Lockard, "You'd do well to ensure your little helpers keep their mouths shut. Because I'm coming to find you."

"You mean from beyond the grave?" Lockard shrugged. "Okay."

Grant picked up his pistol. "Let's go, mate," and ushered Jack to the aft of the plane.

Lockard puffed out his chest as they passed.

"We'll see about that," Jack said, purposely bumping the other man.

"Enough." Grant pushed Jack past the television and around the mounds of cash, then stopped him next to a teakwood conference table at the plane's center. Another built-in table sat against the jet's wall. "Sit there, arms behind your back."

Grant zip-tied Jack's hands around the table's thick steel leg and pulled the straps tight. "There we are, then. Well done, everyone."

As Alex was wondering why they didn't zip-tie her also—again, why they were even still alive—Lockard shoved his mangled hand in her face. "This way, Alex. Thanks to our mutual lover over there, you're now our pilot."

After Jack had distracted Lockard with the threat of coming to find him, then bumping into him, and before Grant had ushered him away, Jack had slipped his other hand behind Lockard's back. A simple flick of Jack's finger, and a straight pull, had yielded Lockard's knife.

He stumbled to to hide the maneuver—not hard given his throbbing leg—and managed to hide the blade at the small of his back.

As long as Lockard didn't notice it missing, Jack now possessed a big enough surprise to take them down. So he sat, he stewed … and he bided his time.

Lockard led Alex to the flight deck where a smooth composite dash housed 3D LCD screens, a touchpad GPS systems, and simple joysticks instead of steering yokes. It was a pilot command center far more luxurious than the Gulfstream they'd trained on in Coronado, but it was intuitive and far simpler than traditional cockpits, and only took a few moments for her to acclimate.

Yet the joysticks were located to the sides of either seat, so it required two hands for proper navigation.

Advantage, Winter.

Lockard said, "Think you can handle it?"

"This and more." She looked at him. "With coffee."

"Why? Are you feeling woozy, all that blood?"

Alex flicked switches as she said, "I have this thing where I black out if I haven't slept in over a day." She turned to him. "It's been almost three."

"Strap in" was all he said, leaving her. Yet he returned four minutes later with a piping hot ceramic mug. Beverage holders were built into the left armrest, and Alex settled the coffee there.

"We have any idea how long the runway is at La Gomera?" she said, prepping for take-off. "I've never seen that on the British Airways destination board."

Lockard gave her a deadpan look. "Four thousand nine hundred and twenty-one feet. This aircraft requires twenty-five hundred, if you know what the fuck you're doing. Which you do." Navy SEALs planned for everything.

He rolled his chin. "Any other questions?"

"I'm sure I'll think of a few."

The plane glided as smooth as a Bentley, and Alex was able to maneuver them out of the hangar and onto the runway with minimal contact from the control tower. Of course she could have screamed *Terrorists* or *bomb*, but she was pretty sure Evan Lockard had a plan for that scenario, too. One that would start with the execution of Alex and Jack.

An execution would be difficult to do once airborne, though, so she pushed forward.

The wide windshield gave an open view of the second runway, the one that the ground crew—consisting of what appeared to be a teenage boy and his father—had cleared with a simple snowplow. The two of them stood off to the side and watched as the jet took off, leaning against the plow, hands in their pockets, hats pulled low.

One minute later, they were soaring over the Irish Sea, headed south-southwest to their destination three thousand and fifty-nine kilometers away.

The Canary Islands.

Alex had to keep pushing thoughts of Jack from her mind. She needed to concentrate, though the Boeing's autopilot computer kept them on target. All she had to do was occasionally check critical indicators and respond to in-flight checks, then land the plane. Apparently Lockard was going to sit in the copilot's seat with his HK aimed at her ribs for the whole flight.

Except for when he was getting her coffee. Finally, after two hours and Alex's third cup piping mug, he decided to speak. "The motorcyclists who jumped you in Piccadilly—are you certain you killed them?"

Eyeing him, she said, "Positive. So, who crossed who there?"

He looked out at the pure blue ocean. "The twins made the drop and then changed their minds. They were going to take you. Ransom you to Edgar for the attaché." He smiled. "Why else would they have missed you with all those rounds?"

Another corner of the operation's landscape came into view for Alex, and she nodded. "Nice team you had there. A bunch of real stand-up guys."

"Right? So I should thank you," he said. "I think they would've succeeded if you hadn't killed them."

"Anything for you, Evan."

He laughed. "You know, you should be blaming Moss. He's the genesis of it all."

"That's one part I don't get. Why would Moss go along with all of this?"

"Honey, that's CIA 101. Everyone has a skeleton buried somewhere. And I found his."

"Must have been pretty damned solid, considering the money you demanded."

"Hey, it was no secret that we'd dumped twenty billion cash into Iraq and proceeded to lose six of it. We only aimed for one. Seemed fair, considering."

Just a billion dollars? Perfectly.

"And Moss orchestrated it?"

"More like guided. The Company had located a cache held by a small group of rebels in a palace. He pointed us in the right direction, and…under clandestine actions, we took it back."

"You mean Draganic, the twins, and yourself."

He nodded. "Your name came up…you know, for the snatch team. I actually considered recruiting you. You're a Talonstriker, and I thought you had to be game for a little payback considering how the Company screwed you and your dad. I even reviewed your file."

"Lemme guess. I was too honest for you?"

"Women lack killer instinct."

Alex decided to take that up with him later. "So instead, you suggested Moss use me as bait, knowing my father would then go after Moss."

"And I knew you'd end up with the attaché."

"And you'd have one less partner to split this with." She motioned to the back of the plane.

"Brilliant, right?"

"And Draganic?"

"He helped in the beginning, but then got greedy. He made his own bed. Right in the dirt."

Alex watched Lockard shake his head, and realized she was sitting next to a guy who considered life to be no more or less than a bargaining chip. He was a machine, unfeeling, unemotional, if self-motivated. Yeah, money was a good way to keep score, but this guy was all about the win and so far he'd outmaneuvered and manipulated her father and Moss and Draganic. He'd either killed or orchestrated the deaths of his teammates, and what was his reward for all of that?

A cool billion in cash.

This world was so fucked up.

Alex unstrapped her seat belt.

"Fuck you going?" Lockard said.

"Fuck you think?" she replied. "Restroom."

Truth was, she wanted to check on Jack. She wanted to be sure he was okay… and she wanted to stir the water up a bit. If the two of them were going to live, Grant and Lockard would have to be incapacitated before they landed. The final descent was in ten minutes.

Lockard finally glanced at his watch. "Make it quick."

She switched the captain controls over to Lockard, and eased out of the cockpit seat and out the door. Standing in the galley, Alex watched Grant and Jack as she put another pot of coffee on the burner. She stretched her neck and touched her own wound, indicating that she knew how Jack felt.

His lip curled up and he nodded.

Grant sat between piles of money on the long sofa, watching the large-screen television. Some British show was on, the kind that featured jokes from Churchill's era, and when Alex emerged from the galley, he seemed annoyed that he had to train his Walther on her.

"Favorite childhood show?"

"Pardon?"

"Forget it." She continued past him and he said, "Alex. I thought you should know, I really liked your father. For the record."

She stopped, and turned to him. "And he thought you were a masterful leader of MI6 operations."

"Really?"

Alex just stared back.

Jack laughed.

"You're a bloody bitch, you know that?" Grant said, but by this time he was behind her.

Alex stopped before Jack. "You okay?"

He glanced at Grant, already engrossed in his show again, then tipped his head for her to lean down.

She dropped a kiss on his forehead as he whispered, "I've Lockard's blade."

"Keep moving," Grant yelled. "I'm happy to shoot you, too!"

The bathroom rivaled that of most five-star hotels, and for a moment it was all she could do not to lay down on the limestone tiles and close her eyes. Instead, after taking as long as she dared without alarming the Dream Team, Alex exited the bathroom with a plan of attack. One that begged for proof of sanity.

Grant barely took his eyes from his show. "Hurry it up."

Jack nodded once and looked away.

Alex stumbled over a packet of cash, calling out and falling into Jack while reaching around his back. As Grant jumped up from the sofa, she sliced the tie between his wrists with the knife he'd readied.

He had it hidden again before Grant could reach them.

"Wait for my move," she whispered.

"Up!" Grant grabbed Alex's shoulder and pulled her to her feet. He pressed the gun into her back as he pushed her down the hall toward the cockpit.

Easy part, done.

Jack could take Grant even with one good leg, of that she was sure. But could he do it quickly enough for them to take Lockard together? At least neither man could fire his gun at this altitude. A forty-five caliber round could blow a hole through the engine block of a Cadillac. A tear like that in the jet's hull would be disastrous for all of them.

Alex stopped in the galley. "I need coffee."

"Oh, bollocks." Grant stood there, waving his pistol. "Make it snappy, then."

The metal pot was still filling with near-boiling liquid, but Alex did the mug-for-pot replacement trick, catching the stream of hot coffee as it fell from the filter. She slipped the pot back under the stream once her cup was full, and

Grant holstered his pistol and turned back to his show. Alex entered the cockpit.

Lockard knew their time was short. He was watching her with an intensity in his eyes; anticipatory, gleaming … wary. "Hurry up. You need to guide the descent."

Alex climbed back into her seat, placed the coffee into the holder, and touched the screens to take back control of the jet.

"Keep it steady, and remember,"—he nodded to the back and smiled—"we're flying with an extra twenty-three thousand pounds here."

"Hard to forget," she said, easing the thrusters.

Alex couldn't see the Canary Islands yet, she but kept her focus straight ahead and touched the thrusters back again, watching as they dropped in altitude.

Taking hold of the handle because the coffee was still hot, Alex turned the mug in her hand.

The altimeter dropped from twenty-five to fifteen, then to ten thousand feet. She waited a bit more. Eight, then seven thousand feet.

Holding her breath, Alex pulled all the way back on the thrusters, all but killing power to the engines.

"What are you doing?" Lockard sat forward and tapped his screen. "It's too early for that."

Alex threw the piping hot coffee in Lockard's face right as he turned to glare at her, and then she shattered the cup on the side of his head.

Thirty-Nine

There really were moments in which time froze. Seconds in which each action unfolded in slow motion due to hyper-perception, your mind clocking at an inhuman pace.

This wasn't one of them.

Though scalded and struck, instead of falling backward like a normal human, Lockard reached for his knife.

"Shit!" he yelled, coming up empty.

He vaulted from his seat and onto Alex, and she drove an elbow into his head while ducking her own. Still holding the cup handle, she tore the jagged porcelain across his face. It fueled him like a lanced bull. Raging, he drove his shoulder into her, taking them both to the flight-deck floor.

Suddenly, Grant yelped from the rear of the plane. "What the devil are you —"

Lockard, turning his weight and bending an arm under her, rolled with Alex on the floor. She clenched a fist on his bad hand and he grimaced, blood dripping from the cut on his face, but he didn't yield. With just enough room, she reached behind him and ripped his HK from its holster.

Lockard, with the kill-or-be-killed expression of an MMA fighter, held her arm high and drove a knee into her pubic bone.

Jack yelled from the back, but Alex's ears were ringing with such pain that she couldn't make out his words.

She slammed the butt of the gun into the back of Lockard's head, but he kept going. She did it again, and he twisted, using his bad hand to deflect the blows before driving a fist into her bandaged shoulder. The strike to the gunshot wound blasted through her, and the gun clattered to the floor as she turned to avoid the next strike.

Lockard pushed a forearm into her throat, grabbed the HK with his good hand, and came back with it pointed it at her head.

Jack held the knife, drawn but ready, behind his back as Alex returned to the cockpit. He spotted Lockard half-turned in his seat, but when Alex glanced back at Grant, Jack knew it was go time.

He pounced at the exact moment Alex threw the coffee into Lockard's face.

At the defense training facility in Lyon, Jack learned that an aggressor could clear twenty-one feet in one and a half seconds, a half second faster than the time it took to draw a pistol from a holster. Even though he had to hurdle bundles of cash with one good leg, he cleared half that distance in two seconds flat.

Grant swung his pistol around at the last second, but he'd spent too many years behind the desk, far removed from his glory days in the Cold War.

"What the devil are you—"

One stiff-arm blow to the underside of Grant's chin, and the old man was flat on his back.

The gun dropped to the floor, and in a clumsy attempt to draw it back to himself, Grant kicked it forward as he fell. It spun all the way into the bathroom.

From behind, Jack pressed the blade to Grant's neck and shoved a knee into his lower back. Grant glanced down at Jack's bandaged leg and moved a hand toward the wound.

"Do that..." Jack pressed the blade harder to the man's throat. "And it'd be the last thing you do."

"Drop it!"

It was Jack's voice, coming from the back.

"Calm now. Calm!" Grant shouted.

Alex didn't dare move. Lockard had his gun tight to Alex's head, and as she stared up at him she could see the calculation moving across his pupils. If he shot her, Jack would have all the incentive he needed to cut Grant's throat and take his pistol. Then Lockard would be in a gunfight with someone with nothing to lose. Causing a plane crash would not factor into Jack's actions.

So Lockard cracked the butt of the gun against Alex's head and stood.

Blinking, Alex turned to see doubles and then triples of Jack. Grant was on his knees before him, the knife to his throat.

"Drop the gun!" Jack yelled again.

Lockard pointed the gun at Jack and Grant, then at Alex again. Then at Jack.

Grant yelled, "Shoot this man, Evan! Do it!"

"Brilliant," Jack said. "Then we'll all die."

Lockard swung the gun from Jack to Alex, back to Jack, then Alex. Back to Jack. Stalemate.

Almost.

"Fools," he said. He began walking to the back of the plane, gun trained on Jack.

Lockard had found a way to win this, Alex realized. He could take Jack on without care of Grant, or Grant's gun, kicked out of Jack's reach. After all, you don't bring a knife to a gunfight, right? Even if you are a few thousand feet in the air.

"Jack, think about it." Lockard took another step.

Alex was struggling to right herself, still seeing multiples of each of them. Looking up at the screens, she saw they were at four thousand feet and dropping faster than normal with the lower thrust.

"Stop right where you are," Jack said, but he couldn't hide the doubt in his voice. Lockard had bested them all. In about a minute, he would be the last one standing. Just him and a great big pile of money.

"A billion dollars." Lockard stepped forward. "Drop the knife and we could share it. You and me, we'd make a great team."

"What are you saying, Evan?" Grant demanded. "For God's sake, get your wits about you!"

"Do shut up." Jack pressed the blade to Grant's throat so hard it cut his flesh this time, a string of red from the man's neck dribbling into his shirt.

Three thousand feet.

Grant began to shake. "Shoot this bloody bastard, Evan!"

Lockard ignored him, smiling at Jack. "Go ahead, Jack. Kill him. It means more money for us. You and me."

Grant said, "Evan, son. Stop this nonsense!"

"I told you not to call me that," Lockard said. He took another step forward.

The jet whined as the computerized flaps moved, dipping the jet into descent. Alex crawled backward, but stopped when Lockard turned to her.

"Stay right there, Winter. Loverboy's life here depends on it."

Two thousand.

Grant said, "Evan, you need me. You need me to pass Customs in the Canarys!"

Alex pulled herself closer to the controls, an arm's length away.

Lockard shook his head. "No, I don't." He raised the HK. "I just need to land the plane."

Alex hauled herself onto the seat, hit the screen with one hand and flipped off the autopilot with the other. She jerked the joystick left. Everyone stumbled.

"Winter!" Lockard spun and aimed at her.

Alex rolled the plane again, harder this time, and Lockard took a shot, hitting the seat as she ducked. The bullet ripped straight through the seat back and buried itself in the flat-screen control on her side of the plane. Sparks jumped from the smoking hole, but the computers remained on.

The bastard had lost his mind.

Alex kept her head below the seat back and her hand on the joystick.

Lockard spun and shot again, the echo of the pop dampened by the hoards of cash on the floor and seats. But Grant's scream rang loud and clear.

"You shot me! You son of a bitch, you—"

Knowing the move had exposed Jack, Alex jerked the joystick again, causing the plane to roll the other way. All three of them tumbled.

Grant crumpled and stayed down as Jack crawled behind a row of seats.

Lockard wouldn't come after Alex, because Jack could then find Grant's gun. If she tried to take Lockard herself, he would just shoot her. His best option, then, was to ignore Alex while he hunted down Jack.

Because right now, Jack only had a knife.

Lockard stepped over a pack of cash as he stalked down the wide aisle.

Taking a deep breath, Alex reached up and took hold of the joystick with her left hand while overriding all autopilot fail-safes with her right hand. She pulled the stick all the way back, raising the nose of the plane into a suicide angle by hiding the tail in the wind shear of the wings. Ten degrees, then twenty, all the way up to thirty-five degrees. She would bury this bastard at the bottom of the ocean. Even if it cost her own life to do it.

Lockard fell forward, dropping the gun. "Goddamn it, Winter! Flatten the plane. Now!"

"You do it." Staggering out of the cockpit, Alex grasped the seat backs to stay upright, the wings shuddering with vibrations as the jet struggled with the angle.

"Push the goddamn thing down! We'll stall!" Lockard said, as his HK slid into a tight spot behind the wet bar.

That's the idea, she thought, stumbling down the hill of the aisle.

Lockard came back toward her, planted his foot, and drove a fist toward her injured shoulder again. Alex anticipated the move, turning her leg out wide and using the full weight of her body to counter with her own punch, a solid uppercut that hit him in the chin. The blow drove his lower jaw into his upper, causing his head to snap back.

Lefty.

Lockard shook it off, though, and against the gravity of the aisle pointing down toward him, he swung a kick that knocked them both to the floor. They tumbled between two stacks of money as he powered them back into the flight deck.

"You crazy bitch!" Lockard yelled as the plane climbed toward vertical, rattling and shaking with the slowing speed and wing angle. The Synthetic Vision System and control panel screamed with warnings of danger and vital instructions. The flight was racing toward unrecoverable.

Needing a few more seconds, she glanced at the controls while driving her arm through his and twisting it for leverage. If Alex could have killed him with her bare hands, she would have, but that was not going to happen with this animal, so she went for the next best thing. Contain him for another thousand feet and let him go. By then it would be too late to recover the plane.

But Alex knew what Lockard would do with it.

Wedging herself between Lockard and the seats, and forcing her own body to stay grounded, Alex fended off a blow with her forearm and another with her wrist, as he swung and swung again.

He drove her between the seats as he tried to grab the joystick, but she pressed her back against the dash and with her foot planted on the joystick, pinned it to maximum lift.

The alarms flashed and rang all over the displays in reds and yellows and oranges, sputtering with final warnings.

Lockard pounded a fist into her injured shoulder once and then again, but Alex held her ground. She fought back with every ounce and every want and every need in her now and in her past. She fought for every woman and every man with a shred of humanity.

Alex did not give.

The jet sputtered in massive vibration and finally entered wing stall, spinning forward like a leaf. Then it began dropping toward the ocean.

The windshield behind her showed a missile on target for the clear blue water, and in the last second left for engine recovery, Alex reached back, flipped open the safety cover of the tiny switch, and pushed it down, cutting the fuel to both engines. She fell to the floor as they went silent.

"You fucking lunatic!" Lockard lunged, shoved the joystick forward, and pounded at buttons frantically, scrambling to do anything to reignite the engines. But it was too late and they were too low. Both engines had flamed out.

Leaving Lockard, Alex scrambled to the cabin, stepping past Grant, who lay on the floor writhing in pain and bleeding from the gunshot wound in his chest.

She heard Lockard strap himself in.

Staggering through the long cabin, she held the seat backs and searched for Jack. He must have gone to the very back, away from the loose stacks of money, because Alex couldn't find him. She searched the floor and under the tables, behind the seats. And then she saw him, crumpled on the bathroom floor, Grant's HK in his hands.

He was bleeding from the leg again.

"Hold on!" Alex helped him up and hobbled with him to the back of the plane, fighting gravity's deadly spin.

As they stumbled down the aisle, Lockard gained enough control to right the plane, though it was too late to bring it back to life. He would have to glide it home and hope for the best.

Like the Talonstrike stall drill, Sui Cadere Dulcis.

Sweet Suicide.

Knowing they had but mere seconds until they hit the water, Alex pulled Jack into the flight-crew emergency jump seat, strapped him in, belts across his shoulders and over his waist. Then she fell into the seat across from him and looked out a window as the water approached.

Five seconds.

Alex strapped herself in. Shoulder belt one.

Four seconds.

Shoulder belt two.

Three seconds.

God help them.

Two.

She closed her eyes, and every muscle and tendon in her body tensed. She felt it as Lockard touched the flaps at the very last second, giving the plane the slightest boost.

Alex thought of Jack.

One.

Then of her father.

Then they hit the water.

The hull skittered across the waves on the barest of an upswing, then tore apart in a gigantic ripping of metal and fabric. Both engines burst into flames, spraying burning gas over the center of the plane and across the bales of cash. Like a giant Jet Ski, the last third of the plane, with Alex and Jack at the back, spun to the side and past the other wreckage. They were spared from ejection by the force of the spin pressing their backs into the seats.

Still, her head jerked forward and slammed into the seat back, and Alex's vision went black. Her stomach crammed up into her throat as they stopped spinning and immediately began to sink. Half conscious, water already up to her neck, Alex took a quick breath as she searched her lap for the straps and buckle but couldn't grasp it. She looked right, but Jack was gone.

Blinking in the salt water, Alex found the metal buckle and yanked it open, then twisted her body from the seat. She kicked with both legs, trying to ignore the insane pain in her shoulder and her knotted stomach as she reached for the surface. The tail was sinking, its plunging force dragging her with it. Kicking harder, with all she had left, Alex pumped her arms out wide and reached and kept reaching until she broke free of the pulling force and rose with the bubbles. A glimmer of surface grew closer.

She tightened her lungs and willed herself not to take a breath.

Focusing on the red light of the fire above and on the rising bubbles, Alex kicked against the burn and the pain. She forced herself higher and higher.

Until she surfaced.

Gasping and spitting, she spun, searching for Jack in the twilight of the setting sun and emerging moon. A trail of money and fire stretched for a hundred yards.

"Jack!" Alex yelled, turning in the water.

But it was Lockard she saw, only twenty yards away.

Floating, he had both arms wrapped around a cellophane package of bills, a two-point-five-million-dollar lifesaver. He turned at her yell, and the moment their eyes met, she found Jack.

He bobbed on the surface and then dove back under, ten yards behind Lockard.

Lockard spun, and when Jack resurfaced closer to him, Lockard dove for him. The two of them thrashed in the water before Lockard pushed Jack under. Driving her own arms through the water, Alex raced toward their fiery silhouettes.

For a moment, they both disappeared underwater, then resurfaced with their arms tangled, Jack coughing and spitting, Lockard with the advantage.

Reaching them, Alex grabbed the back of Lockard's head, and he swung, hitting her in the face with his forearm. Jack dove back under as she pounded Lockard in the back of the head with a spearing elbow. He kicked backward.

Then he yelled.

He looked up, horror and fear frozen on his face. A pool of red began to spread in the fire-lit water below him. He yelled again, a gurgle this time, and peered down into the water in disbelief.

Jack popped back to the surface just as Alex pushed Lockard away, his body beginning to convulse and twitch as he drifted in the growing pool of blood.

A glitter of steel flashed in Jack's hand.

Lockard bobbed twice and reached straight up into the air, eyes wide and mouth open. Then he sank in silence, along with his millions.

Alex pulled Jack to her.

"Payback," he gasped.

Hooked to Jack with one arm, Alex grabbed a pilot's leather seat with the other. They drifted in the cold Atlantic water, kicking away from the burning and sinking money, Jack mumbling now.

"I told you," he said again, looking at her. "He'd gone too far."

"Shhh." Alex pressed her lips to his forehead. "It's okay now."

Lockard was gone.

"You beat him."

And though she was shaking as they held tight to each other, she exhaled hard with the realization.

That they'd beaten them all.

Forty

Bora Bora, French Polynesia
Four weeks later

Lying on the teakwood chaise and facing the endless blue-green of the South Pacific, Alex reached for her watch. It was easy to lose track of time in any luxury resort, but this place downshifted you to a gear right above comatose.

Fine by her.

Though, a few days ago, her physical therapist—she'd found him through her Far East contacts—had suggested Alex schedule something called a Taurumi massage, with local oils meant to "enhance one's emotional and physical state" and "heal the spirit."

Other than the therapy, it was the only appointment she'd scheduled in the last month. And the masseur would be there any minute.

Alex listened for footsteps on the long wooden pier behind her. The bungalow, complete with a plunge pool and ladder extending to the lagoon, was the farthest from the shore at the resort. She wondered if she'd chosen it for the view and seclusion, like she'd told herself, or to prevent anyone from sneaking up on her.

Maybe a bit of both.

Her phone buzzed, and thinking it was the therapist, she checked it. The States. Virginia area code.

Staring at the device, Alex contemplated chucking it into the water, but she'd been completely out of the world-event loop after filing her resignation from the CIA, never mind simple Company developments. She hadn't spoken to a single superior since the new DDO himself called and told her to sit tight. He was supposed to get back to Alex after a careful review of the events. So she'd done as told and pushed it from her mind, focusing on nothing but R&R,

healing, and an upcoming Taurumi massage.

But she wondered about Jack.

She hadn't spoken to him since he'd returned to the London safehouse with Hanna. They'd agreed to part ways for a while, agreeing that neither of them was ready for more than what they'd shared. Still, an ache had bloomed inside her as the first weeks passed, and she was forced to admit to herself that physical injuries weren't all that needed to heal. But there was a strange beauty to solitude, the place where a person can both hear her own thoughts and reflect on them without the interference of others' needs or opinions. Without the need to keep moving at the modern-day pace.

The phone buzzed again, same Virgina number, and—figuring it would be the only way she could return to the sweet silence of solitude—Alex decided to clear this one unavoidable task off the list.

"Yes Director." Alex didn't attempt to hide the slight annoyance in her voice.

"Alex, how's the rehab coming along?" David Wood, the new DDO who'd replaced Moss, asked. There was a faint echo in his voice, evidence that this connection to paradise was forced, unnatural.

Rotating her arm in reflex, she said, "If you count skinny dipping in eighty-five degree teal-blue water as far as the eye can see? Fantastic."

He laughed. "Are you bored yet?"

"I'll let you know after my massage."

He laughed again, then turned to a more serious tone. "Listen, Alex, I called with good news."

The faint creep of footsteps sounded at start of the pier behind her. The only news she was interested in, but she asked anyway, "How good?"

"You've been cleared of all possible sanctions and disciplines from the Company on your most recent assignment." Alex waited as the pad of footsteps behind her drew closer. Finally, Director Wood said, "About your retirement."

Here it came. The pitch to rejoin the ranks and resume her status in Clandestine Service. "I have a proposal."

She stopped him there. "Look, Director Wood, I thought long and hard before filing that paperwork."

"That's the thing. Those papers? They were never filed." The echo was worse now, as if the conversation were being translated through a conch shell. Loud and clear and then fuzzy and broken.

Alex sat up straight. "You're going to force me to keep working for the CIA? What is this, the new KGB?"

"Do you have a laptop?"

Of course she did. "No."

The footsteps from the pier stopped at her door.

"Then I'm glad I came."

"You what?" Alex turned to see who was at her door, but whoever it was had stayed to the side of the entrance and remained hidden from her.

Damned spooks.

Holding the phone to her ear, Alex eased out of the lounger and rolled her shoulder again, then walked through the bungalow to greet the man she'd now hoped in vain was her masseur. Instead, the man who appeared wore a perfectly creased dark almond linen suit that matched the color of his eyes. He held a tan leather briefcase in one hand. She reflexively clinched her robe tight and took two steps back.

Then she noticed that he held a cell phone at his leg.

Director Wood smiled and turned the phone off. Then he nodded to her. "May I?"

Alex moved aside as he stepped forward. Though he was quite a bit older than she, Wood moved with ease and fluidity. Like a man of ultimate experience and confidence.

He stopped before Alex, placing the briefcase on the table.

He gave her a once over. "You look good. Even better than..." he glanced outside, up toward the sky, and continued, "I figured."

Alex fought to suppress the immediate swell of anger at the thought of this man watching her all the way out here, like a damned voyeur. She'd been naïve to blank out the fact that *Tempest*'s reach spanned pole to pole. And with that anything-but-subtle indication, Wood let her know exactly how powerless she was to disappear from the CIA's eye in the sky.

A few more beats of silence passed and he said, "Are you ready, then?"

"For?"

"The proposal." Wood pulled a laptop from the briefcase and flipped it open. After pressing a few keys, he turned the screen to her and stepped back. "That is your new account. The sum of money you see is to get you started."

Alex stared at the numbers and the anger began to rise again. "So you're forcing me out. Giving me, what, three million dollars to keep my mouth shut and..." she glanced at the sky herself this time and continued, "pretend to disappear?"

"Quite the opposite actually." He paused for a second and said, "but if that is really what you want, Alex, then by all means. Take the money. We'll leave you to go live your life. Or stay here in paradise. God knows you earned it."

"Or?"

"Or…consider the money a starter kit. Get you on your feet and set up. Then you'll receive a line of credit to spend any way you like to further your operation. No questions asked. But if at any point you refuse an assignment, no matter what it is, we close the line, drain the account, and set you free."

Alex stared at the screen and tried to make sense of the number before her, the proposition he was suggesting.

"It's close to the same program we offered your father," Wood said. "Similar circumstances, even. Though less complicated." He smiled.

Less complicated, as in, no children left orphaned by the plan.

Alex stared at the screen. That money would burn up faster than the packets Lockard had stolen. She'd need this kind of expense account to succeed in the jobs that would be thrown at her.

"Either way, a star will be etched in your name next week, and there will be a ceremony to recognize your contribution to the Company. How you gave your life to the service. You understand, of course. The President himself couldn't even know."

Translated: *Alex couldn't retire. She was already dead.*

Placing the phone on the table, Alex took a long, deep breath and stared back at The Director.

But Wood's gaze had drifted over her shoulder and to the wall of sketches Alex had made in the last month. Every person, every locale, every important moment. Except for one. She still hadn't been able to draw the Millennium Bridge. She hadn't fully revisited that night yet. She wasn't sure she ever would.

Tracing the lines on Director Wood's face with her gaze, Alex wondered. Could she work like her father had? Could she do this job, chasing rogues, and not only drawing the shadows, but living in them?

Wood said, "We could start with some healing sessions. You know, someone to help you with all that's happened."

"No need." Alex nodded toward the wall. "That's my therapy."

He pursed his lips to that then walked through the bungalow and out onto the deck, where he stopped with his arms crossed and stared out at the water. Alex followed and stopped a few feet behind, watching as a stingray slid along the shallows before shifting to glide all the way out and disappear.

"Gorgeous here," he said.

Alex looked past Wood's shoulder, a quietness spreading through her as she stood on the dock. Like a calming whitewash of the lines that were overly dark and the ones that should have never been on the page, the image of herself now showed a likeness she understood, one she'd come to accept. One she even liked. But the image was still incomplete. The drawing showed solid promise but was yet unfinished. She could take what was already on the page and go in many directions to fill that white space. What she added, though, must live up to that original image's promise. Make it better, even.

Finally, he turned and stared at her. "Too gorgeous to give up?"

"How long do I have to decide?"

He smiled, a predator's grin hidden by the façade of an appointed politician. "Take a week. Two, even."

Alex contemplated the opportunity to retain access inside the foundation where her parent's secrets were buried. The only place where she could find the answers to the questions that had surfaced in these weeks. The ones that she had not just a burning desire to answer, but a need at the human, the primal level.

Director Wood walked back through the bungalow, swept the computer into the bag and moved to the entrance in smooth succession. He stopped at the doorway, glanced back and said, "I'll be in touch."

Pulling her robe tight again, Alex avoided the temptation to glance up at the satellites as she said, "I'll have an answer soon," all the while thinking, I'm sure you will.

You always will.

Author's Note

This is a work of fiction based on fact: between April 2003 and June 2004, the Federal Reserve Bank bundled and airlifted $12 billion of cash, primarily in $100 bills, using twenty-one C-130 military cargo flights to Iraq. There has been much public debate about whether $6.6 billion of this cash was misappropriated or stolen during the war. A final report issued by the independent auditor assigned to situation, the Special Inspector General (SIGC) for Iraq Reconstruction, later claimed to have located most of the missing money. However, SIGC admits that the accounting records for these findings have yet to be fully discovered. Some people believe the money is still missing.

Additionally, the bombing referred to at El Descanso restaurant outside of Madrid, Spain is a real event and occurred on April 12, 1985. The explosion killed 18 and injured 82 others, including 11 American servicemen; police believe Americans were the target of the attack.

I have taken significant liberty and literary license with both events. I should also note that the characters in this novel are entirely fictitious, though there are minor references to actual persons.

Acknowledgements

To my editor, David Downing of Maxwellian Editorial Services, thank you for your insight, suggestions, and perspective on THE SHADOW ARTIST and spy thriller novels as a whole. To my copyeditor Elyse Dinh, your attention to detail is incomparable, and you no doubt saved me from ignorance and humiliation in countless ways. A special thank you to Theresa, your conversation with Victoria about strong women in fiction led to the story of Alex Winter as we see her now. Thank you for thinking of me and for your energy in the process. Alex wouldn't exist without you. And Victoria, you forced me to re-think and re-write more times than I care to ever admit to myself, no less the rest of the world. Without you, I couldn't have done it. Thank you, thank you, thank you.

About the Author

James Grayson graduated from Yale University in the early '90s with a major in Political Science and a minor in Art. He has lived in Boston, New York, Connecticut, and Texas, and now spends much of his time in Southern California and Europe. He is an investor by day and artist by night. When he's not busy working, writing, or drawing, it's a safe bet you can find him with a glass of wine in one hand and a spy novel in the other.

Connect with James online:

www.jamesgrayson.net

https://twitter.com/_jamesgrayson

https://www.facebook.com/JamesGraysonBooks

If you enjoyed reading *The Shadow Artist*, I would appreciate if you would help others enjoy this book, too.

Lend it. This e-book is enabled for lending, so please share.

Recommend it. Please help your friends and family find this book by recommending it to them. Reader groups, social media, discussion boards are also great ways to spread the word.

Review it. Please tell others why you enjoyed this book by reviewing it at Amazon or Goodreads. When you do write a review, please send me an email at *jamesgraysonbooks@gmail.com* so I can thank you with a personal email.